Harper Errant 2

I0673027

King's Raven

Maggie Secara

To believe in faeries is to step into an enchanted space where the rational mind meets the irrational heart, and all things become possible.

—Brian Froud

POPINJAY PRESS   LOS ANGELES

ISBN 978-0-9818401-6-1

First Popinjay Press edition April, 2017
This Popinjay edition has been re-edited and corrected. As a result, it is slightly altered but is otherwise unchanged from the original edition published by Crooked Cat Books.

Visit the author at www.maggiesecara.com

for Jim,
my husband

Mine own self's better part,
My dear heart's dearer heart.

Books by Maggie Secara

THE HARPER ERRANT SERIES

The Dragon Ring
King's Raven
The Mermaid Stair

THE RAVEN AT RANDOM SERIES

Black Dog, Grey Lady

ROMANTIC ADVENTURE

Molly September

HISTORY

A Compendium of Common Knowledge 1558-1603:
Elizabethan Commonplaces for Writers, Actors, & Re-enactors

Time in Secara's tale is a piece of Celtic knotwork. Her narrative loops in and out of history with all the giddy deftness of Dr. Who at his best. She juggles her characters and their adventures without a single ball dropped. It's an impressive feat of literary craft, elevated to art by how effortless she makes it all seem.

Another spirited romp through time with faeries and music...

...The Victorian details and the bits that take place at the Crystal Palace exhibition are priceless!

Fantasy with a great soundtrack!.

...Felt like coming home

...Gentle music, magic battles, and a sense of what it means to serve the king.

...Stalwart and lovable heroes, an unusual and frightening villain, and enough plot twists and turns to keep you on the edge of your seat. I couldn't put it down.

Chapter & Verse

Part 2
The Heart of the World

Acknowledgements

Most writing groups read each other's writing and offer critique and so on. Ours is a mythical refuge served by giant robots and powered by coffee, Otter Pops, and chocolate. The Treehouse of Solitude is the place where a select group of mostly online friends can tell secrets, share triumphs, swear at our editors, ourselves, or the work in progress; get advice, encouragement, or drunk on the palm wine of success; send up fireworks as members of the team cross this year's NaNoWriMo finish line; or simply hum along quietly. Principal among the Treehouse denizens to whom I am grateful are Scott Perkins, who also designs my covers; Deirdre Sargent, and Joel Reid, co-founders; Thena MacArthur, Kathleen Bartholomew, Sharon Cathcart; and Ari Berk, my brother in art, who listens to me ramble and generally has an even better idea.

The Victorianist Society is a group of part-time scholars, devotees, re-creationists, and aesthetes dedicated to the Art of Living Graciously in an often ungracious world, especially Walter Nelson, Marie-Jo Dulade Coclet, Lois DeArmand, Michael McPherron, Frances Grimble, Steven Gillan, and others who provide well-founded advice often on a moment's notice on turns of phrase, apparel, transport, and such questions as whether the piano would be in the front parlour or the back, what sort of pistols are likely to be used, and how many plaids were acceptable for a gentleman to wear at one time (answer: all of them).

While the Elizabethan period has been a nearly life-long research project, I can't claim to know everything, or to always remember what I do know when I need it. Many of those already mentioned are also members of Ren Faire History Snobs, whose assembled knowledge, expertise, research skills, and ability to argue unhindered often for days at a stretch is a constant source of entertainment.

Special thanks to

Ari Berk and Carolyn Dunn, whose wonderful book *Coyote Speaks* gave me the voice and the nerve to create the Secota village and its people with respect and some hope of verisimilitude.

Nan Earnheart for brainstorming with me through the tough parts after I thought I was finished.

And to the gang at the Worlds of Maggie Secara group on Facebook who kept the faith while the Raven's first draft emerged as a kind of performance art in the summer of 2010, and who have held on this long for the final one.

Maggie Secara
Yuletide, 2012

Addendum

Respectful thanks to Laurence and Stephanie Patterson at Crook Cat Publishing who not only embraced a second book, but edited with patience.

M.S.
April, 2017

Dramatis Personae

IVESTON VALE, THE PRESENT INSTANT

BEN HARPER, musician and part-time TV star in the midst of a career change

MELLIS POWELL, professor of music and tolerant wife, currently in Los Angeles with their son Sparrow

ELAINE, Ben's production assistant

MR DAY, landlord of the local pub, Day's Star

KIRSTY DAY, the landlord's pretty daughter

MEMBERS of Faerie Reel, a popular local traditional band beginning to do well:

* DINAH SHORLAND, school principal and leader of the band. Fiddle.
* TOM SHORLAND, her husband, an auto mechanic. Also flute, whistles, concertina
* MORGAN TYLER, a Dartmoor park ranger. Also guitar, mandolin, hammered dulcimer
* BRIAN HOBBES, a drummer

VARIOUS fae great and small, seen and unseen

VARIOUS Dymocks, Satterlys, Days, Powells and other residents

OF FAERIE

AUBREY KING, also known as Oberon King of Faerie

TITANIA Queen of Faerie, an intemperate wife

RAVEN, one of Oberon's principal gentlemen

SWAN, a gentleman in waiting

THE NEW WORLD, 1500s

YOUNG WOMAN, a shaman of the Secota

BADGER, an admirer with a bad foot

I-BRING-THE-RAIN, a demon

MIKUMWESS, the Old People of the shore, faeries of the Carolinas

ENGLAND, 1590s

Mortlake

SIR FRANCIS BROWNE, a gentleman in service to Lord Aubrey

SIR RAFE FITZROY, another of the same

*DR JOHN DEE, the Queen's astrologer. Also mathematician, geographer, diviner, etc. etc.

*JANE Dee, his long-suffering wife

MARGARET DAVENANT, Dr Dee's new housekeeper

MATTHEW, LUKE, AND JOHN, a bit of mindless muscle

AGNES, a very old woman

Kew, at the Anchor

TOM HOBBES, a working man of careful opinions

ALYS, a tavern maid

SIR THOMAS WESTON, assistant to the Master of the Revels, a talent scout

Various working men, apprentices, villagers,

Cowdray House

*ARTHUR GARRET, secretary to the Viscount Montague

MR HANDY, the steward

MR BELLOTT, the Clerk of the Kitchen

SOUTH LONDON, MID-1850S

PROF. ERASMUS LOVEJOY, a mad scientist

AMBROSE CRAY, his ill-tempered assistant

SUSAN PICKERING, spinster, Lovejoy's great-niece, and owner of Hollytree House

EDWARD DONOVAN, a reporter

RALPH FITZROY, a lost boy

ELLEN, DAISY, and PETER, servants at Hollytree House

MRS NIXON, a first class cook

MR SWINDON, MISS KENNEDY, MR HORSLEY, AND MISS DEAN, Lodgers at Hollytree House

OAKLEY, a wee man

PERDITA OF AVALON, a disappointed witch

Numerous shop assistants, tourists, constables, faeries, and supernumeraries

Note: A detailed floor plan of the Crystal Palace at Sydenham may be seen at on <u>this page at maggiesecara.com</u>.

LONDON, SAVOY THEATRE, 1882

*MISS ALICE BARNETT, a famous soprano

BETTY, her maid

FREDDY, a useful boy

VIENNA, FREIHAUS WIEDNERTHEATER, 1791

*JOSEFA HOFER, a diva in the role of the Queen of the Night

*HERR NOUSEUL, appearing as Monostatos

*FRAULEIN GOTTLIEB, appearing as Pamina

* Historical personages

The Crystal Palace at Sydenham, 1855
See http://bit.ly/CP1855

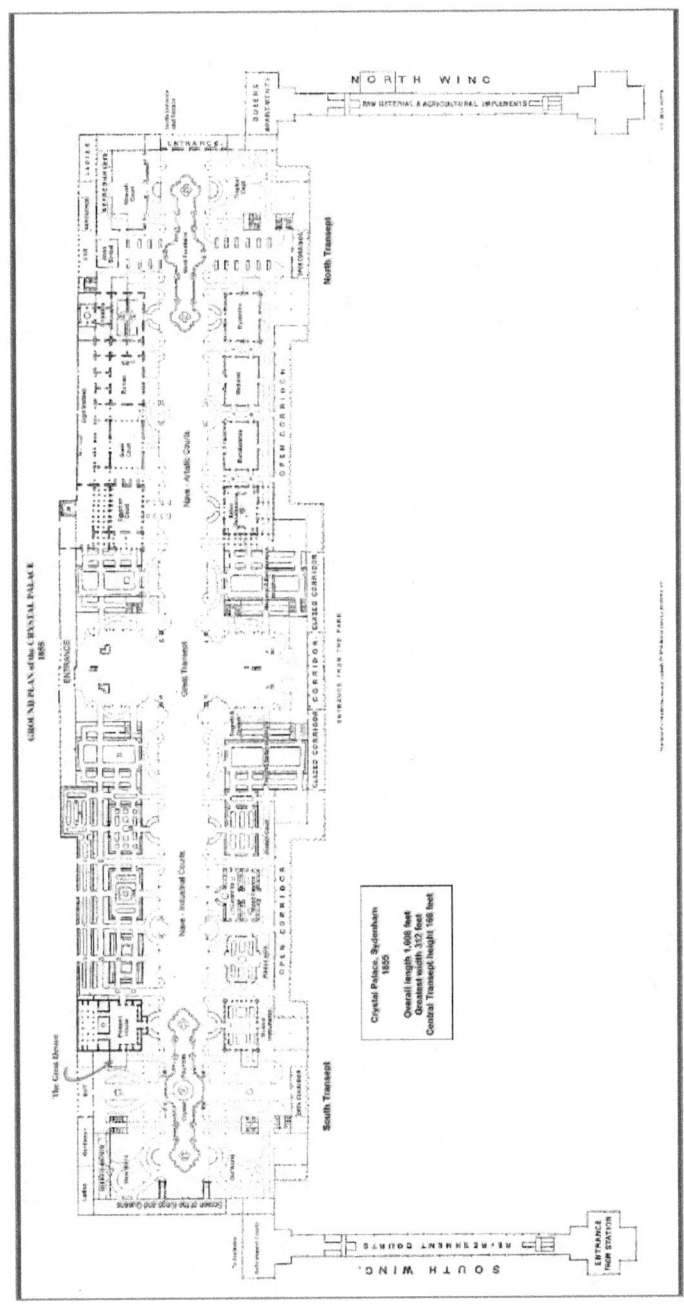

King's Raven

The Heart of Faerie

1
Iveston on Moor, Devon, mid-December

It was getting dark. It was already cold. Two weeks before Christmas under troubled skies and a kissing snow, Sunday slipped across Dartmoor and into the west. At the new recording studio on top of Hobbs Hill, a timer kicked over with a low snap sending a swarm of fairy lights chasing over the windows, the thatched roof, and a discreet new sign: DIAMOND HALL. At once, a chorus of whistling cheers went up from an unseen and largely unseeable audience.

Ben Harper, who could see them perfectly well, just grinned and ignored them. He still had work to do getting the last of the Faerie Reel equipment out of the cars and put away before the band went home.

With *Planxty Irwin* still bouncing in his head from last night's gig, he reached into the van, grabbed a box, and pulled it squealing across the ridged metal floor.

Lift with your knees!

Don't wheeze!

More cheese!!

The little voices that were not, he was happy to say, in his head were "helping" as usual with high pitched, chiming advice and not much else. He had gotten used to that, living on Dartmoor. He'd also learned to appreciate his special relationship with Faerie without being distracted by it, except when they moved his tools. On whimsical occasion, they could also be exceptionally helpful, but the chatter was constant, which is why it took him a moment to notice when they stopped.

Then a lone munchkin voice squeaked, *Uh-oh*.

Two seconds later, an unmistakable ripple of force rolled Devonshire under his feet like a wave of the sea. He straightened, automatically putting up a hand to steady himself for what was coming. The familiar shaking, the almost subliminal rumble, the sensation that not just the earth rippled and flowed but the buildings, too—it had been a long time, but he'd know it anywhere.

A low exclamation burst from him, and he grinned. Earthquake. Cool. Just like home.

Vibration and rumble both gained strength till the van swayed on its wheels. A few yards away, a hairline crack crawled up the concrete back of the aging village hall. The chains of the play park swings clanked against their steel frames. On the other side of the car park, his beautiful new recording studio stood its picturesque ground, though he could hear a creak as the timbers shifted. Aubrey wasn't going to be amused if his meticulous adjustments had been thrown off.

Inside, voices rose in alarm. California boy that he was, Ben was inclined to be nonchalant about the shaking, but the rest of the band, every one of them Devon born and bred, did not expect England to move wholesale under their feet. Almost before they could finish reacting, it was over. Much swearing followed, and something else: the sound of tiny shrieks and giggles, like children's voices, out of sight but quite nearby.

Ben picked up the box feeling just a bit disappointed the temblor hadn't lasted longer. By the shouts coming from the studio, he knew he was probably alone in this reaction.

When he slammed the sliding panel and slapped down the lock, Dinah Shorland squawked, frozen in the studio doorway.

"Sorry," he called, still grinning.

"I should think you would be, Yank!" Dinah snapped. Shaking her head, she trotted down the steps to give him a hand. "What *was* that?"

"Three point five?" Ben suggested the Richter level with a laugh that puffed steam into the frosty air. "Hardly worth noticing."

Dinah didn't find it at all funny. She punched him in the arm, then swung her long braid back over her shoulder, and let him shift the awkward case into her arms. "Well, I noticed, and so did everyone else. That's an earthquake, then?"

"That's an earthquake. No worse than a roller coaster, is it?"

"Well, I hate those, and I didn't much care for that. Dartmoor an't California, mind!" The local accent tended to thicken under stress.

They'd played a nice little club in Exeter last night. Today was about getting moved into the new studio, and it had taken all the short December afternoon to do it. No surprise if all five of them were exhausted and short-tempered with it.

"Are you coming in? I think everyone wants to go home. Mobile service is out, of course."

"Mm, yeah. In a minute," he said, and looked again across the van toward the man who was, if anything, the most important member of the team: the engineer who had designed and supervised construction of Diamond Hall. Aubrey King, who so far hadn't said a word.

He had just come outside when the temblor struck, and yet he'd remained unmoved the whole time as if his feet stood on some other, firmer ground. And perhaps they did, Ben thought. Unmoved, but not unaffected, if the narrowed eyes and tight jaw meant anything.

"Everything all right?" he asked.

The barest hint of a nod, but no more. Just Aubrey, detached and still, watching the sun go down through broken clouds.

A harsh sound, the smell of sulphur, the lean jaw limned for an instant in the flare of a match. Except for the expensive cigarette balanced between tapering fingers, the man might have been a statue, apparently serene, occupied with his own mental landscape viewed through rising strands of smoke.

Below the hill they shared with the hall, the village was full of noises crisp on the air: front doors squeaked open, banged shut as folk gave up waiting for the house to collapse, and went inside. A delivery van rumbled by on the road to Newton Abbot. A motorbike roared out. A voice sounding a bit cross told a child to come inside or Mummy would give her to the faeries. And everywhere phones were ringing.

All the way out to the farms people were gathering for Sunday dinners, urgent with news: Did you feel that? Never heard of such a thing! Not here. Check the internet!

Across the Old Hill Road beside them, where there was a bit of sidewalk and a good steep slope, two boys shot past with the tick and rattle of skateboards. And over the way, Mr Day at the Star was testing the taps, checking for breakage, turning on the television for news. But right here, the empty car park was all their own. The air smelled like snow.

Aubrey took a drag on his cigarette and breathed away the smoke, then he whistled: a pair of rising notes with a peculiar trill at the end. A few seconds later an enormous raven, feathers rattling with attitude, flew out of the cloud-wracked sunset and landed on the Norfolk pine with an insolent cry.

"If you please," said Aubrey.

"Very well," the bird croaked back.

Bright-eyed on the asphalt, something shifted in the world, and the bird was six feet and one inch of fit young man, at least according to the local girls, who tended to swoon over the rakish grin and long, unruly black hair.

"My lord," said Raven with a nod. "Hullo, Ben."

No one who saw the boy would imagine—and who imagines such things, really—that he stood high among the lords of Faerie. Any more than they'd guess that Aubrey, who was also Oberon, wore that realm's crown glimmering on his brow. The king spoke quietly for a minute, for Raven's ear alone. The boy nodded, replied.

Amused in spite of himself, Ben leaned against the van and folded his arms wishing he could read either gentleman reliably. Cold crept under his jacket and up through the soles of his boots. Anxious friends and central heating waited in the studio, but all his attention now was on the fae.

"So," he said at last. "Earthquake. You guys want to tell me anything?"

Tall and ever elegant even in work clothes, Aubrey relaxed slightly. He reached back to pull the hair tie out of his ponytail and shook out the black curls, tossing the ornament away. Raven caught it deftly out of the air.

"I don't think so, no," said Aubrey.

"Okay, but..."

"It's nothing, Ben."

"Not an earthquake, though."

"The earth shook, didn't it?" Raven said with a trace of the old arrogance.

The king of Faerie rolled down the sleeves of his beautifully tailored shirt and flipped down the cuffs. The cold didn't bother him in the least, but with a thought, he found a down vest somewhere and put it on for the sake of the company. With one more taste of his cigarette, he changed the subject.

"Good show last night, I hear."

Ben sighed and pushed calloused fingers through his sandy hair, as ever in need of a trim. He always felt a little like an unmade bed next to these two.

"It was, yes. Exeter loves us. Got rid of all the flyers and the new business cards. Even picked up a client, Mikel Davis. You'll like him. Y'know, you should come with us. Good people, good music."

He broke off, feeling awkward. Ordinarily, Aubrey would have been listening, amused and pleased, but he still seemed far away.

"Sir, we could have this conversation inside where it's warm, but here we are dancing in the parking lot. What's going on?"

An invisible chorus of crystalline voices exploded into delighted, possibly derisive giggles at their feet, until Aubrey snapped his fingers. Wherever they were hiding, they shut up at once. Snow fairies. Pixies.

"Your people work hard for that applause, Ben," he said, and flicked the cigarette away; it vanished before it could hit the ground. "You should know it's your own. If I were there, you might not be sure. And I already know how good you are."

He beamed his best rock star smile, sea blue eyes shining, and stooped to pick up a cardboard box someone had forgotten. Ben made a doubtful noise, but Aubrey remained enigmatic. Faerie feelings and the forces that made them would always be a mystery even to a man who could hear the bells of Elfland, as they say.

When you spent enough time with Oberon and one of his principal gentlemen—and that's something not everyone can say—you had to accept that some questions would get answered in his lordship's own good time, or not at all.

"Have it your own way," Ben said with a shrug.

Raven, whose sharp features gave him an endearingly collegiate look, gently pried the box away from his distracted lord.

"You know it's hopeless when he's like this," he said, flashing the American a sympathetic grin. "Come on inside, sir. It's freezing out here."

"Yes, yes it is."

Ben shook off a sudden shiver, and fell in beside him. Two weeks before Christmas, fae mischief was brewing, and it would probably involve him. Thank god Mellis was in California scoring a film, and had taken Sparrow with her. He hated having to explain these things.

2
(somewhere, nowhere)

She floats. That's all, just floats. Although she has no way of reckoning the passage of time, she thinks—if this is thinking—she has been floating for a very long time indeed. There is no color, although she has the concept "color" in her... mind? There is no sound, no music except the numbers, shapes, progressions that slip and twine around her in the void, each tone an iron brand. Now and then she feels—if this is feeling—that time is passing, changing outside her prison.

She can, sometimes, sense the presence of things when there are things to sense. Which in general there are not. Things. But when she comes near a mirror, that's the word—and this is easier than in ages past—sometimes she can grab hold, latch on to the edges, and look through. The world has altered, she thinks then, forming words with difficulty. At such times, she even has a name.

Perdita, that's it. The lost girl. In the days when the temple was little more than a clearing in a wood, she had been given too young to the goddess, had hung up her girdle in the myrtle grove the day after her first monthly courses had stopped, had been dedicated to the worship of the earth and sea without a clue to what those things were. The first man who came to her was not old, not ugly, but neither was he careful in his devotions, grappling and sweating into her virginity.

In the pain and shock, she forgot she was the earth, the goddess herself. When the sun rose, she killed him with his own dagger, and giggled, and ran away to hide behind the waterfall. When they found her, she was weeping, or so they thought.

After the scourging and after the tears and for long after that, there had been others, and others again. She learned to hide the anger, grow wise, and wait. Then a man came laughing out of the green lands of the North who had caught up her pain and soothed it away for a time. Behind the long blue eyes, curling black hair, delicately pointed ears, and a voice like the very foundation of music, he had the power she sought. More, he was immortal, and almost, almost… Ah! But what is love against the honey taste of magic and the hope of revenge?

She followed him, weeping bitter tears, cajoled and entreated until he agreed to be her teacher and her lover. Was that the right order? Or was it the other way around? He had taught her in the end, and loved her. She had learned, so far as her impatient nature allowed, his music and the magic that came with it, yes, still nursing a thousand hatreds. In time, she became a sorceress, a seer, though it was not enough.

And because he had what she wanted and would not, could not give it up to her, being what he was, she had come to hate him most of all. At last, he had seen through her blandishments into the twists of her heart, and cast her aside. She would have killed him if she could, but his music was truer, and his magic stronger. When he left her, he was not laughing.

Now all the words are gone, and all the music, except a few meaningless notes broken by one harsh cry. When she remembers anything at all, she knows that something has been lost besides herself. Something important. Where she has been. Where she is now. Something about a mirror—another word whose meaning comes and goes. And a name, vanished with her freedom. His name.

Her madness now is quite complete. When she can grab the edges of a looking glass before being swept away, she looks for him, though nothing she sees makes sense. But in those fleeting moments, three things are clear:

> *She is not finished.*
>
> *She will have his power.*
>
> *He has to die.*

3
The Great Exhibition at the Crystal Palace, Hyde Park, 1851

There is little doubt that the exhibitor is a man of ingenious mind and much industry but unfortunately he represents a class of men who venture to invent while yet in perfect ignorance of the truths which investigation has placed beyond all doubts

—Hunt's Handbook to the Official Catalogs, 1851

Ye gods! Steam pressure was dropping! The experiment failing! *Again!* Voltaic energy fluctuating wildly, the Great Device rocked and trembled on its platform, but the vast black mirror that was its inscrutable face persisted dark even while sparks exploded from everywhere else. Something was banging that should not be banging.

"What is it?" cried Professor Lovejoy, whose machine it was. "Newton's wig! What is it now?"

Beneath the old scientist's boots the wooden platform that supported the Great Device shivered and warped. The world dropped out from under him, then spun him off in another direction to carom painfully off the protective rails and fall among the cluttered work tables and stools. A shin slammed into a bench covered with arcane tools. Dizzy, lights dancing in his head like fireflies, his hands flew up too late to keep him from slamming into the heavy desk, slewing through a litter of papers and notebooks; he barked a startled oath, quickly stifled. At least he hadn't fallen to the exhibition floor, and he was facing the right way round, away from the snapping and clanging at the other end of the platform,

He rubbed unconsciously at one ancient hip, while with the other, steadier hand he plucked the horn-shaped end of a speaking tube out of its hanger and shouted to the man in the steam room below.

"What the devil is the matter with you, Murphy! Can you not hold the pressure steady for five minutes? Five... The pressure, man! What's that? Yes, you idiot, what else?"

No time to wait for a reply, certainly not. Not while everything was flying apart. "Damned Irishman." He flung the horn in the general direction of the hook, and glared toward the control panel, willing the arrow on the pressure gauge to steady. The banging stopped.

What now, he wondered. What next?

The Professor propped his spectacles on his forehead and ground sharp-boned knuckles into streaming eyes while the monitors wavered in and out of focus. Again he checked the madly spinning dials in the fitful light. Squinted and checked again. The light was abominable these days, for all the building was nothing but windows. The colored console lights, his own invention, which should be gleaming behind the artfully lettered tiles sputtered, flared, and went out. Lovejoy nearly wept in frustration for his fortune and his fame, his Great Device, his only care.

"Cray!" he shouted above the din. Where was that wretched boy, what was he doing, was he asleep?

A dark head emerged from the crawl space under the platform, then a swarthy face suffused with vexation and sweat. Then shoulders in a streaked and stained lab coat. Finally, spanner in hand, Ambrose Cray appeared, not a boy but a trim man in his thirties with a waxed mustache and a furious expression.

Professor Lovejoy snapped at his assistant, "What are you doing down there, blast you? Stop tampering! Are you trying to ruin everything? Well? Well? Newton's wig! I can't be everywhere at once!"

His own wrinkled lab coat flapping, grey hair floating cloudlike round his ruthlessly shaved face, the old scientist clambered over and swung around and ducked under this cable and that canister, tripped over three copper coils that somehow tumbled into his path when a curious fold in the cosmos—or perhaps just the threadbare carpet—rippled under his feet. After two years with the dratted fellow—a failed schoolteacher from Sheffield, for god's sake—he should know better than to trust Cray with his jewel, his genius, his Great Device.

"Seventy-eight, I said!" Lovejoy barked, and cranked a dial, set a switch, then pulled a lever.

"I set it to 78, you old fool," muttered Cray, unappreciated and unheard under the crashes and bangs. "Now, look what you've— Damn!"

"No, no, *no*!"

Between one denial and another, other sounds: a rustle of papers, a flutter of notebooks, the whir of a spinning gauge. An aura frail as a rainbow began just slightly to rise from every surface disguised as a directionless hum, a buzz that might be pens rattling, or loose bits of metal, silk thread, and reed.

Oblivious, Cray pitched forward, straining to reach the controls though his thoughts were weirdly scattered. If he could just get to the bend of... If he could blind the... What the devil?

In his confusion, he nearly put a foot over the velvet-roped edge of the platform and into the goggle-eyed crowd that had gathered, of course, the instant things began to go wrong.

Things were always going wrong. It made Lovejoy and Cray the most popular exhibit on the ground floor, after the flush toilets and the refreshments area. Explosions daily with iced cream! The crowd loved it.

The grey winter light from the domed ceiling far above began to curl and stretch through the spectrum, trapping the platform, the device, two frantic men in the moment as if in amber. The gaping audience, with one voice, released a moan like the wind soughing through a hollow stone. The thickened light wavered, broke, and scattered. The moment reasserted itself, but the Device continued coughing and straining, spitting smoke.

"Bastard," Cray muttered. "I will tame you, I swear it. I will not be bested, not again!"

"Shut it down! Shut it down!" cried the Professor, waving his arms madly as smoke began to billow and curl.

Gritting his teeth in a snarl like a prizefighter diving into the fray, Cray threw himself forward and, gaining the machine at last, slammed down a massive horseshoe switch to sever it from the power source. A row of colored lamps set into the panel winked like madly disordered stars, then went dark. Smoke rose with one last bang from under the panel. The platform heaved once and, with something like a sigh, relaxed from its extra-dimensional adventures, leaving nothing but shocked silence in the halls of the Great Exhibition.

Exhausted, the Professor slumped into the richly padded velvet chair provided for the device's operator. The crowd burst into mocking applause. He had long since learned to ignore them. They would thank him, one day. By the great Sir Isaac Newton, he swore the whole world would thank him!

A Great Device indeed! The chair into which its inventor collapsed sat in the midst of a Byzantine cage of polished brass and copper, iron and steel. A mahogany console set with beveled crystal panels protected a series of ivory tiles, which displayed the names of cities, countries, continents. These could be flipped and changed by the rotation of several interlocked gears, each cranked by a small ivory handle. Across the top, the seven globes of colored glass, the size of a thimble, each containing a sliver of charred bamboo filament, awaited the excitement of the ether to set them alight, marking the successful stages of the device's operation in the colors of the rainbow, a deep blue-violet indicating perfect operation: a lamp which had so far failed to illuminate at any point, even while the rest had danced.

At one side of the console hung a huge polished oval of volcanic glass, nearly two foot long, set in a wheel of fancifully wrought iron and vulcanized rubber, and suspended from an over-arching iron frame. The whole business was supported by a ring of radiating, stabilizing wires like a mathematical spider's web in a gilded frame of scrollwork and cherubs, each presenting a ball of polished amber. It took the breath away just to consider it. The wires drew galvanic power, when the blasted thing worked properly, exciting its metaphysical properties and harnessing them in the service of Science. At least, that was the theory, yet to be satisfactorily proved.

As he had explained in his application to the Great Exhibition's managers, the purpose of this extraordinary device with its dials and wires and spiraling copper coils, Erasmus Lovejoy's darling, was first to examine the prevailing weather in any area of the world indicated on the ivory tiles, and then, inevitably, to predict it. One day, it might even be used to change it! He reminded himself of this, his great mission, as he fought back despair. Such reminders always restored his sense of purpose.

A network of such devices would end drought and famine, prevent flooding from excessive rains, and mitigate the disasters of blizzards whilst bringing needed rain to the driest lands. Deserts would bloom! It would display weather conditions throughout the world. It would with judicious adjustment, permit the trained operator to move a storm system here to a desert there. Hurricane devastation in the Indies would become a thing of the forgotten past. Before the decade was out, the Sahara would be golden with ripening fields of wheat instead of sand. Under the guiding hand of the British Empire, universal peace and prosperity would result! And Erasmus Lovejoy's name would echo down the halls of time beside Isaac Newton, James Watt, and Aristotle.

The plan was perfect, his understanding of the cosmos perhaps less so, but the device was still in the testing phases, after all. He had the personal wealth and his banker's testy confidence. And he had been granted permission to pursue his experiments in his own twenty-five foot square of space here at the Great Exhibition, the sonnet in glass and iron to the Triumph of Industry that was referred to in the press as the Crystal Palace.

"Professor?" A plain young woman in a plain stuff gown mounted the eight or ten steps to the platform carrying a wicker hamper and two brown bottles of beer. "I've brought lunch for you, Great Uncle, for you and Mr Cray."

"Susan!" the professor shouted, leaping up at once, restored in the instant. "Susan, thank goodness you've come! Just the girl we need!"

Alarmed, Miss Susan Pickering almost dropped her basket. Her Great Uncle had never expressed a moment's pleasure to see her in their whole acquaintance. For the most part he ignored her, in fact. Still she took care of him, and meekly bore his frantic attitudes and appalling manners, because at the advanced age of two-and-twenty with no suitors, no face, and only a modest fortune, she had little other choice.

"Yes, Professor," she said. Not a complete mouse, she picked her way over the cluttered platform, but no more quickly than modesty and multiple petticoats allowed. Not much, as rebellions go, but her options were few.

"Take the chair, child, take the chair. Cray! We'll go again. Watch the readings! Susan, touch nothing until I give the word, then push that red button."

"Yes, Uncle."

"Do you understand? That button only!"

"Yes, Uncle."

"Now watch the mirror, and call out if you observe any changes, anything at all!"

A chattering crowd was gathering again around the platform, drawn from the silk shawls and Venetian glass and the rattling Chinese porcelain in adjoining displays by the violent zaps and whines of electricity and steam engines and action.

Cray pushed a dial three clicks on the steam pressure modulator. Copper coils spun. A flywheel flew. Bars of lightning crawled up the Jacob's ladder and spat out the top.

The panel of lights began to glow a sickly yellow which should, they hoped, grow through the spectrum to success. Lovejoy and Cray both dropped smoked goggles over their eyes, and Lovejoy drew on thick cowhide gloves. Taking a deep breath, he glanced briefly at his assistants, and barked, "Now!"

He brought up the massive horseshoe switch, and closed the circuit. The frame around the mirror began to vibrate, to buzz, then to glow ever so slightly blue. Yes, this was more like it.

For the crowd and the neighboring exhibits all around, voices rose in alarm as wild galvanic energy hummed on the air, caressed faces, lifted hair, snapped from the mirror frame to the massive iron framework of the vast exhibition hall and the lofty ceiling. Those who had read Mrs Shelley's *Frankenstein* gasped in awe, expecting wonders.

Susan dutifully stared at the obsidian mirror, and felt her flesh crawl, though the polished black surface never changed. No, wait. Maybe it did, just for an instant. The flashing lights reflected on its surface seemed almost to be coming from within. Uneasily she wondered why, if the men had felt the need for goggles, they had not provided her with a pair. Perhaps her own spectacles would be enough. Just keep watching!

The air crackled. She could already feel her hair escaping its pins, swirling, tickling her ears. A light draft from the entrance nearby became a whirlwind that moaned, then howled. *Snap!* Both lenses of her glasses shattered in their frames. Susan shrieked, and threw herself forward with hands clasped behind her head.

Over her shoulder, Cray watched the monitor lights dance from red to saffron, from bright yellow to green, thence creeping to royal blue until one, just one glass dome flashed violet. He kept glancing up at the mirror as the lights progressed, making slight adjustments as the professor called out numbers and letters, more deliberately this time, taking care over each setting and percentage, and every spinning dial. Now what was that? The shadows of clouds appeared to drift across the mirror's midnight surface. Ah no, that was coming from sky above. The glass panels that gave the Crystal Palace its name revealed the same clouds. A reflection, nothing more.

But, wait.

"Wait!" he muttered, and clicked a dial back by one notch, then another. "Wait!"

The last light went deep blue, and in the glass a face, a woman's golden face, lovely and desperate, appeared against an open sky, but the image was fogged, hazy, as if seen through a screen. Or through smoke, or fire. For a few moments, moist eyes stared, bare arms lifted in supplication, bare breasts…

Without warning, something exploded, dazzling all eyes, leaving the world about them spangled with light. Then every filament blew out, and the mirror went dark.

"Did you see her?" Cray bellowed over the dying whine of the Device. "You must have seen her!" Frantic to get back the image, he flipped and turned and jiggled everything he could think of. For an instant, he thought he saw the face again, imploring, but no amount of recalibrating could fetch it back.

"What is it?" shouted the Professor. "What have you done? Cray!"

Bang! The delicately etched panes of beveled glass crackled, shattered and blew out across the platform. Lovejoy shrieked and dropped to the floor.

Another explosion and another rocked the floor in quick succession. Patrons and exhibitors alike cried out, though a handful of street urchins were cheering. Sparks fountained into the air, starting a minor fire in a stuffed Barbary ape on the floor above. Furious voices echoed on from all sides.

Someone yelled, "Anarchists!"

No one thought of Susan.

Then just as the air began to clear and the colored smokes faded—and perhaps it was not related, but maybe it was—the earth itself trembled. London had not felt an earthquake in generations. The building swayed and the crowd screamed and each clutched the person nearest him, who might or might not be a family member. Outside, the lowering clouds descended in great masses from the summer sky, throwing the Crystal Palace and half the Thames Valley into shadow. Lightning spiked as well, called and amplified by the fires within. Rain pounded the long glass dome and slapped at the crystalline walls.

In the green and pleasant gardens surrounding the exhibition, under the breaking diamond spray of an Italian fountain, an unmistakable shimmer of derisive laughter echoed in stony halls few mortal eyes could see. The rustic faeries of Hyde Park could not for a moment enter the vast, ungraceful structure buttressed with the iron so poisonous to their kind, but they could dance for its downfall.

Yet it did not fall.

4
Iveston, at the Studio

Neither rain nor snow nor dark of night, nor earthquake for that matter, was allowed to get in the way of the music. Diamond Hall Recording was ready. Rehearsal 1, with Faerie Reel's logo on a permanent placard by the door, had been tested and tweaked to Dinah's satisfaction. Thanks to Aubrey, for whom music and its faithful reproduction were both hobby and religion, Ben was ready to hire a full-time recording engineer, and start scheduling clients. And when Dinah and the gang had settled on a play list, to start working on the CD.

The session tonight confirmed the effort had been worth all the bickering with the County Council who wouldn't let him add on to his Grade 2 listed cottage. And with the Parish Committee who spun ever more fanciful fears about sex, drugs, and rock 'n' roll dragging the village to its doom. At which point, Raven had pointed out the patterns he saw shaping in front of him, and made a suggestion.

So Ben Harper had called a village meeting, as every resident had a right to do. (He did not call a press conference, because that would have been mean.) At the meeting, the star of the BBC's popular *Now or Never* presented his offer to bring in his team to expand and upgrade the 50-year-old village hall, to include a teen center, internet access, and central heating. And oh yes, do it as the final two-part episode of *Now or Never*. His only stipulation, Ben assured them with the smile twice voted Best in Britain, was that his company, Diamond Hall Productions, be first permitted to lease the other lot at the top of Hobbs Hill, and build his studio there. The men and women of Iveston practically fell over themselves to put the agreement in writing.

A few days later, beers firmly in their fists after the first proper practice in the new place, the band could sit back and rhapsodize about how great the sound was, and how brilliant it was all going to be. But in between, they were still comparing stories about the earthquake, each more lurid than the last. Morgan Tyler seemed to be the most freaked out. When a truck rolled up with a delivery, she was inclined to yelp and jump into a doorway, just in case. She'd lived on the moor all her life, worked on it now as a park ranger. Morgan knew the moor could be unreliable, but unless it was quicksand (or a mischievous stray sod), she knew it did not move. And said so.

"I looked it up," Tom Shorland declaimed a bit too carefully. A brawny garage mechanic, he put down the empty bottle of Old Peculiar and stood up. "And there's never been an earthquake in England, not in the last hundred years."

"Till last Sunday," Brian Hobbes, the drummer, rumbled.

"Aliens," said Raven, but nobody marked him. "Or the French."

"This is not California," Tom went on. "It is not Greece. Or Japan. Is it Japan, Ben Harper? Do I *look* Japanese?"

He grimaced cheerfully at the American, the sometime TV star who he liked well enough, and didn't mind drinking his beer. And after all, the man was applying his talents, his skills, and his industry friends to building up the band. And build this great place with the excellent acoustics. And the fine views of Dartmoor out every window. And support the village.

Aside from all that, he was an outsider after all, in spite of being married to Dinah's cousin Mellis, and so were most of his friends. Friends like the sloe-eyed and gorgeous Mr King over there by the window. "That one looks more Japanese than I do!"

The man stood up, sharpish. So did that kid, Rafe, but then he stepped into a music stand and got all involved in catching it before it collapsed. Of course he tripped again and fell about while setting it to rights. Someone snorted. Tom's eyes slipped aside, distracted, and the tension broke.

Mr King adopted a lazy smile, and let the silence lengthen

"Heh. Right," Tom grumbled, eventually. "Space aliens."

"Oi!" said his wife, getting to her feet. Dinah Shorland, founder, fiddler, and school administrator counted up the empties and made an executive decision in plain English. "Right! Everybody out. Before Aubrey has to demonstrate another of his many talents and rearrange my husband's attitude. Some of us have to work for a living, y'know."

A general moaning at having to get up and move again. "But this sofa is so nice!" Morgan wailed, hugging a dark red cushion.

"Yeah, I know." Ben took a fatherly pose. "When the team comes for the village show, you can thank Jilly for the best break room in Devon. But Dinah says we're done, right? As they say down the pub..."

Cheerily, they all chorused, "You don't have to go home but you can't stay here!"

"That's it!"

The fiddler clapped hands twice to refocus their attention and added. "Back here Saturday week, right? Then Boxing Day at the Star. Happy Christmas, everybody!"

Minutes later, car doors slammed, headlamps flared, engines grumbled through the early dark, and Ben was alone in front of his bright new building, watching colored fairy lights chasing across the slated roof, exhausted but very pleased with the choices he'd made since last year.

Oh, there were still obligations to clean up. Next month he had to get back to the London production staff to finish planning the final series. Contractually, he had to produce six to eight episodes of the show, plus the special "Now or Never— Iveston Village" episode, before he could walk away. And that meant a packed schedule of travelling, shooting, writing, editing, and promoting, and at least one appearance with Graham Norton.

The free days were counting down, but he was happy. Time to write a little music, play a little more, make a few phone calls and a lot of plans. Maybe find someone with that puppy Sparrow wanted. As long as nothing else intervened.

"You coming in, sir?"

Raven stood framed in the doorway, hands thrust into his pockets in that way he had: rebellious youth crossed with worldly major domo. Little more than a silhouette, he said, "Or going home? I can lock up if you like, and set security."

There had never been a security setup as thorough as this one, monitored as it was by the more mischievous of the Dartmoor faeries.

"Coming in, for now." So he did, scraping slush off his boots at the threshold like a conscientious householder. "Is his grace still here?"

The kid nodded and stepped back into the warmly lit reception area. Ben had barely closed the door when the low rumble of an aftershock began, as before, with a deep growl he felt more than heard. The building rattled in response, and Ben braced himself as the earth rolled under the parquet floor, the concrete foundation, and granite substrate. Rainbow haloes outlined the lights.

A crash of wood and metal rang from Studio A, and a yelp of surprise.

"My lord!"

"Aubrey!"

The faerie king had just sat down at the mixing board, and had been adjusting his headphones for playback. They found him in a tumble of equipment, just raising himself from the floor braced on the palms of his hands, pale and shaken. And vibrating with fury.

"Oak and ash!" he roared. "Who dares?" He was on his feet before they could help him. He glared wildly, seeking some source, some enemy he could blast. Energy crackled from his hair and hands like popping electricity. "Who dares to conjure me! *Me*!"

The king thrust past Ben and Raven, flinging them aside as carelessly as autumn leaves. With three long strides and a jangle of crystal chimes, he had marched out of the studio and into the perpetual summer morning that by his will was Faerie. With each step, his appearance changed, jeans and shirt exchanged for fine tunic and hose, and the golden tracery of a crown on his brow.

They arrived mere steps from his own graceful palace in its sylvan glade. His people great and small looked up, dropped whatever clever thing they were doing, and scattered, fading or popping out of the way according to their kind. Two or three of his ladies, dressed in little more than leaves and their long green hair, glided forward bravely with sweetmeats and wine, but he waved them off with a growl. Even the towering trees drew back their shadows in the face of the king's rage.

He halted at last, breathing hard, and turned, apparently startled to find Raven and Ben still with him. As one, they stepped back.

"Mirror," Oberon snapped, ignoring them.

A circle of polished silver appeared in the air at the king's eye level, with ribbons of color breaking and shimmering across its surface like oil on rainwater. A little, thought Ben, like a screen saver.

"Chair!"

He sat without looking in the throne of narwhal ivory that was his by long right. Three-thousand years crowned king of Faerie, Oberon swept a hand through the air.

"Who calls me?" he said grimly, and glared into the mirror. "Show me! Who seeks to bind Oberon like a servant?"

Silently, the younger men moved to flank the king, positioned where they could watch over his shoulder, out of sight but near at hand.

A long minute passed while he sought beyond the veils and gates through the worlds that appeared and slipped back into the mirror, scanning images, shapes, and colors that Ben could make no sense of. From time to time, long fingers pressed at his temples, as if resisting a massive headache. At last, he took a deep breath, exhaled, the hard blue eyes still black with anger. He leaned forward on his elbows, the long hands entwined in thought.

"That cannot be," he said.

"Sir?" said Raven.

Oberon turned a look on the boy that Ben wanted to call stricken, but that was just too weird, and too human. It was never safe to guess at fae emotions. "It is not possible. She is…"

Ben started to frame a question, but Raven's hand on his shoulder put a stop to that. They'd spent enough time together, and faced enough royal irritation, that few words were needed between them. Eventually this would all make sense. Or as much sense as Faerie was likely to provide. There would be work for them to do.

I knew it, Ben thought. There goes Christmas!

5
Secota village, Roanoke Island, date uncertain

This was the forest primeval, the murmuring pines and hemlock at the edge of a continent. That summer it was murderously hot, the air almost too thick to breathe. All the moisture of the earth hung suspended in the air, or coated the skin in sweat, withheld from the growing world by the gods of their unfathomable whim. None fell on the corn. Even the mikumwess, the faerie folk who lived beside and among the Secota, gasped when they poked their long, pointy noses into the mortal world, fanning themselves with their mushroom cap hats, and so they came less often. Their dance circles were abandoned even in the deep forest, where the air no longer murmured but stood still and hot as a green furnace. The only things dancing were mosquitoes. The little faerie men and maids could sing and dance in their own lands beneath the rocks by the sea, or somewhere else, who could say. A few stayed behind, always curious about the doings of the Young People of the Shore (they themselves were the Old People, of course). But they never stayed long.

Unaware of them, Young Woman gathered up everything she needed. The reed mats that were the walls of her home had, like everyone else's, been rolled up on all sides, but no saving breeze swept through. Sweat collected in her scalp, rolled down her face without cooling. It dripped salt tears into her eyes, gathered under her tattooed breasts. Distracted, she spared yet another moment to scan the hard blue sky and wish she understood. Clouds piled up like snow drifts, packing the rim of the world, she thought, yet no rain fell.

Across the path, Badger lifted a hand in greeting, his pleasure in seeing her as obvious as it had been when they were young. He had gone out with one of the foraging parties a few days before, like the rest of the grown men and boys, but returned with a broken foot. Young Woman had bound it up for him, so now he just lay on a mat, or sat in the shade and watched, almost but not entirely too hot to complain. She ignored him, concentrating on collecting her magic.

Young Woman walked from her house at the far end of the village to sit cross-legged on a piece of deerskin in the middle of the field where the Three Sisters were trying to grow. Stunted corn spiked up all around her, struggling in their mounds to be tall enough so the Secota could plant beans to climb the stalks and thrust roots down to open the soil so squash could be planted around the beans.

In the sky, she knew, or behind a mountain, or up in a tree, a monster was holding back the rain. Someone had to learn its name and tell it to let the clouds come, let the rain fall, and there was no other but herself to do it, or the People would die. First among them would be the children, like the children who came to her now. A boy and a girl too young to leave the village but old enough to watch the corn and throw stones at birds and any spirits who tried to steal it. But there was none to steal.

"I'm as dry as a turtle," said the little girl, when the Young Woman came to the dying field. Her brother said, "I'm as thirsty as a fish!"

"No, no, no! You must not say such things," said Young Woman, who was not so young any longer but it was her name.

"Why not? It's true!" they whined as only very small children do.

"Don't you know?" While she let them sip from the water she had brought, she told them the story of the monster who held back the river until the hero came and killed it. And when the river flowed again, all the people jumped in to take a drink. And then their words came back to them, for everyone who had said *I'm dry as a turtle* became a turtle, and everyone who had said *I'm as thirsty* as a fish became a fish!

"You must be careful what you say," she said, in case they had missed the point. "Words have power. Now go away." And she sent them back to the watchers' hut on its little platform to scare away the crows that didn't come.

She had put on all her strands of pearls, threaded them through the blue-black hair that swarmed across her shoulders, looped them around her brown neck echoing the pearls tattooed blue and red on her throat and chest. They looped between her breasts and down her arms, around her waist where the deerskin apron, her only garment, draped about her thighs. The spirits would be honored that she wore all her finery for them.

She had brought a burning coal in a clay pot and set it down in front of her. Other needful things she had brought wrapped in a coiled basket. First she pulled out dry moss, so the smoldering coal would catch and turn to flame. Bit by bit she added twigs, sweet herbs, and a handful of precious corn, parched for storage and saved among her medicine things. As she did all this, she sang—quietly at first, then louder as the fire gained strength. And when the kindling blossomed red and gold, she reached into another bowl and brought out a handful of shredded, dried tobacco that she placed on the fire, smothering it. And all the while Young Woman was singing.

> "I make the world, and let it go. See it?
> I make the world and let it go. See it!
> Ai-ya! Ai-ya! Hey!
> Let it go!"

As the tobacco smoke rose up in a column thick and blue, she opened her eyes very wide, and leaned forward over the bowl, rocking back and forth and breathing in the fume, and letting it go. Breathing it in, and letting it go as she sang,

> "I know where the rain has gone, do you?
> Ai-ya! Ai-ya!
> I know where the rain has gone, do you?
> Show me if you know!"

The little mikumwess watched with interest. This sort of thing went on all the time. Often enough, something happened as a result, but mortal magic was not as reliable as their own. If only she would ask them, it might suit them to help her. Perhaps if she asked nicely and left some parched corn for them. As it was, the song was pleasant and they were pleased to hear it, and surely the magic was working. How nice! But even they were startled when Young Woman gasped and sat back in alarm.

The sorrowful face of a girl wavered in the smoke like a face in running water.

"Who are you?" the girl cried. What a queer question! Spirits never asked questions. "Help me!"

Young Woman spoke two or three words she knew and reached for the cover to close the fire pot, but she stayed her hand. The words hadn't worked. The golden figure hovered in the pillar of smoke, a face and a torso, now, and long graceful arms. Almost a whole girl with hair like flame and eyes that burned like a demon's.

"What are you?"

"You can hear me!" the girl wailed. Her grief was palpable and cold as the sea, hard and relentless, buffeting Young Woman, raking at her heart. "Oh, Venus Genetrix, the creature can hear me! Can you help me?"

"What... what do you need? What *are* you?" What help could a woman of the Secota give a spirit? All around her the mikumwess crowded in, peering out from her hair, some hanging on to her pearls like a child on a branch, some sitting on her knees, fascinated.

The golden girl reached out an imploring hand and they all squeaked and leapt away. "Get me out of here!" The voice was so desperate.

Young Woman was not so foolish as that. "Why?" she asked.

For a moment, the strange, snub-nosed face looked thoughtful, as if searching for words. "The North Wind imprisoned me in his fire. I cannot get out without your help."

That didn't sound right. The Bear of the North Wind gave fire to People when he wandered away to eat berries, and forgot about it. People fed the fire, and the fire went with them. Everyone knew that. But the pale girl was beside herself. Maybe she was confused. Maybe it was a different Bear. Maybe she was lying, but who would lie about being enchanted into smoke? Maybe a demon?

A breeze sprang up out of the north, an echo to the thought, and breathed across the fire pot. Bright flames reached up to meet it, stronger than was wise in the tinder dry field. The sacred smoke was filling her eyes and her mind, but instead of drawing Young Woman into the spirit world, it bewildered her.

The girl's face had a sly twist to it. What if she were a demon? It was Young Woman's charge to be careful for the People's sake, but she couldn't think straight.

A slender hand extended out of the pillar of smoke, whole and round as a human being's, but pale as milk. Lifting the hair about her face, the hot air quickened, carrying the girl's voice into her mind. "Help me."

Young Woman sat back to clear her head and the hand retreated. She could see the whole girl now, suspended above the fire pot, wreathed in blue smoke, with the flames of her strange hair floating above her shoulders while lightning— was that lightning?—crackled around her.

Already uneasy, fearful as she had never been, the little hairs on the shaman's arms prickled with the power crawling along her skin. She knew it in her blood as the trance enfolded her at last. She had no will to look up as the air grew dark with storm. The rain clouds were moving, closing in. She had found the demon who held the rain.

The fear slipped away.

"Tell me your name," she said calmly, and her voice carried without effort to the demon in the smoke. "Let the rain fall, and I will help you."

Lightning ripped the sky, and hard upon it, thunder broke and crashed across the world as the bear chased by hunters crashes through the wood. The dainty hand reached out from the smoke again, and hers rose with it, steady and sure, but when she did not take it, the demon lost its temper.

"I-Bring-the-Rain is my name," it shrieked over the roar of wind and power. "The rain will fall. You must agree to help me!"

At peace in her trance, prepared for the sacrifice, Young Woman nodded once. "Yes, I will help you."

She rocked forward and extended her brown hand across the fire. Her blood was the price, and she could pay it. The flames leapt up and licked at her wrist, but she felt nothing, though the skin over the blue veins went red, then black, and began to blister and crackle. The mikumwess jumped forward crying, dragging at her arm to bring it back, but she could neither see nor feel them as her blood began to drip and feed the fire.

Dazed, the shaman's lips sketched a little smile of satisfaction as the first of the rain touched her checks mixing with her tears, spilling trails down her breasts. She sensed but did not see the dust puff up with each fat raindrop. She had won. She had tricked the demon. The rain would put out the fire in the basket, and her people would be safe. Death had come for her. She sighed her acceptance and let her spirit go.

"Not yet, my girl."

The pale hand darted out and clutched Young Woman's ruined arm through the retreating smoke. Red lips shaped a half-remembered word of power, trapping the shaman's spirit just before it could escape along the path to the sky. Naked as Milo's Venus and smelling vaguely of ambergris and bay, golden eyes lit-up with triumph, the demon stepped laughing into the world, mantled in her red-gold hair.

Perdita would have liked to linger, savoring the life as she stole it, but hunger and need overwhelmed all other desire. She could barely stand; better to sit here on the ground, where she could hold the Young Woman against her like a child. The long pale legs slipped down beside brown ones, one arm slid beneath the tattooed breasts and one hand looped through the ropes of pearls, their silken texture tingled the reawakened skin, every sensation new and sensuous, almost painful but splendid.

Lightly she tilted up the round brown face and brushed black hair aside. The spirit remained, though the will slept within Perdita's spell. Tightening her hand in the pearls at the shaman's throat, she laid her lips to the other's like a kiss, drank in Young Woman's knowledge and power with her last breath. When at last she lifted her mouth, she raised a triumphant face to the thunderous sky, and promptly collapsed with the shaman's body in her arms.

The sky opened up, the rain came down in great waves, more than the hard ground could take in all at once. Dust turned to mud and mud to slurry, and flowed around the two women where they lay. It braided through their tangled hair, pooled under their arms and amorous legs, bound them in the earth like lovers. Young Woman's blood had also spilled where they lay while the water ran, mingling with the earth, and the sky had something yet to say.

The witch slept satisfied as her body warmed and the one in her arms grew cold. A flickering remnant of the shaman stirred from the dark corner where it had hidden, and called on the spirits for help. The Grandmother came, then, and dismantled the witch's awkward spell, and sent this granddaughter into the sky with a new name and with peace, then turned her attention. She saw the new one's strangeness, and her vanity, and went away. But she left behind a gift that might remind the woman of her wickedness. Perhaps she would learn from it. Perhaps she would not. All in good time.

6
In Faerie

The king's Great House was not a fairy tale castle exactly. More like a wayside inn in some Ruritanian adventure. The building, if building is the right word for a thing raised by magic and music, and being partly in the mind of the king, was more like layer upon layer of timber-framed cottage roughly the size of Kensington Palace, but cozier, or perhaps more expansive, or sort of folded in on itself. Its bounds merged into the wood and meadow that surrounded it, or billowed into roundel windows and stout doors, balconies and lofty galleries, and delicate traceries that reached into and blended with the forest itself. Fae of all kinds and shapes danced and drank, made music and practiced their peculiar arts or games, or whatever they were, as faeries do when not tickling mortals in their sleep.

The house, as Ben saw it, stood under towering groves of ancient oak and ash and hawthorn, whose boughs supported draperies of silk and light in frail colors that teased the eye. The sound of running water pattered everywhere, even within the house where verandas and whole rooms bridged streams that meandered here and there before spilling away to darker, more obviously perilous corners of Faerie. He suspected that it must be quite different with no mortals present to anchor it in time. Did the house, the meadow, the wood even exist, he wondered, when Aubrey wasn't there, or if the king let his awareness of it slip? An uncomfortable notion.

Most days, tables dressed with fabulous dishes of food and drink were laid out on the vast close-cropped meadow, in the rose garden, by bubbling fountains or across manicured lawns left ragged and rustic at the edges, suitable to more pastoral members of the community. The air was always sweet, the light soft, if the king willed it so. Today was not one of those days. Rooms sat dark, the gardens dreary, laughter stilled.

It was safe to say the king of Faerie was not amused. It was only safe to say it from a distance, because within the sound of his voice, peril dwelt.

To Ben's eyes, privileged to see Faerie as it was, the king had never looked so utterly inhuman. Ben had once told his wife that Aubrey looked like Rupert Everett, and mostly he did, but today Faerie stood stark and alien in the sharp planes of Oberon's face and the set of his eyes.

He spent an hour pacing the length of his banqueting hall, crackling with power barely constrained, while Ben and Raven spelled each other in his close attendance, tense with anticipation. The hall itself was curiously stripped bare of ornament or hospitality. The usual revelers periodically came by, peering in at the windows or from behind tapestries, peeking out of patterns in the ceiling only to languidly depart or scurry away, as suited their age and type, at Raven's sign. Sooner, if they were paying attention.

Eventually, Oberon called for a pipe and for wine, and with a gesture flung open the crystal doors at the far end of the hall. The sky and all else darkened to twilight around him in answer to the royal mood. Torches flared to life, but not the clear candlelight of the chandeliers, and the room took on the shadows and angles of a medieval hall. He stood then on the broad balcony, marked by the cherry glow of the Meerschaum bowl carved like a dragon that writhed through sinuous knot-work under his hand. The vista stretching to the blue and silver distance reminded Ben of the Yosemite Valley under moon and starlight, which it couldn't be. Unless it was.

The temperature was dropping, and the king's face and form were veiled. The music that in Faerie was as constant as the dawn had stopped altogether, too. At least there had been no further disturbances, in the earth or in the ether, that Ben could tell.

The silence was becoming oppressive; he realized he was hungry. There was food on the tables, as always—sculpted sweets and lambent fruits and jellies—but Ben being mortal didn't like to eat anything in Faerie without assurances renewed in advance. He had no intention of trading a life he was finally happy with for one in the Hollow Hills, no matter how pleasant. Nor had he been invited.

There must be something he could do. At last, he cleared his throat experimentally. "Your grace?"

Oberon turned to him, startled at last out of reverie. "Ben?" he said with a slight frown. "Why are you still here? Go home!"

"Sir?"

"It's all right, Ben, and I thank you for your pains." The lofty diction was seldom a good sign. Ben glanced at Raven who had retired to a corner with a book, reading apparently by his own eldritch glow. The boy did not look up.

"You'll forgive me, sir," said Ben, matching the tone. "But it's not all right. You look like hell, and you need to either tell us what's going on or at least let me fetch my harp." At the quizzical look, he added, "Or *your* harp. Or a guitar, or the Vienna Boys' Choir. You may not have noticed, sir, but there's no music in the house. None."

"Ben."

"And I know as well as you do, that's not a good thing." Behind him, a book snapped shut, but he stood his ground. "I could go home, sure. I've got things to do. I need a shower. Dinner would be nice. Mellis will be calling. But I don't like leaving you like this."

A muscle ticked up a corner of the royal mouth, not quite a smile, but a moment of irony perhaps. "You're worried about me, human child?"

Ben stood there, arms folded over his best Brian Froud t-shirt, engaging the master of the Perilous Realm like a schoolmaster. "I'm worried about us all, if this keeps up, sir."

"And you suggest?"

The only mortal in the place gave up. He shoved his hands into the pockets of the jeans he'd been wearing all day, and who knows what time it was now, and sighed a particularly annoyed sigh. "I suggest, sir, we all go to the Star and drink gin, with or without tonic, and play some music until you stop being so damned broody. And if you want to spill whatever it is that's freaking you out, fine. If not, at least there'll be gin involved. And maybe Raven can even get laid."

"I beg your pardon?" said the boy.

"You heard me. Come on, let's go." Ben started for the door, then stopped when he realized he didn't actually know how they'd gotten here. Fine, he couldn't get lost, and he could find his way home from anywhere, including the king's palace of Faerie; all he needed was a tune. Clapton's Can't Find My Way Home crossed his mind like a bad joke. Whatever. They could follow if they would.

7

The Star, Iveston on Moor

i

Was it working? Ben didn't want to look back, but he was pretty sure footsteps were matching his before he shifted through the worlds to enter his own office by way of the garden door. Half an hour later he had Skyped with Mellis and laughed about an earthquake in Devon of all places, and kissed his little boy long distance. When he had turned around a few times in the shower, he emerged to find a hot bowl of stew on the table and fresh clothes, too, laid out by Brownie Meg, his part-time brownie, or hob as they were called in these parts.

Half an hour after that, he was poking through strands of tinsel and plastic snowflakes at the Star, ordering G&Ts for the three of them—just a local entrepreneur, his engineer, and his intern. And it was a damned sight more comfortable than hovering about the king of goddamned Faerie and one of his principal gentlemen, waiting for the velvet slipper to drop.

They'd talk a bit, have a drink or two, he supposed. After a while, someone would notice they were there, local heroes that they were. The neighbors, being neighborly, would make no fuss, no one would ask him to play, not directly. Not that he was too posh to play for them, not at all; they were just too polite to impose.

Everyone knew Mr King—they always called him Mr King, for some reason—and they knew he wasn't with the band. They liked him too, not just because he now then bought a round for the house. Nor he wasn't an idle gentleman, neither, Mr King, for didn't he build fancy recording studios for rock stars and the like. And wasn't he working with his own hands, and hiring local folk besides, and ordering materials through local suppliers, and drinking in their pub for that matter. Not often, but it was always a treat when he did. In a few short months, Aubrey had become like local gentry, which for Devon men in a rather small village was saying a lot.

So, while they wouldn't ask unless he visibly had a guitar or that wee harp about him, Ben imagined someone else might start a song, knowing he and his friends couldn't resist. And a guitar might appear. Or not. As long as there was music, Ben thought, then the dangerous magic Aubrey was holding between his two noble hands along with the gin would be redirected, diluted. It could be put away until a clear target appeared. And that would doubtless come soon enough.

Easing back in the snug booth in the corner between the bar and the unoccupied little stage, Ben stole a look at his extraordinary friend. He saw a man well and suitably dressed, as always, but shockingly drawn for an immortal, who never showed his age much less his emotions. The passions of the Fae are not built on chemistry and hormones, and could be altogether alien, still the signs when they appeared were telling. An edge of anger still lurked there, tightly controlled, but the tension at least had eased a little. It wasn't possible to get Aubrey drunk, of course, but perhaps he could be made to relax. And as long as the earth didn't quake tonight, Ben guessed they'd be fine.

In the meantime, Raven was chatting up the landlord's brown-eyed daughter while fetching the next round. For the village's sake, the kid with the Gainsborough looks had adjusted his appearance in that way that he had. The odd blond streak that flared in his night black hair had faded a bit as the features sharpened, so Rafe Fitzroy looked closer to 21 than 16, more new college grad than junior prom king. As always, he dressed to suit himself, though he toned it down for the village: still a bit Goth-y, and he had taken to wearing a pair of small golden hoops in one ear. The girls hereabouts all thought he was adorable; not one of them noticed the elven glow.

"Americans always want ice," Raven said with a wink as he placed three tall glasses on the table—the frosty one with all the ice diluting the gin was for Ben—then he spun a chair around. He straddled the seat then looked back over his shoulder to blow a kiss and a wink to Kristie at the bar. When she blushed, the boy turned about again and leaned forward, grinning. The Star was busy enough that, like spies exchanging covert information, they could have the most arcane conversation in plain view—conversation which Raven had apparently decided to have.

"I'm with Ben, sir," he went on, staring straight at Aubrey, who ignored them both to share a knowing smile with Molly Downing as she crossed the room.

King or recording engineer, subtle Aubrey gave absolutely no sign that this was a statement unwelcome or unwise. "Are you, then?" he said flatly.

"Uhm," Ben grumbled. "You're with Ben about what, exactly?"

"That thing earlier. The, you know, the earthquake."

"Yes?" Aubrey wasn't, clearly, going to make this easy.

"Sir, I know the feel of power when it knocks me off my feet. You said someone was trying to conjure you, and it rightly made you angry. You know who it is."

The clatter of wooden chairs on wooden floors washed around them along with the crash of glasses dumped into bus trays under the bar, bar taps hissing as they were pulled, and general chatter. Around the low table by the 300-year-old hearth was only stillness and the crackle of the fire.

Aubrey lifted his glass and drank slowly and steadily, and when there was nothing left but a wedge of lemon stubbornly clinging to the bottom, he set it down. The glittering night blue of his gaze rested mildly on the boy. "And Ben, with whom you agree, thinks I'll feel better if I share that knowledge with you both."

"I didn't say that," said Ben. "I said you'd feel better if we got some music into you, but I'd settle for gin."

Aubrey's glance shifted to include Ben. He nodded with grace to acknowledge the correction.

Raven went on earnestly, reckless as a schoolboy. "I think if you told us what's going on, we could help. I could…"

The king's glance stopped him, though Aubrey only raised his glass, curiously refilled. When he had knocked it back, and let his eyes soften just a bit, he appeared to make a decision. Leaning forward on his elbows, he began in a low voice:

"Once upon a time…"

And then he stopped. Sat back.

"On the other hand…" An unmistakable flight of elven mischief passed across the handsome face. He'd been spending too much time with mortals, perhaps, or maybe he just wanted there to be no mistaking who was in charge. A single brow flared over the exotic eyes. "No, no, my boys. Not just yet."

Smoothly, he stood and slipped out of the cashmere jacket and hung it over the back of Raven's chair, looking both more relaxed and more dangerous than he had all day. Well, maybe he could get drunk, if he wanted to. Delighted at their confusion, he shoved the sleeves of a creamy Aran jumper up to his elbows, then ducked briefly under the table. He emerged with a triangular leather bag painted with interlacing floral devices like an illuminated manuscript. He stopped for a hit on a cigarette they hadn't noticed, then flipped it out of the world, exhaling a pale cloud with a sigh. In a moment he sat again and, folding back the cover of the bag, reached inside to pull out a compact harp, a minstrel's harp carved of myrtle wood and strung with bronze and silver wire. Ben brightened, recognizing Dariole, the exquisite instrument he had once played for Alfred the Great. She never wanted tuning; Dariole was always in tune.

"Let's have some Yuletide spirit, shall we?" Aubrey said. He turned in the hard bench seat to make room for her on his knee, then let her recline into his shoulder.

Without a plea for silence, without drawing attention to himself, without even faerie magic, heads began to turn and the whole room modulated to a new key. Darts flew to target, the scores were chalked up, and forgotten. Someone abruptly pulled the plug on the old jukebox at the back. A few mobiles slid open, and someone snagged the phone behind the bar, in case mobile service failed as it often did on the moor. Calls were made. Word spread. Before he was done, the room would be crowded with rosy, eager faces, but he wasn't about to wait.

With a satisfied sigh, Ben relaxed. He had first heard Aubrey give voice to the little harp last spring at a jam session on the borderlands of Faerie itself, just as his first faerie errand was ending, but only rarely since then. This was what he had hoped for. Everything else could wait.

Less content, Raven let something approaching annoyance cross his face, then set it aside, trading knowing glances with Ben who was just happy the music was back. When the king was ready, he would tell them whatever he was willing for them to know. If he also wanted to tell every mortal soul between here and Chagford, he'd do that too.

The first silver chord struck the air. Someone snapped a photo, and was hurriedly told to put the bloody thing away. Mr King, Aubrey, whom they all knew, was playing, running the long, inhuman fingers through the strings, seeking the music he wanted. Ben was right. This was where his strength lay. But where to begin?

It was Christmas time, as the Star's décor was at pains to recognize, with ten days still to go. People would be already sick to death of Rudolph. They might not be quite ready for the awesome simplicity of *Ave Maria Stella*, and besides, this was the pub, not St Michael's church. Where to begin?

For a minute or so he just improvised, his hands finding their own patterns as the room settled in to listen. Instead of a single tune, he wove the old carols together, moving from one into another just where it fit, and the listeners felt how right it was, and what good sense it made. They looked at one another and nodded, beaming, when they recognized one old melody building out of another, congratulating themselves, proud to have a talent like this among them who trusted them to get it, even if he wasn't one of their own.

Folk arrived; Aubrey paused and sipped at the beer someone had put in front of him as greetings were made and wraps put aside, orders made at the bar and maybe just a packet o' crisps, luv, unless there's a taste o' thikky ham and egg pie left. It wasn't a concert, after all, just a man playing a little for friends he knew would like to hear him. Raven went to give Kristie a hand bringing chairs up from the cellar, and sliding back the pocket doors into the bar parlour so everyone could hear. After a few minutes, he reappeared holding Ben's guitar, a classic Gibson, to be stashed nearby until it might be called for.

Aubrey brightened and gave a nod when they called to him, lifted his beer in response to an offered toast, tolerated of his grace all manner of familiarity from the Dymock children and old Mrs Satterly, while Ben wondered where on earth they had all come from on a cold and snowy evening deep in the country.

Then just about the time the pub had returned to almost but not quite normal, a flashy arpeggio rippled from the harp, showing off, just a little. And this time it was *Lo How a Rose E'er Blooming,* and the warmth of his voice created with the harp a sound filled with sweetness and sorrow as deep as the roots of love. It segued joyously into *Deck the Halls,* as if it was the most natural thing in the world, and folk who felt like it joined in on the fa-la-las. And though the moor was as frosty as anyone could remember, the night as dark, the Star was a gilded hub of warmth and companionship, and the phones never rang at all.

Next, it was time to tell a story. Aubrey constructed from gossamer and gummy bears a fairy tale just for the kiddies who might be feeling left out. It came with sound effects and voices and a happy ending and no one dying along the way, although the bad 'un came to a bad end, as rightly he should.

In the applause that followed, he nodded Ben toward the guitar with a wink and a grin. Then it turned out one of the old lads had tucked a fiddle in the car, just in case. A tin whistle appeared in Raven's hands from some impossible pocket, someone else pulled a bodhran off the wall, and the mood changed again. It was time for dancing. More sweaters and coats hit the racks and chairs, the tables were pushed to the walls. If the dancing was as much hopping up and down as it was Sellinger's Round, still round English faces grew rosy with sweat and merriment, and the beer flowed so freely that Kristie's Dad prepared to go out in the deep midwinter to fetch another keg from the shed.

Just as the landlord was grumbling cheerfully and bundling up for bitter weather, Raven caught a word from his boss and went to help. "Trouble, sir? Let me have a look, right?"

He ducked behind the bar and fiddled with the taps, rapped one with a confident blow, looked under the counter a bit and fussed with something noisy before he came back up, beaming.

"A bit stuck is all, Mr Day," he said brightly. "Give it another pull." And wouldn't you know it, the boy wasn't as foolish as he looked, earrings or no. The ale flowed as freely as before, and the music with it.

As so often happens when things are nearly perfect, Ben felt the time slow and stand nearly still, and perhaps it had. It'd happened before, as he recalled with pleasure when it was time to gently lay the Gibson aside. When everyone needed a breather, and threw themselves into chairs and cold drinks, he went to lock the guitar in a closet behind the bar. As he handed Kristie back the key, he couldn't help taking a second look, a proper look, at Aubrey where he sat wreathed in good cheer by the fire. It was another of Ben's gifts to see straight to the true nature of a thing, if he applied himself."

Either way, he could see that trouble was still there, but whatever it was that had left the ancient spirit foxed and full of holes as an old parchment had, as far as any mortal could see it, been filled in with the music that was the source and wellspring of his magic.

Whether the time had been paused or not, and even with the amazingly unstuck beer tap and the uncommonly good company, eventually the evening had to wind down, and so it did. The tunes got slower, and the songs more thoughtful and a little melancholy. Children were falling asleep on laps and on fleecy coats. People who had farms to look after were starting to pack up.

And just as Mr Day was reluctantly announcing the party over, "Landlord!" said the king of Faerie, hardly raising his voice.

And as it must have done in a thousand times and places, that voice carried even across the squeal of chairs scraped over old boards, and the clatter and chime of empties being gathered up.

Mr Day looked over at once. "Yes, Mr King?"

"The good whiskey, if you please, sir!"

A sudden hush fell, and a few people allowed themselves to wonder if it was really all that late after all. That nice chap with the slightly odd accent raised his hand in a regal gesture. "And a round for anyone not driving."

Some sat themselves right back down. Some others, and all the ones with children, sighed and shrugged into their coats, and made their farewells. In minutes, the Star was once again the province of a few courting couples, the old man with the fiddle, the Days, and a few others, hovering.

A bottle of 60-year-old single malt that the landlord kept in just for Mr King made the rounds then arrived at his table with a heavy crystal shot glass. Aubrey poured the glass and held it up smoky and glimmering to the light. He sipped it once, and smiled, once again for the savoring of it, and waited. Then he sat forward, leaning on his elbows and raised the parting glass like a sacrament.

"My dears," said he, meeting their eyes each by each as he scanned the room, collecting their nods and sleepy smiles. "Let us drink to the past, and to the never ending present, and to the courage of your hearts." With a single smooth gesture, he tipped the excellent whiskey down his throat as the others, a bit puzzled at the toast but happy to comply, drank with him.

And now he sat away and pushed his hair back over his shoulders, He pulled the little harp into his shoulder again, and turned so he could watch the listeners, but mainly Raven. Long, untiring fingers traced light and lightly across the strings, keeping company with his tale, illustrating, illuminating, drawing down the magic and casting it up again.

"Once upon a time," he began.

ii

Once upon a time in the dawn of the world when the forests covered Europe from the Danube to the Rhine and half the world besides, there lived a king called Aubrey. I see you have heard of him, said Mr Aubrey King, as his listeners chuckled.

And this king was lord of all the elves, all the pixies, all the faeries, in truth, from Land's End to John O'Groats, and even over the little folk of Ireland, before the Sidhe came. But his kingdom was of music and of magic, not of men, and his rule was light.

In the days of his youth, and that was a very long time ago indeed, he met a woman. A girl, really, though not a maid, of the mortal kind—of humans, aye like yourselves that sit by me here. She had been, as girls were sometimes then, put into the service of an earth goddess. In those days, those far off days, the earth priests brought men for such girls to lie with, to make sure the earth would prosper and oh! So many things.

Kristie Day gave a little shriek and covered her ears, blushing furiously.

One day this good king you have heard of found a girl weeping in a hazel break in the Vale of Apples.

"Avalon," murmured the old lad with the fiddle.

Aubrey's eyes sparkled as he nodded.

Aye, Avalon. Her face was scratched, her arms were covered in blood, and she was dazed with weeping. He took her up with care, for he was fond of mortal folk, and of pretty girls most of all, and she was very fair.

"Ah, you laugh, Billy Clayton! As well you may!"

A light scattering of notes let them all see the young farmer's tendency to flit from pretty girl to pretty girl, to his parents' despair. His neighbors laughed in a friendly way, and the blonde he had his arm around did too. His friend Ripley punched his shoulder.

He took the lost girl and gave her a name. Perdita, he called her there among the apple trees with the white blossoms falling on her golden breast and lighting in her golden hair. Perdita of Avalon. He took her to his hall beneath the hill they called the Raven's Tor.

Under his hands and in his power, Dariole conjured pictures in every mind's eye of wide forests opening out to the broad moor they all knew, and the steep hills just outside the Star's back door, especially Raven Tor with its rocky crown.

First he gave her his laughter. And then they danced among the great lords and ladies who danced by starlight in those marble halls. And then he gave her his songs, and though her voice was not always true, she began to learn his magic. For magic and music, as you know, are one and the same.

As fair as a fox, as greedy as a crow, impatient as a child, she was. All his laughter, all his grace, and all his songs were not enough. She wished, oh, she demanded his power too.

Dissonance uncommon to Dariole's strings raked at their emotions, and the room grew darker. In his mind Ben saw—as if he had been there himself in that star-bedecked pavilion of Faerie to watch the dancers sway—he saw the players move inexorably into their places.

And in the night when the moon died, she wove swift spells about him, made him dote upon her without thought, without care. For a little while, he longed to grant her final wish: to give her all he had.

The harper's hands lifted, stilled Dariole's voice in an instant. Silence.

Alas, poor king! Poor foolish king!

As the harp began tentatively to sing again, the listeners saw before them, like shadows in the room with them, the handsome youth, the king of Faerie, asleep in a twilit glade. And here she came, lithe and clever as a cat and as dangerous in her whim.

But impatience was her downfall, said the harper. Could she have waited—ah, but no, oh no. She came as he slept to lift the golden crown from his brow, and stumbled in her haste, and fell. He awoke and wrathful caught her hand, though she wept and raged. And by his arts he bound her to forget his name, and come near him no more.

A binding spell.

A bitter spell.

To cloud her mind and turn her steps from Faerie ever after.

And while he sang the spell, spinning and weaving the threads of the music in curious modes not heard in the haunts of men, a passing raven in his first summer cried out to hear it! The sound of that cry echoed from the ceiling of the sky through the halls beneath the tor, and the spell snapped shut.

And from that day to this, the raven's cry is part of that great binding, and the song has only one home, in the heart of that Raven. What became of the woman, none can say.

iii

The last chord faded, the listeners sighed, blinked, and wondered how they had come to be here in this cozy pub on a winter's night instead of where they most longed to be, dancing under the hill with the faeries. But shortly, being human and hardheaded, sensible Devon men and women, they pushed the feeling aside with laughter at such nonsense and burst into wild applause. As they crowded round to pump the harper's hand, pound him on the back, or just nod their appreciation, Aubrey accepted their praise with grace and pleasure, feeling restored, and wondered where Raven had got to.

There was more to the story, of course, but that should do for now. Ben, looking thoughtful, helped himself to a short shot of the extraordinary Scotch. Sipping appreciatively, he met the elf king's eyes at last and said, "You realize that raised more questions than it answered?"

Aubrey nodded. "I do." He stooped to fetch the leather bag and cover Dariole. Silver strings shimmered with the movement. "Where's Raven?"

"Not tonight, Ben Harper, if you please." He was pushing down his sleeves and shrugging the coat up over his shoulders, every movement effortless grace.

"Just as well, I guess. I need some sleep, yeah." Zipping up his jacket, Ben added, "Just one, maybe?"

A sigh, a sideways look, the harp on its strap thrown over the shoulder of the man with the waiting expression and a golden crown.

"So you can stop her, right?" said Ben, pushing open the door.

The royal lips twisted up a slight smile to go with the slight nod. "Of course."

"The problem is…"

They waved goodnight to a beaming Mr Day and stepped out into the icy air. Warmed with the music and the magic and the extraordinary liquor, Ben hardly noticed the cold.

"The problem is," Aubrey went on, "that she shouldn't even exist. I didn't destroy her, though I should have done. I banished her, and set aside all thought of her."

"Nice trick."

"I clouded her memories of me, and of Faerie. She should never have become whatever it is she has become. She should have lived a mortal span, and then died, two thousand years ago."

On silent wings, Raven fell out of the sky and into step with them, walking in the dark toward Diamond Cottage. "You didn't make her immortal, then?"

"My, what good ears you have. I did not. There are ways, and she must have attempted them. I fear the results, though."

Ben stole a look at Raven, whose boyish face betrayed nothing. "What do you mean?"

Though his steps were silent as only the fae can be, the road crunched under foot as the kingly harper halted, swearing softly in the middle of the road. "Is this your one question? Or will it be the next one, human child?"

Then he shrugged a bit, and walked on to save Ben's shivers.

Sounding almost apologetic, he continued. "You see, she did have power of her own, and some undirected talents. She could learn, when she was willing, and she was crafty. More often she was too hasty. Impatient, as I said. In the end, truth to tell, she really wasn't very good." The thought made him chuckle. "In fact, her voice was…"

"What?"

"Oh, sir," Raven said, surprised into speaking. "You don't mean…"

"I fear me so," said Aubrey with noble forbearance. "Couldn't sing a note! Well, sing, yes, and with enthusiasm. But always just a quarter tone sharp, and couldn't tell the difference. You can imagine the havoc. When she came to me that last time, to kill me, she didn't stumble over the furniture, but over a transition. Incompetent bitch," he snarled, then recovered with a low laugh.

Past the churchyard, past the school, round the tree-lined curve of the road, they were laughing so hard when they reached the golden lamps at his gate, Ben almost hated to ask the last niggling question. It wasn't his to ask, after all.

So the boy did. "And the raven, sir? At the end."

With a sigh, Aubrey met the oddly sullen look and nodded. "That was you, yes."

"So I'm—"

"You are the key, I think."

"But how? The key to what?"

"The spell that bound her, the song itself, is bound in you. Or rather, you bound yourself into it. A portion of your essence is linked with that single wild moment in the first summer of your existence. (And no, Mr Harper, I am not going to explain where little fae come from.) Thus it is—you are—an inextricable part of that rather complex spell. It cannot be broken except by you. Even if she could steal it from you, even if she has learned to sing it off perfectly and has the will to do it, the spell cannot be broken without you, in your raven form. A happy accident, that, but I accepted it. Now—" And he truly did seem sorrowful. "Now I fear we may both be in peril."

"You might have mentioned sooner. Sir," Raven said shortly, then dropped and transformed, spread his wings and flew away again with a caw that almost rang with sarcasm.

Puzzled, Aubrey looked after him, a shadow glimmering in shadows. "Why?"

Standing at last on his own doorstep, Ben ventured one more thing. He thought he knew the answer, but he had to try. "Who is Raven, sir, really?"

"Enough!" snapped Oberon the King, and this time he meant it. Somewhat more gently, he said, "Do you still have the phone we used before?"

"Yes."

"Keep it by you, please. The diary, too, I think. None of this should be happening at all, and I cannot say what will come of it. I may have need of you, and the notice could be short."

Pleased at the confidence in spite of the sharp rebuke, Ben nodded and said, "You know I'm at your service, sir."

This time Oberon smiled. "Good man."

And with that, the king of Faerie was gone.

8
Roanoke, 1580s

Perdita was not a happy woman, but that was nothing new. In a thousand years she'd not been happy for more than a brief span. No, she was angry. Having escaped one prison, where was she but another, half starved and badly dressed.

Badger, stumbling on his bad foot through the pelting rain, had found her in the cornfield, huddled next to the contorted and strangely shrunken body of his childhood friend. While he wept, the others came and marveled at the strange girl who had clearly fallen from the sky along with the rain, their Young Woman's last gift to them, marked with her tattoos.

The rain might have been as troublesome as the drought had been, but it stopped when she told it to—she had no idea why. Crops grew. The deer returned, women got pregnant, children got fat and the winter that followed was the mildest in living memory. They never asked where she came from. She was their Young Woman now, their hero, their shaman, their spirit chief. When they needed answers about the weather, the planting, the mysteries of the earth, she called on the knowledge stolen, like their language, from the savage she had killed to come into this world.

The Secota treated her as a goddess, and she was vain enough to let them. They wanted to be her favored children, and cowered before the snap of her anger. Her fame spread up and down the coast, and the People prospered.

That was nice, but hardly compensation for being stuck here on the freezing, ragged edge on this wretched continent with no way off. Her powers needed scope! What good was it to have become immortal, and at such a cost as she'd paid, if she was to spend the rest of time trapped among these woodland primitives, wearing a deerskin apron and half a hundred-weight of ragged river pearls?

She had such hopes when the Europeans arrived. But gross and nearly as ignorant as the Secota and their neighbors, they dismissed her as a barbarian, or tried to convert her to their stupid religion which they, apparently, did not practice. She learned what she could of the lands they came from, but it was not enough. She needed to get to one of their countries— Spain or France or even England, which sounded the worst of the lot judging by the peasants they had sent here in the most recent attempt to conquer this wretched place.

The English, under that strutting peacock Ralegh, had even taken two of her men back with them. Manteo and Wanchese were good men, clever boys, and she liked clever boys. Not too clever, though, evidently. Trading with other tribes and taking gifts from the English, she had acquired two precious mirrors of polished and silvered glass, the size of the palm of her hand. She had sent one with each of the boys, with simple instructions for their limited use to send her messages, but no images returned from them, not one. Broken or lost, washed overboard or simply forgotten, they were a treasure thrown away, and she was still stuck here with her little problem.

Little problem, *ha*, she thought, giving her slave girl a slap for being clumsy with her comb. It was one of the weepy English the Croatans had given her, before everything had gone mad. Perdita's problem, her affliction, had kept her from successfully seducing Ralegh or even the nasty little Portuguese pirate who was his pilot. Though in the dark, they would fuck anything that moved, the finicky bastards wouldn't bed a savage woman if they could see the color of her skin unless they were raping her. And though her skin had once been as pale as theirs in the green northern forests of her childhood, it was as brown now as a hazelnut, and speckled with the red and blue tattoos of the coastal tribes.

She really hated the tattoos. Wreathed from breast to belly, from shoulder to wrist, and ringing each slender ankle, they pearled her perfect skin in red and livid blue. Every moment awake, they haunted her. The Secota took them as a sign of her divine origin and fitness to lead them, as if the Young Woman had willed them to her successor. As indeed, in a way, she had.

That, by itself, was not the problem. Her breasts were as perfect as the day when... She couldn't quite remember the day, in the place that had vanished, with the man whose face retreated from her every time she tried to picture it. No matter. Her lips were as inviting, her hair as thick and lustrous, and of a color never seen in the Americas until the Europeans arrived, tawny streaked with red and gold. Beautiful and forever young, all those delicious features drew them to her, along with the obvious invitations of a mostly naked body held just so, draped in copper ornaments they thought were gold and ropes of pearls they thought were fine. They were not subtle men, even witty Ralegh. It took very little to seduce them. Gold was enough.

So long as the sun shone.

By night, when they were happy to approach her, gentle or rough, they threw back the skins that hung across her sleeping place and recoiled in horror. For by night, what was she, and by whose art? A monster of advanced old age, with coarse white hair barely covering her scalp, and shrunken dugs. Instead of gleaming in the firelight, her sallow skin was blotched and spotted with age, and a little wiry beard sprouted under a mouth bereft of teeth—the gross consequence of such great age as none of them could have imagined. Within she was as young and lithe as they, but all outward appearance was corruption and pain.

Crude, vulgar men who would not have scrupled at raping grandmothers while sacking native villages shuddered or worse, screamed and ran, and even her flinty heart trembled just a little in the face of their revulsion. By day, she could cast spells to ensure their silence; they never knew the difference.

But of all the long years she had lived with this, a product of her own stupid mistake, it remained disheartening.

The men of the Secota left her alone because she was sacred, and never met her eye, which made magically calling them to her more problematical. By day, they might have been honored to serve her needs for the sake of some ritual, but she would have none of that. That she had done before and then... something else. She vaguely remembered killing one rutting pig, and another long after, and after that...

She had no idea what came after that, except a very long gap before the next memory.

So now, after all her study while wandering the earth, all her learning, all the death that trailed behind her like bloody pearls, all she had were herbs and chants, dried things and powders, and a column of acrid blue smoke in a firepot with which to search for that unknown man, the faceless one who haunted her imprisonment, her dreams and her nightmares, and who had to die. And for Faerie, as closed to her as the bottom of the sea.

Yes, she had learned of Faerie, too. And though she had no way of knowing how or what had happened to her there, she knew it was real and its walls, she believed, could be breached. Somewhere there was a door that would open to her. There had to be. And there would be the shadowy man and, in his death, the power she sought wrapped in pure revenge.

Her only tools were herbs and charms and sweet woods and poisoned mushrooms, and tobacco on a campfire. It's enough, she thought. It will serve.

If she could only get off this damned continent!

9
Mortlake, Surrey, 1589
On the south bank of the Thames,

There is (gentle reader) nothing (the works of God only set apart) which so much beautifies and adorns the soul and mind of man as does knowledge of the good arts and sciences. Many arts there are which beautify the mind OF man; but of all none do more garnish and beautify it than those arts which are called mathematical.
— The Mathematical Preface to Euclid's Elements
(1570)

i

Mortlake was gloriously rustic, though being within the parks of a royal residence, and in the neighborhood of several great estates, its roads and services at least were kept up, for which Dr John Dee was thankful. Having loaded, unloaded, packed and repacked his books, his notebooks, his scientific instruments, and especially the more arcane materials in their baffling array a dozen times since Leyden, he had exhausted his already sketchy temper. Now the hired wherry that had brought him and his esoterica up the river all the way from

London was at last tied up at the village's landing stage, mere steps from his own home.

Remarkably spry for a white-bearded old scholar of two-and-sixty, he scrambled down from the boat to the shore to sort out his belongings' final disposition. He thanked God that a good-sized wagon was waiting for him, as he'd asked, to transfer everything the last little way to his comfortable if somewhat neglected brick and timber-framed house. He turned to stare at the sharp-prowed boat, packed to the gunnels, and frowned.

It might be a bit over-packed, in truth. Perhaps he'd been a bit mean when he'd thought to be thrifty. It was only just big enough, but he had been unwilling to pay more for something twice too big that would not have been available till Thursday in any case. He was not about to leave everything neatly stacked at the Three Cranes for whatever thieves might be foolish enough, or ignorant enough, to risk stealing from the Queen's pet magician.

It was not everything he owned, only everything he'd taken with him when they left for Holland, and everything he'd acquired since then. Everything, perhaps, except a quiet life and unsullied reputation. Mathematician, geographer, cartographer, scholar of forgotten languages and arcane lore, these were the titles he valued most, and with them, the delight of intellect and the most extensive circle of correspondents in Europe.

Some years ago, his lofty pursuits had led to more dangerous fields: anatomy, astrology, divination. And to his dismay, it was those things which earned him a living, mostly casting horoscopes and compounding love potions and other nonsense for courtiers. Still, that nonsense paid for the rest, though it tried his soul, betimes.

Th'art getting old, Jack, he thought irritably. Be about the day, and give over maundering.

Then his eyes widened.

"Look thou be mindful, fellow!" he barked, suddenly seeing what was right in front of him. "Aye, *thou*, woodcock!"

The hired crew were already ripping down ropes and hauling away the canvas covers at a speed that could only mean his goods would be in the river before too long. Everything was balanced as well as one could expect. Still, unloading his life and work was a delicate operation, not to be given to idle monkeys and flibbertigibbets! "Hold, you, all of you!"

He might as well be talking to himself. Were they deaf? What were they witless? "God's death, leave off!" And he swore colorfully in three languages they could not possibly understand.

"Hold a moment, lads," said a voice like a crystal bell. Jane? No, it could not be his wife, whose termagant humour did not lean toward the crystalline.

At once, the men halted their work. To Dee's dismay, each still held a box on a shoulder or under an arm or in whatever precarious grip he had, frozen as if caught in a painting.

Then the voice's owner glided into his view, slender, graceful, and much too young for these burly ruffians to be taking orders from. Her dress was sober cloth and plain, buttoned to the goffered ruff at her throat, and her hair was bound up under the ordinary linen layers that honest women wore about their heads. Had it not been for a certain look about the mouth, he might easily, glancing quickly, have mistaken her for his wife who had come ahead some days before to open the house.

The woman had not, he realized, raised her voice.

"And who are you, Mistress?" he snapped. From her manner, she might be a gentlewoman, despite her plain dress, or a burgess's wife. Best to err on the side of grace—as much as he was able under these appalling circumstances.

She made an appropriate reverence, hands folded neatly in front of her. The skin, he noted, was remarkably dark, almost golden, like the unsettling eyes. Italian, perhaps, or Greek?

"My name is Margaret Davenant, Doctor." A slight accent, as well, and one he couldn't place. "I am a widow of this parish and, being that you find me suitable, your housekeeper. These men are my nephews."

How was it that, although she did not presume to smile, he had the impression she was laughing at him?

"Well, tell them to be careful," he said, not much mollified. Then he frowned and pursed his lips; the flowing beard rippled like a snowdrift. "Housekeeper? What happened to the other one?" Jane must have engaged the woman, or their old servants had abandoned them. Paid their wages faithfully every quarter, all the years of their absence, and as soon as he returned…

"Her mother, sir, is sorely ill." The slightest pause as he looked doubtful. "In Kent," Margaret Davenant added. "By the sea."

"So far? I thought she was a local woman." She had no reply, but only looked modestly at her hands With annoyance, he detected a thin, unpleasant note in his own voice, and he felt small and fretful, a difficult old man complaining like a child. As a scholar and a man of science, he found the notion revolting.

Finally, she said, "She being her mother's only daughter living, she must make that perilous journey. Her husband, your stableman, I believe? He went with her, of course, for safety. And as I am her cousin, somewhat distantly on her father's side, and being a poor widow in need of employment, she sent for me to come and do whatever needs must for you and your good wife."

There was something wrong with this story; why couldn't he find what it was? Where was his mind wandering? He was tired and he was sweating like two hogs under layer upon layer of linen and wool, and the manky old fur-collared surcoat Jane hated. Eyes half-dazzled by the glitter and glare of the noonday sun that glinted off the river, he wanted only to go home.

"They cannot read, I suppose," he grumbled at last, nodding at the men still standing in their shirtsleeves and leather aprons, waiting with bored expressions. Or rather, with no expressions at all.

"Nay, sir, they cannot, good simple lads that they are. Matthew, John, and Luke, they are, and that's the beginning and end of their understanding."

John Dee had spent most of the last four years closeted with incense and angels—and that lying, bowelless fiend, Edward Kelley—up to his ruff points in esoteric studies and, yes, magic. And this felt like...

Ridiculous. He was over-taxed. He was short-tempered with travel. The sooner they brought him his books and instruments, the sooner his workshop could be restored. So much work, so much to do. And the Queen, stopping at Richmond only a little longer, according to his charts! He must call on Her Majesty at once, today if possible, to be assured of his position and safety. Above all, to secure the stipend she had offered to entice him home.

"Very well, then," John Dee snapped. "If they are your minions, mistress, then you shall manage them. Some of the crates are books, so your fellows may think they can treat them how they may. They must not! Some of the boxes contain instruments for the exploration of natural philosophy, and they are very delicate."

"Indeed, sir, so I understand."

He was pleased to doubt that, but went on. "Since they cannot read the labels, they must treat each box and crate, large or small, as it might be the Crown jewels. Is that understood?"

"Each item precious, aye, Doctor," she repeated in that honeyed voice. "Leave all to me."

With a satisfied grunt, the queen's peripatetic magus turned and walked down the river path without even a glance back. Behind him, the woman who said her name was Margaret Davenant indulged in an antique sort of smirk. Sorcerer, indeed. Men were such fools! As much now as at any time in history.

Turning back to the still idle workmen, she said, "Continue as I bade you." As she reached up apparently to adjust the strings of her cap, golden fingers moved in the gestures that reinforced her real commands. And she added quietly, "Drop nothing, break nothing, as I have told you."

ii
Meanwhile, across the river

"Smoke and mirrors?" Ben wondered and shifted again where he sat. No matter what he did there was no way a leather saddlebag and a granite boulder on a riverbank were ever going to be comfortable. When he stood, the heels of his riding boots dug into the soft earth as he found his balance.

His companion—who was never uncomfortable—thought a moment, concentrating on the tidy figure of John Dee just stepping out of the handsome house partly hidden among the trees across the water.

Ben followed the raven boy's gaze. It was like watching a silent movie, he thought, with only a cricket's lazy chirp and the liquid sounds of the river for accompaniment. On the opposite bank, the mistress of the house and two young children came out, the little ones kneeling piously for their father's blessing. Looking grim, Dee mounted his horse and set off along the Richmond road. The family went back inside.

Abruptly, Raven returned to the conversation. "Nothing but smoke and mirrors. My lord says Perdita was trapped in a mirror for a thousand years or two. Then suddenly, there she was, a priestess in Virginia—trapped among the savages, as you might say. That can't have pleased her. And now, here she is, in the worst possible place, as you might imagine, him being a Hermetic master and all."

Ben looked puzzled, brushed a swaying willow frond out of his face.

"Alchemist," said Raven. "A gifted alchemist of a particularly advanced order."

"His grace found all this in his mirror?"

"He did," the boy nodded. "And more besides, though he's keeping close about it all, of course. She is still safely locked out of Faerie, or things might be worse."

"But he's still pissed off."

"Oh my, yes."

While Ben processed all this, the family reappeared armed with wicker market baskets and the household money, followed by the straight-backed housekeeper with the peculiar eyes. Instructions were given; the witch in plain grey worsted and white linen bobbed a curtsey and went back inside while the others strolled toward the village center and market cross. Mistress Dee, Ben supposed, would call at the church, visit her old gossips, see about a tutor for her eldest son, spend wisely at the weekly market and then, eventually, return some good while later.

"And Aubrey wants someone to keep an eye on her. Not exactly perilous duty, is it? Don't get me wrong," he added quickly. "I was hoping I'd get another chance to— y'know?"

A wry glance from the boy perched at his feet. "To make up for screaming like a girl at London Bridge?"

"To visit this period again! I still think that was you, by the way, that raven hocking a gobbet of rotting traitor at me from the gate. I hadn't been there ten minutes."

Hugging his knees, Raven snorted and rocked back laughing, shaking his head in despair. When telling Ben about his various and occasional hobbies—an immortal has to fill the time somehow or go mad—the fae had admitted to now and then spending avian time with the guardian ravens of the Tower of London.

"On my honour, Ben, I'd have told you if that were so, if only so I could take credit for the joke!"

"I suspect that to be a lie of some sort, my lad," Ben said with a Lord Blackadder inflection his friend did not miss. To punctuate, he picked up the little Italian cittern he'd borrowed from Oberon's music room, and gave it an experimental strum. He sat again on his saddlebag.

"The fae do not lie, human child," said Raven mildly while Ben played a bit, making a pretty picture for passers-by. "As I think you know already. That is a human failing."

"Mislead, prevaricate, evade, dissemble."

"But never lie." Raven said, adjusting his cap and surprised apparently to find his hair still long and caught back in a ponytail. At once it was shorter, of a more soldierly cut, and the jewel that had held it fell into his hand: a sapphire-eyed raven meticulously carved in jet, perched on a branch of gold looped through a fat black elastic band.

"No, no, here's proof of my good heart!" he said softly, admiring his work. "Had I not been so intent on finishing this, and all by mine own hand, mark you, I would have met you as I should have. Mind it for me, will you, good Sir Francis Browne?"

Laughing at himself, he tossed it to Ben who caught it lightly out of the air and tucked it away in his pouch.

"Okay," said the American, who knew the story was true, but still didn't like it.

"Besides, we are at present sitting in the leafy shade of summer—June, I believe—in 1589. You can't very well be angry about something that hasn't happened yet."

Well, never mind. Plucked an hour ago from the snowy chill of Dartmoor, Ben stretched and leaned back under the willows, reveling in the sweet summer warmth and green smells of the Thames. He was ten miles upstream as well as some ten years away from that infamous morning. To the boats on the busy river, to any passers-by on the road above them or watchers on the opposite bank, they were today a pair of gentlemen resting their horses before continuing on some errand for the great lord whose livery they wore.

Two fine horses, in fact, were loosely picketed nearby, cropping the grass, their harness jingling slightly while sharp eyes kept watch on the handsome house over the water. Raven had a flair, Ben thought, for arranging the details.

"So he sent you to get a closer look, okay. And I'm here because?"

"It's snowing at your house. Thought you'd fancy a change." Raven scrambled to his feet and dusted willow leaves from his impeccably cut trunk hose. All black worsted and black leather, of course, with a flash of black and viridian in the fluttering cock feathers on the flat cap tilted over his brow. "Now we need a closer look."

"Okay. Where's the nearest bridge?" There was none he could see either upstream or down.

"Don't need one, do I? Bide you here a while, and I'll just…"

Ben started to object, but Raven cut him off with a lifted hand and a second thought. "No, you're right. Take the horses to the ferry at Kew and cross over. Talk to people, if you can. Collect the gossip, without being too conspicuous. Don't get too tangled up in the town, though, eh?"

"Gossip without getting involved, gotcha."

Raven grinned. "I mean, entertain yourself but don't get arrested. Go on. I'll meet you at the Anchor and we'll sort it out from there."

With that, the fae shrank, folded, shifted, whatever it was he did to wrap his avian form around him in that disconcerting way, and with a harsh cry, the King's Raven of Faerie took wing. As the bird leapt up in a fluttery rattle, a single sable feather shook out, spiraling through the air until Ben reached up and caught it. He wasn't certain, but he suspected it might be best that such a feather not be left lying around, and slipped it into his pouch along with the hair jewel.

Funny, he thought, tracking the Raven's flight path. It was sunny and bright on this bank, and bright too over the brown and glittering breadth of the Thames, as it should be on a summer day. But around the Dee house with its three odd stories of gingerbread half-timbering and thatch, it looked as though a fog was forming, or some kind of smoke, that dimmed and obscured its peaks and ridges. By the time Raven started circling the chimney pots, it was nearly hidden. When Ben looked at it, really looked, he could see the house clear enough though the edges were just slightly blurred: not the haze of a faerie glamour, just fuzzy. He pushed his spectacles up on his nose and wondered what the neighbors and folk on the river were seeing.

Well, he'd find out soon enough. Right now, he packed away the cittern and his modern speech patterns, got the saddlebags squared away. Then mounting up in the boxy but thankfully padded saddle, Sir Francis Browne gathered the reins of both horses, and started looking for a ferryman.

10
Crystal Palace, Sydenham, mid-December, 1854

They were arguing again, Susan observed as she approached the latest version of Great-Uncle Lovejoy's infernal machine, humming on the twenty sturdy legs of its new platform. When to Susan's surprised but abiding relief, the new Committee had accepted Lovejoy and Cray's application, they had moved from the derelict carriage house behind her back garden into the newly restored and reimagined Crystal Palace up on Sydenham Hill. They had also replaced the humid technology of steam—venting had always been a problem—with new and highly experimental technologies, though precedent required them to keep buckets of sand and a sturdy ax nearby, in case sparks got out of hand.

It was a curious thing, and she knew it rankled, that all the other exhibits of British ingenuity—all the ones that worked—were featured in a court called New Inventions quite near to the main entrance. Their past successes at drawing an audience had gotten them in, against all expectations but Lovejoy's. Their remarkable lack of success, however, had condemned them to probationary status in this hole in the wall, as Cray called the southern transept, facing a refreshment area and the ladies' and gentlemen's retiring rooms. That is to say, the toilets.

In three years, the working relationship of the two men had not eased at all. So now, a week before Christmas, the

Professor and Ambrose Cray were again going at it hammer and tongs, as they say. Bickering and expostulating in English, German, and occasional Greek like a pair of erudite fishwives, though as mildly as possible since the work area was surrounded by a flock of schoolgirls. So much for peace on earth.

At last, their barks reduced to manic grumbling, they flung themselves furiously back to the dials and gears, tapping and pounding and adjusting. Eventually Professor Lovejoy stumbled to the padded observer's chair with a groan and began scribbling in a notebook.

"Sausages and some nice pears today, Great Uncle!" Susan said, taking advantage of the relative calm. They ignored her, as always. "And the beer you like. Mrs Knox sent Peter into the City for it specially."

"What?" Cray said, straightening in alarm, as if she had appeared from nowhere, and perhaps she had. The habitual glower returned when he registered who she was. "Oh. You. Stay out of the way!"

Susan, however, had found a streak of stubbornness in the intervening years. Having come into her modest inheritance at last, she had put some of it into improving the old mansion left her by her parents. Uncle Lovejoy, though nominally the guardian of his spinster relative, had hardly noticed. In the course of these improvements, Susan kept her own accounts, managed the household, and ran a respectable, well-ordered lodging house in a respectable district without his help or advice. Life was very agreeable, if only rarely troubled by the occasional explosion.

Whatever else, Susan Pickering had given up her ill-fitting timidity.

"You are not interested. Very well."

With not a clear surface anywhere, and a marked lack of interest from either man, her alternative was to shove the hamper under the plain deal table, which she endeavored to do. Peter could retrieve it the next time

"Wait!" Great-Uncle Ambrose dived under the cloth to snatch out a bottle of Watkins & Son's Golden Sunlight ale.

Oddly for a gentleman, he had a particular taste for the stuff; for a scientist, he certainly had an efficient way with a cork.

With a pop, a long draft, and a wave of guilty pleasure, he sank again into the throne-like operator's chair to stare into the glossy black of the mirror, his Eye of Memory as he called it now, and continue his notes. Susan might as well have been invisible.

"Professor," she said, venturing upon her other reason for coming. It was always a risk, assuming they would deign to eat anything, but it was an excuse. "Will you be working this evening? Some of the lodgers have organized a... That is, Mr Horsley has agreed to read two of Robert Browning's poems, and if there is time we might..."

Sighing with annoyance, Lovejoy put down his pen and dug under layers of lab coat, sack coat, waistcoat until he discovered a worn leather wallet. He carefully pulled out exactly one large ten-pound note, frail as onion skin, and then another which he folded together precisely in half and thrust into her startled keeping.

"I beg your pardon, Uncle?"

"You asked for housekeeping money, stupid girl. Here it is. Now go away," he snapped without sparing her another glance.

Did he think Browning was the grocer? Whatever he thought, she knew the great ugly mirror and this new ridiculous project had his whole attention.

That awful mirror. A glance at the polished obsidian made Susan shiver. A longer look made her feel she was staring into the fathomless deeps of the sea or a universe emptied of stars. And sometimes, she had never told them but sometimes, she thought she saw other things in it, more than mere reflection: shapes, colors, even shadowy people moving through the void in strange, antique costume. Mostly it gave her headaches, as it did right now, along with a panicky desire to run away from it, to get into the open air, no matter how much snow lay on the ground.

Folding the money she hadn't asked for into her reticule, all she said now was, "Nasty thing."

The professor's pen slowed its frantic scratching and stopped.

She shrugged her shawl back onto her shoulders, and picked up her bonnet, moving toward the little staircase. "What is it but a stone, Uncle? A plain polished stone? Not a mirror at all. I don't know what you expect a stone to do."

"What?" His voice rose. Shooting the pen into its stand, he stared at her, hot-eyed. "What have you seen? What are you saying? This mirror?"

Then he stopped and glared beyond her shoulder. His exclamations had fallen into that moment when all the voices around him had stopped at once, as sometimes happens in a crowd. And a crowd had formed. He stood up abruptly, coughed a little, and took up a declamatory pose at the edge of the platform.

So he was, after all, aware of the audience, Susan observed.

"This mirror," he began, "once belonged to the celebrated alchemist, Dr John Dee! It was wrought originally for a high priest of the Aztecs in the deepest jungles of Mexico! And brought around the world at great peril by that most famous of adventurers, Sir Francis Drake."

A smattering of applause rose from the little crowd. About time they got their shilling's worth!

We can take it upon ourselves to confirm at this time, as the Crystal Palace guide book might have said, that Professor Lovejoy's mirror was not Dr Dee's, as Dr Dee's scrying glass was shut up in a drawer in the British Museum with other of his relics, and largely forgotten. It had not at any time come up for sale. Lovejoy had bought his ovoid disk at enormous expense from a colleague who had vouched on his honor for its authenticity—he had definitely stolen it from a dig in Mexico. And despite (or perhaps because) said colleague had taken the money and never been seen or heard from again, Lovejoy was absolute in his confidence of its ability to peer into the cosmos. In that, at least, he may have been correct.

The speech on the mirror's exalted history, nature, and manifest virtues went on for several minutes, then snapped off sharply.

"Thank you," the Professor said, and sat down at the console, writing furiously once again in his notebook.

Away down the nave more than fifty yards away, the sudden voices of carolers burst into *Angels We have Heard on High*. The long cascading *gloria* bounced like liquid silver up the aisle of iron and shimmering glass, a lively counterpoint to the uncanny behavior in this one strange display. Susan hardly noticed.

"Professor?" A young fellow in a bowler hat and three kinds of plaid had pushed through to the front of the crowd. Susan had seen him here before nosing about, memorable for his extraordinary red whiskers. He raised a hand and called again in the accents of Ireland. "Professor! Edward Donovan here, sir. *Illustrated London News*. Can you tell us what your machine is supposed to do?"

No reply but a supercilious stare. Lovejoy was done for now. Susan picked up her things and started to leave. "Mister Cray, your tea is in the hamper under the table," she said over her shoulder.

The man had been staring alternately at his dials and at the black stone for hours. Now he turned weirdly blank eyes on her.

"Go away!" he intoned in a voice so harshly unlike his own, it made Susan stare. Then she turned and ran down quickly to the floor.

"Cray?" called the reporter, shifting his attention. "Ambrose Cray? Will you answer the question for me, sir?"

"What!" Cray whipped about with a kind of wild moan, lips curled back in fury. The schoolgirls squeaked their dismay and jumped as a tremor, a shock, a bolt of energy shuddered through the man's body. Then just as abruptly, the man's eyes cleared and he stood up straight again, looking slightly puzzled. "What do you want?"

"I say," Donovan said, as if nothing out of the ordinary had just occurred. "What does the machine do, Mr Cray?"

But Cray had returned to normal: rude and short tempered, as always.

"Egad!" he snorted. "If you cannot read, how can you presume to write?" Like every other exhibitor, they had posted informational placards on either side of their exhibit space, and more on the front of the platform itself. Sadly, they carried very little information of any substance and were long out of date.

"Wasn't it some sort of weather device, sir? The last time?"

"And weren't you some sort of reporter? Yes, I remember you. At least our work has advanced in the intervening time."

"So, no answer then, eh?" Donovan laughed, enjoying the game. "That's all right, sir. I'll make it up then, shall I? My readers won't mind!"

"Go away," Cray snapped.

"Don't mind me, sir. I can wait till you're ready."

Their two gazes met, the one a glaring prizefighter fierce from the ringed platform five feet off the ground; the other, just as determined, grinning as if he'd won the lottery. At last Ambrose Cray sighed bitterly, and gave in. There were times when just to make the current days tolerable, he had to conjure the desperate, lost years recalling true despair. He did that now,

"It is a temporal displacement device, for all the good that does you."

"A sort of a clock, then."

The gathered watchers burst into delighted laughter, all the tension vanished. They liked a good story, and the Irishman was giving them one.

"It is not a pocket watch! It does not mark the *passage* of time, you fool. The device will allow us to see *into* time, into the past. To peel back the pages of history and observe events as they unfold, that is. I hardly expect you to understand."

"Surely, that is impossible, sir," said Donovan with an incredulous laugh. "A fantasy!"

Sneering, Cray strode to the edge, which made the reporter retreat a step rather than crane his neck to watch the other man's face.

"Impossible? It was impossible to light the streets with coal gas not fifty years ago," he declaimed. Several people nodded enthusiastically. It was true, that, yes. "Most of the equipment you see here—the lights, the voltaic cells, the magnetic coils—was impossible, as you call it, just a few years ago. Who is to say what is impossible? That glass there, of which you have heard the Professor speak, is called *The Eye of Memory*. When activated, and under the correct conditions, it will allow us to witness the great events of history. The coronation of Charlemagne, the building of the pyramids, even the Crucifixion of Christ himself!"

"And is that blasphemy, then?" Donovan narrowed his eyes as if he cared, taking his audience with him.

"Blasph— You idiot, of course it's not. We—"

"And have you had any success?"

Breaths were caught in anticipation, and—schoolgirls, farmers, mechanics from Liverpool—the mob's attention turned to the platform. He straightened and smoothed back his hair, preening just a little. He couldn't see his employer's hot eyes furious behind him.

"As a matter of fact…"

But the professor leapt up and boxed him in the shoulder before he could say another word. Cray turned with a cry, but Lovejoy silenced him.

"Not another word, you, or I'll have your hat about your ears! And you! You scribbler, you Irish ferret!" He pointed down at Donovan whose grin only got wider under his wild red mustache as he scratched in a notebook. "It is the nature of Science to explore, to seek, and not to find. Newton's wig, man! We learn more about the cosmos with every failed experiment than you could discover in a lifetime!"

"No, then."

"We have had small, but significant indications."

"May I quote you?"

"You may go away!"

"Just one more question?"

The audience held its breath. The professor only stood, tight-lipped and arrogant, waiting like the scion of a noble house, which he was. "Well? We are trying to work, here, unlike some."

"What is it you are a professor of, exactly, sir?"

"I hardly think that matters."

Quietly monitoring the exchange, sensible Susan concluded that some other action was required at once if this was not to end in fisticuffs. She took two steps back up the staircase to get a little altitude, and pronounced, "That's quite enough questions, Mr Donovan. My great uncle is a respected doctor of natural philosophy, as you will find if you consult the university of Oxford or any of the usual sources. Now, I believe you have had your turn."

The Irishman turned a charming grin on her and eyes neither blue or exactly green which actually twinkled. For a moment, she thought she was going to blush, then set her jaw, and did nothing of the kind.

"As to that, Miss, you may be correct. Yes, indeed. Another day then." He tipped his battered bowler hat to the platform: "Gents," he said. And turning to Susan. "Miss Lovejoy."

He strolled away with a swagger that she found infuriating, but at least he left. He also winked at her as he passed, and laughed again when she sniffed her displeasure in return.

"It's Pickering, actually," she said primly, but he had already disappeared into the milling crowd. "Irishmen!"

11
Mortlake, Dr Dee's House, 1589

The Raven circled the house a few times in a narrowing spiral, his vision heightened in this form, and his curiosity sharpened, then rode the thermals up and up to scan the district with its villages and orchards and manor farms, and the fanciful palace beyond the next curve of the river. Dr Dee, mounted up and trotting purposefully along the road that cut across the river's loop, making good time though the path was crowded with all the business the Queen's presence stirred up: messengers, provisioners, petitioners of all kinds. Nothing of interest to his king, however.

So he turned a few big barrel rolls for sheer joy then recovered, tightened the circle, closing in and dropping down over Mortlake and Dee's house. Dee's house? Wait, no, there it was. The Raven's bright eye, sharp as ever, picked it out of the almost smog-like haze hovering at the edge of the blue-brown river. Oberon had said mentioned tobacco smoke, and the sorceress making the best of the tools she had. Very well. An unexpected tool in a world that had barely discovered the stuff, but not impossible if she'd been in America.

Fae awareness told him the mist was a thing of magic designed to discourage visiting neighbors, though they would see nothing unusual; being a wild thing of the air told him the acrid stench at the center of the enchantment, though unsophisticated at its heart, would incidentally drive out any fleas and mice. If he hadn't also been a great Fae of Oberon's court, it might have kept even the Raven away. If a bird could laugh, he would have done so for sheer irony.

While the haze couldn't deter him, it had done a good job with everything else. He had thought to gossip a bit with the local crows and jackdaws, collect their news, commend his king's greetings to theirs, but there were none.

The whole house had a shabby, abandoned air. Most of the windows with their lead-framed roundels of glass had not yet been restored since the owner's return. That should be going on now, methodically replacing the framed wicker and oiled paper with the good glass windows retrieved from storage. In fact, the place should be a hive of activity, with servants unpacking boxes, knocking beds together, and putting the kitchen to rights. But if there was any activity in this household, it must be in their dreams; not a mortal soul was in evidence. Did Dee have trouble keeping staff? Probably, but this was ominous.

He could try knocking, sure, but what fun was that. Besides, it would give him away which would not answer his need. Landing instead in the frame of a ground floor window, he used his sharp beak and a little fae magic to tear away the wicker and pierce the oiled covering till he had a good view of the room. The place felt curiously anonymous. Nothing showed that this was the home of a famous astrologer, a mathematician, geographer, and scholar of the arcane. But then, this was a public space, a family space Ben would call the living room as sparsely furnished as any Elizabethan home.

On the other hand... now that was interesting. From a wooden bowl smoldering in the middle of the floor, tendrils of a low smoke writhed like somnolent serpents, insinuating around and about everything, the source of the confounding haze. The smell was foul and bitter with darkness and secrets, not just the smell of the dried leaf. Even if they couldn't smell it, passersby would certainly find themselves hurrying past. The Raven might have quenched it with little effort, but the neighbors were best kept at bay till his surveillance was complete.

That smoke was the only thing moving in a room spartan in its simplicity. A fine, large bed in pieces against the farther wall; a few wooden crates with the nails still in place; boxes and a stack of empty baskets, but no Perdita. Not a servant in sight nor any sound of a bustling household. Had they all gone to the market? Were they asleep? Or dead?

A thrust of wings dropped him into the kitchen and stillroom, equally quiet. The witch must expect to accomplish something quickly and be gone, if she had no intention of keeping up the charade. But where was everyone?

On the next level, half level more like, he found an empty window frame giving light on a boxed staircase and decided it was time to explore more deeply. A few more steps led up to a bedchamber which gave on to the nursery, stacked with trunks and wicker baskets still piled up next to the beds. Mrs Dee was not going to be at all happy about all this.

A sound reached his ears, an oath in a language he seldom heard even among the eldest of his kind, followed by a clang like the beat of an iron bell. With that, Raven unfolded into his usual form, and with a thought, he was invisible. Moving with care, he found a narrow passageway between two larger rooms, an ironbound door standing open with its lock defeated and the remnants of protective charms hanging tattered in the ether. Dee, wherever he was, would know.

Behind the breach waited an even narrower passage—no, a staircase, wobbling and warping through magical barriers, now shredded, into the upper reaches and what must be the doctor's private study, his sanctum. Oh, Mistress Dee's outrage would be nothing to the astrologer's.

Gently, Raven put a hand to the door, carefully avoiding the iron lock and hinges, which even at a distance radiated a burning cold, and pushed it aside. Safely on the stair, where his faerie boots made no sound, he could feel the thready remnants of spells tapping at his mind even as he passed like the wind. He was good, this Dr John Dee. Primitive, over-elaborate, maybe, but a genuine talent. Wards such as these would certainly turn back family members or curious servants, and defeat almost any wizard or Hermetic colleagues. The bell chime that had rung out on the etheric plane, as Dee doubtless called it, was an excellent touch. Pity he'd be entering the palace of Richmond when he "heard" it, powerless to do a thing except control his panic.

But the good doctor's best efforts were simply no match for the faerie-trained if unsubtle skills of Oberon's cast-off mistress. Now, what was she after?

At the top of the stair, the sober housekeeper, the so-called honest widow, was swearing and tearing into cases and shelves, flinging aside bound books and monkish manuscripts, burrowing through papers and notebooks like a careless thief looking for gold and leaving priceless jewels. She had stripped down to her Elizabethan skivvies—linen shift, stays, and petticoat; her skin glowed with sweat under the Secota tattoos.

The fae's eyes widened.

Hovering in the doorway, barely a shadow among the shadows, he resisted the temptation to vanish her clothes away altogether. Instead he moved past her into the wide chamber, thick with gloom. On one wall a stinking fireplace needed cleaning, and the stained and blackened ovens to either side. Dee's extensive assortment of alchemical paraphernalia, much of it still crated, took up most of the available space, awaiting the magister's attention. Three small windows provided the only light, and that grudgingly, through warped seams and gaps in the shutters, though he needed no more and nor, evidently, did the witch.

What was she looking for?

She ignored the books, tossed aside the glassware, picking them out of a box only to get at what might be underneath. As Raven watched he realized her focus centered entirely on the various implements, tools, devices, tablets of parchment or wax covered with curious devices and inscriptions.

Abruptly, she halted, scowling. "It must be here! Where else can it be? How hard can it be to find a misbegotten mirror in a magician's house!"

Ah, that made sense. The famous scrying mirror of volcanic glass, his "show stone". Dee, so Raven understood, had been trying to talk to angels with the help of some con man called Kelley, who he'd finally, wisely, left in Europe. Surely the man had brought his mirror home, and yet, no mirror did he spy. Not even, Raven realized, an invisible one, though he felt it nearby. There were illusions in place here, artfully concealed, but if he broke them for his own curiosity, he'd let Perdita in as well. Ben would go straight to it, of course, but Ben was somewhere swilling flat beer, and no use at all.

The witch was breathing hard and staring around with fevered, red-rimmed eyes. For a moment he almost thought she could see him. She actually looked back twice at the old mantelpiece, stained with age and strange experiments, where Raven lurked as quiet and almost as small as a mouse. Briefly, he considered fading into Faerie completely, but he was having a good time. She might sense his presence, he knew, but she would never see him.

Still, she frowned, nostrils flaring, and governed the barely controlled temper, then bent to retrieve her discarded apron. From a pocket, she pulled a lump of tallow. She chafed and rolled it briskly between her hands; it warmed quickly in the stifling heat. Gently she breathed across it. Then, working quickly, she muttered a charm, pinching here and pulling there, until she had shaped it into a pudgy body with four pudgy limbs and a round stub for a head. Fingernails carved the rough suggestion of a face.

From another pocket, she pulled a twist of scarlet thread, and wrapped it once, twice, three times around the poppet's neck, then held it up between her two hands. Focusing her will and her power with apparent ease, she intoned three old words on the three ascending notes of a major chord. "Be," those words meant. "Move. Seek."

The fae winced. Yes, indeed, a quarter tone sharp on all three notes. How could she not hear it?

The poppet began to swell and grow but not, to Raven's mild surprise, very much. No more than a foot high, it got up, looking a bit like the Pillsbury Doughboy. Then it toddled drunkenly away on its stubby legs, bumped into an almost buried chair, and fell over.

She hissed with what Raven read as frustration. Dee's wards must have interfered with her working. Or perhaps it was simply her musical incompetence. Oberon would be cheered to know that hadn't improved. But from her reaction, she had expected success, as if it had worked for her before.

Ominously, that iron bell sounded again. Raven suspected the show was over and found his way to the door, which was closing. If he didn't want to be trapped behind an iron bound door with a mad witch, he'd better do something.

So he did.

Twirling an insubstantial finger toward the cold hearth, he spun up a tiny, localized whirlwind in the ashes that sparkled with colored lights at its spinning core. Sobbing tones sighed and whined from its movement.

When he had the witch's astonished attention, he split the whirling thing into three, and sent them into the room, circling her and trailing the ash of a hundred foul chemical processes across the floor and over the books and papers. She reacted, flinging out her anger and annoyance in a pulse of energy that Raven caught and dispersed with half a thought. He almost laughed, but refrained. She was angry; he wanted her afraid.

At last, he spoke, his voice a deep boom that echoed in the room and down the stair. "WHO DARES TO DISTURB ME?"

The windows rattled, a jewelled skull spun on its stem and crashed to the floor, and the witch gave a shriek of anger that was, yes, touched with fear. Still she stood her ground.

Back straight, fists clenched, "Creature, name thyself!" she demanded, but her voice trembled. Nothing had countered her will in so long, she had forgotten it was possible, and how it felt.

"I AM THE GENIE OF THE HOUSE!" He managed not to giggle and spoil the effect. "I SEE THY NAME, O CHILD, AND THE NAME BEFORE THY NAME. THY SIN AND THY SHAME ARE WRIT UPON THE WALLS AT THE END OF TIME!"

At that, she shrank back, overwhelmed at last, but the raven boy wasn't done. The three spinning tops of noise and ash sprang up from the floor into the air. Raven flicked his wrist and flung them out through the little windows, smashing the framework, ripping away the wooden shutters, spilling in daylight and a clear summer breeze.

Perdita's nerve broke and she ran. She scrambled down the staircase, blasting the door out of her way while behind her the terrible voice laughed and laughed.

"Oh, look," said the King's Raven. "An open window! Time to go."

Lazily, he flew down to the walled kitchen garden, then walked out to the lane that led past the gate and into the village. He did pause briefly to take all the heart out of that smudge pot and the spell within it. A handy breeze came to his whistle and scoured the smoke away.

As he straightened his gloves and settled the modest but serviceable sword and hanger on his hip, he could just hear her shrieking, stumbling into the parlor and out the door in her underwear and screaming about devils in the house! *Thieves! Robbers! Demons!*

Aye, the house was a wreck, the master's study violated, the servants unconscious in the byre! She had a lot to explain if she meant to stay a while. Which, now, she probably did. He should find a way to fix that, too.

Servants from next door and men from the smithy nearby came running with shouts and exclamations. Unmoved, Raven set his cap at a jaunty angle. More screams, then, as the neighbors arrived. A sudden moaning halt as the witch collapsed in hysterical tears.

"Not a bad actress," he concluded with a smile. "Not musical at all."

He nodded cheerily to a passing chapman with his cart; stood aside, cap in hand, for a nobleman and his substantial retinue—Viscount Montague, he noted by the silver passant lions prowling on the black pennons. When the dust of their passing cleared, he set off again at a cheerful saunter toward the town, sword by his side, Lord Aubrey's oak leaf and acorn on his shoulder, and caroling a song under the hard blue sky.

"Joy, health, love and peace
Be all here in this place!
By your leave we will sing
Concerning our king!"

12
What happened to Susan Sydenham and thereabouts, 1854

Susan Pickering slapped her bonnet onto her head and tied the ribbons under her ear a little more vigorously than necessary. Coat and gloves in order, she collected her temper and her reticule, and turned her back on the appalling device and its disturbing lights.

She had meant to take her sketch book up to the Assyrian Court, but between the awkwardness of dealing with that dreadful reporter, and her annoyance with, well, everything else, she couldn't bear the thought of stopping here a moment longer. The exotic world whence Sennacherib had come down like a wolf on the fold would wait for another time. And anyway, the light was going. Having no lighting of its own (What need, the planners said, when the walls were made of glass?) the place was already filling up with shadows despite the early hour. Better to go now.

So, with a purposeful and not entirely ladylike stride she marched out of the transept and into the nave without noticing the fabulous pink glass fountain towering over its reflecting pool, and stalked passed the industrial courts where Sheffield and Birmingham showed off their ironmongery. She hurried, clutching her coat tight about her through a vast field of statuary: Classical and Medieval gods and heroes, for the most part, their manly *attributi* gamely masked with fig leaves, staring down from their pedestals with flat, blind eyes.

She navigated the queues in front of a kiosk like a medieval baptistery, visitors straining at their last chance to buy souvenir stereopticon views and cartes de visite.

"Good day, Miss Pickering," the guard said, touching his cap.

"Good day, George," she replied with barely a nod, heart pounding, and pressed out the door almost before he could open it for her.

The crisp, cold afternoon assaulted her face as if she'd been hit with a snowball, pinching up the English roses in her sharp little nose and flat little chin. It had snowed just enough to be inconvenient, and a sharp wind was swirling snowflakes up to sting her eyes. There was no sign of the omnibus.

"Get you a cab, Miss?" said George, still in the doorway.

She always said no, and started to now, then changed her mind. Instead she turned and actually registered the pale young face and the bloom of a new cold starting to burn in his cheeks. And after all, hadn't the professor pressed the princely sum of twenty pounds on her, unasked for.

"Yes, please, George," she said crisply.

A fog was creeping up from the river, hugging the cobblestones. Tendrils of grey reached into the snowy lanes, kicked up in ghostly swirls under all manner of cabs and carriages. Safely boxed behind the hansom's beveled windows, Susan watched it come toward them then fall behind as they turned up the gentle slope of Albany Road that parted the once grand establishments—one of them her own—from a once mighty forest. In the grey afternoon, it looked like a street of haunted houses faced by a haunted wood. A good day to be at home, safe and warm, and tonight in her parlour, poetry and music and laughter would hold back the dark.

Like many of the larger homes in the district, the Hollytree, Miss Pickering's inheritance, had seen better times—most of them before she was born. Its many rooms were capacious and afflicted with rising damp, the ceilings high and crumbling. After several years of economy and careful planning, ceilings patched, plumbing managed, it had become a comfortable, slightly shabby but clean and well-tended home. She had filled it with a small handful of respectable lodgers: an unmatched pair of young bachelors who toiled for the Crystal Palace; a sturdily genteel maiden lady who gave lessons in the pianoforte and the harp; and a rather sprightlier maiden of more tender years who lived by the prick of her needle, sewing costumes at the Winter Garden Theatre where she was not an actress. The elderly couple who smiled their secrets over the dinner table seldom came down at all except for meals and an occasional walk in the park.

To keep them all, she had taken on a pair of maids—Ellen, furiously industrious, and Daisy, somewhat less so but good hearted and a fair hand with a needle herself—and a boy for general work. Mrs Nixon, the rosy-cheeked cook from the depths of Ayrshire, kept them plainly but thoroughly fed. If it was not a family, it was certainly home.

Why then, Susan wondered when the cab set her down at her own front gate, did she still feel so unsettled. As she alighted, she noticed the driver's hands were shaking despite their gloves. They trembled so much when he took her money that he dropped the silver coins he couldn't afford to lose. A moan escaped him as he stooped to retrieve them from the dirty snow at the curb, all the while throwing nervous glances toward the wood.

"Are you all right, my good man?"

"Eh?" The face that jerked up to her was white with panic. "Don't you hear 'em, Miss?"

"It's only the wind, you know," she said gently. "It isn't really haunted."

Wild-eyed but without another word, he swarmed up into his seat, cracked the whip, and turned the hansom hard about as quick as a man and horse ever did. As it clattered away, the low mist swirled up behind and followed along, swallowing up the sounds of iron-shod hooves and iron-rimmed wheels in seconds.

And then she heard it. The bright, tinkling laughter of very small children coming from across the road.

She turned to look, squinting a little. The light was dim, and the fog rising, but she could see well enough through the tall iron palings of the fence and into the trees a little.

Nothing, and no one. "How very odd," she said aloud.

But as she set her hand to her low gate, she heard it again, little ones chattering, giggling, then hushing each other, hiding. One little voice began to sing not a Christmas carol but an old lament.

> *Oh don't you remember a long time ago*
> *Those two little babies whose names I don't know*
> *They wandered away on a dark winter's day*
> *Those two little babies got lost on their way.*
> *Poor babes in the wood.*

Susan was shivering; she was anxious, and desperate for a cup of tea. The paving stones icy and slick under her boots threatened to bring her down, but she kept her feet. The wood wasn't terribly deep, though it was old. And she stood there, drawn by an old song.

"Oh now really," said sensible Susan, and she started to turn away.

> *They wept and they cried, they sobbed and they*
> *sighed;*
> *These two little babies they lay down and died.*

She put both gloved hands to the iron gate and pushed. It swung aside for her, gliding over the snow as silent as a kiss. She slipped inside, walking where she knew the path must be and walked—carefully, now!—with only the crunch of her boots for company. No footprints marred the pristine surface ahead of her. There was no sign of anything alive but the ancient trees, a last remnant of the primordial Norwood that slept around her. Once it had been a great forest of oak and hornbeam, holly and tall ash where kings and bishops had hunted and fought since before the Normans came. Its timber had been felled for the ships that sailed against the Armada, and for the charcoal that stoked the fires of Cromwell's armorers.

Now the robins so red, so swiftly they sped,
They put out their wide wings and over them
spread.

There had once been a spring in the haunted depths, known for healing properties, but it was gone now, remembered only in the village name. It must once have had wild boar and wilder men. Now it was no more than a leafy retreat and a path to the Lion pub.

Then why was she trembling?

"Who's there?" Susan called. Her voice dropped into the white, white silence as into an empty room.

A few more steps in, and small changes began to appear in the land and in the light. The shadows that should have been deepening around her instead fled away as she approached, and though the deep fog was folding London into darkness, within she could see quite clearly. And the air was no longer cold.

"Why are you hiding!"

Not hiding, Miss! Right here!

A burst of giggles exploded somewhere over her head. When she looked up, she saw only a cluster of mistletoe in the uppermost branches. The pale buds of new leaves had begun to appear, dotting the fingers of the oaks.

With another few steps she noticed that the snow, instead of drifted and piled, had become patchy, melting as she watched. A week before Christmas, and yet Spring ruled this part of the wood.

Though fancy delighted her when she encountered it, Susan was not a woman given to flights of it. Sensibly, therefore, she concluded that yes, of course, this was a dream, and now that she knew it, she would awaken.

But no waking came, only a balmy breeze that tickled her nose, bearing on it the sweetest perfumes of melons and sweet cherries, and honey cakes! Some new kind of tune hung on the air, light and playful; a harp, she thought. Growing warmer, she took off her coat and muffler and hung them on a flowering branch.

Dreaming or waking, Susan Pickering remained stubbornly curious, so taking her courage in both hands, she took two more bold steps in pursuit of the lilting music. The trees parted and the snow disappeared altogether, her boots finding nothing but green grass springing underfoot, and green leaves bursting from their buds and filling the trees, filling the blue sky over head, filtering the light of a summer's morning. And everywhere, bluebells nodded.

"What is this place?" she whispered. Then she cleared her throat and said more boldly, "Where am I, please? And what do you want of me?"

Silly human!

And there they were, one by one they popped into view before, above, and beside her, six tiny people on impossible, moth-like wings. They took turns dashing forward to touch her face, her hair, her sober dress and giggling as they fluttered away again.

"Faeries?"

"Took you long enough!"

Susan looked down at once, then stepped back. "I beg your pardon?"

Before her, dressed in discontent, stood an old man of sorts, not as high as her knee. He was clothed in a ragged coat of brown and green, with a red hat that was partly leather and partly oak leaves, and a white owl's feather. His nose was so long and so curved down that it came almost to his chin, which was so long and so curved up that it came almost to his nose.

"Say me a riddle!" commanded the wee man, and the winged children—the *faeries*—chirped their agreement, spinning and dancing in the air to the sound of chiming crystal. Other tiny figures, even smaller, she thought, were peeking and poking out to watch her, some from behind the new leaves, some from a tumble of mossy stones where a spring burbled to the surface and streamed away.

Susan frowned, thinking.

"But that is backwards, surely," she said. "In all the old tales I ever heard, the hero is asked questions and expected to answer correctly." She thought further. "Unless an old hermit happens by, I think."

"More stories than you know, human child! Say me a riddle!"

When dealing with the fae, it is best to be honest. Fortunately, that was her nature. "But I don't know any riddles."

The wee man looked disgusted, as if she had failed him. "Say what I say," he snapped in his wee voice. "What is the difference between Joan of Arc and a canoe?"

"Very well," said Susan dutifully. "What is the difference between Joan of Arc and a canoe?"

"One is Maid of Orleans, and the other is made of wood!"

Everyone but Susan exploded with laughter, rolling on the ground or spinning cartwheels in the air. Then one by one as they had come, each bowed to her and kissed her cheek, and vanished with a single delicate chime, except the wee man and his white owl's feather.

"You must take a message to the harper," he said.

"I must— What?"

"The harper, human child."

"But I know no harpers, although one of my..."

Again the sorry look. "When you see the harper, give him this," the wee man insisted, and reached up to give her a little packet like a dried leaf folded into an envelope. Within it she could feel a number of small, hard objects like beads or berries.

"What is it?"

"The harper must give this to the raven boy. Only this and nothing more!"

"I don't understand. What is—"

A single chime shook the air. Sunshine, leaves, grass, wee man were gone along with the summer day, and she was freezing in the dark. Frightened at last, she clutched the little packet in one tight fist, and hugged herself for warmth.

"Wait! Who are you? What do I..." The cold grabbed her by the throat, and the next sound was a whimper. "My coat!"

Casting about, at first she saw nothing but naked trees piled like the earth with snow. Then down the hill and away off to her left, the amber glow of gaslight flickered against the darkness, and yellow lights floated here and there. Black shadows moved—ordinary human shadows bearing ordinary human-made lanterns.

Someone was shouting—not children this time, not a hazy voice out of a mirror, but three or four living men and boys crying, "Susan! Miss Pickering!"

Tears formed into icicles as they fell, and her head pounded. "I'm here," she tried to say, but no words formed. "Oh, I'm here. Help!"

Brittle voices tinkled invisibly, and a cloud of tiny white moths swarmed out of the air around her head, fluttering against her freezing hands and face and somehow warming her just a little. Clever voices urged her, teased, cajoled her to walk on nearly frozen feet to where the old path cut a swath to the road.

"Miss Pickering!"

Her faerie helpers vanished as surprisingly as they had come, and to her utter and permanent mortification, Susan swooned.

13

The Anchor, Kew, 1589

The curve of the river from Mortlake to Kew, most days, is no more than a tube stop in Metro London. For Ben Harper, light of heart and ambling along on a silver-shod mare out of Faerie in Lord Aubrey's fine array, it was a couple of easy, uncluttered rural miles on horseback, and he was in no hurry. He'd brought the diary, and maybe he should be studying it as his grace had suggested, but this was just a simple surveillance mission. And here he was, on a bright summer day, listening to the familiar trill of birds singing out of trees four hundred years younger than the ones he knew, quietly paying attention to everything he saw. Surveillance!

Most of the traffic was out on the busy Thames, but the road that followed it, rutted and dusty in the summer heat, had traffic of its own. A carter with a wagonload of apples; a chapman with his pack loaded with pins, pots, and part songs; a pair of rosy-cheeked milkmaids—all touched their caps or bobbed a courtesy to return his greeting. Both girls giggled, and one of them blushed. Even the hobbling beggar who caught Ben's flung ha'penny tugged his ragged cap and blessed him through toothless gums.

"God save yer Honour!"

"And thyself, fellow. Have a care, and better fortune." This time the cadence and the accent, so different from what he'd expected the first time, settled familiarly on his ear.

Further along, a ruffian with the weapons and sullen look of an ex-soldier turned off without a pension made him wonder what year this was. He'd forgotten to ask. When the fellow stepped aside to piss in a ditch rather than tip his hat, Ben breathed again and moved his hand away from his sword.

Then a whip cracked, and he drew aside and touched his own cap for the thudding cavalcade of some great lady with a curiously familiar look, and arms he didn't recognize. She threw him a dazzling smile as she passed with a dozen liveried riders raising the dust.

This was, he thought with a sense of pride, the England he had saved when he returned the dragon ring to King Alfred a summer and a thousand years ago. All of them and their cares and joys had long ago sighed with their bodies into dust, yet here they were, and he among them. Whatever else came of these adventures, the sheer wonder of it all was a delight he knew he'd never get over.

In the end, Kew itself was easy enough to find; the ferry landing was small but serviceable and the ferryman only grumbled a little to take Ben across—ha'penny extra for the horses—without waiting for more passengers and a full load. An extra silver penny even got directions to the Anchor, though he might have kept his money. Directions or not, he missed the place twice before catching sight of the name painted over one of the lozenged windows that jutted into the inn yard. Over the other, the once bright images of a mermaid wrapped around a ship's anchor had flaked and faded almost to vanishing into dingy plaster.

Still, it looked a decent enough place hugging the road cheek-by-jowl with a busy chandler's that shouldered aside another less savory establishment further along. Stabling in the side street (three pence by the day, four if hay was wanted) and storage sheds behind that, plus a few rooms for travellers upstairs. Not too low for a gentleman nor too fine for a working man, it was convenient to any weary fellow breaking his journey before diving into the mad crowds of Richmond when the queen was in residence. Which, as he quickly learned, she was, on the first stage of her summer progress.

Three stories high, the ground floor where he now sat near the door offered one long room, or two adjoined ones, depending how you looked at it. Tiled fireplaces at either end, he noted, stood clean and well swept but cold on a warm day. In the middle or thereabouts, a familiar enclosure and counter, gave the landlord a clear view of both the door and the staircase to the rooms above.

Draped in the comfortable persona of Sir Francis Browne, pleasant but reserved man of parts, Ben set up camp with his own eye on the door. The livery badge on his shoulder gave him standing; the sword promised some security. His instructions were to watch and listen, and really, how hard could that be? All he had to do was sit back and enjoy the show.

Such as it was. The place was mostly empty at mid-morning, apart from a couple of regulars already lost in their cups. The mostly flat, slightly sweet beer in front of him was odd but a man could get used to it. His whole plan for the afternoon was to nurse a tankard of it, keep to the shadows with his cap down and his boots up on a joint stool till Raven came to collect him.

It wasn't his fault that someone noticed the beautifully made neck and tuning pegs of the cittern sticking out of his pack. There was one hanging on the wall that anyone might pick up, though it was battered and wanting a string. The only thing the two instruments had in common was the name.

"Canst make a tune with that thing, sir?" said one sturdy carter settling in across the narrow room. "Beggin' your Honour's pardon."

"I can, in sooth," Ben said pleasantly. He made no move to fetch the thing out, though, much as he wanted to.

"God knoweth," the man went on, "the singing's been rare enough hereabouts this long year."

"Aye, Tom, aye, in sooth," another fellow agreed, dropping onto a low bench. "'Tis them damned Puritans, an' I care not who knows it."

"Wat, for pity, hold thy peace!" Tom hissed his friend silent before Sir Francis could reply. "Never know, these days, do we?" A bit louder, he went on. "Nay, I say 'twere since Francis Drake whipped those Spanish devils out the Channel, God save 'im."

"Spaniards!" growled a gangly boy in apprentice blue who should have been at work. "Show me them! Them as killed my dad, them murdering, priest loving bastards! I'll—"

But what the boy meant to do was lost when a church bell some streets away started banging out eleven o'clock.

"Away with the glassware, Alys!" the landlord shouted, unlocking a cupboard. The little serving maid went about gathering up the more fragile cups and bowls to lock them away. "And for the good Lord's sake, chick, tie up thy cap. I'll not have thee starting a riot."

Ben tipped his own cap back now, observing everything with the amateur historian's passion and the efficiency expert's calculating eye. For at this hour, he knew, in every busy town in England workshops would be staggering to a halt as masters, generous or grudging, set their wives to feeding the anxious mouths of their prentices, the youngest piping like little birds. The older boys and girls of 18 or 20 in the last years of their indenture, the ordinary workmen whose wages did not include meals, these they released to find their own dinners, to meet and flirt and show off. The youth of the country were loosed for the space of an hour, and the nation collectively braced itself for chaos.

On the last stroke of eleven, a handful of shouting young men shoved through the doorway. The two with white powder clogging their hair and streaking their clothes Ben pegged as baker's apprentices. Another strapping lad a bit older than the others by his beard, had a blacksmith's smudges on his cheeks and brow, and the wary look of an ex-soldier; dark eyes darted into the corners as he pushed his friend aside, though when the others boxed him in the shoulder—which he can't possibly have felt—his lips shaped a merry grin. Vulgar and laughing, shoving back with jolly violence, they shouted for bread and beef and good brown ale, but swore they'd settle for the stew and small beer if it weren't too dear and the serving wench was pretty.

Chaos? Ben scoffed, shaking his head. Every tired old man in every generation from Aristotle to Erasmus despaired of the youth of his day. Flighty, full of impenetrable slang and strange oaths, disrespectful of everything. He couldn't wait to see just how badly behaved these kids really were. He also thought he might want to be a bit more out of the way. You know, just in case a riot did break out.

Sir Francis Browne, Lord Aubrey's man, pressed through the growing crowd with his pack in one hand and his beer perilously raised in the other. Heads turned, curious eyes followed the progress of his sandy head bobbing over broad shoulders. Ignoring them, he smiled, nodded, murmured, "Pray pardon. By your leave. God save thee."

A table near the cold hearth looked too small for a party, perfect for a solitary traveler like himself. He was sidling crab-wise toward it when the scrap of conversation he had just heard sank in. He nearly stumbled as he played it back.

Spaniards in the channel? The Spanish Armada had sailed to its doom, he knew, in the summer of 1588. The whole country had been on armed alert for months. Less than a year later, Great Bess, aging and ruled by her fears, would be mourning the earl of Leicester. Lord Burghley, even older, still held the reins of government, and Sir Francis Walsingham was his spymaster. Walsingham the Puritan.

No wonder the carman had been jumpy. The country must still be gripped in wartime paranoia, seeing Catholic spies under every rose bush, surveying strangers with suspicion. Maybe not such a great time to be a stranger with a peculiar accent not five miles from the queen.

What an idiot! The faerie diary in his pocket would have reminded him of all this, if he'd bothered to look.

With a sigh, he eased onto a bench and nestled his pack into the corner. Then he noticed the other thing. An awful lot of people were staring at him. With malice, he wondered, or only curiosity?

Grinning affably, he tipped his cup in friendly acknowledgement; they noted his fine livery and touched their caps in reply. He tried not to stare back, though a bemused look did in fact cross his face. Strangers attract notice, of course. And he was almost certainly the tallest man in the place. Perhaps that was all. He took a drink, and thought about getting out the diary. No, reading a book would probably cause talk, too. It would not be blending in.

Then in that moment, from somewhere a deeply resonant voice scored across his awareness. "Be that a cittern, sir?"

Ben thought he heard faery giggles coming from the walls. Oh, great. Just like home. With a rush of relief, he grinned and touched a tuning peg.

"Indeed it is, good fellow!"

"Give us a song, then, sir, aye?"

He meant to beg off, keep his head down as promised, but others had heard and joined in. And what's a man to do when asked flat out to play for the hall? Why, he plays, of course. And when the company calls for a song they all know, he tells them to pick one and hope it's one he knows or can fake. Wedged in his corner, facing all those apple-cheeked bluff-natured English carters and farmer's boys, serving men and 'prentices crowding the common room, there is no escape. A man must play or turn in his guild card.

They say if you can name all the songs you know, you don't know enough songs. Happily, as had been proved another time, Ben Harper knew a lot of songs, quite a few of them the drinking songs, love songs, ballads, madrigals and naughty catches and rounds of the time in which he was now a guest. Smiling he drew the cittern out, made a show of fiddling with the tuning-pegs though, being of faery make, it was never out of tune. Heads were already turning his way.

"We be soldiers three," he sang out stoutly. "Pardon-a-moy, je vous au pree. Lately come forth from the Low Countrie with never a penny of money."

Tom the carter came in on the second verse, and the room gave back the responses.

> *"Pray good fellow I drink to thee*
> *Pardon-a-moy, je vous au pree.*
> *To all good fellows wherever they be,*
> *With never a penny of money."*

They wouldn't have much time, no more than an hour, really, so he set about his business with a good will. In a minute or two he had drawn a small crowd that grew along with the volume as voices joined in. Ben the Showman gave them songs he was pretty sure they all knew, nothing fancy, no madrigals or airy part songs. Sir Francis teased them out of any latent shyness over drinking with a gentleman. When someone lifted his glass to shout "God Save the Queen!" he patriotically joined in, shouting it back without even thinking.

Heigh ho for a Husband made the serving girl blush, and *High Barbary* got the blood up among the young bakers and glovers or hosiers who dreamt of sailing away to be heroes.

> *Look ahead look astern, look to weather and to lee*
> *Blow high, blow low, and so sailed we!*
> *I see a wreck to windward and she's sinking in the*
> *sea*
> *A-sailing down along the coast of High Barbary!*

Ben managed to carry on playing, laughing, but not drinking over much though the ale cups kept arriving. He kept his head, the tune, and everyone's temper while they all sang along in great voices and small, even those whose business bade them hasten away.

With a broad grin as the half hour sounded, he let the King of Faerie's cittern make the rounds among those who could play, and watched the faces glow with delight as one by one its magic touched the heart and hands of each man who held it, though none knew why. Afterwards, it might cross their minds from time to time to tell their mothers or their wives how passing strange it had been, and how wonderful, that hour at the Anchor. Then they'd think better of such foolishness, and the sweet thought would pass away. But ever after when the alehouse or the guildhall or the parish lads got to singing of a summer night, one of them might catch another's eye with a foolish look neither of them understood, and nod, and look away smiling.

At last, knowing the time drew short, Ben called the handsome instrument back to his own hands. Holding it silent, he made up three quick quatrains on the spot, vulgar as any limerick. Then he ran them at speed through a complicated catch that was only bawdy when all the parts came together. By the time they'd all collapsed in helpless merriment, the church clock was striking twelve.

Kew had more than the usual work to do with the Court so nearby, so in truth the party had to end. And when it drifted apart, Ben felt he had done a proper day's work, the kingdom's good order assured once more until tomorrow. He waved the last ones off, his cheeks aching with laughter, as the carter he'd first met—Tom Hobbes, his name was—whistled his boy back to work.

The only voice left was the landlord's little wench piping in a tiny voice.

Oh, God a mercy, carman,
Thou art a lively lad;
Thou hast as rare a whistle
As ever a carman had!

Ben leaned back against the plastered wall with a sigh and a powerful longing for a seriously cold beer. With bubbles. Or better, an ice cold Coke, sugar sweet, with the carbonation burning down his throat.

As if reading his mind, a grateful landlord, beaming with unexpected prosperity, sent black-eyed Alys to him with a glass of Canary wine, cool from the cellar, and a pile of silver coins of varying sizes folded into a napkin. On a quick count, he looked up in astonishment.

"What's this then, sweeting?"

"Your share, my master says, sir. He's took in more in this hour past than a whole day and the week beside, your Honour bein' here." She jiggled fetchingly, a clear promise of more than the tip jar, if he wanted it.

Best be polite when you're new in town, and decline offers from pretty girls with grace. So he grinned back, and pretended not to notice the invitation. The money, though; he'd be mad not to take it. Not a man in England could live only on what he earned, especially a gentleman in a great lord's service. Keeping an eye on the main chance wasn't a character flaw, it was a day-to-day necessity. If he left it behind, he'd look a fool, and possibly worse. Not to mention the uncounted generations of busking musicians who would line up to haunt him.

Slave to tradition, then, Ben gave in. Grinning, he flipped a groat back to the girl. "To drink my health!" It was a huge tip, sure, but why not. Then he counted the coins off the polished wooden table, one by one, into his palm—pointedly not biting even the brassy one to check its value—and acknowledged the fee with a gracious salute to the landlord.

With the gesture, he felt a tickle of sweat slide from his armpit along his ribs. Cased in layers of wool, bombast, and fine linen as he was, it came to him all at once exactly how hot the room was. The music and the company—and the ale—had kept his mind from trivialities like weather, but now! Plucking at his buttons, tearing at his shirt points, he almost staggered to the door. Summer heat or not, he stood in the little courtyard and gulped the air, thick with river smells: tarred rope, mud, and moss. A teasing breeze whipped off the water, swirling down the side streets that wound away into the town, leaving a trailing breath behind to dry the sweat beading in his hair and under his eyes. He sucked it in like sweet, fresh water, filling his mouth and throat, opening his lungs.

"Does Sir Francis Walsingham know how you pass your idle moments?" said a tall fellow in a startling yellow doublet. In the tail of his eye, Ben saw he was smiling, leaning casually in the doorframe, but there was a noticeable edge to his voice.

Ben, who had been snuck up on by experts, continued stretching arms and chest, rocked side to side, rolled his neck, and shook out the cramps invading his hands. It wasn't Raven and it couldn't be Oberon, so whatever self-important jackass it was, he could just wait. When he could feel the sodden linen of his shirt begin to dry against his skin, he turned a little.

"I have been," he said, a bit archly, "to the chapel of Our Lady of Walsingham. I have tripped a measure some call Walsingham. I have even kissed a girl called Walsingham, God knoweth why." When a curious eyebrow lifted, he added, "Why it was her name, not why I kissed her. But I have never in my life been called to account for myself to Sir Francis Walsingham, nor to any of his worthy friends."

At this he nodded, finally, with some semblance of courtesy and thought about closing his shirt. And this would be... who then? A gentleman, certainly, not actually a trained monkey, despite the outfit. A confection of pale primrose leather slashed over a silken lining caught with silver buttons, laced with silver aiglets, the outfit alone was worth more than the Anchor and all its patrons combined. Worse, there was a dangerous glint in the those worldly eyes. A man accustomed to getting his way by negotiation, Ben thought. His agent had that look. So did his lawyer.

Ben straightened his doublet and smoothed back sweat-darkened hair, mindful that he no longer looked quite as sharp as he had this morning. He made a leg anyway and took up the thread again.

"Although if you be one of his worthy friends, be assured I am Lord Aubrey's man, and no bench-whistler. How may I serve your Honour?"

Primrose laughed and clapped Ben on the back with the bonhomie of a used car salesman, and led him back inside to a table where pen and ink stood at the ready. A snap of fingers brought a fresh glass of Canary and little Alys. Ben took it and kissed her hand, which made her giggle nervously.

"And are you the devil, contracting for my soul?" he said eyeing the writing materials doubtfully.

"Nay, I am his tax collector."

His timing sucked. Ben nearly choked on his wine.

"By your leave, sir, I think not."

"Nay, nay, man, mind me not!" laughed Primrose as if it was nothing, nothing in the world, all the while mindful of both Ben's glare and his restraint. "'Tis my poor jest, no more. Sit thee down and drink with me. Now I will say for myself and before thou look'st to ask, I am Sir Thomas Weston. For my sins I assist the Master of the Revels in his perpetual quest to entertain her Majesty and her Court."

"Say you so?" said Ben, and found a neutral expression in some pocket of his improv kit. He left the wine on the table.

With that deep, resonant voice and expansive presence, the man sounded like an actor, and perhaps he was that too. Or a ringmaster. "Now tell me thy name, fellow, what dost thou in the Lord Aubrey's service?"

I jest to Oberon, and make him smile, Ben thought with wry amusement. Life is improv. "By name I am Sir Francis Browne, and I serve my lord as he willeth. More than that I may not say, being to some small degree in his confidence. My duty changeth even as his mind."

"Then good Sir Francis Browne, I repeat my theme with this variation: doth the Lord Aubrey know how thou spendest thy time, idling in taverns?"

"And I will ask again, good Sir Thomas Weston." He stopped to sip the really rather good wine. "How may I serve you, and so serve our most gracious queen?"

Weston wasn't used, apparently, to this kind of banter from mountebanks, but he nodded and carried on.

"I heard you play and sing," he said, shifting to a more businesslike address, as equal to equal. "You're very good, sir, in sooth, you are. Better than so modest a place as this likely deserves."

"Grammercy, sir, I thank you." How on earth could he have missed this guy in the audience? He must have been cloaked like Strider in a corner. "I came only to meet a friend who is, I guess, delayed. Happily, I can fill the time."

"And play you for Lord Aubrey?"

"From time to time, and for his lady, too." No use rushing the man. He'd get there at his own stately tempo.

"So you have gentle tunes as well, to beguile the ladies, then?"

He nodded. "So I have, and many more besides."

"What's this, I wonder. Breviary?" With a sudden move, Weston bent and lifted Ben's pack from the floor. Peeking from the top, a corner of the diary he'd been neglecting all day. Weston plucked it out and started flipping idly through the pages, frowning. Perhaps the frown meant disappointment, or maybe he was just near-sighted. Whatever damning literature he expected to find, the wee folk had confounded his vision.

Strong though the urge was, Ben withheld the acid comment poised on the edge of his tongue. Instead he waited, holding his body, his aching hands, quite still. Last thing he needed was to be taken up for religious irregularities. "No Romish thing, if that is your worry."

"One cannot be too careful in these perilous days," Weston said through a thin smile as he slipped the diary back into the pack, gave it a pat, apparently satisfied that Sir Francis was neither spy nor assassin. "And do you go to join your lord at Richmond, while he is there?"

"When my errand is done, I will look for him there, aye. Master Weston, I thank you for good cheer and your merry company, but can you not come to the point?" He was glad the native speech now came so readily to his tongue, even while his imagination flung up a dozen possibilities, most of them dire.

"Very well, 'tis simple. A servant of the Revels, it is my office to seek out entertainments both fine and new for her Majesty. Musicians and poets, players and scholars, voices she might wish to know of among her people, and never would otherwise. Many musicians travel with her upon Progress, but the summer is long and her attention often sparse. Variety is essential, you see."

Weston ran a critical eye over Francis Browne's person in a way that made California Boy squirm just a little, and pronounced, "You're a fair faced man, i'faith, and fill out your hose well enough. She likes that. Aye," he said, as he pulled a paper from the wallet at his side, and smoothed it flat.

Then he dipped the pen, and entered Sir Francis Browne's name and style where space had been left in the text. "Present this at the Magdalene Gate on Monday morning. You will play for her Grace when she dines with Sir Walter Ralegh. And if she so likes, you may be asked again, though no more than twice, mark you. Your lord will be graciously pleased, I am sure, to release you for a day or two."

Ben sat back so hard his head banged the wall. "What?"

Whatever he had expected, it wasn't that. He had thought to retain a professional demeanor, listening politely to the

Maggie Secara

elaborate recitation, but then the words sank in. He could feel a flush rising under his ruffed collar, as a huge bubble of excitement rose through his chest and broke across his face into a stunned gape. "I, uhm—" He cleared the stupid squeak from his throat. "For the Queen?"

"You heard the man, Francis," said an amused and worldly voice from the doorway. "Say 'aye', and let's away. We're stayed for!"

14
The road to Mortlake, a little later

"Did you hear? Is that for real?" Ben was hooting as they urged their silver-shod horses to a hard gallop toward the Richmond road. "I'm going to play the palace!"

Raven just grinned. What an interesting day it had turned out to be. If his mortal friend held on to that pass from Weston, whose signature was as good for its purpose as Sir Edmund Tilney's own, perhaps they could take a day sometime to take up the invitation. Invitation, in sooth? Say royal command!

The way was short and the road somewhat less crowded as the afternoon had trudged on for those upon it. Raven drew them to a halt on a rise over looking the road John Dee must travel home to Mortlake. The fanciful spires and cupolas and fairy-tale turrets of the jewel-like palace of Richmond rose gleaming out of the banks of the river, dominating the town around it. With care, he resisted the urge to explore it from the air. Instead, he trained his fine, long-eyed vision on the road.

"There he is," he said. "Nearly home. He doesn't look happy."

"You can see that from here?" said Ben, collecting himself at last.

"I can, human child. And hear him muttering to himself, if I have silence to listen. He has not had the day he hoped. Gone for three years, and his Queen has not the time to see him, she sends her thanks."

He continued reporting as the black gowned figure on the ambling nag passed a little way below them. "Met with Lord

Burghley. Looked at his gouty foot—that didn't please him, I can tell you. The Council wants detailed reports written up. Not all his correspondence is scientific, it would seem. Our scholar has been doing more than communing with angels whilst abroad, and wife-swapping with Kelley who... never mind, no use repeating the rest of that." He sat back, throwing Ben a cocky grin. "And he appears to be aware that someone has been messing about with his locks but not, I think, of the extent. Money troubles taking precedence."

"He's going to think we mean to rob him, if we come riding down on him out of the sun."

"I have to warn him before he gets home. He may not thank us, but he should be armed against the witch."

Ben nodded and gathered the reins. "Let's do it then," he said. "But slowly, okay?"

They got down to the road, and fell in behind John Dee just as his path joined the river road that skimmed along the outside edge of Mortlake village, which would lead to his home.

John Dee had seen them in the corner of his eye, the two horsemen. He might be old but he was not deaf or stupid, and their harness jingled and clanked as they joined him. And why should he care? It was a public road and he was known here, mere minutes from his own house. Mortlake was not London; the riverfront was not a dangerous place. And he was armed, besides—though the sword he carried to mark himself a gentleman was mostly for show. Still the clever voice raised behind him made him start.

"Doctor Dee?"

He was hot, he was weary, he was frustrated and slightly angry and had no time for idle boys. If it were an emergency, they would not have hesitated. Had they been robbers, they would have stopped him out upon the highroad.

But indeed, two sturdy young fellows—one not entirely young but fit—rode up on either side of him. When one pulled ahead and across his path, crying his name again, he had no choice but to halt. They were smiling, these bully lads in Lord Aubrey's livery, and displayed no weapons.

"I am Doctor John Dee," he confirmed, casting a doubtful eye first on the beardless youth, then on the sandy-haired fellow with the uncanny air. No, both of them, in truth, were out of place, he could not say quite how. "What would you?"

"A word, sir," the younger one said. No, that was wrong, as well. That boyish look belied his age. The elder seeming was in sooth the younger of the two, he was sure of it. What were they?

"One word followeth another, in an orderly world," said the doctor. "Say more than one, pray, and so come to your business. That is Lord Aubrey's badge, I believe."

"It is, sir," said the dark one. "I think you know him."

"He has done me the honor of consulting on several matters. Sent me a copy of Trithemius's *Steganographia* once when I could not for my life come by one. No one could. A man of parts, Lord Aubrey. He does not trouble me with idle nonsense. Nor," he glared, "do his men."

"No idleness, sir," said the sandy one. "I assure you."

"Only news you need to hear, and before you reach your home."

Briefly, for which he was thankful, they named themselves and unfolded a tale he dismissed almost at once. What sort of japery was this? A witch, his scrying mirror, wild magic out of the faerie realm? Faeries, indeed. The housekeeper, though. He'd had his doubts of her—or thought he had. Or was it someone else? No matter, someone had tripped his alarm, and he had the headache to prove it. His memory of the woman, though, even as they spoke of her, broke apart. Ah, of course, and that was the key.

"Ah!" he said at last.

Sir Rafe Fitzroy, the young old one, stopped talking at once. Sir Francis Browne, the old young one, sat back, looking relieved. "He gets it," the fellow said, oddly.

"I find it difficult to think of her. As you speak, I can see her before me, then she slips away. Which means there is indeed some influence at work, as you say."

"You have the skills to dismiss her, sir," Sir Rafe assured him. "And you must. Not only from your service but from your hearth. She will seek to remain with you, I think. She wants your mirror, and has the will to use it."

"Much good may it do her!" he said with a sneer. "The wretched thing—"

"Is worth more than you want us to know. You have hidden it very well, though, not as if it had no value, or she would have it and be gone already."

"Out of habit only!" he snapped.

Sir Rafe smiled knowingly, and the sense of other-worldliness heightened. Though the sun shone bright, and though the river so near at hand glittered, distracting the eye, John Dee could swear the youth had a kind of glow about him, an aura of light not just surrounding him but coming from his long-fingered hands and open, blue-eyed face. And then, he knew.

"Plato's beard!" The awe came harsh and reluctant from his throat, barely above a whisper. "What are you?" His glance shot from one man to the other. The other one, Browne, carried a touch of the same light, as if by constant company he had taken on some of that quality, but... "Are you angels?" Dee breathed.

Browne's brows shot straight up and Fitzroy laughed with huge delight.

"Angels, sir!" For a moment in his laughter the glow diminished, and the boy looked like any young bravo of one-and-twenty. "Nay, sir, we are not angels, though we are messengers. And our messages being delivered, we must leave you to put your house in order. Protect your family, Dr Dee."

"What must I do?"

"Ah!" The boy slapped his forehead in annoyance, then reached into his wallet and drew out a silver coin. "I had almost forgot. My lord bade me give you this token. Keep it by you in your workings against evil, and you can do naught but prevail."

The thing vibrated with power in the palm of his hand; Dee stared at the coin then at Fitzroy. "Not an ordinary silver crown."

"A token from the king of Faerie, sir. Use it wisely."

Faeries, again, Dee thought, wrinkling his nose with distaste. He was not a babe to be beguiled with childish nonsense, but it would be impolite—and possibly impolitic— to argue.

He pocketed the coin to examine later. "But what of the witch? What other harm may she do?"

"Little, we hope, doctor. She will be watched. And so farewell."

Each curious gentleman, old-young and young-old, touched his cap and nodded, then they turned their horses and leapt away.

Still bursting with questions, John Dee watched as they cantered into the west. He thought one of them was singing! And though he was sure he observed them most carefully as they faded into the afternoon glare, when he blinked, they had disappeared.

15
Hollytree House, Sydenham Wells, 1854

Tentative as a whisper, awareness reached toward Susan Pickering.

"Up the airy mountain, down the rushy glen," an amused male voice chanted softly out of the dark.

Around her floated other voices, more subdued, less strange. Other senses touched her: a cool damp, bruised herbs, the sting of aqua vitae. Then flowers. The clean sharp scent of lavender, and something else. Bay rum?

The voice continued. "We daren't go a hunting for fear of little men."

Bay rum, and lime, and a stifling heat. The crackle of fire covering the bare hiss of a gas jet. A gentle pressure on her wrist. A hint of golden light.

"Wee folk, good folk, trooping all together."

Whose voice was that? It seemed to move around her, almost intimate in the strengthening light.

"Green jacket, red cap, and white owl's feather! I think she is waking."

Susan was not at all alarmed when the dream—certainly a dream!—finally released her. The surprise was to find herself laid out, fully clothed except for her boots and stockings, and wrapped in rugs on the chaise longue by the fire in the drawing room, with Ellen just removing an herbal compress from her forehead and clucking like a mother hen.

"What on earth?" Susan tried to rise, but a large hand presumed to replace Ellen's and keep her down. Annoyed, she swiveled her gaze up to meet the smiling eyes and aggressive whiskers of that reporter.

"I suppose that was you, muttering that ridiculous poem."

"It's alive she is, then, bless her," he said, snatching his hand away. "You'll forgive the liberty, I hope, Miss Pickering, for I've taken that and more already."

The voice registered in her ear as more cosmopolitan than it had earlier, less theatrically Irish.

"Liberty?" Mousy brown eyebrows drew together, confused. "What liberties have you taken, then, Mister... I beg your pardon."

"Donovan, Miss Pickering. Mr Edward Donovan, Esquire, but the whole world calls me Ned."

Considerately, he came round so she could stop straining over her shoulder to look at him, and grinned that devastating grin without any shame at all

Single-handedly bringing down the tone of her drawing room, he cut the most appalling figure in the rumpled brown coat and green plaid trousers, the fiery red hair, and that moustache. Presumably the scuffed and stained carpetbag at his feet topped with a battered bowler hat was his, as well.

Now that she was released from captivity, Susan threw back the suffocating rugs and sat up. When the maid objected, it did no good.

"Ellen, that's quite enough, I'm fine," she said crossly. "Daisy, hair pins at once."

With a sniff, Ellen poured a fresh cup of tea and put it in her mistress's hands before grudgingly joining the Greek chorus of hovering lodgers seated or standing among the potted palms. Mr Horsley and Mr Swindon may have been slightly more concerned for dark-eyed Miss Kennedy than their landlady, but that was to be expected. Stout Miss Dean, the music teacher, only looked dour, which could be interpreted as a softening of her usual expression.

With some tortoise shell pins and a pair of combs from the pocket of her apron, and while Miss Pickering sat quite still, Daisy was able to restore some sort of decency to her mistress's demeanor.

Spoiling the effect, Susan curled her bare toes into the pile of the blue Turkey carpet. Bare feet! Goodness, could this get any worse? But without betraying any sign of embarrassment, her naked feet, delicately crossed at the ankles, simply disappeared beneath the rug she drew casually over her lap. In the meantime, her entire household watched her in anticipation.

"My question, Mr Donovan, requires an answer."

He had been watching her, and trying not to stare. Caught out, he took a deep breath, then chuckled a little with chagrin.

"Someone had to carry you in, Miss Pickering. As fortune would have it, I had just paid off the cabman and was coming to your door, when I heard all the commotion. Folk rushing about, shouting and carrying on. Being a helpful fellow by nature, I joined the search party. And wasn't it I who saw you fall, your green dress bright, bright against the white snow."

"I fell?"

"So you did, and out of your senses with it. So what could I do but pick you up—most respectfully, mind—and carry you here. I'd have taken you up to your bed," he added, as free of innuendo as possible. "And laid you down as gently as my own sister, but the rest of the house would have none of it."

"I should think not!" she sniffed.

The lodgers, excepting always the stern Miss Dean, each chorused approval of the reporter's perfect manners, nodding violently in agreement.

"There you have it," he said, insufferably amused, and waited for her to speak.

What was there to say? Sitting in her naked feet, the collar of her high-necked dress open to a shocking degree, and no cap of any kind on her hair, she had to face facts and carry on, as she had always done.

"I thank you, Mr Donovan, for your chivalry," she said with imperial grace.

"I beg your pardon?" He could feel the blood starting into his cheeks. Weren't her ears sharp, for all they were so small and round. "Oh that. Nothing, miss, nothing at all. Just a verse that crossed my mind."

He could tell her about it later, perhaps, if she gave him the chance. For now, he was content that she thanked him.

"And it's entirely welcome you are." Beaming, he bent to kiss her hand, though she hadn't offered it, which brought a blush to her winter pale cheek. After a moment's thought, he added, "I hope I might beg one thing in return."

"I cannot promise you an interview with the Professor, Mr Donovan," she warned.

He thought she might be warming to him. By way of answer, he produced the "Room Available" placard that she had posted on the front gate.

"You're in need of a lodger."

"Oh, Mr Donovan, really! He won't talk to you over the breakfast table!"

"It's all right, I never eat breakfast."

She made a noise like *piffle*, and looked away.

"I have the most impeccable references."

"So you say." Susan cast a doubtful eye over his single carpetbag. "And luggage?"

"I live lightly, bathe regularly, drink little, and am seldom at home. I have honest employment, and no debts. You'll hardly know I'm there at all."

Was he applying for lodging or proposing a sensible marriage?

"Honest employment?" she said archly. "A newspaper writer, lies by the line?"

He shrugged in grudging affirmation. "Also a writer of fanciful tales and tender romances, poems, plays, and whatever I'm paid to, so long as I'm putting one word after another. Except advertising. A man must draw the line somewhere."

She felt she ought to say no, but couldn't say why. He was to every appearance frank, honest, and sincere. He had been kind to her. And since she had no good reason, and a debt of honor besides, what could she do?

When she glanced around the room she realized that, to a man or woman, her residents and staff were nodding and smiling. Even prickly Miss Dean, who seldom approved of anyone, was practically beaming at him. He must have behaved exceptionally well, and she herself must have been in exceptional need, to have earned such esteem in so short a time.

"Well, then," she said crisply. "You have been told the rates and terms already? This is an orderly house. No visitors above stairs, no lady friends, Sunday prayers?"

"I have been so advised by the worthy Ellen." His face sobered and he lowered his voice to speak privately, "And I can tell you how you got those wee pinches on your face and hands."

Uncertain, Susan lowered her eyes. Tiny red marks like little bruises dotted the backs of the square, unremarkable hands folded across her lap. She raised wide eyes to meet his, and delivered her decision.

"Ellen, will you and Daisy see that Mr Sweet's old room has fresh linens, please? Mr Donovan will be residing with us."

They curtseyed cheerfully, and left at once.

At last, Susan Pickering dragged her gaze away from his and surveyed the room. "My goodness, everyone, I am not dying! Please go on about your usual business. I suppose I've missed my tea?"

"Not at all, Miss," said Mrs Nixon. "Just give us a few minutes. Come along, everyone, give Miss Pickering some peace!"

She clapped her hands briskly, and called for Peter to lay the table. It was as if a spell had been broken. Released from their fascination, the rest of the household laughed lightly and chattering returned at last to other amusements.

Susan watched the door close behind them and sighed. What an extraordinary day!

"Do sit down, Mr Donovan, please." He took the padded chair vacated by the worthy Ellen, and sat down opposite the chaise, reaching into his coat pocket with a familiar gesture. "I prefer that no one smoke in this room, if you please."

Caught, he spared a longing look for the fresh cigar, then reluctantly put it away.

Taking pity, she added, "Some of our gentlemen occasionally indulge after Sunday dinner, but only in the billiard room."

"You are a queen among women indeed, Miss Pickering."

"I am a queen in a quandary, Mr Donovan," she said, keeping a keen eye on him. He had jumped up again and was rooting around in the carpetbag. "What did you mean? Excuse me, what did you mean, you know how I came by..."

When he stood, he was rubbing smudges off what she supposed was his shaving mirror with a surprisingly clean handkerchief. Then he returned and shoved it ungallantly in front of her nose.

"Look there," he said, and his expression was entirely serious.

She was accustomed to being reminded of the painful plainness of her face, and so had no vanity to pamper. In the reflection she saw at first only ordinary brown hair sweeping around her ordinary, English face. A sensible spinster of five-and-twenty now, she'd stopped wishing to be prettier longer ago. Still, the reflection so abruptly placed before her made her frown.

"Are my spectacles somewhere about?"

He found them on the mantle. When she had them on her nose, she stared into the mirror again, and gasped. The same tiny bruises as those on her hands, the same but fewer and further apart, were fading on her cheeks and her undistinguished chin. No wonder Ellen had been so careful with her. The girl must have thought it was, well, the small pox, at least! But on inspection, it was clear the marks were under the skin, not breaking it.

Susan handed back the mirror with a nod, and waited. "You say you know what caused this?"

He nodded soberly. "I do that, for I've seen the like before, though not since I was a boy in Ireland. Shall I tell you?"

"Yes, please."

"You've been with the faeries. Ah, now hear me out. Everyone thinks you went for a walk and got lost, but no one sane and sober would have walked into that wood in the dark, filled with snow as it is, and the path all but vanished under it. When I found you, your coat was a dozen paces further in. If you did not run mad..."

A wry smile turned up the corners of her mouth.

"Much too sensible to run mad."

"Or take to drink? Of course not. You took it off, because it was too warm for a woolen coat where you were."

"And where was I, Mr Donovan?"

"There was music, aye? Bells, maybe, or chimes?" Susan nodded. "And something drew you into the wood. Children's voices, perhaps, or a cry for help?"

"Children playing, or so I thought."

"Aye, that would be it, a tender woman such as yourself."

She scoffed and straightened where she sat.

"I have been called many things, Mr Donovan, but never that."

"No matter, you saw them. And being both caring and stubborn, you followed."

Bit by bit he narrated, with her confirmation at every point, her progress into that other place, into Faerie or its Borderland, at least. His only surprise, and a mild one at that, was the little man or gnome or whatever he was.

"And what did he want of you, that wee man?"

Her gaze slipped away from him. One hand rose to push a loose strand of her hair behind one round little ear. Doubt crossed her face, and set her jaw.

The shadows of the room hung more thickly in the corners as the silence between them lengthened. The only sounds, the hiss of the two gas lamps on the wall and the crackle and pop of the fire. In a moment, she jumped up, anxiously pacing as if it would help her to think, and heedless of her bare feet.

"Oh! This is ridiculous, Mr Donovan, as you surely know. It all felt very real, but this, this trip to Faerie as you call it cannot have happened. Fairyland is a myth, a nursery story. I am a grown woman, and long past such nonsense."

That was all there was to it. Her mind made up and satisfied with the decision, she sat down again with a thump, raising a tiny puff of dust and two or three carpet faeries neither of them noticed.

Whee!

Or heard.

"I have no idea how I came to be there, but I clearly hit my head, and have had a dream, which I cannot remember."

Donovan had been observing her as closely as the toughest political interview, marking every glance and gesture. He knew, if she did not, that she was lying.

"Can't you?"

She shook her head with absolute finality. "No!" That stray lock of hair came down again.

"Miss Pickering," he said gently. "Open your hand."

"What do you mean?" She held out her right hand, unfolding the fingers showing it open and empty.

"And now the other one." The clenched fist that had not relaxed even when she was out of her senses came up almost of its own, and turned over. He leaned forward, and gave it a tap with his own left hand. Like a blossom unfolding, the fingers relaxed and parted, one by one.

"What's that, then, eh?"

Their eyes met over the dried bundle in her hand and like a memory of summer, the task she had been given rolled into her mind and snapped into place.

"I have to…" Some natural caution made her pull back, and her hand closed over the packet again, less convulsively than it had before. "I rather think it is only for me to know."

"You don't trust me, Miss Pickering?"

"I do not know you, Mr Donovan," she said firmly, and dropped the bundle in her pocket.

He sat back with half a smile. "No more you do," he said. "You are as wise as you are beautiful."

"Nor am I subject to flattery."

Accepting her decision, he held up an ink-stained writer's hand for peace—his left hand, she noted. So he was cary-handed, then. She wondered if he'd had his knuckles rapped as a child, as she had herself.

"If I wanted to take it from you, Miss, or if I were one of those your Mrs Nixon would call the Unseelie Court—which I am not—I would have it already. But very well. I have told you most of your journey already. I can tell you the end, I think."

So he did. "

You are to give that to someone you have never met, without knowing why or when. Whatever it is, whoever it is for, I guess you are the only one, mortal or faerie, to whom this task could have been given."

She sat with this knowledge for a long minute, considering, and then held up her hands. "And these?"

"Faerie kisses, Miss Pickering. They have no heat of their own, you see. Little pinches are what they can give to make your own blood rise and warm you. They're light-minded creatures and careless of us poor mortals, those little ones. But I saw them in their hundreds, trying to lead you out. They remembered in the end!"

He looked so serious, so earnest, and he had been helpful, if an outrageous flirt.

"Tell me. How do you come to be an expert in the faeries, Mr Donovan?"

"Bless my soul, Miss," he roared in his broadest accent. "Doncha know, I'm Irish!"

That made him laugh out loud, long and delightedly, until she had to join him. And that broke the spell of other worlds and perilous quests, and brought them firmly back to the mundane, palm-filled drawing room in Sydenham Wells.

When a bell rang quite nearby, loud and brassy as a town crier's, the laughter fled away from them in the instant.

Then Susan smiled. "That is only Mrs Nixon with our tea," she said, scrambling to put damp shoes and stockings back on to her cold narrow feet.

When she pronounced herself ready, he offered his arm, which she took, and they went to join the others, squelching just a little as she went.

16
Sydenham Village, 1589

How? How! Perdita raged. How had that wretched little man with his pathetic white beard managed to send her packing with such dispatch? How had he dismantled her spells to see her so clearly, to move against her before she had time even to put her plan into action?

For she had had a plan, a perfectly good one. The family—the plump pigeon of a wife she meant to replace, the scrawny brats—returned from their market day to mayhem and madness, were already asleep under her enchantment; the neighbors, her willing if unwitting accomplices, urging them to rest. She was not finished with him. Not nearly finished!

Now she was huddling in the lee of a crumbling hill, in some filthy peasant hovel, or the remains of one, with the clothes on her back and a pathetic bundle—a pouch of dried tobacco and a copper knife that had come with her against all hope from the Secota town; a silken scarf, a small round mirror in a standing frame. The few precious items she'd had time to gather before barriers slammed down behind her at the garden gate. And as she stumbled from the wretched town into the green and growing farmland behind it, a loud *snick*, like a key being turned in a lock, sealed her out of Mortlake altogether. How?

She had been stumbling across country ever since, through orchards of unripe apples and long fields of barley, looking for a road, even a sheep path, that might take her somewhere before night found her, and changed her.

As the long summer twilight was ending, shelter had become her only concern. She could feel the awful transformation twisting her insides, seizing her bones loosening some and freezing others with the pains of her desperate antiquity. At last, she had staggered through the last stubbled field, clutching her meager possessions, and into the edge of some tiny hamlet—just a few houses, and a ruin of a church. No one noticed the crippled old woman in the grey kirtle who hobbled into the tumble-down cottage furthest from the rest. Shepherds and farm laborers, they rose with the sun, and had long since barred their doors.

Clearing what space she had found, little more than a corner out of the wind, she tried to ignore the aching teeth, the blurring vision, and the inevitable, infuriating tremor that beset her hands. Her anger however, burned as fresh and bright-eyed as it had those few hours before. She had to think, to analyze, try to learn. She had to focus her mind even while her body betrayed her in the dark.

She started by considering the steps that had brought here to this horrific pass, free of her prison but practically powerless. The meddlesome Finch, cleaning her mistress's French looking glass with vinegar, had by purest chance been gazing at her own cow-like face when Perdita's seeking found and snared her. Frightened but willing, the woman had drawn poor, seeming-sad Perdita, naked and tragic, from a sandy bank in the New World straight into England. And without even, the witch noted to herself with satisfaction, any music of any kind. Why that mattered, she wasn't sure, but it pleased her anyway.

Oh, how it had delighted her to take those three quick steps into the box-crowded bedchamber, holding her copper knife. To draw the honed edge neatly under the woman's ear. Best of all, to hold the dying bitch in her arms and chant the old words that sealed the spell and opened Perdita to her victim's memories: language, lore, children's birthdays, whatever was near the surface. It was the most efficient way she knew to blend into new surroundings. And tasty, too.

The essence of the housekeeper's—what, her soul?—had clung to Perdita's lips like the taste of cinnamon, warming and energizing. None of her teachers had mentioned that, keeping the most useful knowledge to themselves, as always. But all of them—almost all of them, she thought bitterly, and that soured her triumph a little—all of those selfish, crabbed old men were dead.

Like the Anatolian seer, as subject to her tears as all the rest. Besotted, he had given up his immortality to her in the end, a spell she had botched in her haste, for which she still paid night after night.

Or the Chinese mystic who had tried to teach her the trick—he called it a skill—of traveling through the mirrors; another disaster with its own penalties. That one had left her trapped for, God's Death, who knew how long—two thousand years. That wouldn't happen again.

This man John Dee was old, like those others, and like all men easily distracted, but his reputation said he had studied widely, spoke languages no good Christian should admit to, and knew much of things both hidden and strange. Perdita might have convinced him to teach her. She had the time, but persuasion and pretense were so inefficient.

No, she wanted the famous mirror she had learned of from Finch and from the gossip of the neighbors in the days while she waited in her new, persona for Dee to arrive. She had knowledge in plenty, she needed a tool! She had contrived her plan, her perfect plan. And then... and then...

It was so unfair! What magic, what clever allies did the old man have that she did not? She who had stolen power from her teachers for hundreds of years. It was almost as if he had been armed against her!

She realized her heart was pounding, her breath wheezing. Her teeth ached, her feet hurt, and she was starving. The light was gone, and she was old, so very old.

Very well, upon review, she had done nothing wrong. Made no mistakes, except perhaps not waiting long enough before acting. The answer lay trapped her memory where some faceless, nameless master lurked.

He was still out there, somewhere, watching her. He knew she was free. She had felt him wake to her. Oh, how he must be trembling among his stinking crucibles and athanors, whatever sort of sorcerer he was! She would waste no more time on self-blame. For now, she would sleep.

When she woke, young and fair, it was a Sunday. After the few wretched residents had bundled off with all their children and aged parents to the next village to fulfill their statutory obligation to God and the Privy Council—more useless information from the neighbors—the witch got up to rifle through each poor hovel for whatever might do her any good. Someone's bed-bound old gammer had been left for pity in her bed, where she snored like a cannonade. It crossed Perdita's mind that death might be in the old woman's best interests, not to mention the family's. They would likely be relieved to lose the useless mouth that must nevertheless be fed. The mean and wretched life at its end could do one useful thing, by enriching her own.

But no, that was shortsighted. She could hide anywhere at need, but not if a trail of death followed her. So she passed on. She found a loaf's end and bit of butter, some turnips and three small eggs. The kitchen hearth fire had been properly banked, and only a little effort brought it back, and so breakfast was accomplished.

In the place next door, the one in best repair of the lot, she found five tarnished ha'pennies tied in a handkerchief and, with a minor finding spell, some hoarded coins, almost a whole shilling in a leather bag under a floorboard. She didn't expect to need much money, but it could be useful, so she took the bag and left the handkerchief.

Against her habit, she took the time to ransack each cottage gently, leaving as little trace of her presence as possible. Then she bundled the meager pickings into her apron and looked in again on the old woman.

Eyelids like yellowed crepe flickered open over wide, milky eyes; the pinched, toothless mouth worked but no sound emerged. Was the hag dying after all? If she were already dying, her people would look no further. Perdita's red, red tongue flicked out over rosy lips, tasting the energy of the room like a serpent. *Yes!*

She sat on the frame of the bed and held the woman's hand, petting and soothing. The trick to this, she knew, would be in the timing, and aye, she had it. The old lady coughed once, and Perdita put one smooth hand over the shapeless mouth and nose, and wrapped the other golden arm around the tiny shoulders. And as the life leaked away, she kissed her forehead as gently as a loving daughter might have, and chanted the spell that stripped the life away, drawing it into herself.

To her delight she found the old woman's essence as warm and spicy as the young housekeeper's had been. As sweet as apples, as heady as honey wine. The memories were hazy and the cultural information hard to sort out, but she—Agnes, her name was Agnes—had lived through dangerous times, borne many children and lost most of them, known terrible fear and danger, and even, once, something tender. As a girl…

Perdita jerked away. Enough of that. It was time to go. Disengaging from the rapidly chilling corpse, she gathered her things, wrapped herself in shadow, and left. She would have to cast a mist about the ruined hovel, as she had in Mortlake to keep people away. She needed some privacy to work, carefully, with the mirror, to find her future, to find revenge.

17

Hollytree House, Sunday before Christmas, 1854

For a loosely associated household such as Miss Pickering's in Albany Road, Christmas might have been a melancholy season. The residents, for the most part young and ambitious with families far from London, had neither the funds nor the time to travel; others like Miss Dean had no family at all. They chose therefore to hang up sorrow and care, and make each other very merry, instead. Much secrecy was involved in the matter of presents, and for days the house smelled of cinnamon and ginger.

The Saturday before Christmas, Mr Donovan, having a rare free afternoon, took Peter, a long ladder, and his clasp knife into the wood to cut white-berried boughs of mistletoe from an oak tree. Miss Pickering graciously permitted a branch to be hung over the parlour door, and sprigs on every window sash. Peter had furthermore scoured the neighborhood for lengths of ivy, which now adorned the mantels; and by happy chance, the two thick holly hedges flanking the front walk, from which the house took its name, were bright with red berries. Judicious snips were made for the gentlemen's buttonholes and hatbands.

The next day directly after church, Miss Pickering's younger residents all went out to scour the wood for a suitable Christmas tree. Their remnant of the Norwood was not much of a place for fir trees in general, and it took some searching, and some throwing of snowballs, but at last a small stand of them was discovered, including one just exactly the size Miss Pickering had indicated. Mr Swindon held the little tree steady while Mr Horsley wielded the hatchet, and Miss Kennedy kissed each of them in the excitement, which made everyone just slightly uncomfortable, but not for long.

They hauled it back in triumph singing *Adeste Fideles* at the tops of their lungs, unwittingly doing exactly what is required when taking a tree from a faerie-haunted wood. As they raised it on a table in the drawing room, Mr Horsley cheerfully noted that a very large one had been put up in the Great Transept of the Crystal Palace. The exhibitors had all contributed miniature toys and tinsel for its decoration. Mr Swindon, Mr Horsley and Miss Kennedy were content to assemble paper chains and gilt paper stars. Ellen the maid found a box of old beads and paste jewelry in one of the closed up rooms to add to the spectacle. And Mrs Knox sent Daisy in to them all with punch and a basket of gingerbread men, sticky with molasses and almonds.

"Is it not wonderful," said old Miss Dean, letting the seasonal cheer conquer her customary disapproval. "Is it not wonderful," she repeated over the hubbub, "how his Royal Highness Prince Albert introduced this tradition of his homeland only a few years ago and yet, thanks in part to Mr Dickens and his Christmas stories, it has quickly taken root in the hearts of all English men and women. Almost as if it were not foreign at all."

Miss Kennedy, ever bubbly in bouncing black ringlets, gave a giddy laugh. "Oh, Miss Dean, will you ever play some carols for us?"

Though she suspected that no one was listening to her, as usual, Miss Dean nevertheless seated herself at the spinet and began a lugubrious *O Come, O Come Immanuel.*

Looking up from her sketchbook, Susan felt the smile bloom across her cheeks, warming to the energy and general gaiety in her house. There hadn't been a proper Christmas in this house since her parents' death. Her mourning period had forbidden it, and Uncle Lovejoy simply ignored it. After that, well this one was nearly perfect. It lacked only the colorful Donovan, in fact. She wondered, as she often did nowadays, where he was, what excitement he was pursuing.

She knew he still chafed over his inability to corner the Professor. If Lovejoy's Great Device had been Donovan's true motivation for moving into Hollytree House, she thought, he must be greatly disappointed, although in his relentless good humor, it never showed. When he was at home, he kept them all entertained with the most wonderful stories of his adventures, providing all the voices, and swearing that some were even true.

And his attentions to her had not failed to be gallant and virtuously flirtatious. After ten days, she almost believed he enjoyed her company for its own sake. Very carefully, for her heart had been misused in the past, she began to think of him as a friend. So when he blew in starving just after the luncheon things had been cleared away, she had Mrs Nixon give him sandwiches and tea. While he was eating, she helped Daisy make up the mid-day hamper for her great-uncle and his unpleasant assistant, and thought of a plan to help Mr Donovan.

Though the Crystal Palace was closed to the public on the Sabbath, exhibitors and staff always had access. Lovejoy and Cray, frantic to become the first trans-temporal peeping Toms, were eager to bicker and swear and run their experiments without the restraints of an audience or pesky reporters.

As Susan flung off her apron and emerged from the kitchen, Donovan was scowling over the *Illustrated London News*, which he momentarily threw down in disgust.

"Why do I write for this so-called newspaper?"

She leaned her chin on her hand, studying him. "Because they pay very well?"

"Not especially. Yes, better than most."

Curious, Susan turned the paper to see what had produced his outburst. His by-line floated comfortably over engravings from a livestock show.

"And they put your name on the story."

"Often enough."

"The *Illustrated London News* is an entirely respectable newspaper, by all accounts."

"Ah, there is that, yes. But there's not a man in that pressroom can write his own name, never mind tell a story with any style at all. You remember the Great Train Robbery in the summer! Of course you do. Who was it cornered the railway guard before all the rest, eh? I did, of course! And last year in Newcastle, when the miners were striking for better wages, practically started a revolution? I was there, talking to the miners and the owners, and the thugs they hired. I filed my reports often at some considerable danger to myself. When the relics from the Franklin expedition came available, didn't I go to Repulse Bay myself and get the story!"

Breathless, she realized it was her turn to speak.

"And they didn't print it?"

"Oh, they printed it, more or less. And stranded me in Canada, they were so happy about it. Something I said embarrassed someone, don't ask me more. But I had to work my way home on a mail packet."

"But how exciting, Mr Donovan!"

"You'd think so, wouldn't you?" he growled, though he preened just a little under her regard. "Filed stories from every port of call from Capetown to Gibraltar. And that bast— ehm, that blackguard Scotchman, Charlie bloody Mackay gutted every one."

She had startled, wide-eyed, at the strength of his language, but said only, "What do you mean?"

"Smoothed all the heart out of the words, he did, and him a poet! And worse, he matched them with pictures you wouldn't put under a dog, begging your pardon. A schoolgirl could do better."

"I suppose you would rather be in the Crimea."

"I begged Mackay to send me, but it was two late. Fenton had the patronage, you see. And a camera."

His glance grazed her face, its expression carefully arranged in sympathetic angles, but he thought she was fighting to keep from laughing.

"That's why I want to interview your uncle, d'ye see! Him, and men like him—the thinkers, experimenters, inventors, the men that are changing the world. I've written a few already about such ambitious, far-sighted men—you'll have read them, I expect—but he'll be the jewel in the crown. I want to do a whole series on him alone, following the progress of his work. If he ever succeeds, even if he never does, I'll be the man who kept the country on the edge of its seat! That story could make a man's career! Oh, *The Times* will be begging to give me a desk."

"But what if his device never works?"

"If I give it the right twist, the right angle, it won't matter. Look, when I write, it isn't just facts but reasons, and motives, the triumph of the human spirit!" He flung his arms out wide as if to take in the whole of human endeavor. "Passion!"

A plate crashed in the kitchen, followed by a muttered epithet from Mrs Nixon.

"And truth?" Susan asked mildly.

"When it's absolutely necessary, yes, truth too," he said with a mischievous spark in his eyes—brown, or possibly green.

"So tell me," he said, throwing the napkin over a plate now burdened only with the smallest of crumbs. "Am I never to meet the fabled Professor Lovejoy properly? I tell you, Miss Pickering, I have stayed up late and got up early to try and catch him, with no luck at all. Does he never leave the Crystal Palace? Does he live there and not here?"

That made her laugh a bit and shake her head.

"Neither, really. No, he lives over the carriage house, behind the kitchen garden. And leaves little notice of his comings and goings, from what Ellen says except cigar stubs and beer bottles. Bloodhound that you are, I'm surprised you have not sniffed him out already. But wait a moment."

With this, she stood and went to retrieve her coat and bonnet. When she turned to him again, a conspiratorial gleam in her eye matched the rare smile. "If you'll come along with me," she said, "and if you will kindly carry the hamper, I believe you may beard the lion in his den."

Almost before she had finished speaking, he was on his feet and reaching for his hat, the soft cap he'd been wearing all week.

"Miss Pickering, I'd be too ashamed to be seen in public again, never mind look myself in a mirror, if I were to let you carry that basket, and I by you."

"Come along then, Mr Donovan," she said with a sudden smile which, he noted, lit up her remarkably sweet face.

18
Sydenham village, 1589

The kind of witchcraft so feared by the people of Elizabeth's England was a long mile away from the magic at Perdita's command. During the week, she went out to the road seducing passers-by for her bread and beer, wine when they had it, and even a few coins, just for practice. Not begging, no. Why beg when she could command! Though having found shelter in this desperate place, she preferred to protect it and herself from prying eyes.

That first Sunday, when the villagers had trundled home weary and broken from practicing their religion, the outcry that had gone up in response to her little thieving efforts had not been quite as amusing as she'd expected. So she maintained the smudge pot, and remained to all mortal intents and purposes invisible. She had heard they burned witches in this benighted country. Best not to find out.

It would be safer, yes, to gather herbs in the woodland, avoiding the charcoal burners at their smoking ovens and the women gossiping as they trudged off wherever they went in search of day work. The curious dogs were harder to discourage, until she chanced on a scent, a combination of vervain and less common herbs that turned them away.

Through the short nights of summer she huddled without a fire in her stolen blankets and shivered. And in the long evenings, after the cottagers had humped their wives and fallen exhausted to their pallets, in the gold and violet hours before darkness fell, before the loathly form came over her, then— Ah then.

Then her magic was strongest, even as the foul enchantment gathered to waylay her. And that was something she could harness, and put to her advantage. A dish to keep a lighted coal alive; a flake of the Roanoke tobacco; a well-made mirror in a plain wooden case; and a copper knife with a razor edge. Sunday came round again at last, and she watched the folk of Sydenham village slink off to their fearful worship. She ate some bread and drank some wine; she bathed undisturbed in the hot mineral pool that burbled and hopped in the deepest part of the wood.

Refreshed, she prepared a corner of her tumbledown shelter, laying everything she needed on a milking stool someone would miss later: knife, bowl, mirror, herbs, and a pair of grey mice asleep in a wicker cage. For safety, she draped the mirror with Jane Dee's silk scarf. The little cow must have missed it by now. How she must have raged and wept! Excellent! That anger, those tears were part of the universe now, and tangible, feeding Perdita's power. The mirror, unwarded, was not. The last thing she wanted was to be drawn back into it, and so the silken cover.

Kneeling naked on the rush mat she had fashioned, she loosed her hair from its pins and combed it out, letting it fall like a shower of gold over her golden breasts. Then she leaned forward and blew gently on her hoarded bit of fire until it glowed scarlet. A few strands of dry straw, the cleanest she could find, fueled it. Flame leapt up. All she had to do was feed it until it was time, as Young Woman's spirit had shown her, to add those flakes of tobacco leaf. Just a few, just enough to swamp the flame and begin to fume.

As the smoke lazily swirled blue and brown into the air, Perdita gently drew the silk away from the looking glass. The awful draw was there still, tugging at her mind like a ring stitched to her throat; but it could be resisted; she could resist so long as the fume obscured the light in the glass.

Now she cast her net. Someone out there in the corridors of time and space was thinking of her, fearful of her. Someone else lived in envy or in fear or stunted passion. And somewhere, in some time, they would hear her calling, and open a door. Her old master was out there, faceless and nameless. She could taste his song in her mind, the awful song that had banished her from solace and joy. And from his awesome power. He too would be seeking for her.

With searching fingers, she pressed aside the wicker bars of the cage and brought out a mouse, still drowsy and compliant. The other hand laid her blade against its tiny beating heart and pressed it home until the blood spurted. With pain and blood came the creature's terror, its struggles as she closed the hand that held it over the glowing coal, and squeezed. Blood and fluids and life drained over the bowl, feeding the flame, and filling the wretched little room with a stench she could ignore with ease. The fume thickened about her.

She breathed the smoke, chanting in a voice as throaty and coarse as her intention, and wove her spell into a summoning, a conjuring, a canticle. Swaying where she knelt, the witch opened her mind and let the chant flow out into the earth, into the twilight, and across the crystal gates that separate the worlds, seeking the seekers, and finding...

19
Crystal Palace, 1854, a while later

Their boots rang on the Crystal Palace's wooden floor—his widely-spaced and sauntering, hers quick and light—as they moved swiftly along the nave past the classic art of the ages, now anonymous and hulking under canvas covers. Stiff-armed Christmas trees were indeed in evidence, spangled with sugarplums and topped with gilded stars.

They had come up from the service entrance ignoring the carriages, reapers, and Machinery In Motion on the floor below, paced off the walls of lion-guarded Nineveh, and ducked under the wide painted gaze of sphinxes and staring pharaohs. They'd passed the forum of the Caesars and Aristotle's Academy, and strolled past the fabulous facades of the Renaissance behind their painted screens, without so much as pausing for the Elgin marbles, copied for the edification of the common man.

As they crossed the broad expanse of the barrel vaulted Central Transept, each felt a low rumble or a hum, a sort of vibration that set the glass panels around them to buzzing. Susan recognized it, or thought she did. Usually the place was so full of ambient noise than no one thing stood out, but this did. She'd felt this before, and hated it.

Donovan, because he noticed everything, felt it in his sinuses and rising through the leather soles of his boots. He ignored it. He had other things on his mind and not just the interview; he'd had that prepared for weeks. No, there were other matters just as important about which he was less sure.

"Miss Pickering," he said, quite casually. A question clearly lurked in his thought.

So much shorter than he, Susan was already taking nearly two steps to his one to keep up. "Yes, Mr Donovan?" she gasped.

The Stationery Court slipped by, its useful machines as protected as the art works.

"As we are more or less alone for a moment. I wonder, would it be an impertinence if I asked you what might be considered a personal question?"

The artistic courts, the glass and ceramics, the goods in the bazaar over head all huddled behind painted screens or under canvas. The ultra-modern goods of steely Sheffield gleamed, fearless in their displays: locks and keys and gleaming sabers.

"If it is not too personal."

"I admit that it's not been so long since we met. And society frowns on too close acquaintance between a virtuous bachelor and a maid, as the poet says."

"Mr Donovan!" Susan gasped, stopping to breathe while he strode along ignoring the mechanized wonders of Birmingham. "Mr Donovan, I cannot carry on a conversation at a dead run. If you wish to speak to me, we must sit down!"

He halted, chagrined, and hurried back to her. Aware of the echoes in the vast, unpopulated hall, he kept his voice low. "Bless me, I apologize! You're quite right, of course. Here, here's a bench. Let's sit a moment, shall we?"

Handsome benches of wrought iron and polished wood had been placed along the artwork-cluttered nave to give foot-sore visitors a respite in their perambulations. Each one was perfectly suited to comfortable examination of a fountain, a handsome facade, or a famous work of art. Donovan put the hamper carefully on one, then with a nerveless hand on her elbow steered her to another they could share in front of the pink-walled Roman house from Pompeii. Graceful goddesses framed the doorway. The mosaic pavement at the entrance bore the image of a snarling dog and the warning, *Cave canem,* beware the dog.

Susan's heart was already pounding; she hardly needed a warning.

"I mean to say," Donovan went on, placing his cap on his knee. He moved to take her hand, but hesitated. "Well, the thing is that I wonder if we are well enough acquainted, if we are friends enough, that I might have the privilege of your Christian name, and if you will be free with mine."

"Oh, my goodness!"

Whatever she had expected, this clearly wasn't it. She straightened, eyes wide, pale lips parted for a quickened breath. The intimacy of names was a gift for very few: family members, school friends, courting lovers. He tilted his head, waiting. She loved how even the grey light glinted sparks from his fiery hair, and softened the lines just crinkling around the merry eyes she couldn't meet.

"Indeed, Mr Donovan, that is impertinent! I hardly think—"

He touched the back of her hand, and when she failed to pull it away, he enclosed it in his own.

"Surely Susan and Ned can share secrets better than Miss Pickering and Mr Donovan."

"I wasn't aware that we were sharing secrets!"

"Why, of course we are. Since the day I brought you home in the snow."

She scoffed, but did not relax. How could she while her hand remained in his? While they sat almost knee to knee?

"That's no time at all, Mr Donovan."

"Ned."

"Don't be ridiculous. What respectable…"

"And I was wondering what you've done with the wee package you were given."

"I… why, I have not thought about it since that day," she lied. "Why do you ask, *Mister* Donovan?"

"A burden shared is a burden halved, as they say. Susan, please. Let me help you."

She didn't like being given orders, certainly not from a man who was so free with her Christian name and with, oh my goodness, such odd eyes. "I wasn't given leave to share it."

"Ah!" His laugh was like a bark, echoing in the hall of watery blue glass and pale red beams, of colored banners and hanging silks. "But you weren't forbidden, either! In that case..."

"It is still in my pocket. Please, Edward."

There. She would go that far. The familiar nickname was beyond her, for now, but at least she had stopped stammering.

"I don't know what this is all about, and I take it very seriously, I assure you. but I don't know what else to do until..."

"Until what?" When she hesitated, he prodded, "I'm a good reporter, Susan. You know you'll tell me eventually."

"We should be going, Mr... I mean, Edward."

Comfortable or not, she got her feet under her, swept toward the crystal fountain among its lily pads. Something in the air was humming, no, it was singing. No, not that, but her skin was tingling.

"Susan!"

Taking up the hamper, honest fellow that he was, he followed.

"Enough, please! Let me think. Let me..."

As suddenly as she had run away, she stopped again, swaying. Her eyes, squeezed shut against the piercing pain, were watering, and her head seemed like to explode. Wincing, she ripped the glasses from her face, pinched the bridge of her nose.

What are you waiting for?

A mocking chorus flittered echoing through her thought.

Fear is foolishness, when we are with you.

"I cannot!"

Silly child! Such a fuss.

"Why are you hurting me? What can I do?"

A chilly silence, and a sense of disappointment. She had insulted them, the voices, whatever they were.

On the ragged edge of their impatience, images of the Borderland flooded her mind, and other things: the scent of bluebells, faerie kisses, and the singsong rhythm of an inhuman voice at her knee. She became aware that her hand had slipped into her pocket. She looked up into Donovan's worried face, and pulled out the leaf-wrapped packet.

"The little man said, 'When you see the harper, give him this.' And said to tell him it was for the raven boy. That he should give this to the raven boy, but nothing else." And she was on the move again, her boots swiftly pacing away.

"Raven boy? What Harper? Susan!"

Now it was Donovan's turn to keep to her pace. His skin was tingling, and the tips of his hair were floating, and unaccountably he wanted to run.

"No clues?" he asked "Or passwords? No carnation in a buttonhole, or a mole on the side of his nose? I mean to say, how will you know who the harper is? I say!"

From somewhere a swirl of air breathed along the nave to flip Donovan's cap to the floor. It slid away to fetch up against the reflecting pool's edge. Impulsively Susan ran back to fetch it for him.

"Perhaps he will be playing a harp?" she said.

With one hand, he slapped the cap back over his head.

"That would make it easier."

Then he hooked his free arm in hers before walking on, more distracted with every step, and not by just the girl.

"You see, now that we both know, we can both be looking for—" He cast about, seeking some source for his uneasiness. "For a harper and a—"

Something crashed, something in the south transept where the Device had its home.

"What the bloody hell?"

The humming had become a hard vibration that washed over them like a wave, travelling up the iron beams and columns, warping the glass walls. A tuneless jangle from every piano in the gallery above, and from lutes, guitars, and citterns in the Music court behind them. Then a single tone pulsed like a great shout; the first panels cracked.

Susan recoiled, throwing arms over her head.

"Mother of God!" Donovan shouted above the din. "What is that?"

"It's the Device! It must be! Uncle! "

"It's going to bring the walls down!" He shoved the hamper at her. "Wait here!"

"I... What? I most certainly will not!" she shouted, shoving it back.

The hamper crashed to the floor between them. Two stubborn glares met, then they joined hands and ran.

20

Doctor Dee's scrying, Mortlake, 1589

There were times when John Dee hated the summer, though the heat of the long days had a more kindly effect on his aging—very well, his aged—joints. He was over sixty, and knew it, and the days spent in study, hunched over his worktable, breathing all manner of noxious stinks and compounds in his cluttered attic, surely did his health no good. But worse it was, surely, to have come home after six years abroad to servants who had betrayed and stolen from him; to books missing or destroyed! Even his private study had been broken into and ravaged. God, the God he knew through the certainty and the perfection of numbers and the unchanging dance of the stars, had looked aside while his faithful servant studied only to know him better.

And then his Queen—either closeted away, desolate with her guilt over killing the queen of Scots, or striking medals in joyous celebration at the Armada's defeat—had barely time to receive him. And yet, when she did, she was unchanged toward him. She flattered him with one voice and consulted gravely with another, listening, disputing, capping his quotations in Latin and Greek. And money. There had been money, finally, and the promise of further preferment.

So it was with a relatively light heart that Dr Dee withdrew the black scrying glass from its wards and settled down at his desk to explore the cosmos. Kelley, that bowelless bastard, that mountebank, that adulterous, lying...

He caught himself and, soothing his mind once more, let the thought continue. Kelley may have lied to him about an angelic presence, and possibly everything else. But the two gentlemen—who had appeared to him just ten days ago—angels of a certainty, though they had spoken of fairies. They, surely they, had been real, as real as a summer's day if more fleeting.

Still awed by that visitation, he longed to see them again, hoped for further aid and guidance. It must be, he thought, his task to find them, to earn their grace and favour.

Workshop windows newly repaired and sealed, the door locked and bolted, wards renewed, he prepared himself with prayer and lustration, donned a fresh linen shirt, lit the candles, and intoned the solemn invocation discovered long ago. Standing before the Aztec disk, he folded the angels' silver token into his left palm. Then he picked up a hazel wand and, with mathematical care, struck six clear notes from the tuned bronze bowls he had assembled for the purpose.

Like bells, the tones rang and blended in harmony, setting up a resonance he had never heard from them before, which sustained and carried and grew. Light appeared in the looking glass, first a tiny hint of a glitter of a flame, that swirled into a growing spiral of all colors. No longer distant, it required no act of faith to see it.

The sound grew with the light, disturbing the focus of his thought. Most disciplined of scholars, Dee renewed his effort to focus on the light, to see a pattern, a face: and there!

Only strength of will kept him from crying out and breaking the contact. For he clearly stared across the void at two men in wonderful costume. Two men, aye, though not the ones he sought: one beardless but by the lines in his face clearly older than himself, with wiry white hair standing away from his head, as if lightning-struck; the other somewhat younger and darkly fierce.

"Who are you?" John Dee commanded in the Latin tongue. The men looked startled, and their mouths worked. They might be shouting, for their arms waved wildly as mad men, but they had heard him. They moved within some sort of device, a cage, or a machine of which they had themselves become a part. Were they men of some other land? Or was it some other—oh, by the Most High God—some other world? He hardly dared to think it.

Then the old one shouted to his minion, who turned away to minister to the machine, and they swirled away into a mist of color and vanished.

"No!" Now he did cry out. "Come back!" He nearly wept. Perhaps the machine would allow them to re-establish etheric contact. He had not thought of a machine. He should have thought of a machine!

There! That flicker again. Calming himself, he turned back the pages of his notebook with trembling hands and made some quick observations in his peculiar shorthand. Then he employed again the only tool he had, and though the vibration had still not utterly faded from the first time, he struck the same brass bowls. The colors swirled again, and faded. Gone.

Very well, he would vary the pattern this time, and yes! A face and body swirled into view, but not those other alchemists. Not they, but the witch, the wretched woman who had posed as his servant, beguiled his family, and ravaged his study in search of this very mirror.

"Be gone!" he commanded, in English this time, and threw a certain gesture of command toward the image. Her eyes widened. The lips moved with apparent speech, but no sound. Then in a flash like bright sunlight, she disappeared to be replaced by a light such as he had never seen before. It swirled and engulfed the whole face of the mirror first with fire, then with colors like the rainbows of an opal, but deeper, more milky, and perilously fair.

When it cleared he saw not a man, as he understood men, but a mask, a face like a man's made all of summer leaves, like the Green Men carved under the eaves of St Anselm's Church.

Instead of diminishing, the bell-like tone from the bowls grew. The sound filled the air, trembling in the crowded room, until it shook the house from Dee's lofty perch to the kitchen tiles, and the earth beneath it moved.

In the midst of all, a pair of eyes sprang open. With a gasp, Dee froze. Inhuman eyes deeply blue and glittering like cut jewels turned and met his own. When they closed, the flash of a bird's wing, glossily black, passed across the image, breaking it so the leaves burst apart, replaced in an instant by that cloudy swirl of fog glowing with colors that sparked and sang. Sang! Oh, such music as he knew could only come from the crystal spheres of heaven!

21

Sydenham village 1589

A few miles south, in the hovel that stood where Susan Pickering's house also stood two hundred fifty years still further on, Perdita laughed and struck her two fists against her chest as the Secota did in triumph. They had come to her call, three strands to twine together, three links in a chain. She had but to join them.

She began again.

> *I make the world, and it is mine. See it!*
> *Ai-ya! Ai-ya!*

The gilded skin tingled with rising excitement. Blue and red tattoos flared to the surface as she chanted; they danced across her shoulders, breast and back, sang in the depths of her sex. She shuddered as each link snapped into place: the old fool in Mortlake seduced by his own curiosity; the two madmen in some unimaginable city of glass, beguiled by their vanity; and herself with all her costly knowledge and the Young Woman's magic, twisted to her need.

One danger remained in the looking glass, even clouded as it was. One spell could yet betray her as it had so long ago; entice her into the tranquility of the mirror world where all strife ceased.

But she would not be trapped again. Even as she gasped under the caress of three questing minds, she grabbed hold of both threads and spun out her own, laced them up like a spider's web, feeding on their need, magnifying, multiplying.

The paths would open, the gates would fall. Her cannon were poised to breach the walls of Faerie.

I make the world, and it is mine. See it?
I make the world, and it is mine. See it!
Ai-ya! Ai-ya! Hey!
I break it!

Behind the whispering smoke, the silken veil, the mask of leaves appeared. She chanted, tightening her grasp, drawing the others to her.

It took longer this time. He was prepared, yes, armored in his will, mantled in his pride but not, no, not enough. He could not resist her, he had never denied her.

And then, at last, she felt him come, felt him in her blood. Behind the whispering smoke, through the veil of silk, the mask of green leaves formed, resolved, turned to her. Glaring eyes snapped open, burning in sapphire flame.

She knew him now. She had his name.

"Oberon."

22
Crystal Palace, about 2:00 PM

As Susan ran with Donovan into the exhibit space and the complex machine in its brass and iron cage, Susan's first thought was no thought at all but shock. She hadn't had the time to come down here in person for some days, and had sent Peter with the hamper instead. The platform had changed so radically, enclosed in a cage of wooden lattice, metal pillars, and wires. Extra battery-boxes had been wired together, and more dials, and gauges, and unidentifiable indicators added.

The great obsidian mirror was supplemented now with smaller, more ordinary mirrors of mercury-painted glass that Susan thought, when she could complete a thought, she had seen in a display of Modern Household Items. Images floated or swirled in each of them. Something had happened! But what?

Professor Lovejoy, his wild white hair standing out in a stiff halo from his head, sat frozen in the throne-like chair, his lips drawn back over yellowed teeth in an almost skeletal rictus. Sparks fountained from somewhere. A sickening pulse thrummed from the mirror system.

"What can we do?" Donovan was saying.

Susan stared, wide eyed behind her glasses, trying to follow the changes. Trying to see what could be done.

And there it was. Among the bells and whistles and the high whine of spinning coils, curiously clouded to her vision, set in the console crowded with tiles and dials: the flat red button. She looked down at her clothes. She'd had already thrown off the bulky coat and scarves, but in her petticoats, there was no room for both of them up there, and her skirts would surely catch on something, probably something deadly.

And there was Ned Donovan, whiskers bristling like a badger's with static. Already on the platform, he inched toward her uncle in the chair heedless of the wires that snaked across the floor. The floor, where Ambrose Cray had fallen among smashed glass tubing, and reels of copper wire, twitching.

"Donovan, be careful."

"I'm always careful, woman!" Even he knew he was lying.

"And if you ever call me that again…" she muttered, knowing he wouldn't hear. The static was tingling the glasses on her nose, and might be getting stronger. "You don't understand!"

And who would? How many people had dealt with power like this? Of all the places in the world he had travelled, the people he had interviewed, had he ever met Michael Faraday, or anyone who knew anything about electricity? "Whatever you do, don't touch the wires, or anything metal!"

He stopped at once, and glanced around, then looked at her in alarm. "What the devil can I touch, then?"

"Wood," she called back, thinking. "Or rubber. Ceramic. Or glass. Except the mirrors! There's power surging across the mirrors, I don't know how."

"How do you know any of this?"

"I pay attention. Now listen to me! Go to the console. That's the panel next to the chair."

He nodded, then gave a look of concern to the professor, transfixed by the images in the mirror. Touching the old man was almost certainly a bad idea; though he sat in a wooden chair, that chair was bound together with iron nails and brass tacks and metal wires under the horsehair and velvet. A glorious construction, but hazardous. They needed to switch all this off first. Somehow.

Donovan turned carefully in place, shocked at all the gadgets and fluttering numbers and the slight wind that passed over everything, lifting the hairs on the back of his hands. "Now what?" he called over his shoulder.

There were images in the mirrors, and Susan was staring at them. In one, a face floated in silence though the mouth was raging, the expression furious. In another, a red-faced old man with a long white beard muttered and stared, drawing or writing in an enormous bound book before him on a table. And in the central one—the Eye of Memory—a swirl of colors, and a face formed of leaves, green and bronze and golden like a spirit of the woodland, dissolved into smoke to be replaced by that cloudy swirl of fog, like a wire in a Leyden jar, glowing with colors that sparked and sang. Sang! Oh, such music!

"Susan, what do I do? Susan!" Donovan's voice rang out, and his cap sailed through the air and struck her face with a soft slap.

She hadn't been staring at it very long, had not fallen into visions, exactly; the distraction of his voice was enough. She was trembling, now, but shook it off. When she glared up at the Irishman, he was staring at her in frustration and anxiety, but no fear for himself.

"Are you all right? What do I do?"

"Do you see the big red button, you great hero?" she shouted.

He turned back to the panel. "I do!"

"Punch it down!"

23
In the heart of Faerie

How long has it been since the last time? Days or only hours? What does that question mean across hundreds of years? All that matters is contained in that moment when another summoning, naked in its ambition, breaks across the gates between the worlds. The chord of power that rolls through the halls and passages of Faerie fractures like a second-rate choir navigating a post-modern oratorio: discordant, promising disaster. Imperfectly echoing, a chorus singing through pain sounds throughout the worlds.

The star-draped pavilion in which Oberon sleeps rocks in the midst of its spangled pool, rippling with awkward harmonies. The witch's magic might be second rate, but it has strengthened, and it rouses the king from his couch in sudden fury, raising a harsh dawn with his look.

"My lord?"

A slender naiad still tingling from his embrace now trembles with fear. He takes a moment to reassure the girl, and sends her away with a word and a twist of the prismatic light that forms the floating image. It is no fault of hers nor temper of the king that has rattled the enchanted realm, though that temper has sharpened.

"What is this?" he snaps.

"Sir!"

Raven parts the curtain of shifting color between them without even pretending he has not been near at hand. The king of Faerie posts no guards because he has no need.

"How is she doing this?" Oberon demands, clothed in shadow, his anger masked in woodland green, lord of the trees. "I thought you stopped her."

Taking to the air, the Raven follows the royal whims through shifting spaces of light and sound, a crystal chime, a fragrance like violets, to the marble halls of the palace, and he tries to think.

"I did, sir," he says when he can speak again. "And the doctor's glass was hidden from her, I know it. There is more here than her own power."

"Was the task beyond you then, boy?" The king's eyes glitter dangerously, his whole being tense with power.

Raven, feeling the perils, says nothing except, "So it appears, sir." Then more boldly, "I followed your orders, and left matters in the doctor's hands, along with your token."

"But nothing more."

"That," he says with certainty, reading his lord's meaning perfectly well, "is beyond my gift, sir. She is your creature."

"Not mine!"

Oberon's snarling thought flings the boy across a couple of dimensions, lets him view in a moment the elegant, fortified structures of time, then draws him back with the lilac scents of scant apology to lie crumpled at the king's feet. The space around them solidifies into stone walls, and the tapestries, soft lights and carpets of the king's great house. The anxious looks of his Court with their almond eyes, their straight, graceful limbs, and alien passions are suddenly bitter points in Oberon's consciousness.

"Neither is she mine, my king, or I would have destroyed her long ago."

Fairest Titania, the queen in her most gentle voice, comes to him from among her ladies. Her pearl white hair curls over a silver white embroidered gown, aglow from diamond crown to gilded sandals.

Their eyes meet and then their hands, as he takes her long tapering fingers to kiss. She can feel a change in him, and he knows she knows it. The blast from the mortal world has, shockingly, struck him harder than he is likely to admit, though from the faces around him, he knows they have felt it, too. Harm to the king is exactly the same as harm to Faerie, and he feels—weakened. Enough that when at last he notices Raven lying still where he dropped him, he is alarmed. He swears, then stoops to wake the boy, and brings him upright with care.

"It's all right, sir," Raven says, shaking it off, though his appearance all in black hose and doublet is a melancholy rebuke. With a nod to the queen he adds, "I'll go."

The Raven's cry echoes in the marble halls as he shifts his shape and flies.

Titania, of course, is perfectly happy to see the boy gone, even though it has cost her something. Nothing is free even in Faerie. Especially in Faerie.

The lights of the hall are dimmer than usual, the colors thinner, the illusion less substantial. All the little folk of forest and moor who should have buzzed and popped and made faces all about them are nowhere to be seen.

"You should have destroyed her long ago," the queen says gently.

He knows that. "I agree. I was too kind."

"You have a great heart."

"I was young and stupid."

"That, too."

"I'm beginning to regret it."

"Only now?"

"Now there are consequences."

Her pale, perfect face is sweet with concern, but the opal eyes like the paths of her mind are guarded. Oberon laughs, knowing her, and goes to the window through the melodious whispers of the Court. Someone fetches his chair, though he hasn't called for it, and another carries wine snow-chilled in a jewelled goblet.

He passes a hand through the air, to open a window screened with summer leaves; he seeks and finds what is knocking at his door. Behind him, the court breathes a polyphonic gasp to see so many mortals alarmingly in concert, and again as moment by crowded moment those mortals appear to become aware first of each other and then, damn it! And then aware of Faerie. And of him.

A woman with tribal American markings and a mad spirit is chanting an ill-tempered magic with smoke and mirror, calling without direction and finding...

An old man in a ritual gown crisply manipulating the power of numbers amplified by a gift out of Faerie, and finding...

Two foolish men who fancy themselves scientists, who scramble, shouting and bickering, to select the perfect settings and to throw a primitive electrical switch...

All nodes in the network of power the witch has forged. The power they are about to add to the connection will boost the spell like a switching station in a city grid. She has found him. She sees through the veils to meet his sapphire eyes, and knows him. Of the many-stranded spell that bound her, one thread snaps with her recognition and delight, and she speaks his name.

"There!" Oberon cries, finding his target and his will. A pulse of white energy flies from his hand, strikes home exactly as the scientists throw their switch, the old man strikes his temple bell, the witch chants her spell to draw him through the mirror. All that power converges on Faerie, yet the king's blow returns it like a shield and drives it speeding back along the nexus.

And yet, the blow is cushioned, restrained by old habit and ancient strictures against abject destruction.

☙

Donovan slaps down the red button; all mirrors go dark, except the king of Faerie's.

Dr Dee stands dumbstruck.

Professor Lovejoy sits in a kind of trance, unaware his assistant has taken a voltaic shock, and some of his equipment has overloaded but the power still hums in the last strands of the network.

Of Perdita, there is no sign.

24
Mad scientists, Crystal Palace, 1854

Donovan's meaty hand came down on the big red button, and the earth rumbled, but the humming vibration stopped, leaving his head ringing with the sudden silence. Susan, at his side as soon as her skirts would allow, waited until the sparks had subsided. The moment the blue and red shimmers in the metal network had vanished with a final snap, she grabbed the great horseshoe breaker, and dragged it down to its home position. She started turning every dial and switch to zero.

The professor stirred from his trance, muttering, "No, no! What have you done, you fool?"

"Turned off the wretched thing, Uncle," Susan said, turning back to him. A quick glance told her the mirrors all were empty, the plain ones reflecting only the world directly around them, the monstrous black one, simply… glowing.

Glowing?

"Mr Donovan, could you please see if Mr Cray is all right?"

"So I can," he replied. "Doing that now." His sturdy boots crunched through glass, kicked aside the copper wire. Cray's olive face was almost paper white, and his hands were twitching like one of Galvani's famous frogs. Donovan didn't know much more about electricity now than he had this morning, but he could see the results.

He got Cray dizzily to his feet. The man slapped Ned's hands away with his usual ill temper.

"Miss Pickering," Cray said hoarsely. "If you would please, eh, bring the broom and sweep?" He waved limp hands in the general direction of the mess of broken glass and everything else.

"I say!" Ned began, but Susan pushed past him with a sigh, the broom already moving in her competent hands.

"It's all right. I don't expect he has any idea how to use it."

Her hairpins, he noticed, had been wrenched out by all the static in the air and been flung to the four corners of well, everywhere. Loops of Susan's hair fell about her ears and one long curl was creeping toward total freedom. Hiding a smile, he stopped her to square up the steel framed glasses on her nose. Then to the clattering pulse of Susan's broom, he turned to see what the so-called scientists were up to; domestic industry ever the counterpoint to the intellectual.

"By the way, Uncle." Her little heels tapped back through the space she had cleared. "Uncle!" she snapped, and for a moment Lovejoy granted her some shocked attention. She gestured to the tall fellow with the aggressive moustache. "Uncle, may I present Mr Edward Donovan. He's our new lodger, so you might at least try and be polite to him. Mr Donovan, my great-uncle, Professor Erasmus Lovejoy. Also, Mr Ambrose Cray."

Ned removed his hat politely and held out his hand. "Professor?"

"Pleasure, I'm sure." But Lovejoy was frowning at his niece as if not sure who she was. Cray just growled. And the social norms reasserted themselves.

"This is a fascinating machine, sir." Even without his notebook, Ned trusted his excellent memory and sense of invention to retain whatever facts might be dropped on him. "Would you call this a learning experience, this effort today?"

But the professor was already ignoring him, consulting his notes, and muttering. Behind him, Cray began flipping dials, turning switches. The cage began again to hum.

25
Faerie Untuned

Oberon sits back, gasping his shock.

"My lady?" he croaks, as if he has been breathing harsh smoke and fire, and he reaches for Titania's hand. In the heart of his realm lies the heart of the world, its creative pulse in the mind of the king. She is his consort and his peer. Their power combined could end this nonsense for good and all. But she is gone.

Fury renewed, he is on his feet, roaring, "Where is the Queen!"

The room gives back only echoes, and he can feel the threat building once more. At each node on the network they are trying again, fascinated, revived, ambitious, ignorant, scheming for power that is not theirs to wield: the power to command the king of Faerie. They seek only power, with no understanding of the cost.

Very well. Now he knows the path as well as she does; better, having no need for her reinforcements and diversions. There will be no restraint. This time, he swears, he will end this.

The witch stumbles from her hovel, dazed but exultant, into a world gone grey with rain. On her knees in the streaming ditch, she lets the downpour sluice the blood and smoke from her hands, her hair, and face as she laughs.

She is close! Very close! He will expect her to give up, but there is time to try again before the day dies, before her minions stray. When she can stand, she smooths back the wet hair and returns to the mirror. Humming, she drops her last pinch of Roanoke tobacco on her tiny fire, and reaches for the wicker cage.

The alchemist in Mortlake takes a glass of wine and makes some notes. He prays as devoutly as he has ever done. Now he pronounces his incantation, touches the hazel wand to the bronze bowls that ring through the crystal spheres of the worlds like temple bells.

"Once again, Cray!" Lovejoy shouts. "Setting at ninety-four, this time!"

Tiles click, dials spin, instruments Ned Donovan has no names for are adjusted and the professor reaches for the horseshoe switch.

Breathing hard, Oberon stands, summoning his music and his will like a sun between his two hands, taking every second to muster his power and tune the weapon of his mind.

"Oh, uncle, no!"
"Professor!"
"Now!"

The switch closes, the bells sound, the witch chants. The king launches his reply even as the spell thrusts aside the veil, penetrates the gate, the mirror....

A harsh cry, a spinning missile plummets from the gilded rafters, and the full mass of the night-black Raven shifting to man-shape slams his master away from the window as the summoning bursts through. Oberon falls aside with an oath; a single jangling thread of the enchantment stabs through his upraised hand.

Raven is gone.

In the tumble-down hovel in the ancient wood on Sydenham Hill, a looking-glass in its wooden stand bursts into atoms, gouting green flame into the walls, and leaps into the rotten thatch, and into her golden hair. She screams and runs while it burns under the pouring rain, consuming everything, leaving her nothing. By some miracle, it burns without spreading to another thing in the wood or to the rest of the pathetic village, though the roar of the flames brings the boldest inhabitants creeping from their hovels to watch in fear. It burns until it has turned to grey ash and twisted slag. If any of her silver coins remain, they will lie there till doomsday.

Up the river about ten miles, John Dee swooned in his pentagram. When his wife pounded on the door a while later, giving way at last to her anxieties, Dee turned the lock from within and met her on the stair, properly dressed, looking more lined and exhausted than she had ever seen him, but dazed with a kind of ethereal joy.

Two days later, Perdita stumbled weeping out of the deep wood and into the Lambeth road clad only in her extraordinary tattoos, and killed the first man she saw.

The Heart of the World

26

Hollytree House, 1854

The boy thought he was awake, but didn't want to check. With every nerve on fire, the headache was the least of his pains. He thought, if this was thinking, that he knew more or less who he was, and even what he was. More or less. He knew, for example, that his name was, ah, Rafe, no Ralph. Fitz, hmm, Fitzroy, yes. Oh good, he had a name.

And he was, ah, hmm… A musician? Without a tune in his head?

Perhaps profession was a concept he could let slide for the moment. A gentleman, though, maybe. Why was he not sure? Perhaps he should open his eyes and do a more complete assessment.

No, there was pain enough already, fiery and constant; he wasn't sure he wanted to know more than that. And, on top of everything, he was cased in linen that smelled of harsh carbolic soaps barely mollified with a hint of lavender. And under that, he thought he might be naked. Oh, he was young and fit, and his figure was no embarrassment, that he could recall, but if he was—as the sounds around him intimated—not alone, well he hoped a pretty girl was in it somewhere, that's all. That made him smile, which hurt, so he stopped.

At least the mind-shredding pain was beginning to ebb, and he could actually form a coherent thought, and start to wonder.

How long had he been—wherever he was? Where had he been before? Falling. He remembered soaring like a bird. No, not like a bird but *as* a bird, then dropping from a great height and… And hadn't there been an awful lot of, what was it, glass? Masses of glass. Massy glass, layer upon layer of glass and time. That would explain the points of fire going out all over his face and hands. And arms. And back, shoulders and…

What was that irritating hum? Aside from the fire in his veins, behind his eyes, circling his brain, a hum like a dynamo, like feedback in an electrical system, familiar but… What was the foul taste in his mouth. Iron?

Actual words began to form in his mind, and in English. Why English? Well, why not? Consciousness began to seem inevitable.

No help for it. He was cold, and he'd never been cold before (except the once), and the distraction of pain was retreating. He couldn't pretend any longer. Voices were gathering around him, chattering, amiable and real. There was no music anywhere.

"I think he's coming round," Ned Donovan said, pulling up a wobbly wooden chair. Ceilings were low up near the roof in the old servants' quarters, and the tall Irishman was grateful to find a place to sit while he stared. "Look, there. See?"

Susan, regarding the boy from the other side of the bed, wasn't so sure. "That's what you said before."

"Yes, well, I've seen men knocked out cold and I've seen men sleeping, and this is sleeping. It's different, see. There, mind the eyes are moving under the lids. Dreaming, he is, or maybe thinking."

"Has anyone looked in on my uncle and Mr Cray?"

"Peter is just back from the carriage house. They're fine, but partly furious. That Ambrose Cray is a vulgar brute for a man of science! It's only this lad that's taken any hurt."

"Can he really have come through that horrible mirror?"

"Thrown through it, more like."

"You know that is impossible."

"Fairies in the snow are impossible, but I know what I saw, and so do you. Hurtled straight through a stone and nearly landed in the Professor's lap. If that's not fairy magic, what is it then, I'd like to know? Now if only he'd wake up. I've a hundred questions."

"Mr Donovan! This boy is not a story for your newspaper!"

Donovan's broad face registered a mild shock, quickly dismissed.

"He is indeed, and mine alone. Oh, I say! Susan, I've noticed you've a fine hand with a drawing pencil. If I had a few illustrations ready-made, even just his face."

Exclaiming in annoyance, she bundled the reporter out of the room.

"Go talk to my uncle, if you must interview someone, you great... Well, as a decent woman I cannot name what it is you are. Just go away!"

The boy did seem to be stirring, in fact, but Donovan didn't need to know he'd been right. Insufferable know-it-all.

The face was beardless; in fact so smooth and unlined, it hardly sorted with the lithe physique that Cook assured her was immobilized beneath the counterpane. Long black hair tangled across his shoulders, though a single lock of palest gold streaked away from the hairline to disappear behind a curiously pointed ear, and his large almost slanted eyes were lashed like a girl's. Long fingers, sharp features, pale complexion; in repose, he looked a bit foreign, a gypsy maybe by the black hair, but his skin was so fair. Irish, or Welsh, maybe.

And his clothing! Largely shredded in his dramatic entrance, it was like some sort of costume for the stage, but too well made: black silk of extraordinary quality, with stitches so small and dainty they were nearly invisible. A fine linen shirt with a tight frill at the neck and wrists. Some sort of fancy dress, maybe? It was Christmas-time, perhaps he'd been part of a pantomime. Which explained everything except how he had arrived, sailing right through the black stone to land on the deck of the Device, as if by magic.

There were faerie paintings on display in the halls of the Crystal Palace, and faerie sculptures. Everyone was printing fairy stories these days, and reporting all manner of nonsense, even the so-called scholars. The ladies' reading club had been discussing the possibilities only last month. But this strange boy had no more than the slightest connection to anything she'd seen portrayed or described. Weren't the Little People supposed to be, well, little? Delicately made the boy might be, but he must be nearly as tall as Donovan. And where were his wings?

With Ned's help, Cook had cleaned all the little cuts, wrapped him in an old night shirt of Mr Horsley's, and tucked him away up here out of sight. If she had found wings, she'd been wonderfully quiet about it.

All the little cuts. There had been cuts and dags all over him from the flying glass. Mrs Nixon had treated them, and she was very good, but surely they could not have healed already. Gently, Susan lifted and turned over one of the slender, patrician hands with its tapering fingers. The bones sat crisp, veins silver blue beneath porcelain skin that almost glowed in the lamplight. Another oddity, the hand was pleasantly cool to the touch where she had expected fever.

"What are you, boy?" she said softly, and leaned close to the exotic face to brush the curling hair from his brow. "And what am I to do with you?"

As if in answer, the eyes opened. Susan jumped at the sudden flash of sapphire.

He whispered slowly through a grimace, as if each syllable brought pain, yet somehow he managed an almost jaunty grin.

"Who art thou, then, sweeting?" The voice was deeper than she'd expected. No, lighter. No...

"I beg your pardon?"

He blinked, and some emotion she couldn't interpret crossed the sharp features. When he spoke again, the voice had modulated a little, as had the diction.

"Who are you, ma'am? And where am I?"

Sitting up quite straight indeed, she adjusted her spectacles and folded her hands in her lap, trying not to notice that she was alone in a bedroom with a naked man.

"My name is Miss Susan Pickering, and this is my house," she said, a bit tartly. "Who are you?"

"My name is," he began, and stalled. Then frowning, he pronounced the name that was bouncing around in his head. "Well, it seems to be Fitzroy. Does that sound right?"

"Does it? How should I know?"

Carefully, he stretched both arms up and back over his head. "Well, it is either that, or it's 'Ben Harper' but... *ah!*"

As one reaching hand brushed the iron bedstead, he gasped and snatched it away as if burnt. Both hands flew to his unmarked face, barely holding back a scream.

Susan hardly noticed. Harper! She stood up at once and moved to the door, keeping an eye on him as if expecting him to disappear like a genie in a story. She went to the door and called down the stairs.

"Mr Donovan!"

"An iron bed!" Raven whimpered through his fingers. "What sort of monster frames a bed of cold iron?"

"What?"

The hands slipped down his face to betray tears starting in the corners of the strange eyes.

"God save you, lady, what year is this?"

Susan took a single deep breath, staring. She said, "It is eighteen-hundred and fifty-four."

"Ah, gods below, then the whole world is made of iron!"

"Ned Donovan," she called again. "Come up here at once! Sir, you're ill, we only want to..."

"Oh, madam, in your kindness you may kill me!"

There was no help for it. His memory for the most part was shocked back into place. At least he knew why he felt so sick, what the headache came from, where the music had gone, even if he didn't know what to do about it. Some sort of fog had descended over his mind, locking parts of it away.

It took all his strength to throw back the covers and sweep his feet out of the bed, hoping not to lay bare skin against the iron frame.

"What are you thinking? Get back into that bed this instant!"

"You don't understand!"

Then briefly he was airborne as he tumbled to the oaken planes of the floor, his limbs a tangle of linen sheets and linen gown but free of the iron cage. Pressing up on both hands, breathing hard but without much pain, he croaked, "Miss Pickering, I cannot abide the touch of iron, not the smallest part, do you understand?"

"No, I— What?" But she did understand. It was impossible, but she did. "Oh, my goodness! It's true, you're one of them!"

Donovan appeared in the doorway, sudden and alarmed. "What's the matter! Ah! Come on, lad. Up you go."

Like a hearty ghost of Christmas Present, the reporter bent to assist the boy.

"No!" Raven's hand went up but without his music he couldn't have held off a puppy, never mind an Irishman. All he had was words and some lingering glamour. "I beg of you. Leave me— Oak and Ash! Let me be!" The hand fell, but not the desperate look.

"No, Ned, don't," Susan said suddenly. "I mean, please just help him to the chair." She looked to the boy for confirmation and got an almost imperceptible nod. "Yes, just that."

Donovan gave her an odd look, then put out a hand, which Raven decided to take. His head pounded almost but not quite beyond bearing. He thought he could manage to get his feet under him, keep from tangling in the nightshirt. Yes, upright, good.

But the eyes were dull as he faced them again.

"By your leave, I need to get out of this room. Out of the house, perhaps."

"I don't understand," said the reporter.

Raven trembled where he sat, the magic as out of reach as a half-remembered tune. The iron pain was everywhere, surrounding him, eating away at his bones, at his heart. He started to fall forward, the world a jangle of splintered chords. "Please," he moaned as Donovan caught him. "I will be in your debt."

27
In Faerie: Queen's play

The room briefly loses a little integrity, then steadies as Oberon asserts his will and locks it all into place. But the harmonies are strained, the song of Faerie sung, as it might be, by a breaking voice, earnest but not entirely in control of its powers. It will recover, by and bye, but at the moment, it is wrong.

His voice is comfortably steady, however, as he stands garbed and crowned waiting for his Court to reassemble. Large and small, bold and timid, fair and grotesque, they will come because he has called them. But not Raven. The king kneads his shoulder through the layers of silk and fine linen. If he were human, there'd be a bruise. As it is, the ache is worryingly slow to disappear. The boy hadn't left him after all, he thinks with a rare smile. No, with his particular gifts he had sensed the pattern and held back for the last possible moment, then done what he could to protect his king. Well, what else could he do? It's not as if Oberon had been open to argument.

But where has Raven gone? Or rather, when? The 'where' appears to be limited to somewhere along the Thames, but with the reliable awkwardness of Perdita's spell, it will take some looking. In a moment, perhaps, when Oberon is feeling a bit less, or a bit more...

Titania? With the thought, she enters to a gentle fanfare of flutes and hautboys, parting the crowd like a flowery parade. There are lilies in her hair and forget-me-nots and columbine twining about her limbs and garlanding her green kirtle.

"My lord!" she says, her face filled with concern that may be genuine. Oberon is her lord and lord of Faerie. If he were to die— but that's impossible—so would Faerie, and with it many other valuable things in this world and the mortal one besides. Also, they have been together so very long.

"Oh my lord," she says again, taking his hand, which hurts. "Forgive me, please, for leaving you. I was afraid!"

"You?" he says. "Afraid?" He is fighting the urge to laugh, and thinks it must be a good sign. He manages to replicate a casual shrug. "With justice, perhaps. The wench was stronger than I expected."

The beautiful eyes widen like expanding pools. "And all those others?"

He nods. "That would be why she was stronger. It seems she has built some kind of network. I don't suppose the others were aware."

"I saw their faces. They knew. Come, my lord, you should rest."

She is the Queen of Faerie; she knows what is wrong as well as he does. How unhappy is she, really, to see him even slightly weakened?

But he lets her take his arm—the one that doesn't hurt—and they walk until the rooms about them are her bower, the attendants her own graceful maidens and lovely boys. The walls are draped in living vines, some bursting with flowers and dancing with their perfumes. They coil and twine at her command to prepare a leafy divan for his comfort. The music of unseen instruments is low and restorative, and just a little bit hypnotic.

Then he is seated, reclining, with chilled wine at his elbow and anything else he can think of at his command, but his mind is troubled.

"Where is Raven?"

"Who knows?" she says coldly. Frost rimes the flowers in her hair. That is a mistake, so her tone lightens. "Never mind, my love. Drink, eat, and let us sing to you. It is over!"

"No, it isn't." He doesn't want to admit that his shoulder, his whole right arm, is numb. If it hadn't been for the raven boy, he'd have taken that blow full in the chest—the blow Raven took on himself instead. He doesn't want to consider what that might have cost him. He can admit to the need for his henchman, however, with no loss of security. "I need to find him."

She clucks as if this is a foolish desire, and perhaps it is.

"No!" It is not. "Leave me."

Oberon throws her off and shifts through the gates with less than usual ease until he is in his own chamber in his own great house again. He gets all the way to the studio before collapsing. At least he makes it, in jeans and a t-shirt, to the desk chair, and no help called for, no special magic.

Well, just one thing. He blocks the queen and all her people from following him, although Titania always knows where he is, or thinks she does.

Well, perhaps, just one thing more. He flips open a drawer, and he picks up the phone.

28

Iveston, Diamond Hall Studios

The Sunday before Christmas, and Dinah and Tom had been defying the spirit of peace on earth since lunchtime. Dinah in particular was on her last drop of good will toward men, as represented by the male members of the band, starting with her husband. Even Ben had not entirely escaped the sharp edge of her tongue.

Everyone, in fact, was cranky. A full day of rehearsal, and the music just wasn't there. The magic of the summer's enchanted ceilidh—which all but Ben remembered only as that particularly excellent evening in Exeter, or maybe Plymouth—was gone. They might not sound too bad in the pub on a Saturday night, but somehow they had lost the delight, the spark.

The tension was not improved when the phone rang, Annoyed, Ben snapped the mobile phone open without even looking at it. "What!"

"Mr Harper, there's a problem."

"Elaine! What's up?"

He listened. She was panicking. Everything was going wrong: staff disappearing, addresses wrong, details she was usually brilliant with sliding out of her control. It wasn't like Elaine at all to be frazzled. He did what he could to reassure her but finally:

"Elaine, love, where is Marcus?" Their producer was around the office somewhere. "Good. Go talk to Marcus. He'll know what to do."

"But…"

"Go," he said softly, "to Marcus. He'll deal with it. That's his job."

"But Mr Harper!"

He snapped the phone shut and shoved it deep into the front pocket of his jeans, then flung open the studio door again to face the more immediate crisis, which had apparently gotten worse.

Dinah was swearing viciously under her breath.

"What's the use?" Carelessly, she practically threw her precious fiddle into its case, and slapped down the locks. "Why do we even bother?"

"Dinah, love?" Even her normally boisterous husband was walking on eggshells around her now.

"Right, that's it," she snapped, as if she'd been insulted. "I've had it. That's enough," she said, louder this time.

Was anyone listening? Why should they start now? Muttering, she tucked the fiddle case under her arm, grabbed her pocketbook, and stopped. Every face in the room stared at her, puzzled, dismayed, surprised

"What are you all looking at?"

"Uhm," Ben began, feeling a very queer energy hanging in the room. "We were going to run through the new songs? Which is why, y'know, you got out the fiddle?"

She glared out of her rosy Saxon face. "What, now? I'm not getting it out, I'm putting it… I mean, I put it away."

"You haven't even sat down yet!"

Morgan cleared her throat. Brian nodded and looked uncomfortable. Tom, clearly confused, turned away, twisting apart the flute he had just assembled.

"Anyway, we sound like crap," Dinah Shorland insisted.

Ben lifted an eyebrow. "And we get better by…?"

"By letting it all go, that's how. This was a mistake. Tom? You might support me once in a while, y'know!"

No one even argued. One by one the others shrugged and packed up their gear and in minutes they were gone without so much as a Merry Christmas. Silence reigned.

It was true, Ben supposed. The energy had been down, but he chalked it up to holiday blues. Only last week everything had been perfect, they'd been rockin'. This morning, for that matter! So no, come to think of it. It hadn't been "all day", just since... Since when?

No, it hadn't been wrong at all until the very last hour, after the... *damn.* After the earthquake. Another temblor he barely noticed because he was bred to it, it had shaken the band a bit before they laughed it off uneasily. And then, only then, things had started to go wonky. Of all the instruments, only Moytura, his Irish harp—which had a Faerie virtue on it—had kept in tune for more than a few minutes at a time. The rest, like their tempers, had soured.

And speaking of Faerie, where was Aubrey? Or Raven, for that matter, he wondered, as he moved from room to windowless room, making sure everything was shut down. Work was complete for now, except in Studio C, which waited on Aubrey's expert touch, his expert ear, to get it just right. Not that Ben expected the king of Faerie to be at his beck and call, but it was odd not to have him here, tinkering and tapping and humming along, giving the place a little class. He'd gotten used to the casually aristocratic presence.

Ben stood for a few minutes in the extra-wide delivery door at the back of the building and stared out at the snowy moor and Raven Tor under the dull winter afternoon. Winter Solstice, wasn't it? Shortest day tomorrow, longest night tonight. A glance at the calendar on the wall assured him it was so. The calendar, courtesy of Iveston Primary School, featuring the children's artwork, was surrounded on the wall by other pictures by the noted local artist, Dominic 'Sparrow' Harper, aged 8. Even a casual glimpse at the wall usually gave Ben a little bump of pleasure, but he was aware, just now, of a cloud hovering about that feeling. Almost as if he didn't care. And that made no sense.

He looked again toward the tor, listening for the bells of Elfland, as Aubrey called the underlying music of the moor and of his magic. But all he heard was wind whistling around the corners. Was it because of the earthquake? *Earthquakes*, he corrected himself. *Plural*.

Then the phone rang, the melodious tangle of notes that could only mean one thing. With two fingers, he fished out the phone and checked the display. "ELF KING". Faerie humor.

With a sense of relief, Ben thumbed it open and said, "Hero Central!"

"Ben!"

"Sir?"

The voice was Aubrey's but strained and strange.

"Can you come to me, now? Can you do that on your own?"

"Of course, sir." No reply, just a long pause, and a play of colors across the face of the phone. Frowning, Ben added, "Your grace?"

"Quickly, please."

29

Midwinter's Eve, 1854

The day at Hollytree House ended rather differently than it had begun. Susan installed the stranger on the horsehair sofa—wooden frame, wool plush covering, and steel springs, not iron—in the comfortable, mistletoe-clouded back parlour. He felt better almost the instant they moved him across the threshold.

As this parlour was the center of their little family life, there was no avoiding the other lodgers. Each had to be introduced, chatted up for a bit, and encouraged to wait for the dinner gong in their rooms or even—to everyone's surprise— in the drawing room, which they were happy to do in order to appreciate their Christmas decorating efforts.

The last thing Susan wanted was to be asked exactly who their visitor was—which she did not know—and how he'd got here—which she could not explain to anyone's satisfaction including her own. She said only that he was an acquaintance who had lost his situation. Fitzroy himself answered all questions mildly, no matter how intrusive, took offense at nothing, and gave every impression—without actually saying so—of being an artistic young gentleman who had fallen afoul of an unsympathetic parent, and been cut off without a bent farthing.

No mention was made of Lovejoy and Cray, though the explosion had been the talk of the Palace last night. Both had been taken home. They were being seen to, but no one had enquired. Most of the lodgers were only marginally aware the two men even existed.

Miss Kennedy fussed over Mr Fitzroy like a new baby, all wrapped in flannel as he was. She also pronounced him an exact copy of Mr Gainsborough's painting *The Blue Boy*, which made the raven-haired fellow smile wanly, as over an old joke.

Mr Horsley and Mr Swindon each gave Mr Fitzroy a wary once-over, then determined that he was too young and clearly too inconsequential to be any sort of threat to their mutual pursuit of Miss Kennedy. They pronounced him a capital chap, and swept Miss Kennedy away to make hot punch. Miss Dean, who had not entirely minded when the last tone-deaf and ham-handed harp student had sent regrets, smiled in her absent-minded way, gave him a few words of Christian comfort but expressed no vulgar curiosity about his origins.

Mr Fitzroy himself, weary but much restored with tea and honey, could still feel the cold poison of the iron radiating from behind the gas lamps bracketed on the wall, but it was bearable. The standing harp in the corner, the pianoforte near it, called to him but the voices were dull and awkward. He leaned his head back against the antimacassar and closed his eyes.

Susan Pickering perched on the piano bench, clearly trying not to wring her hands. At last, everyone had left the room but herself and the Irishman.

"Mr Fitzroy," said Susan.

"Call me Ralph, please, Miss Pickering," he said with a curiously ironic smile. "If you call me 'Mister', I may think you mean my father."

"And your father is...?" said Donovan, clearly trying to lead him. A good scandal was even better than an explosion; both together could do his career no harm at all.

"He is..." The smile broadened as the boy gestured theatrically, "the King of the Fairies."

But when he saw their faces, wide-eyed but not the least incredulous, he withdrew from that path. "Or might as well be," he went on with a shrug.

Mid-nineteenth century, about eighteen fifty-four or -five, he thought, and wondered at the fraying nature of his mind, remembering trivial details and losing critical ones.

Bloody enchantments.

Mid-century, and the "fairy faith" and "fairy lore" were a craze amongst the literati and the artistic set desperately attempting to come to terms with Darwin. Wonderful. He'd just been saying to Ben...

"Mr Fitzroy," said Donovan.

"You know, if I had some proper clothes, I wouldn't seem to be such an invalid. I may need to get a job and," he lifted a midnight curl from his shoulder with two fingers, "possibly a haircut."

"Mr Fitzroy," said Susan.

"Ah!" He raised an eyebrow and an admonitory finger.

"Very well, Ralph," said Susan, and blushed.

Donovan threw her a look, almost hurt, which when he turned it on the boy was charged with annoyance.

Shifting her gaze between the two men, she said thoughtfully, "When I asked your name, you said it might be Harper. The harper, Ned, don't you see?"

With apparent relief, which Ralph found delightful, Donovan said, "And is he the harper? Are you the harper?"

"Am I?"

Ralph Fitzroy considered the strangeness of the question. The woman and possibly, no certainly, the man too, had gifts that he could discern even in his damaged condition. They would help if they knew what to do. If he could think what to tell them.

"I am not a harper. That is, well—" He gestured with somewhat feigned confidence to the instrument standing in the corner of the room next to the aspidistra. "I can play that, a bit. Or I could once. Though I believe the, ah, the violin is my instrument. But I think you mean something else."

Now the woman sat forward and said, very quietly, "I was given a token for a harper."

Her glance went for support to the man with the remarkable whiskers. More accustomed, perhaps, to stating bald facts than she, Donovan said, "A token from the folk of the wood, if y' take my meaning."

Fitzroy nodded slowly, though it felt as if his brain had come loose and was rattling about in his skull. It occurred to him to ask: "Little folk or great?"

"Little," said Susan. "A wee man, and some— Well I did think they were children at first. Across the road, there, in the Norwood."

With that, she told the story as she had related it to Ned. Eventually she came to an end.

"And?" Ralph prompted.

When Susan blinked, Ned answered, "And she was told to give it to the harper for the raven boy."

"I see. Yes." His head was spinning, trying to hold on to everything at once. "The harper is a friend of mine, aye. And the token?"

Without being asked, Ned got up and closed the door quietly, shutting out the busy noises of the house. As soon as it snicked closed, Susan was holding out the little packet in the palm of her hand.

Ralph stared warily without touching it. He took a deep breath, and waited for something to happen. Nothing.

"All right, yes, it's a leaf tied up with string. What am I supposed to do with it?"

Susan frowned. "Just take it," she insisted. "It's for you, isn't it? Aren't you the, the raven boy?"

"Am I?"

"Come on, man," said Ned. "We know what you are. You've as good as told us."

"Then you know a good deal more than I do, Mr Donovan."

"But you..."

This was going nowhere. Rather than argue, Ralph plucked the little packet out of Susan's hand, hoping to feel a warmth, a tingle of power, anything that might restore him, even give him a clue. But there was nothing, even when he clutched it in his fist.

He lifted his hands in resignation, and gave it back with a sigh.

"Perhaps," he said tentatively, "since you were told to give it to Ben, you cannot give it to me. Or something else? Whatever I was, am I still?"

Out in the hall, the gong sounded a mournful clang, and Peter's adolescent voice cracked as he called the house to dinner. Heart and mind straining, Ralph felt for cues in the music of even a dull brass bell, but found only a muddy darkness. The effort must have shown on his face.

"But the iron sickness!" Susan cried. "Your magic. You must be…"

He could only sigh and shake his head. Hiking the nightshirt and wrapper around him, he shuffled over to the harp, crowned with a grey-green clutch of mistletoe, and plucked at a string. It reverberated with a clean, brassy tone.

"My magic? Tell me, Susan. What note is that?"

She shook her head.

So he plucked another, higher and lighter string he thought might be an A.

"Ned, is the tone true or false?"

"It sounds true to me, but sure, lad, I've no idea."

"No more have I. And without the music, there is no magic. That much I know."

Lost, alone, bereft of power, he might be immortal but he felt like he was dying, and the one hope of help was evidently no good to him without Ben Harper, who had no way of knowing where he was. Even Ben, who could find anything, needed something to follow.

He collapsed on the piano bench holding his throbbing head in his hands. "And I can't even phone home."

Someone was banging on the door with considerable vigor.

"Miss Pickering! Mr Donovan!" It was Peter, of course. "Are you coming in to supper, Miss?"

All they could do was leave the room and Ralph Fitzroy, whoever he was, grieving there.

30
London, 1666

Elsewhere on the river and two hundred years behind Susan Pickering, Perdita frowned into a dish of black ink. She was supposed to be scrying for a client who wanted assurances of a superior marriage. A marriage that was never, ever going to happen even if the scheming slut was the last whore in town. Not that "Madame Pellagrini" would ever tell her that.

What the witch saw instead was the clouded image of an elven princeling, weeping. It was the stupid boy who had broken her wonderful spell, had kept his master from his doom, had even let himself be drawn through the mirror in his master's place, but not, oh no, not into her hands where he might be of some use to her. And again! *Again*, it was her own wretched fault! She could tap into the anger, envy, and tears of the world to power her magic, but she could not control it.

With a slap and a curse she sent the silver dish spinning across the pretty little consulting room, dashing ink across the slender-legged table draped with shawls, the fancy French silk wall covering, the client's extensively embroidered gown.

Swearing in three dead languages, she hardly heard the client leaving, or the threats the woman's servants left behind.

31
Into the wood, 1854

Mr Horsley's second best canvas trousers and shirt almost fit Raven's slender frame, even if Peter's boots almost didn't, but they were better than nothing. Donovan wouldn't miss his top coat for hours yet. This business of being cold was as unsettling as it was unfamiliar, and all the worse for standing in the snow in the early dark of Midwinter morning, staring into the depths of the wood.

Once out of doors, he felt better but not well. The wood before him, surrounded by an iron fence, was contained and controlled by the modern world, but the gate stood open just as Donovan had left it. Raven slipped through and somehow found the path.

Snow had frozen and crystallized in grimy drifts under the barren oaks with their crowns of mistletoe, but the vault of the night sky arched over him clear and crowded with stars beyond the reaching fingers of the trees. At the horizon, the setting moon hovered nearly full, a tantalizing promise that made him ache with longing before it vanished.

A ripple of cold shuddered through him, his eyes burning, exhausted but sleepless. On top of everything, Raven thought he might be hungry, and that was wrong. A faerie feast was about pleasure, not hunger, that much he knew. The block on his mind was doing more than keeping him from home; it was changing him.

There were ways for the Great Fae to survive in a city for days at a time, but he couldn't remember them. Even reaching for his name made the world swim before his eyes, and his knees buckle. He didn't know what made him what he was, and the ignorance was going to kill him.

Anxiously he took another few awkward steps. He put out a hand ungloved to touch a tree trunk, vainly seeking the magic under grey bark. Something stirred at the edge of his blunted memory: the susurrus of an ancient river springing beneath the ground, the smell of leaves mouldering under snowdrifts as much as the rumble of the iron city coming awake. He knew but could not sense any of them; nor the secret of springtime concealed within the winter-frozen bolls of the trees; the little lives in hibernation, the path to Faerie lurking beyond the veils he knew were there but could not sense.

And no matter how far he walked in the night-dark snow, no matter how near to the heart of the ancient wood, the magic in it did not know him either. A lord of the Fae, stranded without music; a stranger even to himself.

Surely someone must be looking for him. The king would never abandon him. But how would anyone, even Ben, find him in this ironbound world? He wanted to weep, but he was too cold.

He was shivering again, so much that when he held out a hand it trembled like an old man's: an old, mortal man's. The fair skin that stretched taut over bone and sinew and silver blue veins was nearly transparent. No, not just the skin, the whole hand, as if the bonds that knit his limbs and bones and bound him to this dimension of the mortal earth were dissolving.

The metallic taste of fear was as sour in his mouth as cheap wine, and as unfamiliar. The humming in his ears, just a quarter tone sharp, became a bell beating to his helplessness. His vision filled with snapping, twinkling lights like pin-point explosions as one by one in swift succession his limbs gave way, and one last humiliating thought collected itself:

"Oh, time and rising tide, not again!"

32
In Faerie

It occurred to Ben as he changed his clothes that he had never actually walked straight into Faerie before without company. Into sixteenth century London, yes.

"And we know how well that turned out," he muttered, sliding a belt through his black jeans.

But entering Faerie, Raven had always been with him, or Oberon himself. Now Raven was conspicuous by his absence, and there was clearly more at stake than a white Christmas. It was important enough that, although the king had said *now*, Ben had felt it best to go home long enough to make sure he was kitted out properly. He didn't know yet where he was going, but some things were constants.

Listening to cold rain pattering into the thatch overhead, he moved downstairs to the office, where he shrugged into his favorite black leather topcoat, the one he'd been wearing when they were sent to find Dr Dee. He checked the phone in his pocket to reassure himself it was charged; touched the battered diary in the coat's breast pocket for the same reason. An odd weight over his hip turned out to be that hair jewel of Raven's, the modern version set on a thick black elastic instead of a leather tie. Whatever he put into a pouch or saddlebag always came back with him somehow.

Then he passed a finger down Mellis's rosy-cheeked image smiling up at him from the computer wallpaper. Mellis, his touchstone. How many journeys he had undertaken on the king's behalf, he thought, and how strangely his life had changed, and kept changing. Yet, she remained the still, sane center of his world.

Moving on, he paused to bend over Moytura and strike a bright G chord from the harp's middle range, and wait while the tones caught the magic, vibrated into his muscles, traced along his nerves and settled in his mind. Dinah's behavior had been a warning. He couldn't afford to be out of tune.

When his focus was settled, and a tune cued up, he flipped the last light switch, closed the office door, and stepped out into the rain, which slowed almost at once, then stopped. From somewhere in the country silence, a small, fluttering sound of a pipe and tabor wound toward him, at odds with the tune in his head, until he cleared his throat, and said, "Hey!"

Tiny, fluting laughter followed, then vanished.

"Okay," he said quietly to the dripping dark while his merely human eyes adjusted. "Training wheels off."

Now more than ever, he had to focus on the goal. The path to Faerie was easier than you might expect and harder than you hoped. Whistling O'Carolan's *King of the Fairies*, Ben Harper took a few steps across the slushy garden path, out the back gate and out of the mortal world.

Lights moved, and colors, and the tune in his head went from a whistle to a hum to a complex pattern played only in his mind. The planes and veils and gates he encountered shifted and swept aside in less time than it takes to describe them. As always, he was aware of movement but only barely aware of his body as he passed momentary glimpses of people and events: soldiers and suffragettes, forests and deserts and green fields. He might have stopped anywhere along the way, had it been his intention.

It should have been confusing, but to his continuing delight, the music never left him and he never lost his way, any more than he did in the world he walked every day.

Are you sure? said a silvery voice.

"Raven?"

Ben stopped at once and looked around, feeling springing grass under his boots like a manicured lawn, and about him the scent of apples.

The music spilled away but didn't go far, lingering at the edge of his consciousness like an old girlfriend. Around him swirled an opal light that made him blink until his eyes stopped trying to make sense of it. And suddenly it was cold.

Not Raven then, who might think it funny but wouldn't persist in the joke.

Wait!

The queen stepped out of the milky shimmer, shaping the landscape as she came: a dark hedge and an etched crystal gate Ben had never seen before, with the king's great house behind it, small and insubstantial as a watercolor.

"Your grace!" Ben said, caught off guard. Did the Queen of Air and Darkness answer her own door? *Was* it her door?

"Mr Harper."

Clad in slim blue jeans and a petal pink t-shirt with "Princess" picked out in rhinestones, the face she showed him betrayed something like distress. As if too over-wrought to bother with her usual glamour, her platinum hair was drawn back in a single long braid that fell to her bare feet. Instead of the diamond crown, a narrow band of pearls, crystals, and silver leaves barely glinted at the top of her head. In spite of that and the ethereal, almond-eyed beauty she wore every day, she looked for all the worlds like a wife consumed with worry for her husband.

Were those tears?

"What are you doing here, Mr Harper?" she asked, and did seem puzzled. "My lord is ill, I really can't allow it."

All kinds of smart-ass answers sprang to mind, but he said only, "He sent for me, ma'am."

"Did he?"

It was not a question, exactly. She did not look happy, even with the carved crystal panels of the gate between them, and Ben got the idea it wasn't just because Lord Oberon was ill.

"And you just dropped everything and came, did you?"

"More or less. Ma'am, may I come in? I got the idea he was in a hurry."

"A hurry? Oh, I don't think so"

"He did say 'now' rather sharpish," said Ben, rather sharp himself.

Well done, said the voice in his head with a hint of amusement, and the gate dissolved into prismatic mist.

Titania put up her hands as if to stop it, then sighed.

"Willful child," she said, though it was not at all clear that she was talking to Ben. Then she simply turned and started walking across the lawns.

Find your own way, willful child, said the voice, which had to be the king's.

So rather than follow the queen, who might well be walking him to the servants' entrance, Ben found his tune again, hearing it in his head as if played on the strings of the king's own harp. He stepped out, and in a heartbeat or possibly two, he was in the entry way: the sunny, wood-paneled passage of an English country house, racked with benches and baskets, some pussy willows in a glazed jar, a coat on a peg with a scarf and an umbrella, like a page in an Ikea catalog. His lordship's whimsy always made Ben smile.

"I'm here, sir!" he called.

"As am I," said Oberon from a point about two feet behind him. He grinned when Ben jumped, as he always did. "Nice coat."

"Thanks. You look…"

Oberon—or Aubrey, given the pleated linen trousers and softly green silk shirt, open at the throat. No matter how well appointed, he looked pale, even for him and just, off, somehow.

"So what's the story?" Ben started to take the king's extended hand in welcome, and saw the slight wince. "Sir!"

"I'm fine, Ben, really."

The handshake was firm enough. No problem then, or not enough to worry about. Except that when Ben looked, really looked, his friend didn't seem at all well.

"Sure, okay. None of my business. Why don't I ask where Raven is, then?"

"Long story." Aubrey recovered quickly, give him credit. "Come up to the studio, and I'll tell it to you. I see you got here all right? Good man, of course you did."

They took the long way, spiraling with an easy, unhurried pace through halls of polished granite, grey-traced Italian marble, fine linen-fold wainscoting; gold streaked onyx in one hall, stark ebony in another subtly flowing from one to the next as the trees of the wood alter along a rising trail. Ben felt like a tourist, but his awe was beyond his control as they passed through bedchambers, dining chambers, libraries under coffered ceilings, and galleries graced with paintings and artifacts including some he knew to be lost to time.

While they strolled the king talked, moving with maddening ease from the serious to the silly in his wide-ranging interests, calling attention to the views as they passed. On every level, windows looked out on flowered gardens, tree-covered vistas; and from one small room, Raven Tor with its spiral stone circle fresh, intact, and gleaming on a midsummer morning a very long time ago.

So, Ben thought, the king was giving him the two-dollar tour, which he'd never had time to do before. Or perhaps he was displaying his mortal guest to all his folk, confirming his patronage and coincidentally ensuring Ben's safety in the perilous realm, even without the harp.

Curiously quiet, the chambers and halls were filled with elves and faeries, stately fae in shimmering robes and strange creatures with glowing wings, or limbs and hair of roots and moss; some with twiggy extra fingers, and some with little human about them at all. The music in the air was muted, the dancing desultory, halting as the king came among them.

All bowed as he passed them, reserving the poisonous looks for Ben, as if the king's condition was by human agency. Which of course, it was. As if that made Ben somehow complicit.

By the time they crossed through the sealed walls of the recording studio with its bizarre blend of bleeding edge electronics, Art Deco furniture, and faerie magic, he had been brought up to date with quiet, dispassionate efficiency, and was slightly in shock.

"So what do you need me to do?"

"Simple," said Aubrey, settling onto the wine-colored sofa on the conversational side of the room. The pained look had returned. "Find Raven."

"Don't be stupid!"

Larger and louder than life, Titania's pale face appeared as a kind of projection on the wall that sometimes served as a video monitor. With a gesture, Aubrey dialed down the image and the volume.

"I sealed the room for a reason, *cariad*," he went on placidly. "But you may join us if you promise to—"

"Be silent, I know," said Titania. She was already striding across the carpeted floor, now in very high heels and tight silk pants to match the haughty air. Nothing about her spoke of humility or temperance. The rhinestones on the t-shirt, Ben suspected, were diamonds.

Aubrey returned to the point. "I was the target, but it was Raven drawn through the mirror. I am in his debt for that, at least."

"A faithful retainer doing his duty, no more."

"But Perdita is likely to find—"

"That Raven is her key to Faerie."

"That Raven holds the key that will allow her to find Faerie and, of course, me. She will try to wrest that key from him."

"In the meantime, she's killing you."

"Don't be absurd."

"It's not absurd," said Titania. "You're dying!"

"Madam, enough!" he snapped, and she was gone in a puff of very subtle, very expensive scent.

Tight-lipped, Aubrey stared into the space she had left behind and said nothing more while the tension dissolved by a fraction.

How long had they been together, Ben wondered, suppressing his discomfort. Scrutinizing Aubrey closely, he noticed the awkward angles, the curious translucency that he suspected were the tiny signs of illness. His lordship was, in some way, what? Out of tune. What was the shudder that passed through Aubrey's frame if it wasn't pain?

"How wrong is she, sir?" Ben asked as soon as it was safe.

Aubrey sighed. "I am not dying."

There was no reading that handsome alien face, for all its apparent humanity. Ben had no choice but to accept his judgment.

"All right. But something is seriously wrong. She told me you were ill, and I thought she was just doing her usual anti-mortal thing. Or anti-Ben Harper, anyway."

"Remember the earthquakes, the bloody, buggery conjuring?"

Ben nodded. "Another one this morning. Whatever's going on is affecting the mortal world, isn't it. Practice today? You'd think we'd never played together before. Then Dinah blew up, walked out. I don't even know if there is a band, at this point."

"We won't let that happen, Ben. Everything will be fine, if you can do what I ask. I don't believe the spell was meant to kill me."

"Could it?"

"That's a complicated question with no easy answer, human child."

"But I thought— I mean, can anything kill you?"

"Not exactly. At least..." He shrugged lightly. "I don't think so. We don't die as you understand it, but as you've seen, we can be wounded, and gravely. It's not a thing I want to test."

Titania's voice came from all around them, the queen of Faerie not so easily barred as all that.

"The heart of Faerie is the heart of the world!"

"What does that mean, exactly?" Ben asked, stepping on her echo.

Aubrey's long look of reproof made Ben feel as if he'd said something foolish, and perhaps he had. Before he could withdraw the question, though, the king said,

"You know already, human child. You know it in your bones. I've heard the understanding in your music! The reality of Faerie is bound to my will. Your world and others, too, are bound as well, in different ways. If my will fails, the heart of the world will falter along with the magic of Faerie, and all our enchantment. All this is built on music, you know that."

Ben nodded. He'd learned that the hard way, and treasured the knowledge.

"Creativity, spontaneity, even true love are all part of that. If the music fails, whatever the end of that may be, those things will decline as well, including the tools you'll need to…"

"Save the world, sir?" said Ben, with a small smile.

"Exactly. That is the second part of your task, if you'll agree to it. And I warn you, the longer it takes, the harder it may become. But for all that, you must find Raven first. You'll need him, for one thing. And for the other."

He stopped for a few moments, clearly considering his words.

"He is dear to you, I know," said Ben, sparing the king whatever secret was still too hard to give away.

"He's the only one who knows how I like my tea."

Aubrey paused for Ben to chuckle politely, and went on.

"I cannot find him, which means that wherever he is, he's constrained somehow, or hurt, or worse. Otherwise, he'd simply come home. Still, there are only a few places he can be."

Sitting opposite the faerie king while they talked, Ben thoughtfully pulled out the glossy black feather he'd snatched out of the air on the riverbank two weeks and 400 years ago.

"I wonder if this would help."

A slow, pleased smile turned up the corners of Aubrey's mouth. He leaned forward and took the feather with his steady hand, and sat back, drawing it between his fingers. From the look on his face, it was exactly the right thing.

"Ben Harper, are you sure you don't have a fairy godmother?" he said, and handed it back.

"I'll ask my mom. When did you start using your left hand, sir, if you don't mind my asking?"

When the dark eyes just stared at him, Ben wisely moved on. "So you're saying that when I find him, he might not just be embarrassed because he couldn't find his own way home. He might need a rescue."

"If he is lost among the Victorians, as I suspect, he is in serious danger, or will be soon. The magic itself can't find him. It's as if he's not there. And that means something has trapped his soul."

Shuffling through the magazines and professional journals that littered the sleek, efficiently designed coffee table, Aubrey failed to put a hand on whatever he was looking for.

With annoyance, he looked up and barked, "Swan!"

"My lord!" A tall fellow promptly appeared at his elbow in a shock of golden curls and a green velvet houpeland with dagged sleeves lined with scarlet silk, and the silly hat to match.

"No good trying to hide it from me, you know," the king said sharply. "The boy is coming home whether you like it or not."

"Of course, my lord," said Swan, and produced from his sleeve a gaudy jewelled box a couple of inches square, which he handed to the king without taking his eyes from the mortal guest.

With almost fan-boy eagerness, he said, "I heard you play, Ben Harper, at the Teahouse revel."

Revel? That would be the jam session in the space Aubrey had opened in the Borderlands, outside of time. Where Faerie Reel had played for most of eight hours and made even the great Fae get up and dance. That revel.

"Cool!"

"You're very good."

"Thanks. Uhm, Swan?" said Ben, giving the fae's elaborate costume a professional assessment.

"Sir?"

"Aren't you hot in that?"

The fan-boy demeanor dropped at once, and the fellow sniffed, then returned his attention to Aubrey. "Will that be all, my lord?"

The king his master waved him away. He bowed gracefully and dissolved in sparkles like a special effect. Ben thought he'd ask later what that was all about, but Aubrey provided the footnote.

"He wanted to make you uncomfortable. I'm pleased to see it didn't work."

"Hey, most of your people make me uncomfortable. Does he want Raven's job, or something?"

"Or something. Nothing in Faerie is simple, as you know. Now look here."

The lid of the silver box was thick with gems, polished but not cut, like a jewel from a sultan's treasure house. Inside, however, were two compartments, one holding a plain finger ring, carved of a dark wood, with a single thread of gold wire laid around its equator in a shallow channel.

"Put it on, Ben, please. It will be safer if you're wearing it. It has no virtue as far as you're concerned, but it will allow Raven to return to himself if anything can. Now, open the chamber next to it."

Ben slipped the ring on his forefinger, amazed at the perfect fit. Then he popped the velvet cover that sealed off half the box, and chuckled. The compartment was filled with small, lavender pastilles, about the size and shape of lentils.

"Magic beans?"

"In a way. Let me show you."

He shifted to one of the padded chairs facing the monitor wall, spoke a few words that included Raven's name, and opened what Ben expected to be a view into another time, except there was no picture, just a haze of snowy pixels.

"Static?" he asked.

"The nineteenth century," said Aubrey, nodding. "A world made of iron to a degree the world had never seen before and no longer requires. If he were with Perdita, or even with Dr Dee, I would see him. The third node was here, among all this noise, clarified and refined at the time only because the network was not built on faerie magic. He's there, somewhere."

"I'll find him."

"I know you will. And when you do, he may be very ill indeed. He took the brunt of Perdita's spell, and—because the baggage still can't carry a tune—he wound up somewhere she can't have intended, in no telling what sort of condition, bespelled and possibly injured. That error is hiding him from her, but also from me. And the iron may be killing him."

That word again, killing.

"Wait," Ben said, confused. He waved generally at the recording engineer's booth with its electronics and soundboard, at the microphones, music stands, and instruments that cluttered the other side of the room. "What about all that stuff?"

"Iron?" Aubrey permitted himself a laugh. "No, Ben. Aluminum, steel, gold, silicon, plastic, American walnut, and good English oak. What we have is, well, an allergy, you might say, but it's to cold iron, not carbon steel. And the Victorians made iron their bitch. Curiously, they were also mad to know about the Fairy Kingdom, as they called it, and the 'little people'. It's a quirk of the universe that I have a place in almost every other time, but not in the one where I'm most popular! Unless I'm feeling particularly whimsical."

It was all serious, but Ben couldn't help a chuckle. "Really!"

"But that's another story for another time. I or any of my people can, in fact, spend time in that London as long as we keep those 'magic beans' about us—a concoction of various things with some serious enchantment. Give one to Raven as quickly as you can, as soon as you see him, and another—but only one— every day you're forced to bide there. There's no telling what else will face you."

Ben snapped the box shut and dropped it into an outside pocket. "And then we can get to the other part of the problem."

"Ah yes. The other problem," said Titania, now shimmering like light fractured through a diamond in the space at the king's left hand. Some unaccustomed emotion dusted the fair features.

"Let's take this outside, shall we?"

And by outside, Aubrey meant the clear, frozen dawn of a Midwinter morning at the spiral of standing stones and the rocky pile in their midst. Some said the Raven's Eye was the granite core of the tor, which was true, and some said it was a door into Faerie, which was true as well. From two sides, slabs of stone had fallen or had perhaps been laid by giants against and on top of each other, leaving a squarish archway in the middle. Dawn wind sighed through the opening like an aubade, and the vale around them was empty. No tidy orchards, no Iveston village, no Diamond Cottage, only the high moor. It was the Raven Tor he had seen from the palace window.

"As to the other problem," said the king. He was bundled now in layers of white furs and velvets because they were gorgeous, not because he was cold. A golden crown threw back the pale sunlight. "Here is what you must do."

With that, he delivered a quick set of curious instructions. "Check the diary if you need reminders," he said at last. "Any questions?"

Ben considered, listening to the world around them, half expecting a comment from the queen. There was no sound on the Tor but the wind through the stones, no light except a planet twinkling low in the pallid eastern sky.

"Will you do me a favor, your grace?"

The royal brow lifted warily. "Go on."

"Aubrey," Ben said, as he might to one of his staff interns. "Sing me an A."

"What?"

In that annoying faerie way, Titania stepped through the Raven's Eye bundled in white furs, saying, "Do it, *cariad.*"

The king swore explosively and rolled his eyes.

"Never take a queen for your consort, Ben. It's no end of mischief. Nay, madam, I will not."

"Because you know you can't hit the note?" Ben said, ignoring the interruption, "or because you're not sure? If your magic is faltering…"

"My magic is not faltering, human child," said the lord Oberon testily, and without a second thought he took a breath, reached for and gave out a clear tenor A above middle C without a quaver, which he rode pitch perfect into the high F in the middle of Handel's "Every valley shall be exalted", plus the next eight or ten bars of ornamentation, just to show off.

"Happy?" he said when the echoes had faded.

"For now," said Titania, and turned to Ben in the second major surprise of the day. "Help us, Mr Harper. Please."

She pressed a crystal vial of something green into his hands, and whispered, almost desperately, "The world will not end, perhaps, but many things will. If you need that wretched boy, find him, save him, yes, but do it quickly. This will aid you."

Not one to turn down help, Ben dropped the vial into his other outside pocket.

"Timing is everything," he said with a nod.

He bowed slightly to her and to the king, then holding Raven's feather, he shut out the royal couple and everything else, seeking his focus. And there it was, the tug at his chest, the path clear before him.

"Your majesties," he said politely, and with the king of Faerie's aria still ringing in his ears, Ben walked out of the ancient circle.

33

Midwinter morning, 1854

Ben walked into the last remnant of the Great North Wood that dropped over the clay of Sydenham Ridge toward the Thames. Still winter, of course. He'd rather hoped for the London of Charles Dickens, or possibly Sherlock Holmes, teeming with scruffy, pink-cheeked urchins singing Christmas carols at Scrooge's door. Prosperous men in stovepipe hats. Bustling women in bustles. Was it too early for those? Father Christmas beaming from the newly invented Christmas cards. A fog-bound city rattling with horse drawn carriages.

Instead, snow-laden boughs of vast, thick-trunked trees reached overhead into a grim morning sky like the one he had just left. Snow crunched under his sturdy boots which, he noted, went nicely with the handsome caped coat he was now wearing instead of his leather one. Which meant both that it was in fact Victoria's England and that the king had lent him the glamour to blend in. The year? Ordinarily, Raven could just taste the air and tell him, but it didn't really matter, as long as the kid was here somewhere. Ben clutched the black feather warm and tingling in his hand, which meant he was as good as sitting in the kid's lap.

But where, exactly? Peering downhill through the trees, he realized he could see a hint of the gas-lit streets of the City, and a few factory and warehouse lights a bit closer. Beyond the trees on his left hand, a single street lamp glowed like the wardrobe end of Narnia, illuminating the gates and walks of some grand old homes. To his other side, a circular clearing opened up with snowdrops blooming at its verge, the Borderland of Faerie.

The boy in the ill-fitting clothes, with the pointed Spock-like ears, collapsing in the middle of it with a disgusted sigh, though, that was a surprise.

"Hey!"

In a few steps, Ben had caught the kid, expecting to take at least some weight, but it was like picking up a kitten. And as he lowered him gently to the frozen ground, supported on his knees, the boyish face rolled toward him pink-cheeked with just the faintest eldritch glow in the translucent skin.

"Raven!"

He was breathing, that was something. Ben slipped the feather back into an inside pocket, fumbled in another, and sure enough, everything he'd brought was still there. With one hand he pulled out the little jewelled box, and then he had to pull off his gloves… gloves, right! His fingers were cold, but the latch popped easily. Somehow he managed to get one of Oberon's mottled lavender beans between the grey lips and closed the boy's mouth around it. He could almost hear the pill dissolving with a kind of fizz.

God, Raven looked even younger, more fragile than usual.

"Come on, mate, you're too young and pretty for this. Wake up, okay?"

"Not so young, master harper," said a wee man in a squeaky voice. "Older than me, but younger than this wood."

"What?" Ben snapped his head up. For a change, he was at eye level with one of the little folk, and for a change, it wasn't laughing at him. Which meant that no matter how much the fellow looked like a grumpy garden gnome, he couldn't smile except in recognition. "Don't I know you?"

"Of course not," the gnome said, with an even grumpier shake of his twiggy head. "You know Riddl'didee. Silly Dartmoor fellow. Bad jokes. I'm Oakley, me."

"I do beg your pardon, Oakley," said Ben, and tipped his hat. A hat he hadn't left home with. A beaver hat, in fact, of extraordinary height, which he placed on the snow while he tried to make Raven more comfortable. It did seem the eldritch glow strengthened slightly. "But tell me. You've been here all this time. Couldn't you help him?"

"You're late!"

"I came when the king called, what more could I do?"

"You walk in time—walk faster!"

That was no answer to that.

A bit of color was tinting back into Raven's face, and his breathing sounded easier, but still he didn't wake. Ben chafed one of the long hands briskly, watching for the warmth to return there as well. Warmth, and a bit of solidity. The impression of being able to see the ground through the hand went away.

"What's the matter with him? He's out here, away from the iron. Why doesn't he wake up?"

Oakley shrugged. When he laid a pudgy finger to Raven's hand and snatched it back, the boy's skin went a little pink, but nothing else. "Spell."

"Look, this is the Borderlands, right? This part of the wood? Can't I just take him all the way into Faerie?"

"Did his majesty say to take him home?"

"No, I— Wait! I'm such an idiot."

It was awkward juggling an unconscious man while trying to access all his pockets, but at last he located the crystal vial. He managed to pop the waxy cork and tipped the vial forward. A thick green bead of liquid took ages to collect at the lip. Even anxious as he was, Ben cultivated patience, willing it to drop into the raven boy's mouth.

But as it began to fall, Oakley yelled *"Stop!"* and smacked the vial from his hand. With a green hiss it sailed out into the dark.

No-no-no! cried tiny voices from the snowdrops. *Wait-wait!*

A cloud of sprites, like the flower faeries he knew but moth-winged and baby-faced, rose up suddenly with piping, kittenish voices from what Ben had thought was a snow bank. They crowded around the vial as it flew, until it vanished with a pop and a fall of acid green icicles ten feet away.

"What have you done?" Ben hissed. "She said it would help! The queen said—"

"Our queen, human child?"

The penny dropped.

"Shit. It would suit her to have me kill him for her, while she's begging me to help his grace and save the world." He shivered. "Again."

In his grip, Raven shuddered almost in answer.

"Raven! Come on, man, wake up!"

"What else did King send with you?" said Oakley.

"Damn it, the ring!"

Faerie never gives anything away, does it? Not even simple answers. But in the corner of his eye, the gleam of a golden thread winked on his finger. He pulled it off with ease, and transferred it to Raven's right forefinger, expecting it to slide off immediately. But when he blinked and looked again, it fit as perfectly as it had on his own hand. Half a minute later, it had disappeared, leaving only a thin line of gold as a reminder.

Again, the boy's breathing eased, and while Ben watched, the fragile limbs grew rounded, warm, and solid.

The breath he hadn't known he was holding released all at once as he sat back on his heels. What were the fae, really, other than full of surprises? Where did they come from—so like humanity yet so utterly alien?

Was that it, he wondered with a smile. Space aliens?

He must have said that part out loud, because the wee man snorted with contempt, muttered something incomprehensible, and marched off stumpy-legged into the darkness shaking his head. Then he paused and half turned toward Ben.

"They'll be looking for him," Oakley grumbled, and waved toward the street lamp, its beams pale and dreamlike against the coming dawn. "Over there."

"What? Where?"

"Package for the raven boy. She has it."

"Wait!"

But the little man had vanished.

"Very well, my lad," said Ben, shaking his friend's shoulder. "The game's afoot. Open your eyes, if you please, sir."

The language coming unselfconsciously from his mouth had a mildly Victorian flavor. The clothes had come from Oberon's gift, but the language was new. Which meant… The boy he had thought was dying in his arms squirmed, and the black-lashed eyes snapped open, at once alert and alive.

"Ben?" A hand far less delicate than it had been clasped the harper's arm. "What's going on?"

"Finally!" Ben exhaled relief that turned to steam as the Borderland retreated and mid-winter re-asserted itself. "Next time you lose consciousness, it would be a kindness if you could do it in the summer."

Raven accepted Ben's help as he struggled to his feet, then threw him off while he dusted the snow from the ill-fitting clothes. "What on earth am I wearing?"

Well, his vanity was certainly in place.

"I'm not sure, but you look…" Their eyes met. "Well you look like crap, to be honest. What happened to you?"

"Kind of a long story," said Raven, not smiling at all. "I should get back to the house." He started to walk toward the iron gate, but his knees gave way. Ben hurried to get a shoulder under his arm.

"Slowly, shall we?"

"I'm fine, I…"

"No fainting!" Ben said. "You're a lot of things, my boy, but fine isn't one of them. Ready to try again?"

Raven nodded, gasping a little. "Sure."

"Good. Oakley was here. Do you know Oakley? Never mind. His Grace sent me. The game is afoot. We have work to do."

"Ha! Of course we do. Now, I should tell you. You're going to meet some people…"

With deliberate care, and awkward as a three-legged race, they started through the snow as a thin light began to fill the morning. The wheel of the year was turning on the dawn of the shortest day. In its honor, Ben spoke in short syllables to encourage and cajole, while the little folk crowded around, cheering in their childish voices.

Raven's head came up and he saw them at last, and beamed with pure joy. He could hear them, too.

34
Savoy Theatre, 1882

Bearded by these puny mortals
I will launch from fairy portals
All the most terrific thunders
in my armoury of wonders
—W.S. Gilbert,
Iolanthe, or, The Peer and the Peri

"Places for Act Two, ladies and gentlemen. Places, please."

A quick knock at the dressing room next door, a boy's voice calling the last warning. The diva, cased in stays underpinning the semi-diaphanous draperies of her not-quite-scandalous costume, uncrossed her shapely ankles, sat up straight at the edge of the velvet-covered chaise, and prepared to go on.

The music is all that matters to the fae, and immortality is a very long time indeed. In this century at least, taking stage at the Savoy Theatre was Titania's chief delight. The warmth of her contralto would define, or from another point of view, had defined *Iolanthe's* Fairy Queen for decades. In other voices, at other times, she would do the same for other roles, making names for other deserving singers. Besides, it was fun.

Effortless grace accompanied her every movement, so when the knock came, she was perfectly prepared. Her silken slipper tapping the floor was the only indication of her slight and unaccountable agitation.

"Places, Miss Barnett!"

"Freddy!" she called in a voice exactly pitched to draw the child right through the door, if necessary.

The latch clicked open on a scrawny, smudge-faced ten-year-old in patched britches. Behind him, the muddled sounds of actors vocalizing, patrons shuffling back to their seats, a burst of sudden, unexplained laughter filtered in from the wings.

"Miss?"

"Come here, my poppet," she purred. The midnight eyes, deeply rimmed with kohl and spangled with sequins at the corners, glittered hypnotically.

"But Miss! Mr Sullivan says—"

"Bother Mr Sullivan. Come here, I say."

To his credit, the boy tried to resist, having been subjected to this before. His fear of her was no greater, however, than his fear of poverty. She could have him sacked on a whim, and they both knew it.

"Please, miss, the time!"

Her smile decorated with unleashed sweetness brought him in without another word. The music called; no niggling discomfort should be allowed to disturb her joy, damn it. Not in the middle of the show. She had to know what was happening, and where. And when.

"Don't be frightened, Freddy dear. It won't take a minute. Come here, I say. And close the door."

Freddy really had no more choice tonight than he ever had. There might even be a shiny silver florin in it, if she remembered, and two shillings was not to be sneezed at.

"Yes, Miss," he whispered.

The diva waited until the child stood straight and still before her—trembling but still—and touched his cheek as sweetly as a doting aunt.

"Hush, poppet. Hush, now. Are you fearful? Why are you afraid? There's no need to fear. Hush now."

Once, twice, the long slender fingers caressed downy cheek, brushed unruly curls out of the eyes grown dull. Then her hand drew back and delivered a fierce slap and then another, sharp and swift. Tears sprang to Freddy's eyes, and he flinched, but made no sound.

Peering now into the glassy teardrops as they welled and spilled down his cheek, she sought, and found, and swore.

"Damn it! That blasted harper! Can the man not do one little task for me, just one? I have been too patient with him, with both of them!"

And with Raven, she considered, for far too long. Brought up in her care, cossetted and indulged, he had been the prettiest of her pages, and the cleverest. Most mischievous, certainly. Her favorite and Oberon's, too. Who knew what promises the king had made when the time came for the boy to choose a path?

And there it was. The long contention, the perennial wrangling between them knotted up, as so often, by a child.

Titania would have made him her knight, her herald, not a tool to be sent into danger after danger, meddling in mortal affairs. But handsome, splendid Raven had chosen the king's Court over hers, scorning her gifts, rejecting her favour. Furious, she had, perhaps, over-reacted, lashing out with a force that had flung the boy right out of Faerie, out of time itself. But her anger was nothing to Oberon's, who loved the Raven more, she thought, than he cared for her.

Oh, Perdita had been nothing, a pastime, mortal and temporary. Titania too had taken mortal lovers over the long ages: talented, brilliant men and a few women who amused and entertained, and in return she encouraged, taught, demanded greatness of them, among her faerie gifts even the time to fulfill their promise. None of that mattered. Raven was different. A child of her heart, he had chosen Oberon. And now, there he sat, eating honey, blithe as a summer day. Rescued from Perdita's magic, untouched by her own.

The queen's dainty fingers curled into a ball; her jaw clenched. She hardly knew she'd boxed Freddy's ears until she heard him whimpering, curled up on the floor with one hand clutched to the side of his head.

"Oh, my dear!" Titania cried. "Oh, child, what have I done?"

Returning with swift remorse to herself, she raised him up and took him into her arms, kissed him, and soothed away the terror and pain. It was monstrous to use a child's tears to see through the veils of time, but what could she do? She needed news. The least she could do was remember the vessel, poor thing.

Holding his face gently between her hands, she said, "All better now, my lovely?" And smiled that smile that had dazzled the crowned heads of Europe for uncounted generations.

"Yes, Miss," Freddy said with a sniff. "Please, Miss. Can I go now?" She frightened him, the great Miss Barnett, and confused him, too. But what could he do, poor motherless thing?

"Madam?" Betty, her dresser, poked her curly head around the door, alarmed. "Miss Barnett, that's your music!"

The queen of Faerie rose, temper subdued, to throw off the dragon-embroidered dressing gown and free the little wings artfully hung from her shoulders. A touch of faerie glamour made them appear somewhat more fabulous than the original design, and her papier-mâché breastplate just a bit more like her own.

She flung a coin at the boy, and gave him a sweet from the box on the dressing table.

"Now, shoo!" she said with her tinkling laugh and, enchantment shattered, he scampered off without a backward glance.

Titania and her king had, in the end, reconciled once the raven-brat managed, somehow, to find his way home. Soberly formal and under orders, Raven had come to her later with his apologies set in verse. She, the soul of grace, had accepted them. No promises were made.

"Madam!" Betty called again.

"Anon, good nurse!"

Titania, in the person of Miss Alice Barnett, paused long enough to take a lavender pastille from a quite different box and place it under her tongue where it fizzed brightly, clearing her mind as it eased the dull iron ache in her bones. Another moment, and she had settled into a properly professional frame. The music was calling, and that was all that mattered.

Then away we go to Fairyland.

35

Hollytree House, Midwinter's Day, 1854

Raven's second introduction to the house in Albany Road was somewhat less dramatic than his first, but only by a little. The place had been in a minor uproar since Mrs Nixon had first looked in and found him gone. Donovan was roaring that he needed his coat, and Peter's only other shoes were some second-hand slippers that would wear out before he grew into them. Along with all that, their peculiar houseguest had disappeared, and left the front door standing open besides. The whole house was freezing.

The fuss was short-lived, however. On finding nothing of value missing, and having only a passing interest in the strange fellow their landlady had brought home, the other lodgers went back to bed. Miss Pickering maintained an even calm, all in all, hiding her dismay.

Early as it was, Mrs Nixon had managed to get the kettle on while she retreated to the kitchen to get the first loaves of bread out of the oven, and start breakfast. Nothing more than eggs, today, and sausages, sardines, stewed tomatoes, bread, butter and honey and plenty of tea laid out on the sideboard in the dining room. Feeling lost, Susan took her place at the head of the empty table, pale and silent over her tea.

A moment later, more resigned to their loss than he had been, Ned Donovan stood at the sideboard resting his eyes on Susan, but when her stricken gaze met his, it was more than he could bear. He turned away to slosh some tea in a mug, and then chose the chair nearest hers in silence.

After a few minutes staring at her teacup, she said, "What are we supposed to do?"

Ned shook his head wearily. "I've no idea." At a sound from the hall, he looked up. "Sweet Mother of—"

As if by magic, a bespectacled gentleman had appeared in the broad doorway with their foundling practically in his arms.

"Sorry for the intrusion," he said somewhat diffidently. "The door was open. And my friend said he is known here."

Raven grinned wearily but stood up. "Hullo," he said. "Sorry to have caused a stir." He ran long hands through his hair in an effort to make himself presentable, then gave up and fell into a chair.

After a certain amount of exclamation over Mr Fitzroy's wandering off and in his condition, too, along with some nervous laughter, attention finally turned.

Raven declined the eggs and all, although he did with some eagerness accept a generous slice of Mrs Nixon's fresh white loaf spread thick with honey, and tea with a generous dose of brandy. He also declined to say much, apart from his apologies, even while being peppered with questions. His friend in the beautifully tailored suit and funny accent wasn't much more forthcoming, though he did accept a cup of tea with a few polite words and a worried smile.

"If you please, Miss Pickering, is it? Miss Pickering," Ben said briskly, "I wonder if there is some other place where we can talk."

He was right, of course. The other lodgers would be returning soon enough and that meant the usual morning chaos on top of this new situation.

"Yes, indeed," she said, then she rose from the table and led the way across the narrow passage into the parlor.

Hands folded somewhat primly, she took up a position by the fireplace, framed between the candlesticks, while Ned stood protectively at the parlour door. She hardly knew where to begin, but it was her house; surely it was up to her to start.

"Well," she said.

But the American gentleman relieved her of the burden.

"I hope you won't find me too forward, Miss Pickering, if I come straight to the point."

She nodded slowly, wondering if this were the elusive harper at last. Ralph was obviously easy in his company, and unafraid.

"If you please," she said slowly. "Are you a friend of Mr Fitzroy?"

A momentary pause as the two exchanged a look, as between old friends who shared more than one secret.

Then the gentleman nodded and said, "I am, yes. My name is Francis Browne. I—"

"I beg your pardon?" said Susan in surprise. "I thought... That is..."

"Wait," Donovan said, jumping in with his reporter's boots on. "Are you sure it isn't Harper? Ben Harper, maybe? Or do you play the harp, by any chance?"

That look passed between the strangers again. Ralph shrugged and nodded, and his friend sighed. "*Sic semper* disguises. I am guilty on both counts, sir."

Susan sat down with a thump in the wing chair, limp with relief. At last!

"I am glad to hear you say it. You see, I have a package for you, Mr Harper."

Ned Donovan, however, still doubtful and wary of losing his exclusive again, said, "Talk's cheap, sir, if you don't mind my saying so. The wee man said the token was for the harper. How are we to know you're the man, eh?"

Raven chuckled a bit, then coughed. Collapsing gracefully to the needleworked settee by the fire, the picture of a man who has been very ill but is on the mend. "Go on, man," he said, and waved his friend toward Miss Dean's mistletoe-crowned harp. "Show them."

"On this?" said Ben, surveying it with some alarm. It was almost as tall as he was, and twice the size of Moytura. "The last time I sat behind one of these, I was waiting for a piano lesson."

Raven smiled wanly but the other two simply waited politely while he organized his thoughts. Pillar, sounding board, strings—he could ignore the pedals. All he had to do was find Middle C, and he could always do that. How hard could it be? More to the point, it had to be done.

Follow your gift, whispered a voice in his private ear. What could he do but trust in the magic and see what happened?

"I should warn you," he said as he swiveled the stool up to a realistic height, and sat down. "I usually play a different sort of harp. Let me crave your indulgence in advance."

Taking a breath, he looked up at the mistletoe on the crown, and pulled it down, absently shoving it into a pocket. Another breath, then, and he leaned the harp back into his shoulder, and brought his focus to bear on the strings.

After a tentative start, the music came smiling to him as it always did. He worked gently through a verse of *It Came Upon a Midnight Clear*, then dared to segue into *Silent Night*, hoping as he did so that both were known in eighteen-whatever-it-was. For a few minutes he filled the room with the sentimental carols, and without, to his slight surprise, a single false note. When he stilled the strings, there was a burst of applause from the doorways where the maids, the milkman, and the butcher's boy had all been drawn to listen.

As Miss Pickering shooed them all away again, Ben raised an eyebrow in Donovan's direction. Grudgingly, the reporter nodded, then pulled something from his vest pocket and passed it over.

"This is it?" Ben said. "Well?"

Raven, further improved by the music, said only, "It was addressed to you, Ben Harper. I think it is for you to open it. You know how our Good Friends are about protocol."

So Ben plucked the knotted twine, and at once the brittle leaves sprang open, smoothed, freshened with color—from faded yellow to hazy green to dusty jade—as if reversing in time, and swept the room with an air of ancient forests, cool water, the scent of oak and rain.

Susan gasped. "It's... well, my goodness, it's like magic!"

"Why, yes," said Raven, amused. "So it is."

Cradled in an oak leaf lay three red lumps, bright as holly berries but dry and wrinkled.

"More magic beans?" Ben asked.

"Rowan." Raven picked one up and registered a startled grin as a faint tingle buzzed his hand. "Interesting. Let's see."

Standing easily, he carried it to a window to examine it in the light; as he held it up, washed in the clear light of Midwinter's morning, a faint glow burst where the berry touched his fingertips, and a sound like the shimmer of crystal chimes teased his ears. Could the others hear it too?

He said, "Country people hang them in the doorway to keep the fairies away."

"Does it work?" said Ben.

"Hmm. Are you sure these came from the king? Miss Pickering, what exactly did he say, this wee man of yours?"

Once again she described the encounter in full, even the terrible riddle, which made Ben laugh.

"And then," she concluded. "He said, *He must give this to the raven boy. Only this, and nothing more.*"

"Nothing more?" quoth the Raven with a quick laugh.

"That is what he told me."

"Oh, dear. I see someone imagined this all falling out rather differently."

"I'm told I should have walked faster," Ben said mildly.

"We shall have to work on that."

Without another thought, Raven popped the shriveled berry into his mouth, and swallowed.

"Hmm. An ambitious vintage, hints of vanilla and red currant, with the after taste of battery acid."

He meant to sound nonchalant, with just the slightest touch of charming irony. Hard to do when your ears are ringing. A shimmering jangle rose in his ears, in the room, in the world, starting with the strings of the pianoforte and the harp.

Had someone turned up the lights, or was the intensity of Faerie brightening the air? The others were speaking, or thinking, or crying out, he couldn't tell. But with each word, each thought, the room flooded with light, shadows banished from every decorated corner, every voice a different colour.

In answer, a cool fire sparked in the region of his heart, grew hot and sweet with the ache of his first free breath in days, driving him to his feet, opening his mind. Liquid silver seemed to spill from his heart to course humming through his veins. The air, the house, the world filled with music. Music, at last! The harp responded to his thought in faerie trills, and all the colors of Faerie subtle and fair lent the shabby room such grace as it had never known.

"Oh yes!" he sang out, his voice a cello, a viola, a dancing master's fiddle, more complex in its music than he knew. "This is much better!"

He flung out his arms, lifting his face to a horizon only he could see. His expression unearthly and wild, the long strands of his hair whipped about his face like flame, and he laughed feeling his power, his very self returning: a prince of Faerie walking the paths of home.

He could ignore, for now, the ripple of nausea, the edge of a gauze-like darkness. But against all this it was nothing. Restored to himself, however imperfectly, after so many plodding earthly days, he cried out with a voice to make half of London shake.

"Oh, children, this is wonderful!"

Both of them awestruck Donovan found Susan's hand, or she found his, she hardly knew. Even when the big man's arms folded her protectively to his chest, she did not resist, her gaze pinned just as securely to the dazzling young man whose feet were in her parlour, his head against a strange sky she could almost see.

Ranging in other worlds, the fae had lost track of his own, and never noticed.

"Raven." Ben spoke quietly, "Where are you?"

"Why, in Faerie, of course," the strange voice boomed merrily, more normal but still disturbingly like a string quartet.

"And will you join us here in England, please?"

"Must I? But why?"

"You are glowing like a star!"

"Truly?"

"We have the king's work to do."

"Ah. There it is, then."

Simple as that, Raven allowed the familiar call to draw him back to mortal earth. Outstretched hands closed, drew in the tattered wings of faerie power. With a breath, he abruptly sat down, an ordinary if devilishly handsome young fellow with unruly black hair in need of a trim, and a polite smile.

He was sitting on something. Shifting enough to pull Susan's sketchbook out from under him with a puzzled glance he, with apologies, set it aside. As he did so, a last trill of the great magic sparked like electricity, escaping from his hand to the leather cover, traced the carved pattern, and faded.

Then he turned to the curious tableau at the fireplace: Ned and Susan clinging to each other and breathing hard, flushed with unfamiliar excitement. Both were staring at him wide-eyed and slightly trembling. Even Donovan for a change had no words.

"What is it? What's wrong?"

Raven's pleasant voice had returned as well, and the sparkle in the sapphire eyes.

Ben swore, daring at last to clap a firm hand on the faery arm.

"I think you've alarmed these nice people enough for now, don't you? We should go before you set the planet on fire."

"What? Oh, yes, of course."

"No, wait!" Donovan cried, shaking off the wonder, and Susan.

Miss Pickering jumped with a small yelp of dismayed propriety and stepped to the side.

"Mr Donovan!"

"But what about my story? Pictures? I can prove the fairies are real, not like what all those schoolmasters and country parsons say, dreaming up nonsense over their sherry! But only if I can… If you will…" He threw up his hands in desperation. "Who will believe me?"

The look Raven turned on the big man was grave and sorrowful, but adamant.

"No, Edward," he said, getting to his feet with noble grace despite his rude garments.

"But, can't you at least tell where you came from? Where do you live? Why are you among us now? Just a few questions, sir, please!" He turned imploring to Miss Pickering. "Susan, you must make him stay!"

But Miss Pickering bit her lip, saying nothing.

"It might be," said Raven, "that one day perhaps I can oblige you. But not today."

Ben noted the *perhaps* with interest but kept silent while Donovan sputtered.

"No, wait!" the boy went on, forestalling further enquiry. "You must understand, I—*we*—have a mission, a quest, if you like, which we are obliged to accomplish, on which much depends."

"For your father?" Ned said eagerly. "For the king of the fairies?"

"I beg your pardon?"

Ben laughed, but Raven ignored him.

"For the king of Faerie, aye, and not to be delayed," the boy went on in the lofty diction expected of a hero in a fairy tale. "There is much to do, and we are already much delayed. Be patient, please, and when the time is right, you will have what you desire. Both of you," he added, including Susan, who blushed. He grinned, peering into the future just a little while he could.

"For your great courtesy and your care, madam, I am in your debt. Aye, never doubt it! Faerie is careful of its accounts. If there should come a time when I can repay you, go into the little wood, and call for the King's Raven. I shall be at your service."

With a princely hand, he collected the remaining berries in their strange little packet and gave it to Ben. Then he took the young woman's fingers and bent to brush them with his lips. "For your being drawn unwilling into our affairs, I apologize. And so farewell."

Then the faerie lord and his mortal companion were gone in a glittering mist, leaving only the borrowed clothes behind. The last thing Susan saw of them she could never describe, and except to Donovan long afterwards, never mentioned again. But she thought, perhaps, the two visitors had become a pair of black birds before they disappeared utterly.

When stout little Miss Dean bustled into the parlor a bit later to prepare for her first student, she was not at all amused to find her instruments disturbed and her stool re-adjusted.

36
Above Santa Cruz, California

Raven got them as far as the antique portico of the front door before the magic, over-taxed, abandoned him with just enough glamour to be decently dressed. Replacing the borrowed clothes had cost him, but it was necessary. Nothing taken but paid for, that was the rule. As for the special effects—

"What the hell was all that?" Ben demanded, slightly awestruck.

"Expensive," Raven gasped, leaning against a pillar. "The rowan is mightily effective but soon spent. If you can sing us away safe, do it now, and quickly, if you please."

Ben thought for half a second. Any tune would do, and in a pinch, which this surely was, he only needed a handful of notes and a place to go. Three stumbling steps later, they stood swaying together on a deer track under the redwoods, alone with the whisper of a rushing creek just out of sight, and the smell of... cookies? Sugar pines and Redwoods. Northern California, a few miles from Ben's parents' vacation home in a springish afternoon.

"Fall Creek?" Raven asked breathlessly, then gave up and collapsed to the grass.

"Yep," said Ben, pleased with himself, and sat down. "Fresh air. Sunshine, if you want it. Shade, if you don't. Plenty of negative ions from the creek. *No snow*, I hasten to point out. Summer people haven't arrived yet, not even my mother. Best of all, not so much as an iron nail for at least a mile in any direction."

The last time they had come here skidding to a landing in a desperate run from the ninth century and Titania's temper. That time it was Ben who had lain collapsed and exhausted staring up at the disk of blue sky, and Raven who strolled about appreciating the view and making smart remarks. This time, the raven boy lay back on the grass with his fingers laced behind his head, tangled in the long black hair.

He stared into the clear blue circling above him, and tried to control his breathing.

"There really is a mission, isn't there," he said dreamily. "The world is out of balance, I can feel it. And time, of course, is short."

"Hang on." Ben held up a finger and pulled out his mobile phone. How many people have the king of Faerie on speed dial, he wondered. It shouldn't work, but it always did.

"Your grace!" he said when Aubrey picked up. "Got 'im." Then he listened, his face intent. "And yourself, sir, are you well? Yes, sir, I had to ask." Instructions came, and a single admonition to waste no time. "Sir," Ben finished curtly, and rang off.

"However did he manage before cell phones?" Raven asked of the world at large. "Oh, I remember. 'I am invisible, and I will overhear their conference.' As I said to Will Shakespeare."

In the green and breathing silence that followed, Ben dropped the phone back into his pocket among the usual detritus. The case chimed against something metal—right, that hair tie of Raven's. Also, a pocket knife, a folded receipt from the cleaners in Newton Abbot, Raven's feather, and a dusty half-packet of Mentos. And as he felt for it, finally, the jewelled pill box. Balanced in his broad palm, almost before it could throw back a spark in the dappled light, he could feel the pull.

That was his gift, Ben knew. Well, one of the three. Aubrey called it True Finding. He could find anything that was lost if he had a connection to it. The feather had led him to Raven. This jewelled trifle of the king's would lead him straight to, what? A key. The key, the king had said, would lead to a lock. And then?

"Bring what you find there to me. Stop for no reason," he had said on the phone. And repeated the warning. "The longer it takes, the more difficult it will become."

There was no reason to think either the key or the lock would be what Ben expected it to be, but that didn't matter. He knew where it was—at the other end of a golden thread that hummed in his chest like a harp string.

"That was the Crystal Palace, did you know that?" he said suddenly. "Where you tumbled into the nineteenth century. It appears we have to go back."

For an answer Raven managed to produce a breathy cough. "Great. A building made entirely of iron and glass. I can be incapacitated, stupid, and on display, all at the same time. But, okay," he said, rolling up onto one elbow. "I'm ready."

"Sure you are. Lie down." A single finger to the shoulder was enough to push the fae lord back to the grass.

"But…"

"Don't make me call for backup. I need to check the diary. You still need to restore or recharge or whatever it is you do. And then we need to talk."

"My favorite conversation starter." When Ben chuckled in reply, the boy added, "You're enjoying this."

"I surely am, mate. No question. Now be still." More seriously, he said, "I should have thought to keep the cittern, but I didn't, so his grace said you should look for the music in the world around us. And for that you need to be quiet and listen. It's getting fainter, he says."

A few silent moments later, Raven said on a deep breath, "We should have gone to Dartmoor."

"Getting sentimental in your old age?"

More thoughtful silence, then the boy said, "Places have meaning to us, Ben. How could we make music if we had no feelings? Our passions aren't based on hormones and enzymes and red blood, but we have them. Anyway, it's my home, if any place on this plane is. That's where my heart is, and my music."

Looking around at the green and golden landscape of his own childhood, tasting the crisp mountain air, Ben could only lay a sympathetic hand on his friend's shoulder for a second, and then get to work. He pulled the diary from the other coat pocket.

"Okay," he said after a bit, scanning the faded remnants of last summer's notes. "Did you really tell that Donovan guy that your father is the king of the fairies?"

The boy sighed, eyes still shut. "I was delirious. I was babbling. I had to say something."

"But you can't lie."

"I can make a joke, an exaggeration. They wanted to believe it. It just sort of came out."

More silence, broken by birdsong and the sigh of wind in the evergreen boughs high overhead. "Are you going to tell me whether…"

"Ben!" Raven snapped. "It's a meaningless question. Let it go! I'm trying to listen to the grass grow."

Elven prince or not, Raven lay flat on his back in the wild mountain thyme, listening to the birds calling overhead. Dressed in his customary black doublet and hose, with just a frill of white open at his throat and wrists, palms flat to the earth, the long eyes closed, he was at last altogether still.

Until he said, "And somewhere up there is a stellar jay with domestic issues. Better than a soap opera."

"Tell me about the rowan."

"I told you, they keep the faeries away." The boy twisted up a lazy smile. "It works because we know better than to touch them except at need."

"And?"

"Are you writing a book? They enhance power. Sometimes in uncontrollable ways, as you saw. It would have been a bit less dramatic if I hadn't already taken one of my lord's magic beans, as you so charmingly call them. Or put on the ring. And if you hadn't added your excellent music into the mix. (For all of which I have neglected to thank you, by the way.) And that's why they're in your pocket, not mine."

"That's a lot of charms. So why aren't you all better? Up and at 'em? Here, hold my coat while I run to Chicago?"

Raven snorted. "You know, I'm not sure. It was a powerful spell, powerfully delivered, compounded by dragging me through a stone into an iron cage. For all the virtues of ring, rowan, and harp string, I'm still a wreck. Now, would you mind?" And with that he got up and strolled over to the riverbank, disappearing among the ferns.

No matter how often he encountered it, Ben was still surprised to find that immortals had weakness and weariness, could exhaust their energies or weep with pain. They could also, as in the diary he examined now, provide useful notes to events and places even before he knew he needed them. It had never been clear just who was writing it, or how, but it was way past time to give it some attention.

They called it a diary, but that was probably not the right word. About the size of a large paperback book, it was like an enchanted cross between a scrap book, an advice column, and *Hitchhiker's Guide to the Galaxy* with vulgar cartoons, some passable poetry, and terrible jokes all in the most appalling, spikey handwriting. New pages, which appeared only at need, provided useful advice, original maps, and background among the food stains, with occasionally animated scribbles, and goblin wit, such as it was. And whatever he read in it, Ben remembered. A gift from Oberon, it had been his guide on that first nerve-shattering mission on the king's behalf. All in all, it was the most practical magic ever.

The fact that it had notes for him now meant that things were probably far worse than he realized.

Today the new pages contained a quick summary of events so far, rendered in a crabbed scrawl. Then it continued with train schedules from all over England to the Crystal Palace, omnibus schedules within London, the names of security personnel (with hand-tipped portraits) and their rota. Also testimonials, opening and closing hours, and clippings from *The Times* quoting Prince Albert and praising the designer, Sir Joseph Paxton. And finally, some riddles suitable for conversing with garden gnomes, with a note in the margin: *I so funny!!!!*

Ben smiled grimly at the predictably self-congratulatory goblin humor, and turned the page. An insert of tissue paper folded and creased like a road map started to fall open into his hand. Putting the book on the grass, Ben proceeded to carefully unfold the insert, opening it down, then down once more, then out on both sides to show the layout of the three levels of the Crystal Palace. And if he touched any spot for a few seconds, it expanded as if through a magnifying glass for detail.

"This is just so cool," he murmured.

Settling in to study, he gave the map his whole attention, reading the captions, admiring glimpses of the interiors, till he thought he could smell the perfumed air, hear the trilling songbirds that perched in the highest reaches.

At last, sensing more than hearing his friend's light step on the grass, he let the page go and watched it fold up neatly by itself. Sometimes he felt like he'd wandered into a Harry Potter movie. Whatever, he slipped the Raven's feather between the pages and put the book away.

Raven dropped down next to him, looking troubled. "Remind me. I transform into a raven—an actual raven—sometimes, right?"

Ben pushed his glasses up his nose with a practiced finger. "You do. Are you kidding? Isn't that your true form?"

The expression on his face was one Ben had seldom seen before: barely disguised panic. "But I can do it, yes?"

"Sure, why?"

"I can't." He breathed a quick hard breath and considered. "I thought I would just fly up there and give that jay some sage advice, see where the river goes, stretch my wings. I've never given any thought to how I do it. I just— I just do it."

"Okay, so… Go!"

"What do you think I'm…" The heels of both hands pressed into his eyes. "But it doesn't work! Something is still… I felt it even after the rowan back at the house, underneath all the flash and dazzle. There is a darkness that still clouds a part of my mind. It was worse before, much worse. I thought it was just the iron sickness, but I'm free of that."

He exhaled forcibly in frustration and jumped to his feet. "Shit."

"What can I do?"

"Nothing. I don't know. My lord would know, but—"

There was nothing more to say.

"Here." Ben held up the jewelled box with its cache of lavender grey pastilles. "You may need another. His grace said one a day, but I think this is special circumstances. Then we should go."

He got to his feet, brushing away the detritus of the forest's ferny floor. Then he held the box out again to Raven.

The fae gave in and popped one under his tongue, closing his eyes while the charm worked. When the blue eyes opened, they were brighter, but Ben could see the disappointment.

"Any luck?"

"Still there, but I can live with it," Raven said, setting off. "Tell me about this critical mission that we are obliged to accomplish, on which so much depends?"

"For your father, the king of Faerie."

"Leave it!"

Ben threw up his hands in defeat. He conjured a conciliatory smile and pitched his voice just above rattling leaves and the river hissing over flat stones beside them.

"Okay, short version. Perdita's spell was amplified, networked in some way with Dr Dee and a couple of mad scientists—"

"Susan's uncle and his assistant, she said."

"—and Oberon himself."

"No kidding."

"You saved him, yeah, but you didn't take the whole blow."

"I beg your pardon? It practically killed me! Is he not all right?"

"This will go a lot faster if you don't interrupt. The king caught a fragment of it, or a sliver, or whatever, just as you slammed into him. He says it wasn't meant to kill him but to stun him, and draw him through the mirror to wherever she was."

"So of course, it went wildly wrong."

Ben nodded. "The queen says he's dying, he says she's exaggerating, you know how they are. But it's worse than he's admitting, or he'd have just told me to bring you home."

"And we would be sitting at the Star toasting Yule with tumblers of honey mead. Instead?"

"Instead, we have to find a key."

"A key? To what?"

"That part's a little hazy. Hopefully the key will lead us to it. Quiet now, please."

A particularly thoughtful frown engaged Raven's already troubled features as they split off from the path that followed the rushing creek.

Cradling the jewelled pillbox in one hand, Ben found his gift, the tether that attached him to the thing he sought, and touched it with his thought. The music of it came to his lips as a curious little tune, tasting of filtered light and clear water. Setting sunlight flickered through the rattling leaves, and the path shifted under their feet and altered.

The first gate parted for them with a sound like tubular bells tossed in among the fluttering aspens. The next, with the sound of garden chimes. Others opened in quick succession until together they pushed aside the last veil into the busy shopping level of the Crystal Palace in December, 1854, at the opposite end of the hall and nearly a quarter mile away, by Ben's reckoning, from the king of Faerie's key. He'd had better landings, and others far worse.

They were higher up than he expected, closer but still very distant from the vaulted dome. The view of London from here would have been excellent, except for the clouds and the slanting rain.

"Of course," he sighed, pocketing the pillbox.

"And yet you're always surprised." Raven in quietly gorgeous afternoon dress tipped his tall silk hat to a pair of pretty twins examining the sheet music in the shop above the Musical Instruments court.

"Merry Christmas, ladies," he said genially.

The poisonous emanations of the structure beat at him from all sides, without harm. Restored and inoculated as he was, Raven snapped his fingers at every painted iron bar, and allowed himself to relax.

37

Plague year, London 1666

People were more addicted to prophesies and
astrological conjurations, dreams, and old wives'
tales than ever they were before or since.
— *Daniel Defoe. Journal of the Plague Year, 1722*

In the year of the Great Fire, London had already been a city
in panic for most of a year as plague ravaged the population
sparing neither peer nor peasant. Even the physicians had fled,
their useless university degrees fluttering behind them, their
skills insufficient to a sickness no one understood and for which
there was no cure but Fortune. Winter slowed the course of
the disease, but by the time King Charles II was persuaded to
return to the capital in February, one Londoner in five had
succumbed. When the Fire began in September, sweeping
away most of the old medieval city with its wood and thatch
buildings and riverside warehouses filled with train oil and
pitch, hides and paper, mice and rats, the disease had already
moved on.

In the summer of that year, between plague and fire, when
the rents were excellent even in the better districts, and even
the most aloof trembled over the future, the long cast-off
mistress of the king of Faerie established herself in the
metropolis as a diviner, a spiritual advisor, and for the right
price and assurances, a medium. Calling herself Isabella
Pellagrini, she took a modest house in Woodstock Street near

to Hanover Square where she received the great and good, and those less great and far less good besides, so long as they could pay her fees.

She dwelt in an aura of mystery. There was a certain amount of conjecture amongst her clients as to the source of her wealth. She appeared to be a widow. She was thought to have married a Florentine banker. The envious claimed to know she had been a laundress, or worse, but such rumors never prospered, and those who spread them always laughed nervously and withdrew early from the conversation. She was presumed by some to have Gypsy blood, and by others, Moorish, though no speculation could explain the wonderful amber tone of both her complexion and her hair. The latter was generally thought to have been dyed, though how exactly, no one would hazard to guess.

She lived on the fringes of Society, going to the theatre only in the afternoons, taking chocolate or coffee with friends, and all the while quietly maneuvering toward a position of trust with people of power. Their wives at first, of course, then with their secrets comfortably in her keeping, the actual keepers of power.

Losing her temper in the middle of a session had been unwise. Naturally she had sent a beautifully worded note of apology and returned the fee. The woman was someone's mistress and doomed to a syphilitic end in any case. She'd be sweating the cure in Leather Lane soon enough, and it was just as well to have her out of the house. Still, no point in alienating anyone while they still had friends.

Especially when it really had been her own bloody fault, the witch thought as she bade good afternoon to the day's last client.

Servants were not permitted in the consulting room, of course, except in her presence and then only for ordinary dusting and polishing. And to clean up Madame's ill tempers. So she set about putting the tools of her trade into cupboards and drawers and a sideboard, all locked with a simple charm.

She moved through the room in her silken gown the color of the deep sea, aware of the music in the sweep and susurration of the fashionable train that followed along from room to elegant room. In daylight, at least, she could please herself and all manner of men with her exotic looks, though she had failed to find any solution to her nightly problem. The tribal markings of the Secota she had sponged away with cosmetic washes, the passage of time, and a spell until they now only appeared when her passions got the best of her.

Perhaps, she thought, humming a dance tune as she put the Tarot deck away in its silk lined box. Perhaps she was learning patience, after all this time. A little.

"Do you think so? How refreshing!"

With a little gasp, Perdita looked up. A swarm of tiny rainbows burst across the walls as if the window were filled with a thousand crystals. She saw nothing else, but she had certainly heard a voice. A woman's lovely voice, filled with music, and magic. And the air was tinted with roses and musk.

"Come, don't be difficult, girl. Face me!"

She stiffened and turned. Perdita had not submitted to such a tone in a hundred years and was not about to do so now.

And yet, a very great lady indeed stood bathed in the brilliant shaft of sunlight pouring through the garden window, shining with the most extraordinary beauty. From her silver gown with its cobweb lace, the jewels shimmering at her throat and in her pearl-white hair, she had to be a duchess at least.

Patience.

"The door is locked," Perdita said as if merely surprised. "My servants admit no one without an appointment, not even the Duchess of York. So I must ask you, Madam, by what means you have entered this room. What are you?"

"An excellent question," said Oberon's queen. "And I will set you another. Do you know me?"

Perdita's brows drew together in a frown as she considered. She had lived a long time, even before the mirror captivity, and had met many people. Since returning, she had encountered many more. If she had known and forgotten this lady, it could only be by design—her own or someone else's.

At last, and with caution, she said, "I think I am not so fortunate as to claim my lady's acquaintance."

For good measure, she sank to the floor into a perfect curtsey. She'd hired teachers to make sure she had all the graces required for moving in the best circles, and had never regretted the cost.

Stepping away from the window with perfect grace, the lady drew the glitter of sunbeams with her. "So you have found some manners, excellent. However your memory, as ever, is faulty."

"Madam?"

"I am Titania."

Now the queen moved further into the room and took a chair, arranging her splendid skirts with care. Everything about her sparkled. On her head, a crown that might have been cut from a single diamond caught and spangled the room with light.

Dumbstruck, the witch stammered and reached for the table's edge. She could feel the color rising in her bosom in a flush that pricked the exposed skin with the Secota pearls.

"Come and sit with me, human child."

Titania gestured to another chair at a little table that Perdita had not known was there—that had not been there. More than that, a steaming pot of tea appeared with cups of pale green celadon from China, with cream, fine white sugar, and dainty biscuits crisp and brown.

Next to these treasures, the royal lady placed a kind of knife shaped not of metal but of white porcelain; a dainty thing, fit for a woman's smaller hand. About the hilt twined blue forget-me-nots. The edge, as sharp as broken glass, held a faint blue glow constrained along its fine-ground bevel.

The magic sang with a purity Perdita had long forgotten and never understood.

The witch stammered her confusion as she failed to control her trembling. If the queen of Faerie meant to kill her, surely she'd have done so without the elaborate game. Or would she?

"You have done my consort some small bit of harm, though not as much as you hoped. That deserves some reply." Oddly, the queen offered no more than this mild reproof, and spoke without rancor, as if reporting the state of the weather. "So, you will listen to me, very carefully."

38
Crystal Palace, two days before Christmas, 1854

Out flew the web and floated wide;
The mirror crack'd from side to side

—Alfred Lord Tennyson, 1833

Though they had brought him home unconscious, stunned by falling equipment, Ambrose Cray had, like his employer, taken no major injuries apart from the obsidian shrapnel that peppered his face and hands. His pallid skin was an itching collection of gashes. The headaches, though, were monstrous. Once restored to consciousness and speech, he had rapidly returned to thinking and planning and, finally, swearing.

They had been so close! Far more than they had imagined possible. He had actually witnessed a living man walk through the black mirror from some unknown world! At least Susan Pickering said he was alive, and had been alive when he left just hours before Cray learned of his existence.

When he left! Almost incandescent with fury, Cray's mind raced.

Stupid girl. It was her fault, failing to make so much as a note of the device's final readings—could she even read? Then letting the fellow go without discovering who he was or where he came from. Or so she said, but you know how women lie. Even that new fellow, that Donovan. Supposed to be a reporter, wasn't he? What kind of reporter is witness to an extraordinary event—a History Making Event—and then lets the principal actor slip away? Well, the girl had him tied up in her apron strings, that much was clear.

Then, when Cray had raised a corrective fist to the moon-faced slut, the big Irishman had grabbed it and held it, forcing the hand open and down till it slammed against a wall. Cray's arm still ached from fighting back, the wrist printed with bruises.

Well, the girl would wait. Temper banked for the moment, he flung himself out of the house and onto the omnibus, never mind the cold.

He had work to do. There were so many questions to answer, so many avenues yet to explore. They needed to know more, but by God, it had worked!

As it turned out, the professor agreed. They couldn't get back to work soon enough, though Lovejoy was battered and sore, the yellowed parchment of his face a map of bruises and broken capillaries. He recovered with remarkable ease for a man of his age, or so he insisted to his doctors. But his imagination spun a tangle of half-formed ideas and urgent possibilities, and there was much work to do.

"We will need," Lovejoy declaimed, "more power, larger batteries, more scope if we mean to move on. Excelsior!"

Thankfully he had a standing account with the glazier. The black mirror, though, was another problem yet to be examined. Not merely expensive, it was irreplaceable. The tolerance of Lovejoy's banker was substantial but not limitless.

Then there was that difficulty with the Crystal Palace Committee. Within hours, a letter arrived stating in severe terms the end of their managerial patience. The explosion, which they called "the inevitable consequences of an ill-conceived and crack-brained scheme" had blown out a large portion of the western doors, frightened horses in the street, and terminated a piano tuner's efforts in the gallery. A rather famous sculpture of Cupid and Psyche, or rather its plaster copy, had been denuded of its fig leaf, causing at least three women to faint!

After a notorious history of disaster, the latest antics had finally tipped the balance between uplifting scientific entertainment for the masses and a threat to public safety and, incidentally, to profit. A half-dozen exhibitors were threatening to sue. Sir Joseph Paxton himself arrived in person Monday morning to throw them out.

Throw them out!

While Ambrose Cray seethed in his lab coat, put to sweeping up like a housemaid, Professor Lovejoy calmly, contritely negotiated the extra week they would need to arrange for the porters and carters to remove everything, the cleaners to tidy up after and, of course, to compensate their neighbors. Not to mention the Company.

"All that glass must be replaced," Paxton had said testily. "And the claims will be coming in for months."

"Well, let them claim!" Cray muttered, fiercely grinding a boot heel through a pile of shards. "Pitiful, small-minded apes. We should never have come here. Bad enough putting up with Lovejoy, the old fool, but the sooner we leave this damned greenhouse, the more swiftly we can proceed."

Still muttering, he bent to his work, scooping yet another shovel full of broken glass into a wooden barrel with a crash. Gradually he found the mindless physical labor to be curiously calming. The anger drained away as the simple activities first emptied his mind then admitted the leisure for analysis. He began compiling a list of what must be tested and what could be replaced, what repaired, what re-designed. And moreover, what would be gained.

What would be gained? That was the greatest curiosity of all. His heart, a shriveled organ unaccustomed to emotions of the tender sort, beat a little faster as *her* image floated into his open mind: the golden girl. The perfect woman. Uncannily beautiful, exotic, excitingly wanton in her person, ultimately compliant. Compliant? Well, of course she was, he knew that instinctively. Just as he knew she was meant for him. That she was—yes!—his destiny. Her face and form, so briefly glimpsed, so thoroughly known, filled his thoughts while all around him the graceful columns of the hall, the iron cage of the Device, the hanging baskets of flowering vines peering through the arches of the gallery overhead all quite, quite disappeared.

A superstitious man might have recognized, or at least suspected, witchcraft. Would have wondered how after a lifetime's abstemious avoidance of entanglements with the inferior sex he had become in a few moments so enthralled. But Ambrose Cray, man of science, had rejected such fancies in the nursery. Had the simple-minded Miss Pickering even hinted at the word Faerie, he would have delivered the corrective blow as he had intended, for her own good, and called for her removal to a madhouse. Fancies and fairy dust, the stuff of peasants, fools, and the undisciplined mind.

Absolute rejection of the perilous realm had left him unprepared, without defenses, when it appeared.

"Ambrose?" said a voice like liquid gold.

"What?" He glanced up, snarling. The broom fell from nerveless fingers. She was here. Or rather, she was there and speaking, apparently trapped within the great Aztec disk, her honey-gold perfection blemished only by the jagged crack across the surface of the stone. The impossible hair floated loose about her naked shoulders as if stirred by zephyrs. If she was gowned in anything else, he was unaware of it, drowning as he was in her eyes.

The last sensible part of his battered brain wondered momentarily how he might have come by such language and such fraught images. Without a drop of romance in his nature, he knew no more about poetry or art or the literature of love than he did about Faerie. But the limpid pools of her eyes drowned that question along with all the others. He had no idea what "limpid" meant, either, but it didn't matter. The divine creature had spoken to him!

"Oh!" he whispered, pulse driving. In those other brief visions, she had had no voice.

When she smiled her glorious smile and touched two fingers to her lips to blow a kiss across time, he reeled as if it had reached him. The taste of honey filled his mouth, and oh, how he hungered.

"Ambrose, do you love me?" The sweetest voice in all the world echoed slightly, as if resonating in the spaces between the stars that swirled in the black glass, or possibly the confines of a small, featureless room.

"Oh, I do, I do, but... Dearest lady, how do you know my name?" Some tiny spark of the experimenter remained curious.

Her slender arms reached for him. "Ambrose, my love, let me take refuge with you."

Oh, who cared how she knew.

"Yes!" he said, trembling to the tips of his black mustache.

"Will you save me?"

"Yes, yes! But how?"

"It will not be easy," she said, her words as hypnotic as love talk on the pillow. "Blood must be spilled. For naught of worth was ever accomplished without blood. I cannot come to you unless you bind yourself to me, do you understand? Only and utterly to me. And that bond must be sealed to me with a life. Bring me a life warm in the palms of your hands and I shall cross to you. One small death only and no more for our happiness. A small price surely for eternity. And then, oh my love, then, shall we become immortal!"

The horror of her meaning barely touched him; someone had to die, he accepted the need, that was all. He would have accepted much greater terms had she asked. For his part, the only questions were merely practical.

"Whom shall I kill? And when?"

Perhaps some part of him survived under the spell of her voice; even madness may have a semblance of reason. For Ambrose Cray, what thrived was not his better self. Who to kill?

So many grudges leapt to mind, the interfering Miss Pickering, for one. For another, his doddering employer who paid him a pittance and used him like a dog, as if all those dukes and marquises cluttering the family tree made Lovejoy the better man. Then there was the bishop who had stripped young Ambrose of his father's legacy, denying the young divinity graduate the living and career that should have been his—on the slender excuse that he had no faith. Or the supercilious headmaster later on who had sacked him, leaving him without resources or references in a shabby suit. Was there time to make the trip to York, he wondered, or must such a deed be done at home?

"Ambrose!" snapped the woman, less sweetly now. "Pray attend!"

"I will," Cray sighed. "I do."

But he didn't. Half-drowned in over-heated fantasies of lust and bloody vengeance, his body swayed where it stood longing to come to her without delay. The unfamiliar passions that clouded his brooding intellect now moved him inexorably toward her image as a growing seed sways with the passing sun.

She had sent him a kiss, he remembered suddenly. He must return it! Surely that would please her. Stiffly, Cray, whose manner with women had always been abrupt at best, lifted a bruised hand in an unfamiliar gesture to dry lips, and offered it to her image in the stone.

"No, you must not!" she cried. This was not the plan. It was never the plan. "Stop!"

Too late. Though the questing fingertips barely grazed the surface, the spell collapsed, the connection broke with a snap and a tiny spark. Shocked, he jumped back, hot tears springing to his eyes.

A strangled cry, and Perdita's image shrank in a gilded spiral to a blue white dot that floated for an instant, then vanished. Cray looked in shock to his fingers' ends, as if some clue might be there. Angry blisters were rising, but that was all.

39
Faerie Dartmoor

Bowered in a leafy glade deep within his kingdom, pillowed in silk, Oberon reclines in the arms of his queen finding little comfort and no joy. The dull heaviness all through his right side might not be pain, but it is foreign, a distraction. More aggravating still, the music that fills the air is just the slightest bit off, as if played without care. And that, he fears, is his fault.

The damage is greater than he thought, certainly greater than he admitted to his Court when he dismissed them, or to his mortal henchman when he set the man to his task. This would bother him more if one of the side effects weren't an abiding lassitude. He is not dying. At least, he doesn't think so. But he is no longer entirely confident of his high A.

Sleep, he thinks. Sleep and let the worlds roll on unaided for an hour, or a day, or half a hundred years.

He frowns slightly, uncertain in the watery light. This isn't right. He sees that Titania's side of their bed is cold. How long has she been gone? How long has he been lying here waiting to care enough to wonder?

He calls for his harp of ivory and myrtle wood, set with strings of silver. And when it appears in his hand, he strikes first one chord and then another, and stops. There is music in it, but no song.

With an effort, he flings himself from the bed, naked under the stars. Lean and beautifully made, he kicks down the gates as he goes, careless of the fear flying behind him. He marches along his own halls calling some sort of garments about him out of habit, but his face is the mask of a horned beast, and his eyes hard as adamant. When he bursts into the midst of wintery Dartmoor, the heart of his realm on earth, he is an enormous red stag out of ancient times. He bugles a challenge, letting his mind be washed in simple earth-bound passions.

There is no answer, not even a friendly echo; the air is wrong and he is alone on the high moor in a sorry drizzling rain.

And that's not right for December in this age of the world. Just yesterday, or whatever day that was, the land had been buried in snow. Puzzled, Oberon is a man again, mostly. The horns remain, and the hard glitter in the eyes, but he needs the clarity of thought that comes with this form.

"This is not possible," he says aloud.

He turns in place to survey the land that is his special care, and swears in a long dead language. The snow is gone, but nothing is green, the freshet that should be bubbling from a spring a few yards away is silent, no birds sing. Breathing in, he tastes the air and frowns. He has not been merely idle or careless of the calendar, sleeping while the seasons turned. The world itself is damaged, as he is. The song that binds it to him falters.

A bitter smile creases the king's lips. The witch has wrought more than she knows, or could have known. If her curse reaches his heart, his command will waver, all extremes high and low will decline over time into a single, featureless average, and the human heart will die. Sufficient revenge for a spurned lover.

ii

"Hullo? Is anybody there?"

A woman's voice broke the air along with Oberon's preoccupation, and mortal time asserted itself. The world brightened a little, as if he'd pulled off dark sunglasses, though what met his eyes surprised him. Around him ringed the standing stones, raised by the local clans in his distant youth, whose spiral march ended on the level top of Raven Tor. Their broken teeth reared up out of a dense fog that poured away from him like the waves of the sea, filling Iveston Vale to an uncertain horizon. In the distance, the other nearby tors—Hay and Hound and Shattered—were already disappearing as the mist engulfed them, billowing from the earth.

"Who calls?"

The question fell dead at his feet, smothered in the soggy air. Impatient, his will provoked, he halted the mist with a thought, thinned it, and swept it back to the perimeter of the stones. When he asked again, he got an answer.

"It's me. Where are you?" The woman sounded unafraid, almost dreamy, yet he sensed an undercurrent of panic. This had to stop.

"I'm up here," he called. "At the top. Where are you?"

"I don't know. I can't see the way. I can't see anything."

He knew that voice, though he knew her mandolin better. "Miss Tyler? Morgan?"

"Yes. Who's that?"

In his mind's clearer eye he could see her staring into the mist on the trail that led from the original settlement to the Raven's Eye. Though fairly flat where she stood, the track under her feet was stony and uneven, broken with winter weather, growing slick with rain. Worst of all, she had blithely wandered toward the winter-burnt edge where the hill dropped sharply away from the path.

"Stay where you are," he said. "I'll come to you."

They never listen. Raven Tor promised a hundred meters of slithering, bone-crunching tumble through snow-flattened grasses splashed with granite outcroppings to the ruined abbey at the bottom. In disbelief, he watched her take a wobbling step; a rock must have rolled under one sturdy boot and cast her off-balance. Hands grasping only air, sturdy shoes insensible of the danger, she'd be over in another second. One foot started to transfer her weight to empty air.

"Hold!" Aubrey snapped, and she froze, but too late. The earth gave way under her heel.

Morgan shrieked, kicked out, and would have fallen had he been anything but what he was. In the next moment he had her standing firmly on two feet well away from the edge and breathing hard.

It was good to know that enough of him remained, he thought, a little wryly, for a simple maiden rescuing. At his command, the fog swiftly drew away, breathed in again by the moor remembering its master.

"What were you thinking, Miss Tyler?"

"Thinking?" she said, and the eyes she turned up to him were dull and strange.

Bare arms, no coat, charmingly brief walking shorts, and a North Face gillet over a—well not quite nothing—but a thin cotton tee shirt, as if the sun shone hard on a summer day instead of palely loitering too close to the horizon on the day before Christmas. With the snow gone, and the drizzly fog cleared away, she was as good as naked in the tor's perpetual breeze. Every patch of fair skin dimpled with goose flesh.

Her moment of clarity had disappeared with the threat.

"Pixie-led, as they say," he murmured, though he knew it unlikely.

Experienced and knowledgeable Morgan Tyler would never have been turned about, not by his folk nor by sudden weather. She would hardly have set out unprepared. Oak and ash, those weren't boots, they were running shoes. Not pixie-led, he thought, so much as enchanted, a victim of a battle she knew nothing about.

He considered a moment, tight lipped. This was what his injury was doing to the moor, and to the human world that lived on it. Surely, it was something he could fix. He must fix it.

"What?"

"Never mind."

Aware that his current aspect was probably not ideal for rescuing sensible women lost on the moor, he robed himself suitably before laying a hand across her brow. While he watched, the cornflower eyes cleared, brightened. She took in his face and gasped, then smiled uncertainly.

"Aubrey King?"

Satisfied, he released her, whistling her walking stick to his hand. He held it out. "You dropped this."

She stared and took the staff from him. "Just came for a walk," she said, blinking. "Then, mist."

"Someone who doesn't know the moor as you do might say it's a touch chilly to be hiking the tor in summer clothes."

"Am I?" Distracted, she looked down at her clothes. "I'm freezing."

"Of course," he went on. "Here." For good measure, he made sure Morgan saw him in a cozy fisherman's sweater so she wouldn't mind taking the coat he offered: a long boiled wool Royal Navy topcoat that would keep her warm all the way home. He wrapped her in it, idly adjusting the length and fit for her, chattering lightly.

"Heard one of your talks once at the nature centre. Quite impressed. Very knowledgeable."

"Don't know what I was thinking," Morgan murmured huddling into the coat. "I was watching the telly, and the programme ended. Then I... And it just... well, it just seemed too much bother. Clear my head."

"I'll just walk you back to the car park, shall I? These fogs are maddening, coming up all at once, out of nowhere like that. Wouldn't want either of us to get lost again, eh?"

"Uhm, yeah, okay." She glanced at him sideways a few times but wouldn't meet his eyes. "Listen, Aubrey, an' no offense, mind, but you don't seem yourself. Are you all right?"

He smiled a little, catching the irony.

"Sure, fine," he said shortly, and shut up. At least she was moving, and at a good clip too. No need for chat.

A silent walk later he was putting Morgan in her car and a small enchantment around her thoughts to make sure she didn't drive into a bog on the way home. She mumbled a thank you, still unwilling to look at him directly. He might never have understood except that, as the town car pulled away in a flurry of loose stones and rock salt, he caught his reflection in the smoked glass of the windows.

Clothes: period appropriate. Eyes and hair: familiar and ordinary. Everything else, fine, perfectly fine, and utterly out of key with the roebuck's horns that pricked the sky so nobly above his head.

iii

Sitting an instant later under the gate called the Raven's Eye, high above the world again, he is amused but weary, angry but exhausted with the effort of holding on to his throne.

Now he looks down at his feet, the stones and peaty earth. It is too quiet. His people should be here, the snow faeries and pixies, the little ones that love to laugh and dance in the moonlight and lead unwary travelers astray. Where are they?

When he calls, there is no answer, not even an echo. When he sings to them, there is a rustling under a drift of dead leaves washed up against the stone, but all he hears is tiny snores. Any other day, it would make him smile but a growing numbness creeping down his side reminds him, this is his fault. If he had dealt with the witch properly to begin with, none of this would be happening.

So this is only fair. Now there is little he can do but sleep. Sleep. He can always sleep.

"No!" he shouts, and calls out: "Ben Harper!"

The sound vibrates in the empty landscape. In a moment, the harper's voice speaks anxiously in his ear.

"Not a good time, sir."

"Ben, can you give me an A?"

"A what—uhm, hang on." After too many anxious seconds, Ben's confident, creditable baritone softly hits the note that matches, almost, the one in the king's head. "Really got to go, sir!"

"Thanks. And Ben? Be swift!"

His music has begun to decline, his magic to thin, but there is time. If there is anything he can do, then he must. Ben and Raven must do everything else.

Changing shape again, a golden Eagle mounts the air with less than perfect grace. He favors the tawny right shoulder just slightly, and cries out, calling up the moon.

40

Crystal Palace, 3:00pm Christmas Eve, 1854

The twins blushed and giggled when they noticed Raven's attention, and hid their faces in their bonnets.

"Mad, bad, and dangerous to know, oh yes!" he said, employing a particularly refined accent. "Pretty girls everywhere, an entirely admirable suit of clothes—ooh, a pocket watch, I love these—and the chance to save the world without a clue to what we're doing. What more could a young man want?"

"A young man who's how old?" Ben wondered.

"I am the very spirit of youth, young Harper! Did you not know that?"

"Mm-hmm."

Like any dedicated tourist, Mr Harper was studying what appeared to be the *Guide to the Crystal Palace and Park*. It wasn't, of course, or not entirely; Faerie glamour accommodated the diary as well as their appearance. And it did have the maps, even though, as it turned out, they wouldn't be printed for two more years. The best little folk could do, he supposed, considering they couldn't safely come inside.

The broad gallery where they stood ringed the vast structure a good thirty feet above the main floor, and echoed the world below with commercial enthusiasm. For every exhibit below, the heights above held associated samples, souvenirs, and exotic trinkets of all sorts, even clothing and housewares. In handsome gilt script, *Crystal Palace, Sydenham* shone from china plates and tea cups, throw pillows, and plaster busts of the Caesars, not to mention the assorted tin-ware statuettes mounted on Genuine Cornish Serpentine Marble. The guide book called this level The Bazaar; the gift shop, Ben thought with a smile.

"So where are we exactly," he muttered, glancing up to compare the dull line drawings in his hands to the reality in front of him. Opposite, a display of etchings he couldn't make out at this distance, but below that in grandeur, the lotus, papyrus and staring ushabti of the Egyptians; cream and honey-colored columns ringed with sacred symbols in ochre, blue, and green: the eye of Horus, the feather of Ma'at, the stately march of hieroglyphics. That meant he stood over the delicately polychromatic façade of the Farnese palace and, behind it, the Renaissance courts.

The space to his left would be the Great Transept, dropped down from the main entrance, cutting across the width of the thoroughfare called the Nave. Lesser transepts did the same at north and south ends. This one, at least the breadth of an NFL football field, seemed to be cluttered with all sorts of sculpture—statues, crosses, architectural wonders all dazzling white—with a good-sized space left over in the middle for people to mill about. Beyond that, the Industrial section: artifacts of mining, weaving, manufacturing Britain. With relief he discovered that, when he felt for it, the harp-string tug at his breastbone was drawing him north and down, away from the industrial south end and its muttering iron.

"What are you doing, Harper?"

"Just getting our bearings," said Ben. The book snapped shut and disappeared into a pocket. "I wouldn't mind if when following my precious gift it actually dropped us on the spot instead of taking the scenic route."

"Another thing to work on. As well as your temporal targeting."

"Why? What day is it?"

Mister Fitzroy took a deep breath and held it for a bit, tasting the air. Then he let it out as a sigh. "Aye, me," he said. "Christmas Eve already, my dear Harper."

Something in the stylish drawl made Ben look up sharply. The boy had dressed himself as a dandy—hardly a surprise—in a dark blue coat with a nipped-in waist, and trousers of some remarkably subtle plaid Ben assumed was the essence of style. His own attire was just as fine if a bit less desperately fitted. Apparently today he was the responsible foil to the more dashing but less respectable friend. Not his favorite scenario.

"Fitzroy?"

True to form, his lordship had already wandered off among the last minute shoppers, sauntering easily with silk hat and a silver-topped walking stick, sporting a sleepy, careless smile like someone mildly wicked out of Dickens. When he bumped into a display counter filled with papier mâché Venetian masks, he murmured an automatic apology and bent to peer at the contents as if he had meant to all along.

"Fitzroy!"

"Hmm?"

"Are you stoned, sir?" Ben said when he caught up to him.

"Ha!" Raven barked, and moved to the next table of curiosities. "Silly ass. Can't get stoned. Nor drunk, neither, remember?"

"Maybe not, and maybe you shouldn't have taken that last pill after all. Come on. We just need to get out of the nave and…"

"The nave!" Raven brightened. "Of course! A cathedral to Industry! Naves and transepts, too—side chapels to the twin saints of science and commerce. Oh look! Venetian glass."

"Oh, no you don't!"

Getting a firm hand under the faerie gentleman's elbow, Harper guided him away. Some days in Raven's company left Ben reeling with awe; today it was more like shepherding a hyperactive toddler. And oh, good, now they had drawn the scowling attention of a burly fellow in a blue uniform with copper buttons and a domed hat Ben had only seen in silent movies.

That would be Security. Time to move.

Somewhere a clock struck three, echoed by bongs and bangs and clangs and a cuckoo from the Clockworks section, and the railway clocks suspended over the central transept. More important to their needs, the afternoon was fading even as the clouds broke to reveal a pale winter sun sinking toward the western horizon.

"I beg you, remember who you are," said Ben in all seriousness. "We are losing the light. They'll be closing."

Visibly asserting his will, fighting the urge to mischief, Raven nodded. "No time to play, then."

And as they strolled down the gallery, the fashionable slouch straightened, the impulse to sarcastic observation became a sophisticated chuckle. By the time they reached the end, next to a display of clothing and supplies for travellers in antique lands, he was himself again.

Instead of following the wall, as it did everywhere else, the gallery terminated on the far side of the north transept, overlooking an avenue like a processional way flanked by Egyptian sphinxes, twice the height of a man. In fact, they nearly walked into a frosted glass door with "Tropical Department: Conservatory" etched on it in sober copperplate lettering. Below it, a notice said, "Patrons are asked to close this door behind them."

Hardly pausing to register the information, Ben pushed through the door and into a wall of summer. Raven put out a steadying hand as the soggy heat rocked Ben back a step, then he closed the door behind them. The echoing noises of the exhibition broke off at once, leaving only a ringing in their ears, the hum of useful insects, the calls of parrots for whom windows had been opened in the curtain wall of paned glass. Rich scents of moist earth and burgeoning growth reached up with the heat, alive and vital. The fae, clear eyed, breathed in the life of green and growing things like a sustaining tonic.

"Well done, Paxton!" he said, admiring.

According to the guidebook, the winter temperature in the main hall was about 55 degrees Fahrenheit in winter, but behind the wall that closed the Conservatory in its corner terrarium, abetted by hot water pipes hidden in the floors, it held to a balmy 85 with attendant humidity, no matter how bleak and chill the wintry winds. From the top of a winding staircase they looked out into the tops of palm trees bedded far below.

"Are you all right?" said Ben.

"I may live, after all." Then the boy winked and said, "But it's going to wreak havoc with my cravat." When the laughter burst from his friend, he added soberly, "I do appear to be myself, or as much as I can be till we get out of here. I have to thank you again, haven't I?"

Ben leaned way out over the rail into a view of layer upon layer of split leaf and clambering vine in every shade of green, and whistled. "It's like the Swiss Family Robinson tree house."

Accepting the change of subject, Raven asked, "And the key?"

"Down there, somewhere in Adventureland."

"Ha! Among the hippopotami! After you, my dear Harper."

A rustic construction of wood and bamboo, the staircase spiraled down into to a quarter-acre jungle close-packed with the broad-leafed natives of Niger and Sumatra, elephant ears and feathered tree ferns, the stately columns of date palms. As elsewhere in the Palace, flowering baskets suspended from the galleries softened the hard lines of industrial iron; tendrils of flowering vines twined about the cross beams, as sedate as the ivy on the stateliest home. But here in humid air intensely rich, they blossomed with abandon, whispering rose and violet, bold crimson underpinned with azure to tease or surprise the eye seduced by endless green.

In the farthest corner, a burgeoning wisteria had already threaded its lilac-burdened arms to embrace the first gallery, flourishing upwards toward the next. One remembered that Paxton, the genius behind the design, had begun his career as a gardener, a builder of greenhouses, of which the Crystal Palace was only the most extensive. His winter garden might be confined to this one corner, but it was a triumph.

As they went down, the jungle closed about them, each genus and species neatly identified on lacquered cards. At the bottom, they had no choice to but to walk the winding path that gave patrons their lesson in tropical horticulture. A stream in a rocky bed sometimes paralleled the path, sometimes cut beneath or disappeared for a minute leaving only its music to remind them. Everywhere, water tripped and chuckled over bronze and stone, and artificial waterfalls, lightening their hearts even while the clock was ticking. Ben bit back his frustration each time the path turned them counter to the goal.

The walk ended at last in a open space where wooden chairs and benches allowed the weary to rest and admire yet another fountain. Crowded with ferns and still more gaudy flowers, a modest version of the elaborate Monti sculpture in the nave bubbled serenely in its pool. Stylized dolphins frolicked with modestly voluptuous mermaids on a wedding cake of fans and shells, bronzed and baroque, while clear water spilled through the ferny base to smooth stones brought from a hundred rivers.

"Well," Ben said. "Here we are."

At the water's edge, the thread that guided him ended. It hadn't failed, he realized; it just sat there humming to itself, waiting for him to do his part and see what he was supposed to see.

"I don't suppose it will actually look like, y'know, a key?" Ben said, adjusting his glasses to peer into the intricate design for anything like a clue.

"My lord will have made it long ago," said Raven, on alert while Ben did what only he could do. "Although he must have renewed it from time to time. I don't expect it will look like the ones on your key chain. Or even like it did when he first made it."

This end of the Palace was deserted now, so near to closing time. Behind the glass curtain, the silence was broken only by the hum of insects, the occasional flutter of a bird's wings, until a tiny sound fell on the fae ear from high above.

Probably nothing, he thought, glancing around. Just a petal dropping from a basket, maybe, or a dragonfly. Or the cop frowning at the top of the staircase. Perhaps it was his sore feet making him miserable, and maybe he just didn't like a pair of rich kids playing in his pond, but he didn't look pleased. Plodding deliberately, the fellow started down.

"Ah, you might want to hurry."

Ben grunted in response, but his focus was elsewhere. He took a deep breath, and thought, remembered: *Follow your gift*, as the king never left off saying. Bad enough he'd been looking for clues that weren't there, but more to the point, that wasn't how his gift worked.

Finally, he made a face and muttered, "What an idiot."

Ripples and refraction shifted images. The slip and tumble of water falling, pooling, falling again confused the ear, no matter how musical. So he tuned his mind to the base line, listening for the continuo underneath. And there it was, calling to him like a mermaid's song, like a story being told in an undertone, or in a strange language, in another room.

Hitching his trousers, he dropped to his knees and swept his hand through the water, passing over every river stone within his reach.

"That's it, talk to me."

To one side especially, dozens of tiny fish with fins like flowing veils swarmed over his hands, tickling his fingers. When he moved elsewhere, they scattered.

Oh, clever king.

"These goldfish seem to think they're piranha."

"You're sure you're looking in the right place?"

"Dead sure, just... hang on." It was right under his hand, but when he waved off the attack koi, all he could see was a rough, moss-covered rock about the size of a baseball. When he reached in to grasp it, the top part of it came away in his fingers, and he sat back with a bump on the deck. "Damn it!"

"What?" Raven was beside him in a moment.

"Look!" Within the broken shell, the ugly rock hid a hollow center crowded with a small treasure of violet crystals and a flecks of sparkling mica.

"It's a geode."

"Yes. Gorgeous. But how is this a key?"

Thoughtful, Raven took it from him, rotating the crystal cave to catch the watery daylight.

"Hmm," he said. He leaned forward to hold it again under the water, then tipped it just slightly. "Now look at it."

As they watched a shape resolved within the crystalline glitter, still amethyst but shadowed and limned with gold.

"Oh!"

Ben reached in and flicked away some loose bits, then grasped the shape between two fingers. With a snap, he had it: a flat ring with a little bar projecting from it, notched at one end; undeniably key-like though certainly not what he'd expected. When he brought it into the air, the color faded to dull bronze. Behind it, a slender chain formed as if from the water itself.

"What's all this, then?"

Raven unfolded easily to his full height, the haughty peer, diverting and holding the constable's attention while Ben slipped the key into a pocket.

"I beg your pardon?" he said icily. "If you must know, my good man, we were taking a closer look, if it's anything to you, whoever you are."

"I 'appen to be," said the bobby with all the narrow-eyed confidence of his authority, "the constable who's asking you what you might be about, sir. As it is my job to see no 'arm comes to any of these 'ere exhibits."

Lord Fitzroy rolled his eyes and struck a pose. Lightly he let the homely stone with its flashing center drop to the water with a splash.

"And an excellent job you're doing, constable. Excellent! Do you see, Harper? I told you the place was in excellent hands!"

"And so you did, my lord," Ben said, flicking the water from his fingers as he stood. "Forgive us, constable, I was only pointing out to his lordship here some of the finer points of the geological elements inherent in the natural history of that extraordinary piece of, uhm, granite. Why, did you know the rocks in this basin alone come from as far away as Java, Africa, Tahiti, and even South America? Why, that one stone alone…

Or no, where'd it go? That one. Or was it… Wait! I can show you!"

The man did not seem either impressed by titles or baffled by bullshit, and surveyed them both rather more closely than they liked.

"Oh, are they, sir?" he said, in exactly the accents of a man who will not be diverted. "Well, that's very nice I'm sure. You're an American gentleman, I take it, so perhaps you might not be aware of the customs here, so I shall say no more. However, I should take it very kindly if you would do me the very great favour of taking your friend and your air-you-dition toward the exit, as it is now closing time. Sir."

He gave a slight turn to gaze pointedly at the blushing western sky.

"Yes!" said Ben, deeply relieved. "Yes, indeed! Happy to oblige, indeed."

"Really!" Raven sniffed, and drew himself up from the aristocratic slouch he had adopted—on purpose, this time. "Do you have any idea who I am? I… I say, is that a dragonfly?"

"Come along, Fitzroy!" Harper, the picture of helpful enthusiasm, tipped his hat and grabbed his over-bred friend by the elbow, and hustled him away. "Time to go. Sorry to be a bother, constable. Merry Christmas!"

The constable watched them sourly as they found the door and exited the 'mild and genial heat of Madeira' promised by the guidebook. Shaking his head, he turned to continue on his rounds. He never had this kind of trouble with Hob Hobson from the country. Never.

The shock of the temperature change smacked them both in the face as they emerged under the sphinxes and the looming aspect of Abu Simbel. The paired statues of a long dead pharaoh rose six stories to the dome of the northern transept. Restored to the original brilliant colors (speculative), impossible to miss, it dominated as much now as it did then although the eyes were a bit alarming. Ben shuddered and slid onto a handy bench.

"You're not going to recite *Ozymandias*, I hope," Raven said.

"Well, not now," he said. "They look surprised."

"Probably just astonished to find themselves in England."

"Think how the Elgin Marbles feel."

"Time for us to move on, then."

He had the key, and no idea what to do with it, and time was getting shorter with every delay. In fact, he fancied he could feel inspiration tip-toing from the world. Hopefully, he drew out the key and held it up dangling like a pendulum from the insubstantial chain, curiously dull for a thing made of mist and moonlight.

The raven boy had taken up a jaunty pose with his coat open to display the fine tartan waistcoat, hands in his pockets, but his expression was somber. "It's a part of his soul, isn't it, this thing that's locked away."

"I think it must be, yes," said Ben.

"So it will be hidden especially well. And what does he mean, a lock? A locked box? A canal lock? A lock of a maiden's golden hair?"

Ben lifted his hands. "Not a clue."

"You've got the key. Won't that lead the way?"

"It should. I thought it would, but... nothing. Weird."

He tried holding it in one hand then the other, just in case. He put it on his finger. He closed both hands around it protectively and whispered sweet words. He even slipped the chain around his fingers and looped the first figure of a cat's-cradle. The voiceless song of its own making and the king's cleverness remained, but that was all.

Well, the gift had whims of its own, sometimes. And the king of Faerie even more so. Maybe when they got outside it would give him something. Not that he was looking forward to the cold. More likely a sidestep to Faerie for further instructions.

He put the chain over his head, and tucked the key behind his waistcoat. "Are you hungry?"

"Seldom." Raven smiled and nodded to a weary tour guide with the last dazed group of the day. "I wouldn't say no to a drink, though."

"Well, my stomach thinks my throat's been cut, as my granddad says. There's supposed to be a refreshment station around here somewhere. Let's see if it's still open."

41

Hollytree house, at about the same time

Fire crackled in the grate, warming the sitting room where Susan Pickering sat sketching at the writing desk, surrounded by Christmas. Festooned from end to end with swags of ivy and scarlet-jewelled holly, bedecked with tinted cards of robins, chubby babies, and Father Christmas with his pack, the sitting room itself had become a present from her lodgers to themselves. Their splendid tree glittered with tin stars and spicy gingerbread men, and little packages tied with colored string, but Susan as she drew saw none of it.

The cheerful ticks and pops of the flames had already disappeared into the hissing scratch of her pencil moving swiftly over the drawing paper. One rebellious strand of hair lay across her cheek as unheeded as the spectacles sliding down her nose. Her left hand flew, desperate to capture the memory of strangers. Skidding across the rough paper with the scrape of skaters speeding over ice, images emerged from the paper almost before they formed in her mind's eye, as if her hand only called them forth from some other world. Bypassing conscious thought, the figures leapt to the page.

A pale boy as she had first seen him, launched broken and impossible out of a stone mirror in the instant before it cracked in two.

Again, crumpled and broken on the platform at her feet, whimpering like a kitten in the iron cage of the Crystal Palace, caged twice in the framework of her uncle's terrible machine.

The same dark-haired young man, this time awake and frightened, a pair of slender hands reaching up from a tangle of linen sheets imploring her to set him free.

She turned the page and started again. Ralph Fitzroy in her parlor, leaning over Miss Dean's harp to pluck a shivering note. The same sharp features, high cheekbones, tilted blue eyes dulled with pain under a cap of sable curls like a fairy tale prince. The boy who said his father was the king of the faeries. And then...

Harper, conjured by his name, who had appeared at her door with an American accent and fine English clothes, and a prince of Faerie in his arms rescued from the snowy wood.

She caught a startled breath and stopped. This face, she realized. Ben Harper's human face, she remembered exactly as she drew it. But Ralph's... Oh, she knew that wasn't his name, but was it even his face?

Her hand moved again. She dashed the suggestion of a gleam over one lens of the American's glasses, then sat back to examine the scene that had come from her pencils. What wild, scarcely human face was that blinking at her out of the cape of a borrowed topcoat? Startled, curious, she flipped the pages back, examining each with a practiced eye, recalling each study hastily done, some little more than a suggestion to finish properly later on. But this one... Somehow, very faintly over the page, the shadow of a raven appeared that she didn't remember drawing.

Susan drew in a breath and let out a sigh so deep, she wondered where it had come from. The air tasted deliciously of Christmas. The log on the fire. The beef roasting slowly in the kitchen. The spicy fir tree that brought the living world indoors. Cinnamon and ginger, nutmeg... and bay rum with a touch of limewater. Donovan!

"You are very good." His voice, strangely unsteady, made her turn around, pleased if slightly embarrassed. "Better than most of the hacks I work with."

"How long have you been standing there? You might have made a noise."

"I knew it would make you stop, and it seemed some need maybe was on you to do this."

Her breath caught, wondering how he could have known, when she hardly knew herself.

"You may be right. I don't generally show my sketches."

"No?" He nodded toward the room so filled with color. "The framed one over the chimney piece. All the little cards. They're everywhere."

"That's different. They are finished. Besides, when I was a girl, my grandmother made it very clear... Oh, never mind," she concluded with just a little irritation, and slapped the sketchbook shut.

For a moment she closed her eyes as well, marshaling her feelings. If she never talked about her family, there were reasons, good ones, which she had no intention of explaining tonight. When the brown eyes opened she smiled at him and said, "Merry Christmas, Edward."

"Merry Christmas, Susan. And don't change the subject." He pulled up a chair and while he held her gaze, reached over and pulled the book from her hands.

"I wish you wouldn't," she said automatically, but did nothing to stop him.

Where the images had poured themselves onto the pages with mindless speed, Ned Donovan lingered over each one, his expression sober. There were more than a dozen, some detailed vignettes, others just a study of angles and expressions, the turn of a wrist, the bones of an elven hand, the tilt of a brow. The arched curve of a Raven's beak, and a bright black eye.

As he moved from one to the next, he let the pads of his fingers touch only the paper's edge, gently turning the page as if handling some rare manuscript. At the last one, he sat back with a low whistle.

"What do you see?" She expected something polite, possibly flirtatious, but nothing more.

"This is how you saw him, our fairy prince?"

Her brows drew together in a considering frown.

"Not exactly. I think— I think it may be his true face, somehow. It is like the one he shows us, but more strange.

What is it, Ned? What's the matter?" He was staring at that last sketch with an expression she found alarming.

"This is the last one, is it? The one I watched come from your hand? Harper and Fitzroy together?"

Without looking, she flushed a little and said, "Yes, of course. Have you changed your mind about my talents?"

But he was already on his feet, pressing the sketchbook back into her hands. "I have to go. At once. Forgive me."

"On Christmas Eve? Ned Donovan, what can be so important?"

He was already buttoning his coat, but he looked back at her and stopped. In two strides he had plucked her out of the chair and taken her in his arms, and before she could react, his mouth was on hers, the ridiculous whiskers scouring her cheeks.

"You've been given a great gift, dear Susan," he said at last. "Open the book. Look again. Now I must get to where I'm meant to be."

Then he was gone, her pictures rattling on the walls with the slamming door, again when the front door closed behind him. Susan, light-headed and trembling with six kinds of shock, sat down before her knees could give way. When she realized she was still hugging the sketchbook to her bosom, she returned it carefully to the desk.

He'd kissed her! Surely that was gift enough. But what else? Oh yes.

Quite.

The picture.

Collecting herself as far as she might, Susan turned again to the last drawing.

"Now what did you see, Edward?" she whispered. Her breath rushing across still tingling lips almost bubbled into a girlish giggle. And then she saw it, and every other thought went away.

The marginalia, test studies, incomplete portraits of the fairy and his mortal friend were as she had left them, she thought, drawn by her own rebellious, unmistakable left hand. Except for one.

"What on earth?" She frowned, and pushed the loose lock of hair from her eyes, straightened the spectacles, and looked again. "That can't be."

Instead of penciled lines given a suggestion of life and movement by her art, she saw the two men peering over the observation deck above the central transept, the massive lobby of the Crystal Palace. In one moment they had turned to face each other, in the next Harper's image seemed to speak, Ralph's to laugh.

I am dizzy, she thought. Her heart was still pounding with Donovan's impulsive kiss.

As she shook her head to clear it, the figures froze, ordinary sketches again, as they should be. But then she shifted her gaze, and there, as if rising up from the bottom of the paper, a few strokes she cannot have made became Ned Donovan's unmistakable hat, broad shoulders draped in that awful tartan topcoat, arm raised to hail a cab.

Her eyes fixed on the impossible vision, Susan tried to believe it was an illusion, a hallucination brought on by the heat in the room, the fading daylight, the honeyed scent of whale oil in the lamps, the unexpected elation of her first—oh lord, her first kiss!

Another page, another unfamiliar scene. Her two strange guests were examining something in the Tropical fountain. Her head swam as if she walked a ship's lurching deck. Rising to her feet, she cried out, "Stop!"

And so it did.

In a strip along the bottom margin, a series of scenes suggested a narrative: Ned arguing with a constable at the entrance to the Crystal Palace. Finding another way in. Above, Mr Harper and Ralph—no, *Raven*! The boy who could not abide the touch of iron. They were somewhere within the Palace itself, barely visible among the ornamental shrubbery and shadows. It was closing time, surely. If there was trouble, why didn't they just leave?

That she even asked the question made it clear, she had accepted the truth that lay before her. Biting her lips, resolved to keep her head, Susan allowed herself to collapse, but in a very sensible way, into the writing chair, thinking. Beset by interruptions, she was always leaving her sketchbook about; Raven had moved it aside the other day, as people were always doing. Moved it, but what else?

"An extraordinary gift," she murmured. "But what does it mean?"

She didn't really expect an answer, and of course, none came. Best not to waste it whatever it meant.

Perhaps a pot of tea would help her to think about it. Or better yet, it occurred to her that there was a tantalus in the one of the cupboards; brandy for a toast tonight, and sherry for the punch. The key was on the ring in her pocket. Well, it was her house, and her brandy, wasn't it?

A quick shot to stiffen her resolve, another for reinforcements, she took the glass and the book to the chaise and opened it on her lap.

"Show me," she whispered.

42

Crystal Palace, Christmas Eve, 1854, 4:00pm

And moving thro' a mirror clear
That hangs before her all the year,
Shadows of the world appear.
—Alfred Lord Tennyson, 1833

Every clock in the Palace had just struck four. The corners filled up with shadows and a few yellow lamps as the sun dropped behind a low bank of cloud. At the Industrial end, nearest the exit and across from the retiring rooms, the platform on which had hummed the Eye of Memory, Lovejoy's pride, his Great Device, was piled with boxes and ringed with heavy crates, partly filled. The workmen hired to knock them all them together and load them up had been paid their shilling and sent home for Christmas, and the banging hammers that had bothered the neighbors for two days fell silent. Little more than the supporting framework remained, and the platform itself.

Within his brass and iron cage, Professor Lovejoy, feeling older and more fragile than ever, slumped in the red velvet chair almost hidden among the strapped bundles of iron pipes and copper tubing, coiled rubber hose, gutta-percha joints and dead batteries, and crates filled with random bits of brass, porcelain, and glass. Gaslight from the refreshment stalls and tables flared across the surface of the fractured Aztec stone still suspended in its frame, casting rainbows over his face. Dull-eyed, he sat and stared. Now and then a sigh escaped him as if, drowned in his fate, breathing had become a burden.

He still had money, he knew that. There was no shortage of money. If money were the only concern, an obsidian disk could be found in no more time than it took write to his agent in Mexico. But it would not be the mirror of the great John Dee. The spirit of that remarkable man had, he believed, reached across the ages to take his hand. To guide his work. To put the miracles of modern technology to the service of Dee's knowledge. Alas, that it should be so—the tool on which he had placed all his hopes destroyed in an instant of chaos he could not even explain.

Had a man really appeared out of nowhere? Impossible. Madness and delusion, even though he had seen it himself. All, all was lost, as lost as the dead past itself. His mourning had taken on the garments of epic tragedy.

To continue the work, in spite of Ambrose Cray's enthusiasm, would mean starting again. And he was feeling old, so very old. Perhaps it was time to rest. Perhaps he dozed a bit in his chair.

"Erasmus?" A voice throaty and cool soothed away the beginnings of a dream. "Erasmus, dear."

Eyelids he had not realized were closed fluttered open, and his mood lifted as it always did at the sight of a lovely woman. The deep lines around his mouth began to rise toward a pleasantly puzzled look. Young women often smiled at him, and called him "dear". Silly flibbertigibbets, of course, but it was charming all the same. And he had, had he not, cut quite a figure as a younger man. A much younger man.

But who was she, this girl, with her golden hair and wanton expression? And more, how could she speak to him out of the black mirror though no power flowed across it?

"Who are you?" His weary form still frozen in his seat, his voice was a hoarse whisper. "Where are you?"

Dark winter though it was for the old man in 1854, Perdita spoke to him from her noon-flooded studio in another time, weaving enchantments with her power at its height.

"I am your destiny, Erasmus," she purred.

"Nay," he snorted. "My destiny has failed me!"

"Erasmus, do you not know me? Have you forgotten me?"

"Tell me your name, O nymph!!"

She threw back her lovely head and sighed with pleasure. Bare, sweetly rounded arms reached to him.

"I am your muse! Your beginning and your end! Come to me, Erasmus, and let me teach you all my secrets!"

He sat forward now, enjoying the dream, as he knew it must be.

"But how? How shall I come to you, dear creature, while you are in the stone and I, poor mortal, am trapped upon the dreary earth?"

To his alarm, she moved closer, her face filling the cracked disk until he could count the transparent lashes beneath her tawny eyes, which all at once grew wide.

"Traitorous bitch!"

Behind the chair, a mad voice shrieked and swore. Thick-soled boots slammed echoing across the platform.

"Ambrose, my love!"

"What are you babbling about?"

Lovejoy spun about in the chair to see his assistant approaching crazed, almost gibbering. Fist clutching the ax they kept for fires, he beat aside every obstacle that blocked his way to the control panel.

"Cray, you idiot. Put that down!"

But Cray heard neither of them. Eyes rolling wild in their orbits, furious tears streamed down cheeks blotched with crimson; spittle flecked the once fine mustache. All pretense of civilization abandoned, his chest heaved with each breath. He never responded to the sound of his name.

From the gathering crowd a man with a napkin tied under his chin waved a cold meat pasty and shouted, "I say, look out!"

Others turned to look and, horrified, cried out as well. "Who is that man? Someone stop him!"

The dream had gone too far, too far, the Professor thought as he struggled to find his feet. He commanded it to cease.

Maggie Secara

"I've had enough of your tempers, sirrah. You are dismissed! Now put that thing down and go away!"

But the younger man shrieked and flailed the ax like Hercules with his club.

"I shall have her, not you, old man, and no other! Do you hear! No more waiting! No more standing aside for lesser men to rise above me. She is mine, my reward! I have earned her, and your blood seals the bargain!"

"Ambrose!" she cried, her words a joyful welcome. "Yes!"

With a garbled cry, he swung the ax high and brought it whistling down toward the old man's head, crashing instead into the back of the red velvet chair. As ancient as the professor himself, the chair exploded, flinging the frail old scholar over the gutted control panel. Roaring, Cray advanced again.

"Oh, yes!" Ecstatic, the voice echoed throughout the transept. "Ambrose, come to me!"

Then a movement beyond him caught her eye.

"You!" she gasped. "Oh, this is excellent!"

And she started to laugh.

The staff from the Pompeii house, disturbed from their tidying up, gathered to peep out of their rosy atrium. Patrons being shepherded toward the trains paused, exchanged looks, then hurried back to stare and wonder. Then the screaming began.

43

And shine in at the casement, Christmas Eve, 1854

The Palace is opened on Mondays at 9.0 a.m. ; on Tuesdays, Wednesdays, Thursdays and Fridays at 10.0, a.m. ; and on Saturdays at noon ; and is closed daily at sunset.
—Guide to the Crystal Palace and Park, 1856

i

The king of Faerie's key hung about Ben Harper's neck, silently unhelpful. The search for a restorative snack had failed. Anxious to get home themselves, vendors were unwilling to provide so much as one more cup of tea when Christmas punch awaited them at home. The refreshment stall behind Nineveh had closed before they got there, along with all the exits in the north end of the building. Frustrated with the wasted time, desperate to get out of doors, they had no choice.

So they fell in with the homeward bound and the tardy being swept along the nave with the tinsel and fallen pine needles. Sensibly they kept to the garden side, avoiding the iron-rich industrial courts opposite and walking quickly.

Assistants in every court, in every gallery shop were covering their goods and locking up cabinets. Optics, Ceramics, British Textiles, each dimmed their lamps as Ben and Raven reached them. Others simply drew down painted curtains to show decorative but politely regretful messages as the staff found their coats, scarves, hats. The forest of sculptures in the great central transept threw down wild shadows across each other, altering their shapes in the gloom: a leaping horse became a dragon, the winsome saint an ogre.

Ben drew up in front of Musical Instruments to admire a spinet inlaid with marquetry and ivory quillwork, his mission momentarily driven to a secondary level by thoughts of his wife. Already an antique, the spinet was a beauty. In his mind's eye he could see Mellis in a taffeta gown sitting down to it, listening, trying the action, then wakening it to elegant music under her expert hands—Purcell, perhaps, or Bach. He sighed when a young man apologetically pulled an accordion of etched glass panels flat across the entrance.

As they crossed into the south transept, Raven slowed and turned his glance across another long reflecting pool with a fountain tinkling in its center, a flowery spire of rosy glass. The crowds were, almost to a man, diving into a doorway marked TO THE TRAINS. Nearly hidden in a vast oaken screen carved with nine hundred years of kings and queens of England it was, however convenient, utterly closed to them. The very thought of a Victorian train platform with its massive iron engines made Raven shudder.

"Hold on."

Still preoccupied, Ben was hardly aware that they had stopped until he felt the hand print on his sleeve. "Hmm?"

"This way."

They had to retrace their steps to get around the pink fountain , which put them at odds with the flow of traffic diving for the exit. Or should have. Without thinking, and without a word, the way simply cleared as he required. Not one patron made a fuss, and only one small child even glanced at them. Raven permitted himself a thin smile of satisfaction.

Then he froze. Took two steps back. It had looked like a safe exit, an ordinary door at the end of the transept, but something ugly barred the way. The outer wall of the rose and white replica Pompeii house shaped one edge of the transept.

Slapped on to it like a wart stood a raised platform shrouded in melancholy. Some sort of technical display had been abandoned whilst being disassembled, apparently, and from it a sense of evil. The world was out of balance, and the fault lay here.

Ben asked, "What is it?"

"Up there," Raven said, nodding toward it.

"An unlocked door! Excellent. So why are we standing here?"

His friend wasn't listening. Over the platform a smudged banner announced:

PROFESSOR ERASMUS P. LOVEJOY, DPHIL
presents
HIS GREAT DEVICE & THE WONDER OF THE AGE
THE EYE OF DESTINY

In much smaller letters beneath a muddy illustration:

ASSISTED BY MR AMBROSE CRAY.
LECTURES EVERY TUESDAY AT 3.0 P.M.

His eyes narrowed feeling the patterns of the world slide and shift. Miss Pickering's people, Perdita's unwitting minions. His own pain-filled, unwilling entrance to the nineteenth century. Other misty shapes moved maddeningly beyond his reach, so he concentrated on the merely physical things he could see.

Above an almighty mess of boxes and baskets stinking of cold iron bars swung a long piece of polished obsidian. Cracked right through, its heart gouged open by an ugly diagonal gash, a gutta-percha band and the cupids of its gilded frame barely held the pieces together. Susan had described it to him, not hiding her distaste, and now he understood. Its elaborate supports curled and sprung, it hovered over the platform on a last frayed cable swaying lightly in the heavy air.

Facing it, a wild-haired old man who must be Lovejoy appeared to be asleep in a chair. Asleep or dead, since he gave no response to the imprecations and wild gestures of a choleric younger man in a lab coat pacing, kicking boxes, swearing behind him. Shortly, the less than admirable Cray growled his frustration and gave up, hard boots rocking the platform. He marched down a short flight of steps and disappeared into a curtained supply area just beyond.

"What's the matter?" Ben asked, though his focus was elsewhere.

Emotions shifted across Raven's observing face that no mortal would have recognized, except for one. The fae merely nodded toward the skeletal platform, sensing new, unexpected ripples forming in the patterns of the world.

"I know this place." Shoulders rolled uncomfortably in his fine clothes; he was never uncomfortable in his clothes. "I've been here before. And didn't like it."

"Not exactly cottage loaf and honey, is it?"

"What?"

Stomach rumbling, Mr Harper had missed the banner in favor of a sign, this one on a staircase, pointing out visitor services not revealed in the guidebook. "They'll be closed, of course."

"Which one?" Raven smiled tightly, giving in to the moment's diversion. "The snack bar, or the men's room? You don't suppose they're in the same place?"

"I'll just go and find out, shall I?" Ben said in his most genteel tones, and disappeared almost at once behind what seemed to be thirty feet of hedge maze labeled "Natural History: The New World."

"At least he's a better navigator than Columbus."

The stream of humanity swirling around him had thinned to a trickle; just the very last patrons, the security staff chivvying them along, eager to get home themselves.

"Christmas Eve, you know, ladies and gents. Closing time."

"This way to the Egress," Raven said, gently deflecting all passing glances. The sense of wrongness rolled over him again. That stone.

"Move along, if you please. Yes, closed all day tomorrow, madam. Come see us on Boxing Day."

"Happy Christmas, Miss Jordan, Miss Arbuthnot. Merry Christmas, Bill."

A few of the heavy lifting types from the Automation Department below paused as they rumbled up the stairs to laughed at the mad old man on the platform, as they probably did most days. Lovejoy was awake apparently, and talking to himself, still staring up at that bit of volcanic glass he called a mirror, even with his famous machine in pieces around him.

When the workmen failed to get a rise from their target they lost interest. One even shouted, "Merry Christmas, Professor!" before giving the platform a parting thump, then lengthened his stride to catch up with his fellows.

All Raven's attention was on the polished stone, the mirror, damaged but not destroyed, the source of his unease and his cold fury at the malign will on the other side of it. At this distance, he could sense though not exactly feel the native low-level power, ill-used but not in itself corrupt, radiating from the cracks braided across its surface. Such power came from earth, not from art. And it could still be used.

Too soon, Ben returned empty handed but otherwise refreshed.

"You do realize we've just strolled through one of the great wonders of the age without seeing any of it?" he said. Then he caught the look on his friend's face. "God, man, what is it?"

"Don't move."

Summoning his will, Raven stepped forward into the mirror's range. As if a door had opened on some dark dimension, he reeled under the assault of a sudden deep malevolence—not the stone but a trap lying in wait behind it. The muttering shadow that still blocked his music, blanketing the core of his magic, roared into his mind with a noise like the static of a dying sun, redlining the meter.

He moved away, slammed that door shut; the threat retreated to the dull white noise he had lived with for days. But he knew where he was, now. Something had changed ever so slightly, frayed the edges of the shadow just a little, and he thought he might have a weapon left after all.

He could not change his form in his current state, but the song within himself remained, complex and flexible as the veils between the worlds. He was the King's Raven still, and knew it.

With a push, the Raven within stretched out a talon to flick up that frayed shadow. The shining point of a hooked black beak darted in, reaching for even the smallest part of his power. It would take a few minutes to collect what he needed for even one command, but it would come. Breathing, he set the image aside to work as it would.

Focused on his need, he never noticed when Cray returned, leapt snarling to the platform swinging a long handled fire ax like a cricket bat. Never registered the man lumbering like a bear baited by dogs, trapped between bonfires, insane. The old man's imperious voice, the woman's laughter, and the rising sounds of violence cut the air.

ii

"Raven! Damn it, snap out of it."

Night blue eyes opened on Ben's worried frown, lifted to the drama on the platform. How had they wandered so close to this train wreck? The professor was screaming, while the other man moved in for the killing blow.

Ben shouted "Hey!" and lurched toward the platform, but his friend's inexorable grip had him by the arm, and anyway, it was already too late.

Every witnessing voice screamed in horror as the ax came down with a wet crunch, a single agonized cry swiftly cut off. The weapon, released with a twist and the whimper of a sick animal, rose up clogged with blood and brains, and fell again with equal force. A third time, more fierce than all the rest. Screams echoed from all around even as Cray, spattered in blood, flung the ax aside.

"Look out!" someone cried as it arced into the open air, grazed a kingly statue, landed ringing and clattering on the wooden floor, where it skidded almost to Ben's feet. He skipped back to avoid it, then leaned forward, as curious as his own son reaching for a bug.

"Touch it not, human child," said Raven's low voice, perfectly calm, adding, "Security is certainly taking its time."

Ben snatched his hand away, looked back and gasped while Raven watched, coldly disinterested. None of this involved him; it had nothing to do with their quest. It was not for him to intervene or even participate in mortal affairs without being asked. Unless it was amusing, or at his king's command. This was neither.

Cray was crimson to the elbows, oblivious to the slaughterhouse stench of thickening blood and voided bowels. His hands clenched in the old man's coat. Face contorted with rage, he lifted the battered body and roaring shook it like a broken doll until the blood flew, splashing the mirror and everything and everyone nearby. Then choking with disgust, he flung it aside and staggered back to face the glass.

His face twitched into a parody of yearning lust. He reached out to the laughing girl shimmering beneath the surface, cracked and crazed. Like the Lady of the Lake but less discreet and spattered with death, the ends of her fingers slipped easily now through the surface, followed by hands, arms, the rosy tips of her breasts leading the rest of her body, ready with another step to walk into this world from whatever strange place she was. He had only to draw her to him as he had been told.

"Ambrose, my love! Take my hands, yes, and I will come to you! No, my hands, take my hands, you fool! As I told you!"

What man remembers what a woman has told him?

As impatient as she, Cray rushed to her, but his senses and her ill-tuned luck betrayed them both. Half blinded, mind occluded, he touched his reeking fingers not to the sweet promise of her body but into the glassy surface of her mirror.

"No!" she howled. "You idiot!"

Muttering endearments like a prayer, Ambrose Cray stepped through the polished stone into that other place and took her in his arms.

The image collapsed and the lights went out, the woman's desperate curses suddenly cut off, connection severed. Only Lovejoy's body remained, one shattered arm draped over the edge of the platform, the fingers still mindlessly twitching.

Dark blood dripped much too close to Ben Harper's shoulder. He jumped back, sick with horror, and turned on his friend.

"You could have stopped that!"

Dark eyes and light voice lifted together in a kind of apology.

"How? And why? Though I may wish otherwise, it's not for me to meddle. And here's another problem."

Ben turned to follow the fae lord's gaze into the nave where the fountain pool lay placid under giant lily pads, and beside it, a lady heavily veiled in black seated in a wheeled bath chair. Bending to hear her whispered instructions, the man they had just seen vanish into a mirror, now clear-eyed and clean-shaven.

"It's the same guy," Ben breathed. "Is that her?"

"The spurned mistress, the fair Perdita, still unhanged."

Straightening, the villain met Raven's cool gaze as he rearranged his face into a convincing expression of shock and horror. Next to him the woman's crabbed hand painfully lifted the veil on a visage of unimaginable age and pain. She winked at them over a toothless smile, and let the veil fall.

Then she howled. "Murder!"

On cue, Cray bellowed, "Murder!" and thrust a pointing finger straight at Ben and Raven. His voiced bounced off the girders and around their heads. "Foul murder! Those brutes have murdered the Professor! Police! Help! Murder!"

Security, as stunned as anyone and grateful for some direction, shook off their torpor and rushed forward. Police whistles shrilled and other voices took up the cry. Almost at once some poor thief hurrying away with a coat full of pocket handkerchiefs was collared, and hauled away protesting loudly. It wouldn't help for long.

Ben looked back over his shoulder, confused. "What?"

"That would be us!"

"But everyone saw…"

"When we get arrested, you can explain that," the boy snapped. "Right now—"

Impatient with speech, he shoved Ben into the hedge of the New World already deep in shadow. "Don't move."

For a few minutes, the whole length of the transept was nothing but shouting figures dashing in every direction but mainly toward the exits, panicked by the smell of death, identifying murderers in every shadow. If Security was counting on those last stragglers to join the hue and cry, disappointment was in the air.

Raven watched with growing dismay as the one exit they could use slammed shut, leaving them alone in an iron cage with a handful of uniformed officers and a few bully boys. Cray and his ancient lover were nowhere to be seen.

iii

Black billy clubs swinging, the beefy, red-cheeked constables and their beefier volunteers marched ponderously forward with hard eyes sweeping left and right. The line broke as they turned into the nave, split around the fountain.

"We'll need lanterns here!" someone called.

One pair of copper-buttoned peelers split off to check everyone pressing through the screen of the Kings and Queens. They left one man, a civilian with a decidedly uncharitable attitude, stationed near the retiring rooms.

"How efficient of them. I was so hoping for a quick solution. Just for the novelty."

"That would be too easy."

"I like easy, but I will make do."

Calmly, Raven took a first step out into the open. The next glance that swept across them slid smoothly away. He wasn't sure that would last, though, given what he had in mind, so he retreated again, thinking.

Ben hissed, "I don't suppose you've got a plan?"

"Not much of one."

"Magic?"

"A little, but you may not like it. You?"

"Hmm?"

"You got us in here. Can you get us out?"

Ben closed his eyes, trying to focus. He only needed six true notes. Or no, this was different than before. The century, maybe, or the era or the Palace itself, had its own song, and would not release them for so little effort.

Nine good notes, then. Maybe eight, if he didn't care where it took them. If he could summon just that much of a song, any song, or hell, just the rising notes of a C-major scale he could get them out of here, but not now. It was hopeless against the echoing din of voices, the shrill blare of police whistles, all bouncing up into the dome and back again.

Finally he shook his head, hopeless for now. "It's quieter than it was, but I've got to get out of this echo chamber."

"Then it's back to me." The look of determination on the raven boy's face was one Ben knew, a warrior's look. "You told me to remember who I am. We—you—have a mission. I told you before, I am your sword. Failing that, as I must today, I can at least be the shield. First thing, I have to get rid of that damned mirror before she can use it again, right?"

When his friend nodded, Raven added, "Better cover your ears, then."

So Ben covered his ears and waited, while Raven, as if he had all the time in the world, took a calming breath, found the shining thread he had been spinning, husbanding the magic in the unblocked corners of his mind. It wasn't much.

"Pitiful," he muttered. "Have to do."

Calmly, he sighed the breath away and stood up, stepped out into the nave, raised a closed hand in front of him. He had to let go of the look-away, but he couldn't do both.

Someone shouted, "There's one! That's 'im!"

He paid no mind. With three words, he opened his hand on three tiny balls of eldritch fire crackling blue and white over his palm. Another word, and he sent them, three slender cracks of lightning one after the other snatching power from the last hint of twilight, to drive golden into the braided rifts of the Aztec mirror.

With a crash like an exploding orchestra, it burst into rainbows and shimmering dust, a mushroom cloud that boiled in the air to the height of the dome, dazzling, deafening. And abruptly gone.

In the stunned silence that fell while every other human in the place cringed, Raven turned looking impossibly pleased with himself.

"Nice," said Ben appreciatively. "What now?"

Night had definitely fallen, the hanging greenery and potted foliage marking every exhibit softened the hard iron lines and threw every corner into shadow. Raven turned his gaze overhead, and sighed. It meant going up into the iron again, but there really was no choice.

He shrugged and said, "They're looking down, so we go up. And look, stairs!"

Gaining the gallery level with no more cover than the night and elevation, they retreated through the shrouded displays to the glass wall, looking out over the snow and ice-blanketed gardens. The glow from the mirror's destruction had faded, and so had the last streak of the sunlight. They were running in the dark, which meant little to him and could be used to advantage, at least until someone fetched the lanterns out, and even then.

Ben whispered, "Now what?"

"Find a door, we will exit," the boy said simply, stopping to stare down the window to the snowy earth and the terraces of the garden side. "Look. There's an open terrace right down there."

"The gardens aren't ready, nothing opens on this side."

"Can't we just break the glass?"

The harper shook his head, looking back the way they'd come. "It's specially made. Almost a quarter inch thick. If you could break it, we wouldn't need to. Hang on."

Grinning suddenly, he sidled between the counters, flipping up canvas covers, scanning as he went: sheet music, guitar strings, harmonicas, pan pipes; *Teach Yourself the Harp, the Pianoforte, the Violin*; plaster busts of Bach and Beethoven.

"Is this really the time for souvenirs?"

"Come on, come on," Ben muttered. "Be here. Yes!" A simple museum display case, a wooden table with a class top held pitch pipes, tortoise shell guitar picks, and a cribbage board shaped like a mountain dulcimer, plus exactly what he needed.

"Damn it!" he hissed, rattling the locked case.

"Here," said the fae at his side, not even questioning. "Lift when I say go."

A shove and a smart twist. Lift. The lid came up like the top of a school desk, no magic spent.

"Yes! And yes, a tuning fork! Christmas!"

Ben sighed happily, and rapped the tool on the edge of the wooden case. Just a second or two to let the overtones settle out, and there it was, the pure, clear concert A soaring across every other note in the hall. "A reliable marker, just in case."

The raven boy's heart leapt to meet it, but one note is not a song. In his current state, he could no more use one note alone, no matter how perfect, than he could fly. But he could stash it away, let the Raven within add it to the gathering lights. It would be useful soon, maybe, but not yet. For now, he reached into the case and picked out a shiny toy for himself.

A voice from below rang out.

"They're up here!"

"Shit."

Well, Raven thought, his head might still be cloudy, but the path ahead was clear enough, and he hadn't led anyone a merry chase in ages. Hard boots were pounding up the stairs they had used themselves, four sturdy men with billy clubs and attitudes bore down on them, clearly looking to break some heads.

A weird, uncanny smile spread across the ageless features, betraying a mood like Peter Pan, excited and wild. Himself again, in other words, or nearly so.

"Come on!"

They paused only to overturn as many display cases as possible into the walkway behind them, and another for good measure. Tuning forks and all the rest bounced and rang against the boards setting up an echoing hum, almost a feedback, that stalled and confused the pursuers for a minute or so.

Keeping to the less direct but less obvious path, they ran for the next section.

"Textiles." Ben called out their location from memory, confirmed by the colorful stacks of knitting yarns, silk scarves, bolts of tartans, and carpets and whatever else they could fling behind them. From the cursing and irregular thudding in the distance, a six-foot roll of silk brocade was the ideal road block.

"Manchester Court: Glass and Ceramics."

Gleefully zigzagging through the department, Raven plucked up a stack of blue willow soup bowls and every few feet turned to send one sailing into the troops behind, calling his shots.

"Shoulder! Elbow! Kneecap! Kneecap... damn! Sorry, constable!"

"Good thing they're not armed."

"Except for the batons."

"Lenses, Optics, Cameras."

"Ha! Special effects!" Raven hooted with delight at the prospect, but had to be disappointed.

Somehow all the jasperware and blue flow ornaments of Manchester had transitioned into housewares and prepared foods—gutta-percha buckets and Pear's soap, jars of pickles and apple-peeling machines. The anticipated reading glasses, stereopticons, telescopes of Messers Negretti and Zambra, Opticians, had evidently been removed to the shop at ground level. All Raven could find to throw was a few fringed cushions expertly aimed and a tin of Coleman's mustard. *Greetings from the Crystal Palace.*

"Next?" he said.

"Great Transept. Decision time. Stairs down or go around?" Except there was no stair where Ben expected. "Damn it."

He stood staring over the edge in dismay as Raven joined him. The diary had never failed him before, but this time it appeared the map was out of date. The Opticians' shop took up the space meant for stairs on this side of the transept, which forced the traveller to go back or continue around. The gallery wrapped around the outer walls, which would send them down into the viewing area at the far end of the massive corridor and back again before descent was possible.

"Can you jump?" said Raven.

Ben stared back at him. "Are you nuts? It's like a three-story drop!"

"I'll catch you!"

"You won't."

"Oh, Ben, where's your sense of adventure?"

It was not a happy face.

"In a box at home with my discretion and my common sense. Which way?"

Peering over the edge while gingerly avoiding contact with it, Raven assessed the pattern, drew reluctant conclusions. Satisfied, he stepped back and whipped off the beautifully tailored coat. He laid it doubled across the iron rail, looked up through the layers of ceiling, and broke out a wild grin.

A milk-pale moon was already riding high in a clearing sky. He blew her a kiss with a whispered hope, put his hands to the rail, and vaulted over the side.

Ben watched his friend land lightly, then turn and throw a gesture up, urging haste. A deep breath, a thought of home, and he followed if not quite so dramatically

Someone shouted. Voices consulted. Feet turned to go back while the rest of the posse stared into the shadows that flooded the ground floor.

Screened from view by a dense hedge of ficus and juniper, and grinning like an idiot, Raven monitored what he could hear of pursuit as he watched his friend drop from gallery to false rooftop and clamber down the opticians' decorated façade. Lattice work to hang on to, an x-frame to stand on, another short drop, then only a few feet of sliding along the plasterwork over the door. Foot here, hand there, heart pounding a little and breath coming fast, but never hesitating, seldom misjudging the next step.

He sometimes forgot just how much courage was there, and what the king had seen in Ben Harper, which he himself had dismissed at first. More than just a gifted musician, certainly more than the efficiency expert he'd been, he was bolder and more graceful, too.

Now one last move found the right handholds, the harper swung down and dropped the last five feet. If the landing wasn't perfect, he could blame the fancy shoes.

"I always forget about the Dick Daring parts of this job." Ben slapped the blood back into his hands. "Anything?"

Raven's grin twitched a little. He looked aside, his own hands still burning from the iron rail. If he'd had to climb, he might as well have fallen. The beautiful coat hadn't helped much, and now he stood here with the brilliant white sleeves of a dress shirt gleaming like a beacon in the half-light.

"Not yet. Everyone seems to have turned around or passed us by. Cray and the witch are still out there somewhere, too. Any other time, I could... Never mind. Those boys will be going door to door in a minute. Where are the exits?"

"According to the map," Ben said, almost without thinking, "except for the railway access, they're only on the north side, or all the way back the other side of Adventure-land."

"My favorite part of the park. Let's go, then."

They each put a hand to the rattling ficus on either side, and peered out carefully. "We still have to do a broken field run across that bloody football field out there in the dark, without running into..."

Ben stopped, listening. Into the crowded silence a voice clear as daylight dropped on them from above. "I've got 'em! Over here, Sargent! You're under arrest, you two."

Both heads turned up to the gallery they'd just abandoned.

"Oh, we are not," Ben shot back in disgust, turned, and slipped away.

Before the man could react, Raven reached into his pocket, pulled out something small and hard, a souvenir of the Crystal Palace he'd pocketed above.

"I say!" he shouted, then cocked his arm and threw.

The sharp corner of a pocket harmonica popped the fellow square between the eyes. He yelled and fell away.

His power might be low but his other skills were schoolboy sharp. Grinning, he followed Harper out of the passageway into a picture gallery still devoid of pictures.

Barely slowing they dived into the Sargasso Sea of the central transept, dodging the sculptural wonders of France and Italy faithfully copied for the improvement of the masses. Ghostly white on polished stone plinths, some delicate, some colossal, all appeared to float unaided in the darkened transept.

The vast lobby was filled with moonlight, and the Palace took it all in like a night garden. Then someone found the lanterns, and the place lit up like Christmas.

"I see 'em!"

"Crap!" Ben gasped, slamming into the statue of *Psyche Borne Up by Zephyrs.* "What happened to the look-away?"

Hissing with annoyance, Raven turned back in the shadow of an equestrian figure of Richard the Lion Heart to stare back down the nave.

"I don't know if it will work at this distance. I'm beginning to appreciate the size of the hall. Wait!"

He could make out the lump of constables, but the shouting had stopped, the lanterns halted their advance.

"What is the matter, gentlemen?" said a smoothly composed voice, and Ambrose Cray stepped into a slanting beam of moonlight, holding a pistol. "Are you lost?"

"They don't know," Perdita wheezed from somewhere very close, "whether to be more afraid of the police or me."

The two men exchanged glances, minds racing, but said nothing. Ben started to raise his hands, but Raven went for an air of studied nonchalance. If he'd still had a hat, he'd have tipped it back. He settled for loosening his tie.

"I'm afraid I'm not afraid of either of you, y'see."

"Shall I show them, my love?" Cray pulled back the cock and raised his pistol to Raven's head.

"Oh no, no, no, not that one, Puppy, dear. I have something special for the faery. A gift from his mother. The man is nothing, though."

Ben lifted an eyebrow along with his hands as the barrel swung over his heart. Raven shifted his weight back and gave in to an enormous yawn.

"How nice, Perdita. A little yappy dog for company in your old age."

"How dare you!" the former scientist hissed.

Raven ignored him. "Oh I see, he's the gingham dog! Then you must be the calico cat who side by side on the table sat. No, wait, that hasn't been written yet."

"Shut up!"

"I don't suppose he's house-trained."

"I said shut your bloody mouth!"

Teeth clenched, even the pretense of refinement fled. The back of a closed fist smashed across the boy's mouth. It rocked his head around, but Raven stood his ground. When he beamed his most adorable smile, he felt a trickle of blood sketch a silver thread from the corner of his mouth, but no matter.

"Now that's the face of apoplexy that I remember," Raven said, beaming, "from, what, an hour ago? Bulging eyes, inarticulate rage. All for your coy mistress. Only, you cocked it up, didn't you? And now I've unmade your mirror."

"It's all right, Puppy," the creaking voice cackled, pushing in short bursts to maintain its strength. "He'll be sorrier, soon. But you miscall me, faery. I am a proper Englishwoman now. You must call me Mrs Cray."

Ben snorted and looked away, while Raven went on, sliding into a vulgar register.

"Do I understand this correctly? You seduced this buffoon into killing for you, but instead of being drawn into his time, he stepped into wherever you were. You trained him, even gave him the spell that made you immortal—and got it right this time, though still unable to reverse your own sad mess. Ooh, my dear, that must just keep you awake nights!"

"Clever child. I saw you behind my dear Puppy on that day. Today. And tonight I will put an end to your meddling."

"And all you had to do was wait, travelling into the future as most humans do, one dreary day at a time."

"I have always hated waiting, faery child, but I have made the best of it. Puppy, however, is such an impatient fellow. You shattered his looking glass, he blames you for his errors. He thanks me for his immortality. We are…"

Swathed in velvet, a trembling claw that must be her hand extended from behind the pedestal. Without glancing away, her lover raised that hand to his lips, and said smoothly, "Inseparable."

The hand retracted but the lisping challenge went on. "Now he hardly knows whether he wants you to die slowly or all at once, he has waited so long."

There were noises at the southern entrance again, rattling and banging on the glass walls. Ben cleared his throat, but Raven wasn't done.

"Best make up Puppy's mind for him, missus, you'll lose your chance. The rozzers are practically on top of us now."

Oh, she didn't like that much, he could feel it. Her power must have limits, too, in this decrepit state. How she must hate winter with its long, terrible nights.

"They'll see you exactly when I want them too, or not at all, stupid boy! Did your master teach you nothing?"

"More'n he taught you, from what I hear," said Raven. "Little lost witch."

With an eye on Raven, Ben dared to add, "Lunatic."

"*Tone deaf* lunatic."

"Tone deaf lunatic serial killer."

The boy's eyes snapped with mischief. "Old woman."

"Be silent!" she shrieked.

So they were. And so were all the other voices. Which gave Raven a moment to feel for his tiny little horde of power and wish there were more. The binding on that damned cloud was humming again, and he was not yet whole enough to break it. What was missing?

He wanted rather badly to see how Ben was managing, compliment his wit, share the joke before the world ended. But holding Cray's attention on himself was, he thought, keeping Ben from getting killed 150 years before he was born, and that had to take priority.

Then into the moonlit stillness floated three clear notes played on some kind of flute. The three unadorned notes of a C-major chord. He waited for the fourth to cap it, but no, that was all. Enough. And in tune. When had she ever been in tune?

When the last vibration died, a ball of thin red light floated up from where she sat alone behind the Lion Heart, casting a feeble glow.

"That's it?" he said mildly. "But this is a child's exercise, a toy. My friend's son..."

He bit down on the rest. Yes, Ben's son Sparrow had learned the basic principles in an afternoon last summer, but he wasn't here to chat.

"Is it?" said the witch. "I do not think so."

The trick, as Raven knew, was that the ball gathered energy out of the air. You had to keep ahead of it, gathering as it grew if you didn't want to burn the house down. He'd started his own share of fires in the green woods of his youth. But once you nailed this one, you had the first element of many things, including the lightning he had used to destroy the Aztec mirror; including, come to think of it...

Oh.

In the milliseconds it took him to remember, the thing had grown to the size of a tennis ball. Light as a soap bubble, it started to float away. Distracted, Cray broke eye contact to follow it.

The floating ball was hovering almost at Ben's nose, spinning itself into a disk, winking with gold and blue like a Catherine wheel. The harper went a little cross-eyed trying to keep an eye on it, then just turned his head away, whispering his wife's name and an apology.

A flare, a whine, and a sharp syllable.

Raven shouted, "No!"

The disk roared past Ben and down the nave to where the searchers still huddled together in terror. The explosion rocked the Palace as if the earth had moved under it. A man's disbelieving scream broke off with a crack Raven recognized, and he trembled.

Perdita, though, clapped her hands like a little girl. Bitter scents sailed back to them with random sparks flickering a poisonous green, and winked out leaving a strong smell of salt. Her own power might be diminished in the long winter nights, but she had brought Titania's with her.

Ben coughed weakly, and turned to meet his eyes. The boy in his pride lifted his chin, suddenly feeling very young. This was the queen's handiwork. At least this time, he thought he knew why.

The witched cackled.

"I see, oh yes! She said you would remember! Puppy, you idiot."

They swung about to find Ambrose Cray in a heap behind them. A crack, a ragged sigh, and a thud like a pile of laundry slumping to the floor, and the empty wheeled chair spun backwards into view.

A pleasantly Irish voice said, "Will one of you remarkable fellows remind me what it is that goeth before a fall?"

"Monologing?" Ben suggested, deeply relieved, as he moved to steady Raven who was not, after all, collapsing. Remarkably, the boy tugged the handsome waistcoat straight and raised an eyebrow.

"I believe Mr Donovan is thinking of pride, though I don't know whether he means these two, or me."

Raven took a knee beside Cray's motionless body, touched the pulse, and sat back shaking his head.

"Alive."

From the sound of things, what was left of their pursuers were picking themselves up, having found themselves back at the starting point—whether of their own will or Perdita's, he couldn't say. Soon enough, they would find their feet and their anger.

They had just witnessed an impossible thing, some of them for the second time in an hour. Now they weren't just angry, they were afraid. And every atheist, trades-unionist, and bomb-throwing anarchist from here to Assyria was about to get what was coming to them.

"Time to go, gentlemen," the boy said already wrapping himself in gloom. "And no dawdling. I believe they've been set back a bit. We can't waste the gift. Mr Donovan, my debt to you continues to mount. Now go home."

"Wait! Where's that pistol?" said Ben.

Donovan pulled the gun from his coat pocket. "I lifted it when I set him down. The man has no head at all. It's safe enough now."

"Leave it," Raven snapped. "Or get rid of it."

"But man, it's a Colt revolver!"

"Worse, still. For everything you love, human child, toss it in the sea, but do not keep it. It's not for you. Now, come on."

Jaw tight, he faded into the forest of medieval and Renaissance sculpture, Cellini's *Nymph*, Donatello's *St George*, heroes and saints and martyrs with their gridirons, virgins with their dogs. His senses as reliable as ever, all they had to do was tread lightly and follow.

"So, what was all that about your mother?" the reporter asked as soon as he dared.

"And the Artful Dodger routine?" added Ben, softly.

The King's Raven shook his head in despair.

"In order? No idea. I loved Jack Wilde. And I thought I told you to go home, Mr Donovan."

Raven turned on the Irishman as they broke into the void between Ancient Egypt and the Elizabethans, the first of the Artistic courts. "We are very grateful for your help, but you must get out of here!"

"But, you sent for me!"

"This way," said the fae. "What do you mean I sent for you?"

"The sketchbook. You laid a charm on it, I guess."

"Did I?" Raven said, puzzled, listening to the sounds of the hall, the voice of the Raven within, and the London Irish lilt in his ear.

"Man, Susan's a grand artist, but even she can't make a picture move." As efficiently as possible, he told them about the last page. "If that's not a message, I don't know what is."

"You didn't bring her with you?" At the man's look of horror, Raven smiled, "No, of course not."

He thought for a moment, allowing himself a small feeling of hope between long strides. Sliding behind the next court, he let his gaze travel up with longing to the moon shining through the vaulted dome, inviting, promising safety. If only he could spread his wings. Wings he could feel straining under his shoulders.

"All right. Ben has a diary with similar properties. I don't suppose Susan drew me changing into a black bird?"

"No, but," Ned said thoughtfully.

"What?"

"There's one. When Mr Harper here brought you in from the wood, all wrapped in my coat and you're face all but hidden, nothing but shadows all round the eyes. It sounds mad, I know, but from one angle it looks like feathers."

The fae who hadn't yet made a false step, even crippled as he was, stumbled into the barrier surrounding a knightly sarcophagus, and came to a halt.

"Feathers." A slow smile curved up the mobile mouth, till he very nearly laughed as the last piece fell into place. "And that's the real reason he's here, our illustrative journalist. Feathers!"

Ben gave a short nod, not understanding but willing to go along. The man really had to get out of here before he got arrested as an accessory or blasted into dust.

Out in the nave and much too close, an authoritative voice yelled, "Spread out, all of you. Open every door. There's no need to rush when they've no place to run. No need to be over-nice when you find them, either!"

More shouting. A glow of lanterns sputtering into life one by one and being hung up from cross beams. And creeping into all their bones, a growing cold.

They might look like Keystone Cops, but by the change in tone he could tell reinforcements had arrived, probably the Metropolitan Police, and after all, a man was dead. Two men, as far as the coppers knew, including one of their own. Their Christmases ruined, a comrade killed, they would hunt door to door like wolves, flinging aside curtains and throwing down screens. Hobnail boots banged across the galleries above, stumbling and swearing in the iron dark. Some brave souls had even ventured up to the third gallery, a narrow observation deck barely wide enough for two men to walk abreast, but giving a grand view.

Raven picked up the pace; still doing what he could to make them invisible, but not interested in anything except getting out. By the time they stood at the arches between gothic England and old Byzantium, they had come most of the length of the nave, nearly back to the Conservatory. Out in the central transept, the clock struck half-past four.

"Ben?" said Raven across the Black Prince's tomb. "You realize we're running out of cover. And I can leap that reflecting pool in a single bound, but you can't. Nor, I think, can our friend here. There must be a delivery entrance or something? Ned?"

"Paxton's tunnel, you mean. Staircase 2 takes you all the way down. There's a tunnel takes you out by the Queen's suite."

"No!" Ben was shaking his head soberly. "It's all machines down there. Printing press, drill press, McCormick reapers, even a locomotive engine or two. Full sized, fully functional, cold black iron. It will kill you, more surely than any spell of the Queen's."

"I was afraid of that. But there's your way out, Donovan. No arguments."

The man said nothing else so Ben went on.

"Options," he said, counting them off. "We can stay under cover, which means we cross the nave now and take the long way around, or we can dare the straight run through the sphinxes and hope for the best. Either way, it's going to be dark."

"Straight run," Raven said at once.

"The north doors, you mean?" asked Donovan, "Locked already."

The boy waved away the objection. "I laugh in the face of locks."

"You laugh at everything," said Ben. "People are trying to kill us, you know. It's a lot of open space."

"You'll be wanting a diversion of some sort, then," said Donovan.

Two pairs of eyes turned to the Irishman, whose resolve had not wavered. But Raven shook his head, "No, human child, you've already done what you were meant to do here. Whatever cover I can give, you must use it."

Hard-eyed, the reporter said, "I am not running. Put me to work."

Then the phone in Ben's pocket went off, buzzing like a hornet.

"Sweet Jesus!"

"Damn it! Now?" Ben scrambled to grab the mobile out of all the other crap in his coat pocket, while Raven put a hand on Ned's shoulder and took him aside, clearly stifling an urgent desire to laugh.

"Not a good time, sir! What? Uhm, hang on." He moved the phone long enough to wave Raven on. "Two minutes, tops. Donovan, go home and marry that girl. And thanks!"

Raven nodded, and rolled away taking his fae glimmer and the reporter with him.

"Here's where it gets exciting, Ned."

iv

One note, the king had asked for. Just one good note, not a whole song. But in the explosions and light shows and running in the dark, even Ben with his gifts felt no more confident of his music than did the ailing Oberon.

Then out of the jumble of images rattling his mind, one bright one sorted out and dropped into his hands, and made him smile. Grim though the day had been, the king of Faerie needed an A, and Ben Harper just happened to have one in his pocket.

"We have the technology," he murmured as the right tool came into the workman's hand. "Here it comes, sir."

Holding the steel handle just so, he struck the tuning fork on the Black Prince's golden helm. Within seconds that pure concert A rang sweetly through the chamber. Then he took a breath and sang it, soft and clear and perfect, into the phone.

"Now I've really got to go, sir!" he said.

"Thank you," said Oberon quietly. "And Ben? Be swift."

All was not well in his own time, that was clear, but at least the ripples had not yet reached Christmas Eve of 1854.

Or so he hoped. Be swift? That was his goal. But once they reached the terrace and the snow, what then?

The key over his heart, when he listened for its voice, babbled cheerfully but said nothing useful. He still needed those nine notes and a place to go. His music had never failed him in all his service to the king. What if… He sucked down a sudden rush of panic.

"Stop it," he snarled, and fixed his mind again on the task at hand.

He had heard but not noted anything after Raven left. A lot of things can happen in two minutes. Carefully he peered around the saint-rimmed doorway of Rochester Cathedral to look across the back end of the fountain pool, its surface as still and black now as an Aztec mirror.

Beyond it, a thousand miles away, or maybe only fifty exposed yards, the laced and fretted tiles and pudgy lions of the Alhambra, at once the mightiest and most graceful castle of medieval Granada. Off to the right, that far away again, almost invisible in four hundred feet of glass, three doors gave on to an icy terrace. But not, apparently, a single soul to stop him.

Out of nowhere, pain shot through Ben's head as if he'd taken a blow. Over the building pressure, he thought he heard a cracked voice bark a string of words in a strange language. The reptile back-brain took over without consultation, and he tucked in his head and rolled away, eyes tight as a pulse of white light lit up every shadow. Men cried out for their seared eyes, and much too close, the sound of a painted ceiling giving way to a falling body. There was no explosion, though windows rattled, and he could hear a crash of tinkling glass fallen from a height.

Ben sensed it wasn't the same spell that had killed the constable; more general, less personal, careless of what damage it did so long as it was messy. Either way, the witch and her minion were at large. In the silence that followed, Ben could only hope he hadn't delayed too long.

He took the long way, just in case.

Maggie Secara

44

It hath a dying fall, Christmas Eve, 1854

He found Raven waiting for him under a shaft of moonlight just inside the Assyrian Court, eyes bright and a little manic, leaning back against one of the gigantic winged bulls. Otherwise, the place stood silent, haunted only by its long dead kings in their chariots and the tales of their glories in arrow-headed cuneiform on the walls.

The fae bounced forward eagerly, indulging Ben in a rare embrace filled with warmth. "You're still with me, I'm glad to see."

"Too late to bug out now," Ben said with a grin.

"And the king?"

"Not well, though of course he didn't say exactly. Any trouble here?"

"Just getting Donovan to go home. I had to drop him down the staircase myself—no, not like that. You were right, I couldn't get close enough. But I gave him what glamour I could spare to keep him safe." As he had just done for his friend, transferring what he could with his touch.

"I don't suppose he's really gone."

Raven snorted lightly and left it at that.

"Come along."

They slipped under the crimson columns with the bull-headed capitals, passed beneath the gimlet eye of a pair of winged bulls with warriors' heads. Ben gasped, then almost laughed at a staring giant when it loomed out of the dark, strangling a lion with thick-fingered hands. In the main room, four massive pillars, a tall case of glass bowls and ornaments of gold, enamel, mother of pearl. And no one calling a challenge. No tingle of twisted magic.

"Where is she?" he whispered, but Raven only shrugged.

The side chambers led back to the nave, contrary to the notes in the diary. But in the back, a pair of colossal winged lions loomed out of the dark, and the passage between them dropped the boys into a seating area under a pink and white sign reading "Ices and Sweets". Crossing in front of it brought them straight to a passage along the northernmost wall. The one with the doors in it.

A gas lamp that glowed in the avenue above them cast dim golden circles over the snowy curbs, but the building's terrace and drive lay quite dark under the moon and stars.

Raven hovered as near as he dared to the wall, registering the poison radiating from the iron frames, reaching for the hoarded power to withstand it. There were wooden doors—six of them, widely spaced, not three as the map said—each hung with a chain locked over a single bar.

In their midst, standing watch like the blue-maned lions of Assyria, the copper who had thrown them out of the Conservatory so firmly. Alone and grim, the last Spartan at the gates of Thermopylae frowning into the shadows, he might have been just another of a thousand statues, but for the steady beat of a nightstick smacking the flat of a beefy hand.

Turning to Ben, Raven gave a few quick instructions. The harper nodded and went quickly back the way they'd come while the fae retreated to the shadowed corridor.

A minute later or maybe two, Ben reappeared, approaching with care from the opposite side, sandy hair a-glimmer in a wash of moonlight. The fae held his breath as the guard's searching eyes scanned right across Ben's position, and slid away seeing nothing untoward. In the deathly silence, he could hear the floor boards give and release under his friend's careful steps, and one thing more. The labored squeal of a bath chair's iron shod wheels. It was time.

Grinning like Peter Pan, he sauntered out to the nearest of the doors and called his challenge down the wall, almost dancing with excitement.

"Still don't know who I am, do you, constable!"

The man's head snapped around, eyes narrowed, recognizing him at once even hatless and in shirtsleeves.

"You!" he shouted, and took a step. Behind him, Ben moved into position.

"But it's not me you want. I swear it!"

"Is that so, your lordship? And what about all them men you killed today? An' the poor old professor?"

With no patience for banter, the man was quicker than he looked. But Raven was a lord of Faerie, and the cop only one middle-aged man. The fae lord already had his hands on the locking bar and his will focused on the power he'd been gathering for the best part of two hours, even conjuring back the lone note Ben had given him. Time lengthened, the charm assembled, and set. Not with the first thought but with the second, he brought that charm to bear and in a single heartbeat the bar, chain, and locks on every door dissolved into airy nothing.

When time caught up, the man was staring not at him but at the couple approaching at a steady, inexorable pace like some strange automata.

"Constable, you can't stay here," Ben cried in horror.

"Ben, now!"

"Constable!"

With one move they flung wide the doors into a frigid night breeze dashing across the snow. Raven, free at last, broke left with a run and a hop, tumbling like an acrobat as if he had no weight at all.

Moonlight showed Ben too little, his eyes too slow to adjust. The stylish but useless leather boots slipped under him and sent him sprawling, sliding toward a drop he knew was there but couldn't see. He flung out his arms hoping to grab a baluster or something, when a massive weight slammed into him out of the dark, and a deep voice said, "No, you don't!"

A second later Ben and Donovan spilled together over the slope of snow-filled steps. A little voice in both their ears whispered, *Heads down!* Ben dug fingers into the snow and ducked.

Deep in the building, Perdita's broken voice screamed out her curse. Lightning flared, lit up the building like a beacon, and the doors exploded. Glass and iron spat outward bearing death across the carriage drive, battering the water tower, clattering on the roof of the fire brigade, as far as the frozen surface of Paxton's reservoir.

The thick glass panes above the doors, each row carefully depending on another, trembled, cracked, shivered. As the music hovers breathless in the orchestra eager for the downbeat, the central panels of the shining wall hung suspended in place for a second, then two, then with a sigh, a thousand million crystalline shards surrendered to gravity and plunged like daggers to the ground, and fountained up, a fantasy of deadly rainbows. Clattering, chinking, chiming to the floor again, the tinkling sound hung on the air while faint echoes danced back into the nave. Then all was still.

It wasn't over yet, Raven knew in his hiding place, but he didn't care as he tumbled gaily across the terrace. He could breathe again!

Even with the iron monster at his back, he could feel the magic coursing through the earth beneath him, the swift currents of Father Thames and all his hidden daughters. He could even sense the stresses that the king's decline laid over them all. But he was free, and the smiling moon was in the sky, almost within reach. Laughing, he flung up his arms to embrace her and she, a doting mother, poured moonlight over him.

"Sweet Moon," he cried, "I thank thee for thy sunny beams!" Then he snorted, tickled at his own joke. Well, Shakespeare's joke, which tickled him even more. "For by thy gracious, golden, glittering gleams I'll trust to taste of... You'll see!"

Best of all, he knew exactly what to do, if he could get a free second to do it. One last thing.

While the raven boy revelled, Ben and Donovan were both scrambling to their feet. Before the reporter could say a word, Ben rounded on him and nearly knocked him down again.

"Just how crazy are you? Will you get out of here before she kills you like all the others!"

But the man was staring at Raven frolicking with a dozen ice fairies, chattering in their bird-like voices, more manic than the Irishman had ever seen anyone not in an asylum.

"What is he doing?"

The crunch of glass, the light squeak of an over-taxed wicker frame, and a painful wheezing meant she was there, silhouetted in the space where a wall had glittered. The boy looked over at his friends as if only just remembering them.

"Hush," he urged. "Go!" He shooed them away, blowing kisses, then leapt to the balustrade where he sat down at the feet of some noble Roman in a toga to watch his master's old girlfriend approach.

"What, still here, faery boy?" she said.

He laughed. "Where else should I be, thou sad old woman?"

"How should I be sad, boy, when I'm about to gain all?"

He chuckled lightly and shook his head.

"Shall I tell you? I remember this fellow, this Marcus Aurelius," Raven said cheerfully, delightfully, giving the statue a pat. "Very wise, for the human kind, he was. He always said the first rule is to keep an untroubled spirit. But you, poor hag, have not done that, have you? There art thou unhappy. That and in the other troubled spirit you keep as a pet."

"Am I unhappy, faery?"

"Oh, very. Just look at you. Oh, but there, you see? That's the second rule. The good emperor said, he said the second rule is to look things in the face and know them for what they are. And sorry as it is, I have looked at your face." He shuddered. "Ooh, you can't have done that in a while. And it's wicked through and through. There too art thou unhappy. And then, of course, the tattoos."

The witch's gasping laughter as she rolled to a halt had no humor in it, but each note of her ancient voice fractured the frozen air.

"Such a playful fairy child," she said. One of her shawls slithered clear of the hand that held the spell-bound knife made by better magic than her own. "I hope you don't mean to leave without your mother's gift."

Raven rocked back on his perch and cackled. "I can't imagine what she told you, the fair Titania. Because she—" He flipped into a quick handstand on the narrow balustrade. "Is not—" To one hand. "My mother!"

"I know what will slow down this mad Jack," Cray snarled. From somewhere, a pistol appeared in his hand.

"Now hadn't we got rid of that gun?" the boy admonished, shaking a fatherly finger at a bewildered Ned.

Always unimpressed by firearms, Raven cartwheeled to his feet again, walking back along the snow-heaped balustrade like a balance beam. "Must I stand very still? I fear I cannot stay, all in the pleasant open air, the pleasant light of day. You see, I have to talk to my friends, first. I shall be over here!"

The boy had set some lesser sprites to tease and distract—a lesser magic within his scope, with some help from Robert Herrick.

> Come, bring with a noise,
> My merry, merry boys,

Pixies sang in Cray's ear to make him jump. It came from the air, from the floor; even the glass shards in the broken framework found voices.

> The Christmas log to the firing;

Above their heads, behind her chair. Cray turned again, confused, and again.

> While my good Dame, she
> Bids ye all be free—

It bumped along the terrace into the snow-mounded gardens while the man twitched and trembled each time he swung his aim to meet the fae who each time was not there, until

And drink to your heart's desiring.

Cray brought the noise. A flash and thunder, he fired once into the empty dark. Fired and clipped a lamp post.

"Stand still, damn you!"

Having set his little folk to work Raven, quite calm, strolled to where Ben stood with Donovan shivering in the snow. He held out his hand. "You have something of mine, I believe."

Well, that remark met with a blank look.

"Sorry?"

"Come on, human child! You can't have forgotten. You've been using it as a bloody bookmark!"

Understanding washed over him. Ben patted his pockets until he pulled out the diary, from which he withdrew a long, shining black feather. "You can never just ask for what you want, can you."

It brushed the outstretched hand with a sprinkle of chiming notes and the Raven, taking it with a sigh, stepped back.

"Gentleman, stand aside if you please," he said, his eyes fixed on his missing piece. It had been here all along; he'd only forgotten how to remember it with his waking mind. But now…

Eyes glittering, Raven in starlight breathed gently across the feather until it began to glow with his own telltale radiance. Enchantment crackled in the air as it curled and shrank, faded and melted into his hand like a snowflake, restored at last. Within, the last remnant of the complex spell, meant to bind greater powers than his, vanished, and as it did released his music. All barriers dispersed in a jangle of chords that burst, roared and resolved at last into the harmony of mind and magic that was the King's Raven, shimmering on the night air.

At a sound, he looked up, laughing. Behind them, Cray shouted and fired. The report echoed across the sparsely populated neighborhood. Suburbs or not, the explosion had wakened dogs, and those had wakened sleepers and their servants, and messages had gone out, enquiries made. There would be letters to The Times in the morning. The fire brigade down the road was finally scrambling.

But for Raven, the dam had burst, the clouds ripped away, and he knew himself entire, the King's Raven of Faerie unique in all the worlds. When he brought up his head, he was singing, simply vocalizing up the tonic scale until some note of joy grabbed him and he burst into *Deck the Halls with Boughs of Holly*. He faced the witch and her deadly knife and just sang.

Cray's pistol roared again. Ben shouted, but too late. This time it caught the boy full in the chest, spinning him around right in the middle of the fa-la-las.

The American watched through disbelieving tears as, silver as mercury, fae blood blossomed across the handsome waistcoat. But as he watched, a second raven seemed to overlay the first. The fashionably dressed young lordling collapsed and disappeared even as the King's Raven sprang up into the night sky calling to the moon. It soared and tumbled and stretched its wings, powering over the horizon.

Perdita, bright eyed and eager, grasped the porcelain knife, calling up Titania's deadly gift, preserved and rehearsed through so many long years.

Compose your mind, the queen had said. You must rule your heart.

I am composed, Perdita had snapped.

Then get up. Try again! You must be ready.

"Damn you!" the witch growled. "I am ready."

Titania's gifts. The first, thrown away on an unplanned demonstration, had been meant only to remove the human companion, to leave the boy friendless. For the boy she had another, more terrible, the key to her desires.

Dainty as a tea cup, a spell rose as a green flicker on the knife edge where she held it, keeping back the last sharp syllable. She forced herself to stand, stepped from the chair, bringing her twisted form as upright as she could.

Lesson after lesson, what had she learned? What did she need to learn, she who had been taught by the king himself. The queen of Faerie was on her side. She had the spell and the will to use it.

She shrieked, "Come here to me!"

Gamboling a thousand feet up, barely visible to those below only by the moonlight glimmering on sable feathers, the Raven heard her and looked down, registered the irresistible glitter, and cheerfully dropped for the terrace.

Pointing with the knife in her outstretched hand, she tracked him as he came, leading the target as she had learned to do until he disappeared behind the bulk of the darkened Palace. When he reappeared, he called twice to be sure she knew where to look.

"Yes," she hissed.

The black bird was skimming the snowy surface, mirroring the rise and fall of every hillock and hump on the garden. Over the terrace itself, he came in low and slow, balanced on the span of the great wings. She would have him as he rose again.

Together, Ben and Donovan shouted, "No!"

The part of Raven's mind that was always a fae lord understood, and made his plan.

Eyes only on the black bird, she judged the moment, launched the spell as he committed to his trajectory, then fell exhausted into her chair. But it was Cray, angry Ambrose Cray who had never understood the magic, who missed the cue, and stepped in the way. Ambrose Cray who screamed just as Raven, as fast as thought, shifted away.

It was a spell designed to shred a lord of the great fae and spin the ragged atoms out of time, beyond all hope of rescue or return. It began by creating a vision of that fate from beginning to end, so that Cray saw in an instant what the rest had to watch unfold before them, and even unconsciousness was no release. Merely mortal, Cray's mind collapsed at once. He screamed, but not for long.

Skin and organs, teeth and tendons, even the fabric of his clothing began to swell, every molecule to wander away from every other. The bonds that held them softened and grew thready, attenuated, and began to part. The expanding human outline, bubbling with internal turmoil, quickly lost its shape. Growing toward transparency like a heaving balloon, it began to leave the ground.

Open-mouthed, Ben and the reporter stared in revulsion, tracking its rise. Even the witch was silent, following it narrow-eyed, and gripping the arm rests of her chair. She may have gasped when each trembling particle lit up as if with fire. Already way past his limit for horrors, the harper turned aside to be sick over the edge of the stair. Donovan—well, a reporter can look at anything, but his eyes were wide.

No longer remotely like a living man, it was a single-celled grotesque roiling around a cloudy nucleus of exploding stars red, blue, and green.

The breeze at the top of the ridge was a steady constant. As the cell expanded, its only bond a twisted vengeful magic, it should have caught the air and sailed down along the slope toward the river and the city. Yet almost as if a thread of consciousness somehow remained, it pressed instead toward Perdita, a puppy seeking a kind word. She shrank away from the leading edge, but it persisted. In disgust, she made to push it away.

Ben turned when her shriek broke the air. The bubble, he saw, had grazed her hand, and with that touch, compressed, dwindled to a milky swirl. The magic found its note and made it a bronze bell, and then a single crystal chime. Then it was gone.

The witch howled with pain and fury. Unable to rise unaided, she tried to bring herself about with the spell knife in her hands, but she had run out of time. In the moments before the fire bells began to clang up the hill, the unmistakable ratchet of a revolver's hammer being pulled back broke the air.

Ben watched Ned Donovan, poised and calm, take good aim and fire, and fire twice more. When the echoes died, the witch lay broken over the edge of the chair.

"I don't suppose it will do any good," the reporter said, slipping the Colt back into his pocket. "But it needed doing."

"Did we mention? She's immortal."

"Ah, well." Donovan shrugged. "Isn't that always the way."

"I don't suppose you'll be going home now?"

The reporter's face was strained, but his eyes were alight. "Of course not! Work to do, Mr Harper. Look at all this! Policemen murdered, fire brigade on the way. Untold damage. Can't you see the headlines? Unexplained Christmas Eve Explosion at the Crystal Palace. Story by Edward Donovan, first on the scene."

"Illustrations by a new kid? One S. Pickering, maybe?" Ben smiled. He held out his hand to Donovan, who shook it warmly.

"I'll do my best."

"And the rest of the story? The more, hmm, uncanny parts?"

Laughing, Donovan buttoned up his top coat and found his hat. "Bomb-throwing anarchists! I'm sure that's it."

"I look forward to reading it."

Now, where the hell was Raven?

The smallest demi-quaver of Titania's bitter spell had grazed the uttermost tip of a single feather as he flung himself away, but it was enough to send Raven hurtling through the gates of time. To his endless relief, he found he was both conscious and all in one piece even as he tumbled to a stop, a gorgeous blue-eyed stranger, on the beach at Ipanema.

In 1966.

In the middle of a *bossa nova* party.

Without a thing to wear.

Cooing like brightly colored doves, a number of very pretty girls in very small bikinis ran to help and oh, that was almost heaven. Especially when the *caipirinha* started flowing.

But he knew he couldn't stay. Blowing kisses, promising to be right back, he ran off down the beach. Moments later, he was powering toward Sydenham on Christmas Eve in 1854, and his song blew aside the clinging veils of time and space with effortless ease.

Exhausted and getting frantic while the various auth-orities swarmed over the site, Ben became aware that no one except the snow fairies seemed to notice him hugging himself and stamping his feet for warmth, and of course they thought that was hysterical. He still wasn't sure exactly what had just happened, and certainly didn't want to be questioned about it, so he was grateful for the neglect, all in all.

Then a rattle of coal black wings, the glint in a sapphire eye, and a cheerfully vulgar expression. Twice.

"You talk to your king with that mouth?" said Ben Harper.

The hooked beak bobbed, cackling, the light shifted and Raven, perfectly appointed in black jerkin, ruffled shirt, and jeans, was standing right there with black curls long on his shoulders, and a pair of golden loops gleaming in one ear.

Grinning they started walking and, on nine joyful notes, they sang the iron world behind them.

Fa-la-la-la-la la-la la-la!

45

Freihaus Wiednertheater, Vienna, 1791

Der Hölle Rache kocht in meinem Herzen
Hell's vengeance boils in my heart;
Death and despair blaze around me!
If he feels not Death's pain at your hand,
Then be my daughter never more.
Disowned forever be,
Forsaken forever be,
Shattered forever be
All bonds of nature
If death's pallor takes him not because of you!
Hear, gods of vengeance, hear the mother's oath!
—W.A. Mozart, Die Zauberflöte

She was the Queen of the Night, staged against a vast screen of painted stars. In the week since stepping into final rehearsal at the *Freihaus*, Titania had made Josefa Hofer famous; already an extraordinary talent, her voice would be in Wolfgang's thoughts even at the moment, so they said, of his death. Perhaps she would call on dear Constanze Mozart then, just to see if it were true.

It had been a joy—it always was—but it was time to go and let Hofer enjoy her glory without interference. Just this one last night of applause and champagne, roses and oh! the most glorious music, then she would let it go. The mortal woman retained the queen's memories—her own memories, in truth—and all the pleasure of debuting this extraordinary music. Titania meant only to inspire, never to steal.

The next act began. Waiting for her cue while the slave Monostatos attempted to seduce the daughter, she felt through the layers of time, memory and surveillance, a part of her tied to events she had set in motion. Her music began.

Cue. She descended to the stage from the star-filled rafters, half her thought a hundred years away from the sparkling glory of Mozart.

Cue. London, between the Plague and the Fire. In the shimmering glory of the Queen of Faerie, she explains to the witch, once the whore stops trembling, that the raven boy's death is the price of her return to Oberon's realm. The raven was part of the binding spell, she said. If he dies, it will end.

It is not a lie, but a special kind of truth. With Raven gone for all time, the spell ends unbroken and unbreakable. With the boy gone, Faerie can never be breached. Oberon will be safe, and the world with him.

She placed the dagger in Pamina's hand, showed her how to hold it, what to do with it, how to kill the priest of Isis who held her prisoner.

She places the dagger in Perdita's hand, sings the spells into place for her, and tries to train that awkward voice to just this once be true. Offers a suggestion, and a flute with three notes.

Cue: In a voice that pulled the stars down with her fury, the Queen of the Night's aria floated to the tessitura's high F with harsh grace. "Hear, gods of vengeance, hear the mother's oath!"

Cue: The Crystal Palace. Across time, she can feel the rage and power growing, she hears Perdita's vengeance bound with her own. She could not have hoped for a more perfect moment. All the fire of her passion compressed and controlled into the aria will pulse through the threads connecting them, fuel the spell when the whore casts it and take the faithless boy out of time forever. She exults when it launches. Cries out when it fails, all that power wasted on a ridiculous mortal.

"No!"

The audience exploded to its feet, never even hearing the very last and less than perfect note. Herr Nouseul, as Monostatos, had to hold his pose over Fräulein Gottlieb's cowering form while Fräulein Hofer, breathing harder than she remembered ever doing, stepped to the edge of the stage to receive their adulation and applause.

Somewhere, Josefa found a smile, blew kisses, curtseyed deeply, then raised gentle hands to quiet and settle them, and beg the audience let them continue. A hand on her pounding heart, she curtsied one last time and resumed her place. She nodded to the conductor, but before she could take the downbeat, Titania was half way to Faerie.

46
Home—Diamond Cottage, Dartmoor, UK

*They started at once, and went about among the
Lotus-eaters, who did them no hurt, but gave them
to eat of the lotus, which was so delicious that those
who ate of it left off caring about home, and did not
even want to go back and say what had happened to
them...*
—from The Odyssey, trans. Samuel Butler

The fragrance of hot beef a perfume on the air; the crackle and
pop of chipped potatoes hitting hot fat; an awareness of home.
Though he sang with gusto, the last veil parted reluctantly to
Ben Harper's command. Darkness followed after, but no
dreams.

Some hours later, one eye opened on a silver-grey world
not at once familiar, but no one was trying to kill him or, as far
as he could tell, blow anything up.

Both eyes, now. World still grey, but with some open
beamed detail. Ah, the ceiling. Other sensations began to
assemble. Nerves fired off random twitches in legs that had
done too much running, climbing, falling in too short a time,
too long out of practice. Fingers which no longer, Ben noted
thankfully, stung with cold, pressed the somewhat threadbare
surface of a battered but serviceable sofa. Out of the air but
quite nearby, the sprightly ripples of *Bransle Gai,* played
swiftly and well on his long-suffering Gibson under the

distinctive fingering—he would have sworn—of John Renbourn. Since he hadn't seen John in a couple of years, either he was dreaming pleasantly or it was time to turn his head and assess the situation more directly.

He blinked, twice. The pale grey light came from the picture-window wall of his office, shutters open on a solid Dartmoor mist. The tumble of black curls, the long-fingered hands dancing across the strings belonged to Raven, which came as a mild surprise; he'd never seen the boy pick up anything but a tin whistle or his own glorious voice. Ben put his feet to the floor just as a flurry of notes resolved the medieval dance tune, and the fae lordling tipped up an expression remote and alien, lost in the music. Then the glittering eyes, the charming face relaxed and opened into a broad smile.

"You're looking better."

"That's good, considering I feel like crap."

The kid hopped down from the desk and handed Ben the guitar. His first guitar. It had come with him through every move and change of fortune. Last summer when it was damaged almost beyond repair, Oberon's people had returned it to him a few days later, whole and sound, with none of its temper lost and a wonderful inclination to stay in tune. It was good to feel it in his hands, something of his own, after so much terror and strife.

"I didn't know you played." The blunt tipped fingers strayed across the strings, touching a note, fingering a change, a harmonic. "And after listening to you, I may never play this thing again."

The left wrist curved; fingers flexed across the strings. An open G chord fell out of his right hand. He let the resonance die on its own, then he set the guitar aside.

"There's food for you," said Raven, grinning.

"I love magic," Ben said with feeling. On the work table facing the desk, the steak sandwich of his dreams, tangy coleslaw, and a pile of chips, still fragrant and sizzling as if they'd just come from the oil. On a real plate. With a cloth napkin. And oh, dear god, "Coffee!"

"And a change of clothes laid out. Brownie Meg was yawning mightily but she made your tea, when I asked her to. Then she sniffed and said she didn't mind the world slippin' away s'much, if them teller-phones 'd fall t'sleep as well."

This last given, grinning, in the brownie's own Devonshire brogue, around a finger full of honey.

"Phone?"

"I think it's a suggestion to call your lady wife."

"Any messages?"

"None. From anyone." When his friend looked doubtful, Raven added, "It's worse than we expected, Ben. I've been on the computer for more than an hour. The headline at the *Guardian* hasn't changed since yesterday, the *Sun* since last week, if you can imagine. Even financial news is just a trickle. Some passions die harder than others, it is safe to say. Skype is down. Facebook's a ghost town. The trending topic on Twitter is hashtag just-fine. Systems are more or less working, but..."

He turned away, hiding his expression to gaze into the fog and the dying light behind it. "It's like no one's there. As if they have come to the Land of the Lotus-eaters with no thought for their return."

Frowning, Ben could sense the idleness creeping through the world, a low, stammering pulse that lurked out there in the mist. He could feel the nudge against his own consciousness: *why bother, what's the point, it doesn't matter, it will be fine.*

"How could this happen so fast?"

He had spoken to Raven's slender back, but the bleak voice from the window told him more than the words alone.

"The queen said it. The heart of Faerie is the heart of the world. And Faerie is dying."

"Now don't you start," Ben demanded.

The boy didn't answer but the meaning, Ben realized, was clear enough. They had the key but no lock to open, and the world was, as promised, going to hell. The time and so much else was running out. He was exhausted, his own edge dulled quite apart from the world's malaise. So he ate, showered and changed, clinging to his purpose for Mellis's sake. For Sparrow's.

Sick with apprehension, he made the call to California, and apparently woke Mellis too early to be coherent, which was very odd. A quick check told him it was almost eight in the morning, there in L.A. At home, she'd have been happily tormenting graduate piano students by now. Her news, delivered after much delay in a languid drawl utterly unlike her own voice, brought him to his feet.

"What do you mean you're staying in L.A.?"

"You're not angry?" Mellis drawled in a languid voice not at all her own. "Nobody is angry anymore, haven't you noticed? It's so peaceful."

"Mellis, honey, snap out of it!"

"Oh, Ben, don't fuss. I don't even know if we can travel. I think our flights have been cancelled."

"You think..." Fingers flew across the computer. Found her flight number in his calendar. Opened the airline's web page and scrolled, staring hard-eyed at the screen.

CANCELLED.

CANCELLED.

CANCELLED.

DELAYED.

Flight after flight showed grounded. It must have been the last responsible act of a scheduler who could no longer be bothered, taking pilots out of the air who felt no urge to fly. The last On Time confirmed was at least a week old. He couldn't even go to her, not even if it would help.

"Look at this," he breathed. He felt more than saw Raven's head come up, felt him move.

Mellis sighed, but not too heavily, contented as an angel.

"It's all right, love. Perry's kids have new puppies, so Sparrow wants to stay anyway. He's fine We're all perfectly fine."

His throat constricted, he managed to croak, "Sweetheart, are you stoned? Dr Mellisande Harper Powell, stop sighing and talk to me!"

The fae lord seeing his own fears in human shape just a few feet away, crossed the room feeling his soul swell and fill with every step. Closer to Ben, closer to the key still hanging around his neck. That meant the key had some power of its own, that was some hope.

"Ben!" Raven was at his shoulder, saying gently, "I don't think she can."

Firmly, he slipped the phone from Ben's trembling fingers and pressed *Speaker*. They could hear the woman breathing, the beloved, talented, passionate wife that Ben adored. Calmly, the fae said her name, but she seemed to have forgotten it. After awhile, the call dropped away. Ben, stricken, threw the mobile across the room, and put his head in his hands.

"Good," said Raven. "Your passions at least are intact. It's up to us, now. You have to be Ulysses, so she can come home, yes? Let us go and see the king."

47
Faerie in dreamtime

The king's great house in Faerie offers him no comfort. His Court is empty, his people withdrawn to their ancient strongholds prepared, it seems, to fade away. What has been by his will a long, pleasant summer morning now matches almost completely the dreariness of the commonplace world. The lawns between the embracing, translucent arms of the house are brittle and sere, except for the patch where his pavilion is set, and even that is sad and seedy. The light dims, colors retract, music fails.

Even the ghosts and monsters are failing. Old roads, abandoned houses, lonely moors are safer than they have been since men first came to the island of Britain, but no one cares. All fears, all doubts are quieted, along with joy and love. Even quarrels have become too much trouble. The world is at peace, but it is the peace of the sick room.

A numbing cold has claimed his whole right side and he can neither make music nor inspire it. Oberon sleeps now more often than he wakes. His strength remains in some part; it is the will to use it that slips hourly away. Some spark lingers and when occasionally it flares into life, he longs for his henchmen to call or come to him. He has set them a task, his two best men, though as time goes on—and he is subject more than ever to time, now—it becomes harder to remember what it was.

The little silver-strung harp rests beside him, but he is forgetting what it is for. Sleep is easier. Sleep, and fade away.

Which explains his surprise when he dreams a sprightly tune that he has not thought of since he gave it to a blind poet, oh, long and long ago. He smiles a little, stirred to pleasant recollection. When the tune ends, there is another touched with sadness and longing that reminds him of an ancient love and ancient loss, and he is moved within the dream almost to tears. Then quite without warning, the harp is still, and two pleasant voices he ought to know rattle off a filthy limerick.

"Ha! He twitched," says one.

"That should do it," says the other.

"Give us the one about the Peeler and the Goat," he says in a broad country accent, and opens one blue eye. Raven and Ben exchange a look and collapse on the brittle lawn with laughter. So he gives in and sits up, not the horned man nor the forest spirit, nor the king—just Aubrey.

Aubrey will do.

With a perceptible jerk like a train taking up slack, time asserted itself nudged by the presence of a mortal man in Faerie.

"Whoa!" Ben said, feeling the shift as a kind of burp. "Okay, that was weird."

"Have you brought what I sent you for?" said Aubrey.

There were clothes around here somewhere. Oh yes, thrown over an old milk crate upended at his feet. Indulging in the tediously physical, he forced himself to notice the sensations, the textures, the scent of silk, leather, velvet as he drew on stockings and trunk hose one leg at a time. Shirt. Jerkin. Without a word, Raven stepped up to lace and tie ribbon points at waist and sleeve, while Ben made idle music on the little harp.

"Just the key, your Grace, I'm sorry," the harper said. "Bit of a problem, though."

"We have no idea where to go next."

"When did you two start finishing each other's sentences?" Aubrey said under a tilted eyebrow.

The two exchanged a glance and said together, "Do we?"

He responded with a lazy smile.

"You should come with us, sir," Raven said casually. He knotted the last jewelled lace on his king's shoulder around a sprig of Susan Pickering's mistletoe to hold back the dark. Then he sat down cross-legged in the grass at the king's feet.

"Maybe next time. Just now..." Aubrey yawned and blinked, looking somewhat improved for their attentions. Did the air seem just slightly brighter than it had? "I fear I'd only bring the problem with me. Gentlemen, if I may ask— why are you here?"

"Honestly, sir, we've had a very long few days."

Aubrey looked down at Raven as if seeing him for the first time, and took his hand. "Everyone else is leaving. It's good to see you."

Abruptly, the music ceased.

"Sir," Ben said. "I don't think you understand. The key isn't leading us anywhere."

"What?" Aubrey chuckled lightly. "Must I say it again, Ben Harper? Follow your gift."

But Ben met the long eyes in sorrow. "It led us here, sir, back to you. You've hidden the lock very well. What if, well, what if it's in a world I can't see? Can't you just, you know, tell me?"

"He's right," said Raven, and nodded at the harper to keep playing. Ben's music always helped. "Tell us where to go, and what it looks like, we'll fetch it at once."

They waited on his pleasure while Aubrey sat on the edge of the cot and stared into the middle distance like an undergraduate just becoming acquainted with a hangover. He idly rubbed his chin, somewhat surprised to find it rough with a growth of beard he hadn't sported in centuries. No wonder the boys were staring. Eventually, he shook his head, the long tangled hair shifting on his shoulders.

"Hmm, no, apparently I can't. Hidden."

"But— Forgive me, sir, but that can't have been part of your plan when you made the thing and put it away."

"I think I left something with John Dee, didn't I, boy? Long ago. Or was it in Mycenae, under a sphinx? Theseus knew, once."

The younger men stared at each other, and Raven shrugged. "I don't know, sir," he said, "but we can check."

He was awake now, more or less, and thinking, and that was probably a good thing. Still the cold crept toward his heart, and into his mind. Thinking was a challenge when all he really wanted to do was dream.

"Show me the key, please."

Dutifully, the harper drew up the silver chain and the amethyst ring from under his buff jerkin. Here in Faerie, he was pleased to see its true nature glittered in royal violet and gold. In this world it had a glow of its own, as things of the fae often did. He pulled it off and held it over the king's outstretched hand, letting the ring swing from the chain like a pendulum. Graded around from pale lavender to deepest violet, where it spun lazily in the air it cast a ball of light. And wherever the light fell, every color grew richer, brighter, restored. When he let it go, the chain dropped after it with a ripple of water, home at last.

"Ah," said Aubrey, folding ring and key and chain into his fist. His complexion warmed and he sat up straighter. "This would be why your music is true, Ben, when everything else is out of tune. I wondered. Although I admit I didn't wonder very hard. I did put some excellent magic into this, didn't I?"

"Indeed you did, but— By your leave, sir, you asked for haste."

"So I did. And I think you can see why that is." Almost reluctantly, he laid the cool, liquid chain over Ben's head again. "You must be off."

Raven grabbed Aubrey's hand before he could release the ring itself. While the glow still filled the little bower and lightened the king's mind, he said, "My lord, you have not said where we are to go."

"Haven't I? Did I mention that the lock you seek is not always in the same place? For that matter it is not always the same thing?"

"What?"

"No, sorry," said Ben. "Your grace neglected to mention that."

"But I did tell you to use the diary, didn't I?"

"Which is how we got to the Crystal Palace—and there's another story for another time. Also some clean-up. But now? No one knows, if you do not."

The king disengaged the boy's hand and stood up, looking about as if truly seeing the devastation about him for the first time.

"John Dee knows," he said. "Show him the key, and he'll tell you. Now please, gentlemen! By all the Powers, go!"

48
Cowdray House, Sussex, July 1591

We see that the Moon in her shape and her
proximity rivals the Sun with her grandeur, which
is apparent to ordinary men, yet the face, or a semi-
sphere of the Moon, always reflects the light of the
Sun.

—*Dr John Dee, Theorem IV*

i

They'd been lucky in the weather on their Elizabethan
journeys. The red summer afternoon they rode into now was,
to Ben's intense relief, warm and fair though thunderheads
were forming to the southwest, and a lively breeze chased
patterns through the barley. He'd already seen too much snow.

When they passed through a village, they found the people
of merry England both as merry and as cross as ever. Back on
the road, still fretted with ruts and torn with hooves, they
stopped to help a carter gone off the side into the mire at the
plowed edge of a field of ripening grain. Each put a shoulder to
the wheel, straining and swearing until Raven remembered
what he was and whistled it out of the ditch. The ill-tempered
fellow spat and cursed his mules roundly, and drove off
muttering without another word of thanks or otherwise.

Happily, the faerie-bred horses had waited dutifully, even
cheerfully, at the side of the road, knee-deep in the green

Sussex corn. Ben slapped the mud and muck from his hands, and grabbed the reins, hauled himself into the saddle.

"Well, someone has to say it."

"What?" said Raven, mounting up. "That it's too early in the day for gin and tonic?"

Ben sighed. "That this isn't Mortlake. And I don't think it's Mycenae."

"It's Guildford," Raven said, "or nearly. Flowing gently on our right is the sweet river Rother. The village opposite is Midhurst. The year is 1591 and there beyond the apple trees, rising before us out of the mist—"

"Mist?"

"Orchard (don't quibble) is Cowdray House where you are, I believe, a distant relation of some sort, Sir Francis Browne."

"All quibbling aside?" Ben Harper looked up and nearly stopped breathing. "Oh."

Slowly, appreciating every moment, he raised wide eyes to the stately view as they broke through a stand of apple trees and stopped. Two fine octagonal towers lifted over the gatehouse, glazed and painted in the long afternoon. Beyond, the sturdily graceful house spread wide arms, its golden walls battlemented by special license in the old King's day, though it had never stood a siege. Within, he knew, a perishing amount of glass in mullioned windows filled the Hall with light. All that glass long vanished in his own time, along with too much of the house itself, still he could walk it, he thought, blindfold.

Staring, Ben gulped and said, "It burned to the ground in 1793, you know. The last viscount died the same year. It's been nothing but a ruin all that time. The current owners only restored the walled garden a few years ago, for weddings or whatever. They have self-guided tours now. Conference center. Not in the ruin, of course. That big wind last year made a mess of the place, though. Oh, the hall was called Stag Hall, see, because..."

"Come on, Sancho," Raven said tolerantly. "We have work to do, whatever it may be, in the house of your putative fathers."

Thus, with Ben rambling in tour-guide ecstasy, two men in Lord Aubrey's livery nodded to the porter, who clearly knew them, and trotted through the gate.

Anthony Browne viscount Montague was not at home, being required to continue on Progress with her Majesty after giving her two nights of his hospitality. The Lady Magdalen, his viscountess, had retired shortly afterwards to her house at Battle Abbey near Hastings to be seditiously Catholic in peace. By the time Lord Aubrey's gentlemen arrived, the steward, Mr Handy, and Mr Bellott, his lordship's Clerk of the Kitchen, were both in a state of nervous collapse, relieved beyond speech to find the two men did not need accommodations, what with all the Queen's furnishings moved out and most of their own not yet retrieved from the barn on the lower manor.

The Queen with half the Court and all the progress had left after breakfast. It would take days to put Cowdray in order again even after only two nights' stay, assuming the other half of the Court—the tardy half—got their backsides moving.

Arthur Garrett, his lordship's secretary, was booted for riding and practically on his way out, but he stopped to see what service he might be to Lord Aubrey's men.

Ben found it hard to keep from staring like a tourist around the high wide Hall—it would have fit comfortably inside the Assyrian Court—with carved stags on the corbels, trefoil tracery under the crossbeams, the high hammer-beamed ceiling. He had only known it as a grey and shattered ruin, a collection of faded engravings.

"The tardy half?" he said.

Master Garrett who, on an ordinary day, was the most composed of men, permitted himself a profound sigh.

"Gramercy, gentlemen, but nay, 'tis not so many as that. A few of the young gallants who could not be bothered to rouse themselves, and one or two of the hungry ones who follow the Court hoping a benefice will drop from her fingers in passing. You know the sort, Sir Francis, I am sure. They wear themselves out with groveling, and now other, hopefully

308   *Maggie Secara*

worthier men, will be first in line at the day's end, though I may say it as shouldn't."

"Anyone I know?" said Ben, pleased with the confidence but wondering all the same.

This man, whose name Ben had in his notes but not much more, knew him well enough to be comfortable with a little gossip. Perhaps one day he'd find out why.

"Doubtful, sir, for you keep far better company."

"Such as I?" said an unexpected voice. Older than when they had last seen him only by a couple of years, John Dee's eyes still wore that wariness Ben remembered.

"Well met, Sir Francis, Sir Rafe. Has Lord Aubrey sent you to be my escort?"

From the look on his aged face, he remembered them, too.

Raven smiled comfortably, leaning on his sword. "If you wish, good doctor, with all good will."

"Then Sir Francis, by your leave, I must be off." Garret gestured meaningfully to the surrounding chaos, clearly happier to be in the saddle than in the midst of cleaning day. Ben nodded, of course, and wished him farewell. The man bowed and was away.

Raven went on, "Whither can we take you, doctor, if not to rejoin her most gracious majesty's train, as we mean to?

"Ah, but that is not why you are here, is it, either of you?" said Dee. At their startled reaction he permitted himself a small smile. "I thought not. And yet, I knew you were coming to see me. Well, come along, come along, gentlemen. I believe I have something to show you."

The doctor directed them first to the far end of the hall where a broad oaken staircase led to the private sections of the house.

Ben's pulse was racing. He'd visited this place so often in imagination, it seemed unreal now he was here. He wanted to stare into every corner, examine each carved finial, stop the servants to talk, but that's not why they were here. A fact that was brought home as they mounted the stair; beneath his fine linen shirt, he felt the king's key grow warm. At the first landing, it became almost uncomfortably hot.

At the next floor, heart pounding, Ben laid his hand to the half-open door Dee indicated, and pressed into a room smelling of account books and ink, new parchment and quills—an office or study, lighted like the hall by a generously glazed window.

"I should like to come back here with more leisure," he murmured.

"Down, sir," said his friend, a bit sharply.

Alert only to his own purpose, Doctor Dee led them to a table, bright with color on carved and painted legs, and covered with a carpet of exotic design almost hidden under bound document boxes and papers.

"The Queen has found much for me to do since I saw you last," he said, waving them airily to sit. "All this is why I am delayed so in following—or so I thought. I have been aware for some months that you would visit me again."

"Oh, aye?" said Raven, unaccustomed to accuracy in mortal divination.

Still in awe Sir Francis Browne pulled out a bench and hesitated before sitting his road-filthy bum on its embroidered cover. Then with a pinch from the fae, he got over it. Raven took up a watchful position at his shoulder.

"Aye, indeed. Almost since I saw you last. After, well, there was an experiment, as thou knowest. Two experiments, rightly said."

Dee seemed quite ridiculously pleased with himself. Well, how often could a man actually test his prophesies? He could tell you what the Great Cham of China was having for dinner, but who could say whether it was so? He was practically dancing in his old bones as he rummaged through the boxes.

"Experiments wherein I saw you, sir, Master Fitzroy, in my mirror, along with others. Fitzroy, a curious name. The old king gave his eldest bastard that name, as all know, to signify he was a king's son."

"As all know," Ben echoed. He glanced back at Raven who pretended not to notice.

"In sooth I saw your master in my mirror, as well," said Dee, burrowing into a new stack of papers. "And those other curious men—who were they, I wonder—as well as that accursed witch. By the time I understood how she was using us all, it was too late to break free of her net, that she-spider."

And if he hadn't tried very hard, being enmeshed in scientific curiosity, clearly he did feel some regret now. There was more in enthusiastic Greek with parcels of Latin and some apt if esoteric quotations that neither of them could follow before he ran down and said,

"Eureka! I have it!"

Dee turned holding a small wooden folder, like the covers of a book without the book, carved with twining roses.

Ben saw nothing unusual about it; the key, however, practically flew toward it. More impatient than ever, he said, "Doctor, we were sent to ask you for something. Lord Aubrey told us..."

"I knew it!" Dee shouted, nearly dancing.

A maid's head, wreathed in linen, poked around the doorway looking like she had lost a bet.

"Sir?"

"Not now! Not now! Go to, busy woman. Away!"

The maid vanished as if conjured. Against the key's eagerness beating a pulse to match his own, Ben saw nothing in her except a servant trying to do her job. But Raven's hand on his shoulder suddenly tightened, radiating cold. Better hurry, then.

"The lord whom we serve," said Fitzroy, "bade us come to you and ask where we may find a lock that you know of. Though how you know it, I admit, I do not."

Dee's face fell. "A lock?"

"Aye," said Francis Browne as, opening a few buttons of his doublet, he drew out the key on its wonderful chain. "A lock for this to open. He bade me show it to you, and you would tell us where the lock can be found, or of what sort it is."

Now the fellow's expression went thoughtful, meeting their eyes in turn. Then he laid the flat wooden case on the table and said, "What you seek is within, sir, or so I believe. Sir Rafe, of your courtesy, will you open it?"

Under a flaring eyebrow, Raven considered for a moment, then reached forward and slid it closer. Unerringly, he touched a fingertip to the carved rose in the lower right hand corner. Lightly, the boards sprang apart like an oyster and lightly, he flipped the cover aside.

Within, where another man might have had wax tablets for quick notes, was a drawing or engraving of German design, about the size of a playing card, the corners captured under ribbons to hold it in place. Under the caption, *Der Rychman*, a miser in his barred strong room surrounded by his riches, exclaimed while the skeletal figure of Death collected his gold in a basket. At their feet, more sacks of treasure leaned against a locked casket. Behind, a door was locked and barred.

Ben looked up in alarm.

"A *picture* of a lock?"

In Nürnberg at the book fair, Dee explained, he had came upon a series of cards by Master Hans Holbein depicting the Dance of Death, wherein it was shown, as here, that death comes to all both great and small. He paused, chuckling at the inadvertent rhyme.

"Curiously, there were two of this one in the packet. I had thought to sell the odd one, or mayhap make a gift of it. However, I chanced to meet with your good lord while I was examining them."

The narrative faltered, though John Dee covered it with a cough. What Aubrey had said, or what they discussed, disappeared with a distracted breath.

"Go on, Doctor, if you please," Raven said, which made Dee jump and pick up his thread apparently without noticing the gap.

Thereafter, he said, he had taken to carrying this one odd card about with him, a talisman of sorts, though he couldn't say why exactly. Being of a curious mind, he had tested it for any esoteric properties, and discovered that the card could not be burnt or cut, pierced or torn.

"Moreover, the door in the back of the scene here, which is closed as you see, appears to be open when seen in a mirror. With flame behind it, the Latin words *helio trope* appear in the lines of shading on the wall. It is a remarkable piece of work.

Would I knew how it were made. Think of libraries impervious to fire! The knowledge that might be saved."

Ben frowned, and slipped the card from its bands. What was it besides a three-by-five inch parchment stiffened with size, printed with ink? In Latin, *helio trope* ought to be "it turns to the sun". Or maybe, in the curious way of medieval magic words, it meant simply "turn this to the sun" or even more esoterically "turn the sun". One way to find out.

So he went to the sun-filled window and held it up, turned it over in various ways, but no word appeared, and nothing changed. In spite of Dee's slight appearance of panic, he handed it to Raven. For a moment the boy held the card over a pale flame hovering above the palm of one hand, while the queen's astrologer sputtered with annoyance.

"Ah. There it is. See?" He gave it back to Ben.

"Hmm." Not two words, but one: *heliotrope*. Odd.

"Gentlemen!" Dee couldn't bear it any longer and snatched the card from their careless touch. "Grammercy!" he breathed.

Between the dazed look on the old alchemist's face and the twitching of aged fingers, Ben could almost hear a hissed *my precious!*

"Isn't heliotrope a color?" he asked abruptly. "Or some kind of flower?"

"A color, a flower, a perfume, a herb," Dee recited as if from a list. "It is also a name for a kind of chalcedony otherwise known in the vulgar English as—"

"Bloodstone," said Raven.

Something was moving in the air around them, not merely the bustle of a great house righting itself after a two-day binge. He could taste enchantment forming that was not in this room. "Doctor, forgive me, we must take this with us and go."

"Nay, thou must not!"

The man snapped the cover closed and laid his hand over the roses.

Ben frowned at the fae lord, but he too could tell something was wrong.

"Rafe, you know we cannot. It's already in the time stream. Not for us to displace it. If this is the lock, then the key will open it here and now. Good Doctor, an thou wilt."

With a gentle pressure, he nudged the old man's hand away, and opened the boards again. Swiftly, he pulled forward the key on its chain and put the amethyst ring on his finger. Oberon's name slipped from his lips like a prayer as he touched the silver key to the lock in the picture.

And nothing happened.

ii

"Oh, come on!" Ben swore and stabbed the ring into the card again as if main force could penetrate the world it contained.

"Master Browne!" Dee cried in alarm. "Sir Francis! Stay thy hand!"

Calmly, Raven's hand came down over his friend's and stilled it. "Enough."

"But it has to work!" Tension sang in the air between them.

"There must be something else, a detail we're missing. Doctor?"

Dee sat back in his chair. In a moment, though, he had resumed the mantle of mysterious authority he cultivated, glowering at them both.

"I believe," he began with scholarly speculation, "that another item is required."

Thoughtful, Raven tapped his companion's shoulder and said, "Rowan, if you please."

"What? Wherefore?" All the same, Ben fished around in his pouch and handed over a wrinkled berry.

"Wherefore I have a mind to," said Raven, and took it between his fingers, then laid it on his tongue. "By oak and ash and thorn!"

Ben watched the power take him as it had before, saw his friend receive it like a lover, familiar, welcoming its embrace. The room itself began to hum, as if channeling the song of the world that bound them to it while Raven smiled, a lord of the Great Fae triumphant in his full powers.

No ironbound invalid this time, the magic had no healing to perform, no weakness to counter, and perhaps no boundaries to contain it. Taller now, laughing lightly at things mere humans could not hope to perceive, his presence filled the room, the hall, the house, the island of Britain.

When Ben glanced at John Dee, the old man's face was a fixed mask of stern disapproval, and he had taken more than one step back. The pale eyes betrayed some awe and envy, too.

"Raven!" Ben ordered, calling him back by his own name as he had before. This was beginning to feel like his principal role. He said the name again, more gently. The fae shook his head a bit, and visibly dragged the power into his control, himself again.

But Dr Dee was furious.

"Are you so reckless, sir? Are you mad?" he sputtered. "You toy with perilous things as if it were a child's game. You call up such power, a danger too perilous by far, to yourself and all this house, without so much as invoking the patience of the Divine."

"Doctor."

"Do you put yourself above God, sir?"

Raven had the grace to look chagrined; he had forgotten where he was, and even Ben was not entirely amused.

"Peace, good doctor, peace! I do cry your pardon," he said humbly. "I am of Faerie. That is not our way. Still, I assure you, the danger was to me alone."

Ben lifted a doubtful eyebrow, and cleared his throat meaningfully.

"Too much?" the boy asked.

"A little too Star Trek, if you know what I mean."

"I see, then I'm also guilty of excessive melodrama, and that will never do. Nay, Doctor, I cannot answer your questions or teach you aught. The effect is but fleeting and our errand bespeaks haste. Therefore, Sir Francis, if you will lend me the key."

With the violet band around his finger, Raven marshaled his will, pleased to feel how the rowan, for all its melodrama, had heightened his awareness of the magic in all things, not only in himself, When he touched the key to the picture, a crystalline tingle and the echo of a familiar voice assured him that this was the lock's form for this time and place and, just as certainly, that it would not open.

He sat down suddenly. His head was pounding, but the eyes shone.

"Extraordinary!" Dee breathed, objections overcome by avid curiosity. "And what did you learn?"

"It is most surely my lord's working," Raven breathed. "Wonderfully complex and many-layered, like your multi-foliate rose, sir, and quite beyond my understanding. However, I know now that you are right, dear doctor, and the lock we seek exists only as the reflection of this one."

"You see," said John Dee, slapping the table in triumph. "My scrying glass, as I told you. We must set out at once."

"But we have no time!" Raven insisted, springing to his feet.

"No, Rafe, 'tis well," said Ben with a knowing look, and added more quietly, "It is in Great Russell Street. I know it, for I saw it there but lately."

A firm knock rapped at the door, and a woman said, "Dr John Dee?"

"What!" all three men snapped at once.

The mousy chambermaid did not, this time, run away. In fact, she strode boldly into the room, for all the world like the lady of the manor.

The niggling sense of wrongness that had been growing on all their minds suddenly flowered into full blown danger. Raven, senses still singing, stepped forward to shield Ben and Dee and all the esoterica.

The woman's stretched one hand toward them, fingers stiffened as if to cast a spell while she chanted.

Ai-ya! Ai-ya! Hey!
I make the world, and I—

The shaman's blue and red tattoos rose like jewels on the backs of her hands. With swift understanding, Raven cried out, "You!"

She stopped and stared at the faerie lord seeing him cloaked in an aura of power she longed for. Her eyes widened with recognition.

"You," she sneered. "You interfering brat, I saw you in the mirrors. We destroyed you!"

"You tried." And would try again, but he needn't mention that. "You have no idea what I am."

"I know what you are," she hissed. "You are the impediment to my return, the barrier to my success. But you are no more than a child's whimper in the night!"

When the chant began again, he only cocked his head curiously. "Do you use that because you expect it to harm me? Or because you still can't carry a tune?"

"Monster!" she cried. "I sing to destroy you!"

At this, Raven laughed out loud, almost relieved. "Oh, where is Ned Donovan when I need him?"

Ai-ya! Ai-ya! Hey!

Unimpressed, still filled with more power than was good for him, he indulged in an operatic pose, waved his arms a bit and shouted, "Aroint thee, witch! Abracadabra!"

The power that pulsed from his hands sent her flying, slammed her into the linen-fold panelling with a crack of good English oak that wouldn't please Lord Montague at all when he got home. Another gesture, and she fell forward to the parquet, panelling thoughtfully restored.

"Abracadabra?" Ben asked with a wry look. Raven just grinned. "But you didn't finish her."

"Not within my gift, I'm afraid. Pray forgive us, doctor, we have to go, and this must come with us."

"Again, no," said Ben before the alchemist could protest further. He folded the Holbein neatly into its case and restored it into John Dee's desperate care. Then a wink to his partner. "Trust me. We'll go to Sir Hans Sloane."

"Very well, but uh…"

"But first we must to do something about her."

"Quite."

"Of course." Raven took only a moment, then clapped hands with delight. "Doctor, do you remember the spell you used to dismiss the witch from your house? Do it again, please, just as soon as we've gone. Protect this house as you did your own."

The old scholar nodded. "Gladly."

"Now, we do need a mirror."

"I have told you," Dee began.

"Nay, only an ordinary looking glass, such as she dare not use, like…" Raven scanned the room and to his relief, found a small gazing mirror framed over the livery cupboard. He smiled broadly. "Just like that one. Come along, Francis."

The image reflected the room in small, perfect for his needs. With enough light, it would do nicely, and he could provide the light—and the dark.

With a single undramatic word, he plunged the room around them into deep night, as if the sun had left the world.

Dee cried out, "What have you done?"

Moonlight or something like it spilled in through the casement illuminating the mirror and little else. A bubbling wail emerged from the pile of pain and crippled age that had been a pretty chamber maid an instant before. Other sounds filtered up from a house thrown suddenly into panic.

"It will pass when we have gone, Doctor. Be well," Raven said.

His hand on Ben's shoulder, they stepped through the mirror to the courtyard of the British Museum, Great Russell Street, London, on a drizzly twenty-first century Christmas Eve just around lunch time.

49

British Museum, Christmas Eve

*I remember that the officers and men were all
gathered together round the canteen tent. It was
quite cold, and I was glad that some heavyweight
kit had caught up with me…. Everyone was
playing whist. There wasn't much else to do. They
had tried to decorate for Christmas using strips of
fabric and bandages as decorations. There were a
few bits of signalling ribbon that had been used as
well.*

—Harry Turner, letter, 1941

i

"Home!" Raven shouted, spinning a cheerful and somewhat
questionable pirouette. "Well, London, anyway. Christmas
Eve. *Welcome Yule!*"

He had brought them through, fiddling the time streams
as they went, to the broad front steps and stalwart Doric
columns of Hans Sloane's museum, which had stood there in
one form or another for more than two hundred years.

"And… We've already done Christmas Eve, remember?"

"Yes, human child, in 1854. Which, you will notice, is not
the same day as today, as the worlds turn. The great virtue,"
Raven said, straightening his tie as he hopped up the icy
Palladian steps without a care. "The great virtue, as I say, of
the twisty nature of time is not being bound to doing things in

order. In fact, strict chronological order is somewhat meaningless when you can step in and out of the stream. As long as you don't meet yourself coming and going, of course."

"The universe explodes?"

"No, it's just awkward. And since we haven't been in this century for the last two days *of this century,* heh… it's very unlikely."

Ben shook his head. Some days it really was like traveling with Dr Who, and he was pretty sure Raven knew it. He buried his hands in the pockets of his own black leather jacket and followed, a bit more careful of the ice. It had snowed, apparently, but not lately. The remnants, grimy and crystallized, lay piled in shadowed corners. He should be freezing but it wasn't especially cold, as if the weather hadn't made up its mind. Fat drops of a desultory rain slapped the pavement.

"You do realize the museum is closed, right?"

He pushed his glasses up his nose with one finger, reading the enormous Holiday Hours banners on either side of the door. By their reflection in the glass, he decided Raven would pass handily for a museum security guard. Ben, however, was dressed just as he had left the house in jeans and jacket over a Faerie Reel t-shirt.

"Not a problem."

"Fine. And you're Security. Who am I supposed to be?"

Raven peering in the door, turned with surprise. "Why, you're Ben Harper, of course. Star of television, chat show, and book tour. Who else would you be?"

He nodded. "Point taken. And I need immediate access to the museum on Christmas Eve. Why, exactly? Again, closed."

"That's what makes it so perfect!"

The boy placed his hand over the electronic keypad that secured the door. When nothing happened, he frowned at it sternly and whispered something. The front door sprang open with a sigh. Raven smiled.

"That and the fact we're a hundred feet from the street behind locked iron gates, and that the street is—and how odd is this—nearly deserted."

Ben had jumped back, expecting a mad clanging of alarms and the full might of uniformed Security, the Metropolitan Police, and possibly a platoon of ninjas to descend from the coffered ceiling of the portico.

No alarm. No guards. No ninjas either. The museum was as asleep as the street behind them. Then it came to him. There had been no sign, four hundred years distant, of the spreading weariness at the heart of the world unless a few slugabed courtiers meant something. But here, at home, it was all that was left.

He followed the boy into the Great Court, wondering if he should have made notes first, in case he forgot what they were supposed to be doing. Well, too late for that now.

In the middle of a courtyard the size of a tennis stadium, the vast central cylinder that was the Reading Room rose to the latticed shadows of the glass and steel canopy, staircases climbing around it. Grey skies and spattering rain above.

To one side behind a Classical façade of pillars and porticos lay the sculptural treasures of Ancient Egypt, testimonial to the taking ways of the museum's founders and their heirs. To the other, the old King's Library, now called the Enlightenment Room, housed among other things the display of John Dee's tools and books with identifying cards and an engraving of his portrait from the Bodleian. Ben brought Sparrow here just a month or two ago. Curiously, he realized, the big coffee table book Sparrow had made him buy made no mention of Dee's things, but he had seen them there, hadn't he?

At the base of the Reading Room stairs, Raven stood at ease reading a placard about the architect and design of the building. His costume had changed again to leather pants, waistcoat, and dashing topcoat, over a fine silk shirt.

"So, what next?" he asked, and yawned. Raven never yawned. The rowan must be wearing off. That couldn't be good. He stumbled a bit, sauntering to the information desk.

"Well, we have to bring together the Holbein card—always assuming that the lock is still in it—with the key, which we have." It was good to rehearse the steps, say them out loud, to keep them from slipping away. "And to do that we need John Dee's obsidian scrying glass. The real one."

"Yes. Excellent! But that first part, the Holbein."

"Okay, I believe it's here, somewhere. I know the mirror is behind that wall, or it was last month. But we have to find the Holbein. It's probably in, uhm, with the, uh, etchings and… There's a document room. There would be a lot less security to worry about if we just…"

"What security?" Raven asked over his shoulder.

"Uhm…" Ben looked around, up the steps, down the corridors. Not a sound, not a resonating footstep. "Have we had this conversation already?"

"It's the king's illness affecting the world, remember? Weariness, lethargy, terminal boredom. Like, you know," he yawned some more. "Like this. Oh! I need a nap."

"No napping!" Ben punched his arm, which made him stand up, at least. "He did say the longer it took, the harder it would get."

"And because of me, we've taken a lot of time."

"Hardly your fault. So if we just go back a few steps…"

"No," Raven said sharply, flipping through a *Guide to the British Museum* on the information desk. He was trying to hold on to urgency, but it kept slipping away. "Look, Ben. Why did you leave the card with Dee?"

"Because you don't take things out of their proper place in time, you know that. Oh!"

"Yes, exactly. You knew something. What is it?"

"For two hundred years the scrying glass was stored in some drawer or a storage cupboard. Everyone says it's always been here, but no one really knows. But I was just here. And we—"

"And you keep getting distracted by the one thing you're sure of! Where's the card?" the fae said. He sounded drunk and looked worse.

"It's here, in plain sight. I just… Sparrow dragged us all over the place, so maybe…"

"Stupid directory!" Raven swore and slammed the display case with a petulant fist.

Ben could hear the glass crack across the echoing room. Even that might be a good thing, he supposed. At least it was feeling, movement. But there was something else. Something of stomach-churning familiarity was growing as well, shaping, like a window sliding open, like a door swinging away from the latch.

"Hang on." He patted the front of his jacket and located the diary that had never let him down yet. Flipped to the end. Layout of the museum, yes. A couple of bad jokes, of course. Help? "Nothing."

"What?"

"Nothing. It just sort of runs out, like they got bored or... The last page is just scribbles, round and round. With a big red X in the middle, and 'You Are Here'."

"X marks the spot? It's worse than I thought. Oh!" Raven suppressed a huge yawn, but another one followed close behind. "Oh! Damn!"

Ben looked around, frowning, cudgeling his brain for clues, but he felt like he was trying to think and drown at the same time. Then he clicked his fingers.

"Got it. The Dee collection is right behind that door, with the, the uhm... Enlightenment Room. That's where I saw the mirror. But what about the, uhm— Damn, I'm doing it again. What about the Holbein? Raven?"

The fae had rolled to the side and now with his back to the damaged case, while a long crack went exploring, Raven was sliding to the floor with it, singing softly.

"I dreamt I dwelt in marble halls,
with vassals and serfs at my si-i-ide."

"Oh no, mate, not again!" Ben dived to catch him, too late. All either of them could do for the next half minute was lie in a pile on the floor of the echoing marble hall.

"Hmm?"

"I must have seen it last month, and in 1591, I must have remembered where. Was it a Holbein exhibit? Some art grouping? Think! Okay, it's usually up in the Prints and Drawings room. Christ, that's three floors up, that can't be..."

"What?" murmured Raven, half-asleep. He waved a limp hand more or less toward the door to the King's Library. "Oh, it's, uhm... hmm. Where is it?"

Ben had shoved the diary back into a pocket, wondering what had happened to his problem-solving skills.

"Don't worry. I can find anything, remember. I always do. But I can't do that and carry you too. Get up!"

"Uhm, Ben?"

"No, you can't just sleep here. Y'know, I'm getting tired of carting you all over the place."

But the boy gave a sleepy chuckle, fighting the lethargy, and started pawing at Ben's pocket. "Human child, I think you have something of mine."

"What? No, we did that already."

"No, the, uhm thing, the..."

"Pill box? But there's no iron here, I don't think, anyway. They..."

The long fingers, trembling slightly with effort, slapped the leather jacket again, persistent as a drunkard. "No— No, that's not— Not what I meant. Tree and leaf, I can't think. Right! Empty your pockets, come on."

When laundry tickets and pencil ends, pocket knife, receipts and sweets, a red Lego brick, bits of leaves and a single dusty rowan berry had spilled into a pile along with Oberon's pill box, Raven smiled and plucked out the one thing that had somehow clutched at his memory: a raven carved in jet with a brilliant sapphire eye, perched on a golden branch, and looped on a thick black hair elastic. He closed his hand around it, and sighed, and sat up.

"I put enough of myself into this thing. By my lord's will, this should work," he said, and dragged the band onto his wrist like a bracelet.

Ben watched as the long blue eyes blinked a few times and brightened.

"Come along, then, human child," said the fae lord as he got to his feet and dusted down his clothes. Straight and tall at last, he bent to his toes again to pick the jewelled box from the rest of the pocket detritus at his feet. He opened it and took one pastille, just in case, and thought to drop the last rowan berry into the extra compartment. He might need it later.

"I wonder what else these are good for."

Not much steadier than his friend, Ben put an hand against the display case, fighting to keep upright.

"What," he wondered, "what if I took one of those?"

Raven shrugged, though he didn't precisely know what they were made of. He held one up.

"No idea. Open wide, then."

Without thinking, Ben did as he was told. Then he jumped slightly and straightened as the thing fizzed on his tongue.

Raven ticked up a grin and, satisfied, dropped the box in his own pocket. Sidekick's prerogative.

"Oh, God save us!" Ben gagged on a taste like black licorice and bile, but then it was gone and his mind was clear, even over-bright, as if every particle of light in the huge white hall had entered his brain at once. He shook his head, "I haven't seen this much color in a white room since college."

The amethyst key under his shirt had started to grow warm, or perhaps he had finally noticed it. And something else.

He was staring down into the information case, but this time he actually registered what was there. Looked up to stare across the room, and down again to be sure, then up and across the room to his right, then down to be sure, then up again.

Raven watched him bemused and amused together. He put a hand on his friend's arm and said, "This would all be much funnier if it were animated. What are you doing?"

Wordless, Ben pointed to the faint glow of an open doorway tucked away under a staircase. Under the banner "The Changing Museum" a standing sign read "Dancing with Death". Reproduced under it, a Holbein engraving—not the one they needed, but one of the series.

"Come on."

I love dispatch, I strike at once
The wit, the wise, the fool, the dunce;
The steel-clad soldier, stout and bold,
The miser, with his treasured gold.
   —William Combe,
    The English Dance of Death, 1815

It was a smallish, octagonal room, more sleek and modern when Raven turned up the droplights than Ben expected. Not at all the setting he imagined for the macabre and sometimes ghoulish reminders of the even-handed nature of death, however artfully arranged.

Clockwise from the door, the history of Death as an artistic motif was laid out in paintings, illuminations, and three-dimensional art, from its late medieval Dance of Death to a chapel built of skulls, from the Victorians to the Second World War, where Death itself wandered the bloody fields perplexed at the carnage. The soundtrack, inaudible from the lobby, was still quietly running, the disturbing and sometimes frantic violin Ben thought of first as the theme to an old detective show, before remembering it was Saint-Saëns's *Danse Macabre*. Eerily appropriate, he hoped it wouldn't be the soundtrack to the rest of the day.

In the middle of the room, apparently supported on a bier of skulls and bones, the largest display cabinet featured. "Death's Dance with the Soldier": dice and gaming tokens whittled from bones, a hand-drawn deck of cards with swords and skulls in place of spades and hearts; Willie and Joe cracking wise under fire; a newspaper clipping and post card from the Queen; a soldier's letter home:

> *"After breakfast we had a game of football at the*
> *back of our trenches! We've had a few Germans*
> *over to see us this morning. They also sent a party*
> *over to bury a sniper we shot in the week… A few*
> *of our fellows went out and helped to bury him."*

The image of Death stalked battlefields through the clash of pike squares, of cannon belching smoke. Arrayed in Landsknecht ribbons, laughing skeletons unfurled the banners of noble causes or noble houses, caressed lascivious camp followers, spilled treasures into the sea.

And there among images of arms dealers and war profiteers, smaller than Ben remembered, sat *Der Rychman*, its black inks as crisp as they had been an hour ago in the sixteenth century. Still secure in the folder of exquisite marquetry, displayed on a velvet-covered stand. Behind quarter-inch glass. Wired to who knew how many alarms. Which, as far as he could tell, no one would answer. Had the whole world died already?

"How would you suggest we remove it without destroying everything else?"

Raven sighed. "After all you've been through, you still ask."

With a fingertip, he drew a largish rectangle in the front panel, which vanished when he pressed it. Then he reached in and plucked the card from under its ribbons to place it in Ben Harper's hands.

"It hasn't even aged," he said.

Carefully, Ben tucked it into the inside pocket of his jacket. "Now we just have to hope it's still the lock we're looking for."

"Our luck will hold. Next stop, enlightenment!"

Only a few yards away, Raven fiddled the lock on another pair of doors to open the Enlightenment Room. Once the personal library of George III, now given over completely to remnants and reminders of his brilliant century, it was cluttered, tastefully, with marble busts and Classical statuary—some looted, some copied—and books. Lots of books.

"Remember that cabinet of curiosities we had to search in 1763?" Ben mused. "I think this is what that room wanted to be when it grew up."

A mantle clock chimed noon. Outside, against all hope or likelihood, the weather appeared to be breaking. Some pearly grey light was trickling in from the high, tree-crowded windows on the street-ward side. Matching windows opposite caught shifting shadows of grey cloud and grey-blue sky. A few rays arced in from the latticed foyer skylight to land on the opened scroll of a XVth Dynasty *Book of the Dead*: Anubis weighing a heart against a feather.

A select handful of themes governed the room, as the informational card explained at the entrance. Voyages of discovery, the beginnings of archaeology and scientific classification, 3ancient languages, modern science. Doctor John Dee could be said to have contributed in some way to most of those fields, but the artifacts the Museum had in hand encouraged them to pass over his work in mathematics and navigation in favor of fortune telling. They had placed him under Religion and Ritual. "Magic, Mystery and Rites", said the modest banner a little beyond the middle of the room.

Of his vast collection of philosophical equipment, so little remained. Between a golden figurine associated with the Eleusinian Mysteries, and a seventeenth century ring engraved with the Lord's Prayer, sat John Dee's crystal ball, his set of round wax tablets scribed with all manner of esoteric detail, and the thing they sought—the mirror Perdita was so willing to destroy the world for: a round, slightly convex disk of polished obsidian, no more than a hand's span across, an inch or so thick—his scrying glass, displayed on a Lucite stand. It even had a kind of handle at the top with a hole in it for a hanging cord, long perished.

Mirrors like this, said the card beside it, would have been used by a Mexica (Aztec) priest for divination and healing, especially when a patient was afflicted with 'soul loss'. Such mirrors were also associated with the Mexica god of rulers, warriors, and sorcerers.

"That would certainly be Aubrey," Ben observed. Dee and Kelley ("that bowelless bastard") had used it to talk to angels. Erasmus Lovejoy would almost have killed to own this small thing. Ambrose Cray had done so, for much less.

"I don't think the good doctor would find this at all amusing," said Raven as they stood together, staring into the display. "Queen's Sorcerer, indeed."

"They never could make the sorcery charge stick."

It was their usual careless banter, but tension was growing with every word that echoed across the polished oak and mahogany. Then they stopped, and their eyes met.

"Do you hear that?" they said together.

A low humming had begun, and a vibration in the floor that came in waves, like the pulse at the low end of a radio band.

"I've got a bad feeling about this," said Ben.

The coffered ceiling began to tremble, the glass in the cases, the statues on their plinths.

"It's got a great beat, but you can't dance to it," Raven said, but his eyes were hard.

Both looked up the gallery beyond the Piranesi Vase, past the Book of the Dead, the works of John Locke, *Psyche Borne by Zephyrs*, to the doors at either end.

Doors. One they had breached themselves and not closed behind them. The other, slightly closer, opened toward the Montague Place entrance. Or would. So far, it remained bolted, secure under card lock and pass code.

"What the hell is that sound?" said Ben, keeping his voice low. His teeth were starting to ache.

Raven raised one hand and pointed at the double-door they had come through, then crooked a finger. *Come.* It shut with a ringing slam and a whoosh of stale air.

"Door closing," he said, expression set and grim. "Let's get to work."

The humming increased. Its nature changed, the reedy trill of pan pipes pierced his ear, then something like an oboe. And as it changed, so Raven's expression hardened, his eyes a sapphire storm, and he was older, Ben thought. Much older than he had ever seen him.

"It's a recording!" he snorted as he returned to the Dee display. "A bloody recording. How many centuries and the bitch has finally learned to let something else make the music for her."

In a moment, he was handing the mirror and stand to Ben, while he prepared a place to use it. First, find the strongest sunlight on a rainy day. One shaft of light had found its way from the clerestory windows but no more. It would have to do.

"A book that old shouldn't be in direct sun anyway," he muttered with annoyance. He gestured a case aside, avoiding the bust of Voltaire and narrowly missing a bronze Cernunnos. "Table?"

Ben glanced around and saw nothing but slanted document display cabinets like the one Raven had just moved. He gestured to a point in the middle of his chest "Something about this high."

"Got it." With care, Raven vanished an exquisite figure of Artemis—it would be safer in Faerie anyway—and slid its mahogany pillar into the strengthening sunbeam.

"Perfect. The noise, though…" The whining melody grew more insistent; another instrument joined, in a different key. "Is it getting cold?"

A stream of cold air, not unpleasant but unexpected, had begun to flow across their feet. What the hell was she doing?

"Get set up," Raven said. "I'll take care of it."

Eyes closed in concentration, he squared his shoulders. Both hands went up, out-thrust as if bracing himself against the doors, Samson between the pillars. And he began to sing, almost to himself. A simple melody from a forgotten world, with words long lost. He set the simple purity against the noise.

At the same time, Ben set up the mirror in its stand. Adjusted the angle to be sure it caught the light. Held up the card and checked again. He considered, evaluated, and rotated the stand a hair to the right. The feeble sunlight that slipped through the windows needed to wash against the night-black stone for as long as possible.

The music grew more raucous, and a pounding began at both doors. They bowed in; the fae pushed them back. Easy enough now, but for how long?

What had been a curious draft now ticked up into a gentle breeze. Little whirlwinds rose near the doors, lifting and tumbling a delicate Dionysus to the floor with a crash. Briefly, Ben hoped it was a copy, but blocked the concern as just one more distraction. All his attention he brought to bear on the picture, the mirror, and his task.

"*Helio trope*," he pronounced against the rising noise, and held Holbein's Rich Man to reflect its image in the mirror.

The wind whipped his hair, tugged at the parchment, trying to tease the card from his fingers. Something small and solid flew across the room and slapped his face on the way to smash into a glass case. He gritted his teeth but did not let go. Shattering glass no longer made him jump.

A powerful voice roared into the wind, filling the gallery. "Open to me!"

"Be gone!" Raven bellowed back, as the music grew still louder and more discordant.

Rocking in the wind that rattled the windows and flung flint hand axes through glass, somehow the mirror stood fast, anchored by other forces. Ben squinted from the reflection to the card in the bouncing light. With more sunlight, the reflection took on more detail, more depth and dimension. Both the rich man waving his arms in horror and the smug figure of Death seemed poised to spring into life and leap from the surface.

While Raven strained a few feet away, one of the money chests in the card stood out from the other. In the reflection, there was only one box though Holbein had drawn two, and the closed strong-room door at the back of the picture stood open, just as Dee had said.

"I know what to do," he shouted over the rising howls. If there was music in this wind, it was lost behind the sounds of shrieking metals and yelping hounds. "Ready?"

"Just do it!" Raven roared.

In his other hand, Ben shortened up the silver chain, letting the key hang steady as a plumb bob at the eye of the hurricane. Easy and slow, humming a tune he knew the king loved, he moved the image of the key toward the reflected strong box. Steadily the harp string of his gift out reached for the thing that was hidden until, letting his listening mind slide beneath the cacophony, Ben felt the connection click into place. A single vibrating silver note, sustained and holding true.

"Raven?"

"Go!"

He went. Oh, that was strange. He was inside the picture, inside the reflection, surrounded by a blue-green glow like the light at the bottom of the sea, cut off from the sounds of the real world. There was air, at least; he could breathe, but he felt slightly dizzy and his sight blurred at the edges. He wasn't meant to stay long. He didn't mean to.

"Hello?" he said.

No reply, no challenge, not even an echo. The rich man in profile, the gloating skeleton, now life-sized, both held their peace. He half expected them to spring to life, or speak, or for the flat black eyes at least to follow him, but they were as lifeless as they had been for four and a half centuries, hardly more than cut-outs; like the furniture and the candles, mere set dressing. So Ben forgot about them and went to his knees in front of the metal-bound strong box with its round, medieval lock.

At a muffled sound, he glanced over his shoulder to his own world. The Holbein card itself must have fallen when he entered the mirror. He watched as Raven threw up his arms, covering his face as every sheet of glass in every windowed book case exploded around him.

"Glass again? Really?"

A catch in his throat reminded him to hurry. The sunlight was moving more rapidly than he'd expected. Or he was moving more slowly. *Walk faster.*

So he set his mind to the song, and set the key to the lock, and turned it. A click, a tinkling of crystal chimes, the lid popped up.

A pirate's fortune in gold coins spilled over the edges and into his hands, gilding the room with something like sunlight. Blinking, he thrust his hands deep among the doubloons until they landed on a smaller casket of chased silver engraved with images of a royal wedding party. It was heavy, and he had to shift it back and forth a bit to clear away the coins.

It came free in his hands to the chiming music of gold sliding on gold, the song of wealth, but Ben ignored it. He had money. That was not why he was here. Harder to disregard, the light tune that came with it, an eerie descant to the one in his mind. The amethyst key opened this one, too.

From the silver casket, he scooped out a treasure of glittering jewels, some set into rings and chains, brooches and carcanets. A ruby the size of a pigeon's egg came into his hand. He admired it briefly and set it aside to find another, much smaller coffer wrought of fine gold, enameled on the lid with the figure of a goddess, arms open and welcoming. Ben frowned at the cheesy clichés, clearly meant to deter thieves with less good purpose and less need. He left the glittering baubles on the floor, and lifted out the golden casket.

When it opened, diamonds spilled away, glittering and perfect, from a still smaller treasure, giving his music back to him with cathedral variations: a tiny box carved of a single emerald. It sang in his hand with Oberon's own golden voice, gently chiding, soothing, encouraging him to look away, to take any of these riches or all of them, and seek no more for things no mortal man requires.

The harper listened, and nodded, swaying, longing to obey even while the air around him thickened. Then out of the swirl of sound and color, the image of the king as he had last seen him appeared, and the scent of violets.

"Now, stop that," Ben snapped, and shook off the enchantment. "Sir, you're needed."

Gently, cajolery became a lilting laughter and faded, leaving behind a sense of acceptance and permission.

The emerald case needed no key but his thought alone. It opened almost before he touched it. Cradled in violet silk richer than anything he had ever seen lay a small, almost ridiculously ordinary polished stone in shades of sea green flecked with crimson. Not jade, he thought, but heliotrope, sometimes called bloodstone, its natural shape suggesting a heart. The heart of Faerie.

For some immeasurable moment it was as if as he held every song there ever was of shared hearts and lonely hearts, broken hearts and hearts of stone, and hearts unchained or full of soul. He wanted to touch it, but drew back. That temptation might still be a trap. Instead he closed the emerald box and dropped it in his jacket. Maybe the distractions weren't so cheesy after all.

Finished here, he got to his feet and went to the barred door behind the table. It swung wide easily to his touch.

Now Ben Harper looked back again, trying to see beyond the mirror's face, and shouted, "Raven! Come on!"

No response. He reached his hand toward the surface; the image of the room around him fish-eyed and distorted. He called again, and thought he heard something, weirdly muffled as before. Even his own voice sounded like he was under water, and breathing was as strained as on a smoggy day in L.A.

He couldn't leave, he thought in anguish; but he couldn't stay. Raven would be fine—everything would be fine—if he could just complete his task and restore the king.

With a last glance outward, Ben turned and walked through the open door, and into the chilled heart of Faerie.

50

In Faerie

What is Faerie really, and where does it come from? Who are the Fae, and what sustains them if not mist and moonbeams? As well to ask what art is, or music, or love. The heart of Faerie, the queen had said, is the heart of the world. And Faerie had fallen into slumber as surely as if it had pricked its finger on a spinning wheel.

Ben Harper felt the pen-and-ink door close behind him and dissolve away without a sound. He stood within a deep wood, feeling neither threatened nor welcomed but surrounded with a deep stillness. No breeze stirred, nor bird sang. The limbs of giant trees reached high over head, their leafy canopy blocking out the sky; others dipped almost to the earth. There was no path, only silence and forest, dense and still as the world before men came or fae sang.

"Y'know," he said tentatively, as much to hear any sound at all as to address some unseen, unknown intelligence. "Hiding the path won't help."

As he sought for the direction, he could feel his gift flowing through him, and something else, as well. A tingle, a fizzing, an anticipation as if the magic waited for him suspended and hopeful. An intermission, not a finale.

When he took a speculative step, leaves rattled, a twig snapped. Yes, that was the way: not to the great house, not to the floating bower, but to the king himself who was as lost as the sleeping beauty. The faded wood wasn't a tangle of thorns.

Ben wasn't Prince Charming. A sword wouldn't help. What he needed, he thought with a sudden easy smile, was a harp.

Carefully he fetched the ring-key from under his shirt, feeling as he brushed the emerald box a pulse of warmth and urgency. Trusting some weird instinct, he held the key between his two palms and thought of Dariole, Oberon's silver-strung harp. A few moments of glitter and shimmer, and the harp was in his hands, carved of myrtle wood and strung with silver wire where the key had been, suspended from a worked leather strap instead of the silver chain. He could walk and play at the same time, then. This should be interesting.

He greeted the instrument as a familiar friend, whispered an endearment, and set his fingers to the strings. He struck a chord, then another. At the first phrase, the light shimmered around him, and a patch of opal sky opened overhead. At the next, the vast tree that stood directly in his way slid ponderously aside, and the one behind it, too. At the third phrase he realized he had started into *Greensleeves*, and as he played, the wood began to open and the sky to clear. When he stepped out, a faint track appeared with bluebells flourishing to either side, as if they had always been there. And perhaps they had.

The verse led into the chorus, and then to the verse again but he chose not to sing, only to play, becoming more elaborate, more complex with each cycle as the tune came round again. He had given Faerie the Vaughn Williams version of the simple melody once, this time it was all his own invention. With each round, fancy broke away from the clouds that beset him, the path widened into a tunnel of trees, the brittle grass greened up, spreading new life as each leaf touched the next. Bluebells and harebells, cowslips and columbine nodded, hurrying over the rolling hills. A dull grey ditch that crossed his path grew dark with moisture until a freshet burbled up swift and cold, so that by the time he came to it, he had to hop across.

But Ben Harper alone had not the power to restore the heart of Faerie, and so when he came at last to the dusty pavilion, not silk bright and crisp but plain, war-weary canvas, he stopped and released the harp to be a ring again of amethyst and gold. Around him, a sigh of disappointment blew through the faerie wood rippling the sad pennons that hung from the finial posts by the door. Inside, all was as he'd left it, a bit cluttered but almost unchanged. Faerie or no, it had an air of spent beer bottles and empty pizza boxes. Last call.

They were both there, king and queen, looking like nothing so much as a Waterhouse painting. Oberon reclined in his velvet divan asleep, still dressed as they had left him, the curling black hair plastered to his brow. Titania, graceful even in despair, knelt on cushions beside him, her arm and lovely head draped across his body. The opal sheen had faded from the pearl-white hair falling loose about her. The precious embroideries of her gown looked in the dappled light like stage costumes, cheap and tawdry. Her dainty feet were muddy, and no flowers grew. But Oberon's arm was laid over her shoulder, the one hand lightly caressing the curve of her white neck.

Ben stopped. The king's small, domestic tenderness was almost enough to break his heart. The sadness here was more than his music could counter, no matter how enhanced his gift might be.

"Your Grace," he said softly, and bent to touch the king's shoulder. Then louder, "Your Grace?"

The sapphire eyes fluttered open, blue as the summer sky over the moor, and the handsome face turned to him. "Ah," he sighed, and the eyes swept shut.

"Sir!"

Ben drew out the emerald box and went to one knee at the bedside. In the next breath, he took Oberon's hand and tipped the heart stone into his palm, curling the long fingers around it. Then he laid the closed hand over the king's heart, and rocked back on his heels.

"Lord Oberon," he said firmly. "Rise you. It is time and past time to come home."

Long seconds passed in uneasy quiet, then from outside the pavilion came the unmistakable trill of birdsong. The little stream changed its course to dash over mossy stone behind him, cheering the air.

Shadows flew from the king's face. The eyes opened, this time bright and clear, and the American realized that he had almost stopped breathing himself.

"Ben Harper!" said the king in soft surprise. He sat up easily and opened his hand to see the last shimmer of the heart-stone disappearing into his palm. A deep breath, a rumbling laugh, he reached to clasp his henchman's shoulder.

"You have done it. Well, of course you have. Once again, I am in your debt."

"All part of the service, your grace. I should mention…"

"And what is here?" He bent to place a kiss on Titania's head, and see her stir. "Wake you, my sweet queen!"

The sweetly-rounded shoulders rolled back, the graceful fingers of her hands catlike closed and stretched. As if she had only just fallen asleep, the lovely face came up, perplexed, a pattern of the king's jewelled belt pressed into her cheek.

"Oh!" she said with the voice of a young girl surprised to waking. "So, we're not to sleep away the ages after all."

Standing now to give her room, Ben bowed and ventured to kiss her hand, which she graciously allowed.

"No, my lady. Not this time."

As she yawned and sat up, his smile echoed the king's, seeing the violets spring up under Titania's feet as she put them to the ground. And as she did, like a time-lapse film, color swept over everything in the tent and the tent itself—glowing silk again and not dull canvas, with golden plaited ropes and embroidered banners snapping in the breeze. It swept up the walls and out into the lawns. The sweet air sprang to life, scented with cherries and sugar cakes, as lively as if there were dance and music somewhere just beyond hearing.

All the folk of Faerie were rousing, and their laughter with them. Ben nearly expected a golden lion to enter and roar the world awake, but the lion of this world was Oberon and he was whispering instead into his queen's shell-like ear. Laughing, she leapt up and gave him a deep curtsey, then kissed his cheek playfully and skipped away with her silk sleeves flying, crying to her maidens to lead out the dance.

"The king at his pleasure will join us presently!"

Around them, the pavilion sparkled swiftly away, no longer needed. Joyful laughter filled the glade again, and from all sides the Great Fae and the little folk awakened and ventured to return as the king's will restored streamed out into the whole of Faerie. In fact, the only one not merry was Ben.

"So," said Aubrey, comfortable in pleated trousers and silk shirt. "You look like you need a beer. Come, sit and tell me everything, both of you." He paused, frowning. "Where is Raven?"

"Well, your grace," Ben said with a touch of irritation. "Here's the thing."

51

King's Library, Christmas Eve

Raven watched Ben step into the mirror, saw the Holbein fall, whisked away by the howling air. He had no time for more. A blast rocked the door on his right. He drew on his power and his king's name, and fired back. The answer came like a blare of trumpets, and the double doors blew off their hinges, splintering everything in their path until the pieces banked off the ceiling and slammed bouncing on the floor.

Fine. Door was just in the way anyhow.

The king's old girlfriend strode toward him out of a smoky cloud, dressed in her golden skin and flying golden hair, perfectly balanced on an impossible pair of stiletto heels, but Raven was unmoved. Much as he loved a pretty girl, rage had never been the way to his cool faerie heart. If she meant to intimidate, this was not the way.

She smirked as her music, her *recorded* music, beat at his senses; percussive, atonal, electronic, loud. He heard a Russian men's choir and a modem squeal, and the old Secota chant buried upside down under a bagpipe for good measure. She had finally found her world, her music: random, bent, as untuned as herself. It was so perfectly suited to her, even the indelible Secota pearls rested calmly on her skin. She probably had a music review blog and a fan club.

Already exhausted, gathering for a final push, well aware that it might not be enough, he ran a quick inventory on resources. All his remedies had worn down. The thin line of gold on his ring finger had almost disappeared. The rowan's power, too, was all but spent. Even the king's magic beans had, well, he couldn't remember what had become of them. In Ben's pocket, probably. And the old iron pins left behind in the walls and ceiling of George III's library had been filling him with ice since they walked in from the Danse Macabre.

All he could do now was sing and buy Ben time.

Defiant, he pitched his song against hers, the ancient laughing cry he had lifted to his mother the Moon. Perdita flinched, reminded of defeat, but still came toward him, until between her cacophony and the old iron searing his lungs, he broke. It took only a moment to glance at the mirror and see Ben calling for him. If he were quick he might just make it, if he could reach the mirror, touch it just long enough to…

"Not alone!" Perdita shrieked.

Faerie was almost within her grasp! When he crossed into Faerie, she would be with him, let no faithless tyrant deny her right.

Raven threw himself at Ben's retreating image, diving for the blackness and swirling lights.

Her fingers raked into his long black curls and tightened.

The disk was under his fingertips, the light changed, his breath caught as he touched the stone.

"Oberon!" he cried in anguish. "My lord!"

But in the moment the door should have opened to him, stripping the witch away, it spat them both across the length of the ruined gallery. The landing did what Faerie's rejection did not; it forced open her grip, flinging him into a wall, depositing him under a tilted statue.

She slid through drifts of shattered glass, bouncing like a pinball off ancient sculpture and the beginnings of modern thought, until she slammed into the fathers of the Age of Reason, which she had lived through without understanding any better than the age before it. Voltaire, Rousseau, and Adam Smith crashed to the floor around her.

The king's binding held as he had meant it to. Perdita was bound out of Faerie for all time by a magic more complex than she could ever comprehend. She could not steal into the perilous realm, not even on another's back.

Aching and exhausted where he lay crumpled under the truncated but un-fig-leafed Farnese *Hermes*, Raven managed a weak laugh even as she limped toward him, with that damned ceramic knife, again, shimmering in her fist.

"Gods below, will I never learn? Never leave a weapon behind! Even if the wench has been shot three times in the head by a quite excellent marksman."

If she understood the joke, she failed to laugh. Titania's gift was building in her hands and that, she believed, was all she needed. It probably was. Well, Ben would have to save the worlds without him; Raven had given what he had. On another hand, or two, he was himself still holding on to the good doctor's scrying glass like a slippery life preserver. For whatever that was worth.

She stood over him, shaking but resolute, consumed with malice. The whirlwind died. Papers, books, pamphlets, gold foil gods spinning at the ceiling all clattered to the parquet floor. Her horrendous music broke off.

"Oh, thank every god," he groaned, the silence ringing in his ears.

When the crashes finished echoing, there was no sound anywhere but the crackle of power. He braced himself. He'd been thrown out of time once at Titania's command, and fought his way back. Who knows, he might even do it again.

Was it likely? Ah, well, truth to tell, it was not. The girls of Ipanema would be so disappointed. And then it crossed his mind to wonder if perhaps he could afford to be a hero after all, as well as the faithful man-at-arms.

Ben has done his job, he thought. My death will serve nothing. And I do have this mirror.

So instead of closing his eyes and going nobly, but pointlessly, to his doom, when she raised the knife he thrust up his hands with the black disk shining between them, daring her to destroy it. Then something, a flash within the mirror caught his eye, just a flicker of a moment of a thought of a light like a star just before it winks out at dawn. What?

"Wait!" he cried into the vibrating silence. And she did.

"Why?"

"I know what you want!"

He managed, more or less, to sit up while holding the disk in front of him like a breastplate. She would hardly destroy the one thing she wanted just to kill him.

She paused without lowering her hands.

"What," Perdita sneered, "do I want that you can give me, *boy*? If I destroy you, the door will open."

"No!" he gasped. Was that what she thought? Really? "If that is what the Queen let you believe, madam, I swear, you were misled."

"And you would lie to save yourself."

He shrugged a bit, and winced for the pain it brought. "You would lie. My friend Harper might lie. I cannot, being what I am. I know. You want to dance in the fields of Faerie as you did in old times. You want revenge on the king, and you want his power for your own. I am the King's Raven, and the Queen's rival in his affections, and I know it is so."

It was all true, of course it was, if not quite how it sounded. Waiting while it sank in and her own notions filled in the blanks, he watched her fury shift and change: a lifted brow, a cheek grown pale, an eye brighten.

Finally, she sneered and said, "How can you give me revenge or power? You're a child."

"Oh, I'm older than I look. Mine was the other voice in the song that bound you, and made you forget," he said, and silently thanked Aubrey for sharing that story. "I know what will un-bind the spell. Kill me, and you will be flung away from that door till the sun goes cold."

There were textiles somewhere on display in the Museum. She summoned them to her, wrapping herself in bitter scarlet ikat from Sumatra while she considered.

And while she considered, Raven held himself very still, feeling his strength seep into the floor boards. Which would soon be visible through the delicate transparency of his body, if his arm were any indication. He might as well have died in 1854 as go through this again.

Witches, Neil Gaiman had said one day, are often betrayed by their appetites, and to Raven's certain knowledge it was true. He could use that, but she had to get him out of here first, and she was certainly taking her time.

Apparently she hadn't noticed that the world around them was changing, recharging, filling up with light and life, color and energy. That Ben had gotten to the king in time. Uniformed Security and the Metropolitan Police (with or without ninjas) could any minute descend on the scene in all their destructive glory, just as Ben had feared.

"Very well," she said at last in her curious accent. "But how?"

He permitted himself to breathe again, and shoved the scrying glass, his talisman now, into the pocket of his top coat, where it tapped against the king's jewelled pill box.

The pill box? The latch, which should have been proof against mere accident, had popped with little more than a touch. Snatching at it, dozens of lavender pastilles swam free, slippery as a handful of peas. All those little charms, and one other thing.

"Just, just let me make this secure," he said, "for safety."

The agile fingers combed through them, his blood tingling, until the last wrinkled rowan berry brushed against a swollen knuckle. He clutched at it, held it, and felt the surge of power rise through him, bubbling and tickling his soul like champagne. He wanted to laugh, but caught himself. Instead, he raised the other, no longer quite transparent hand in pitiful supplication.

"My lady, touch my hand," he said, and watched her eyes widen. "I will take you to the doors."

52
Raven Tor

It was snowing again on the moor. Tomorrow would be a picture postcard of a day. Tonight would be a proper Dartmoor Christmas Eve as the world recovered its sense of humor, among other things. As the afternoon wore on toward an early sunset, the witch, never known for her patience, grew edgy and more anxious. Raven wanted to say something snide about her two thousand year failure to conquer her night-time handicap, but forbore. Heroes, he thought, do not indulge in cheap shots, unless the timing is really perfect. Besides, he was hoping for something more subtle.

He had brought her through the gates with her fingers curled around his arm like vulture's talons, and so come to the stone circle and the gate at the flat top of Raven Tor. Although like him she did not notice the cold, as a show of deference and defeat he bundled her as they came in a silver gown under piles of white furs—snow fox, white wolf, an ermine scarf—and placed a tall crystalline tiara on her head, which pleased her all out of proportion to the joke.

Raven, arrayed in something black, fur-edged, and whimsical from a Burgundian winter court, bowed to her very low and very seriously, and bade her take the seat he had provided, a broad-backed chair on a dais that she could take for a throne, if she liked. Of course, she did.

Now, all he could do was wait for the hope he thought he'd seen in Dr Dee's glass to manifest in some useful way. If he were mistaken, it was all over.

It was like waiting for the phone to ring. Hell, he'd have been happy for the phone to ring, but Ben's mobile was with Ben, of course, and Ben was or should be with the king. Maintaining this delicate courtly relationship with Perdita was wearing on his nerves. Except he didn't have nerves. Well, it was delicate, no matter.

What if Oberon were waiting on *him*? What would Ben do?

"I've been here before," said the witch, patience flagging. "I know these stones. What is this?

"As you wished, my lady," he said. "I have brought you to the gate of Faerie. If you will allow me."

The boy drew the black mirror from the folds of his furred velvet surcoat and considered. No lights played across the polished surface now, no images appeared. When he looked up at the tumbled stone of the Raven's Eye, though, he got the distinct impression he was being nudged.

Very well. He was new at taking the lead. Any hints would be appreciated. It felt a little more Buck Rogers than Beowulf, but he was ready.

He bowed again gravely before turning his back to her, and walked to the low, squarish archway that formed the Raven's Eye itself. He raised one hand and lifted his boyish head, and sang a silvery phrase. Usually too low for a grown man to stand under, the gateway shimmered and the ground fell away to a steep slope into Oberon's country. The road to Faerie lay open beneath the stone.

"Lovely," Perdita drawled. "But if I put a foot to yon bonnie road, I'll be thrown back again. You cannot trick me, boy."

Ignoring her, he spoke another word and positioned the mirror so that it hung at his eye level in the gap. No, too high. He hadn't realized until she was standing next to him just how small she was. As if directing invisible hands—and they were here, he could sense snow faeries urgently whispering nearby—he lowered the disk to a level she would not have to strain for, assuming the king allowed it. When it was ready, suspended in the air, he stood back to make sure he would be seen, and bowed to her again, the perfect major domo at her service.

She nodded as she had seen queens do, bidding him begin.

"My king!" he pronounced. His voice rang across the stony hills and along the hollow road. "The Lady Perdita of Avalon who is known to you bids you come to her and hear her complaint."

The face that filled the glass was not the stylish Mr Aubrey King, nor even the glittering king of the enchanted wood, but the horned king, the lord of the trees. His shirt was open under a leather coat and a collar of oak leaves green and gold. And though his mouth shaped a smile, the eyes that glittered hard as adamant from the leafy mask had no humor in them and no grace.

"Her complaint!" he roared, and his voice filled the circling stones of the hilltop. Even Raven took a step back, and another, just in case.

Unafraid, the witch was on her feet, the queen of Faerie's spell pointed straight at the raven boy.

"Oberon!" she cried. "Aye, I know your name, and you will hear me."

The king sighed and spoke a name that had been hers before all the others, the one Raven had never heard but once, all unknowing. It caught her off guard.

"Thou wast broken," he said as a teacher to a wayward pupil, "and I healed thee. Thou wert a child without a voice, and I gave thee magic which thou didst not merit and music beyond thine abilities. I loved thee, little one, sweetly and with care."

"You used me and cast me aside!" She came off her dais marching fearless to the hanging glass.

"You sought my life and my power!"

Her flung gesture drove the boy to his knees. Her free arm whipped around his throat and held him there in shock. "Aye, and now I have the life of your henchman, your sweet Raven, in my hands. What you took from me, I can take from you! And your Queen will only thank me."

And before he could speak, she had raised the spell-knife to drive it into the Raven's heart.

"Wait!" commanded Oberon.

"Why?"

But she held her hand, the white-hot spell poised above the boy's breast where he knelt quite still, waiting. He breathed, tasting the cold and the time, the day and the year, the life of the moor all around like flavors in his mouth. The leaden sky and the air on his skin, all tingled and spoke as it might be for the last time while Oberon let the moment hover between them, fury burning from the image in the glass. Raven had the idea that someone else was speaking to the king, Ben perhaps or possibly Titania. He hoped it was Ben.

At last Oberon spoke, his voice tight with control. "What makes you think this boy is precious to me?"

Perdita threw back her golden head and laughed till the Secota pearls shone like jewels. "You are such a fool, my lord. Look to your bed! Is that not where trouble always begins and ends? Your queen has told me so, and the boy himself!"

More silence from the king of Faerie, who spared no glance to the child of his heart. Raven was shocked enough for them both. Is that really what Titania had told her? That could not be true. The silence on the Tor stretched until the boy simply closed his eyes. His death would come if the king willed it.

"What is it you want of me, then, girl?"

Raven's eyes snapped open, round with delight. There was a plan after all. The king was not going to give her anything and he was not going to let her kill, well, anyone. All he had to do was wait with the patience the golden girl had never learned.

She drew herself up haughtily to what height she had and said, "Unbind the spell that keeps me from you. When we are together again, Beloved, we can discuss the rest."

"Release the boy!"

Slowly, the knife lowered, the sparkle at the edge of the blade moving away, though her other hand still lay across his throat. "Unbind the spell."

"He is part of the song. I can do nothing while you hold him."

Her mouth twisted with contempt, but she let him go. Raven wasted no time but stood and moved aside at once.

"And put away Titania's spell," said the king. The knife winked out as she tossed it among the stones, where someone small and curiously obedient scurried to hide it under a stone, never to be found.

Satisfied, the imperious eyes turned toward his henchman. "Raven, the song is locked in your mind. Can you find it?"

"Forgive me, lord?"

"It's all right, lad." The mask dissolved to show the kingly jaw and curling hair, Aubrey's sapphire glinting in one ear, and the eyes to him were gentle. "You have carried it all along, though you knew it not. Listen!"

From all around, from the air and the stones of the earth a tune began, just a few phrases like a silver flute rising over the hill and far away. And he realized that he did know it, though he had heard it sung only once, interrupted by a Raven in his first summer, reveling thoughtless and beguiling under the moon.

So he sang. It began simply enough, an ancient tune in a minor register bound up with words that came to him in a language he barely knew, of longing and sorrow, remembered laughter, and lost worlds, and the dancing light of the stars. It wasn't long, but it needed three repeats, each in a slightly different key, and the modulations would be a challenge even to the most practiced of the fae.

Raven could feel the power grow as he settled into the second phase, sensed the king's will emanating from the glass suspended between the mortal world and Faerie. When he shifted into the third variation, the energy crackled about him, visibly snapping at the ends of his fingers, the strands of his hair. Whatever Perdita thought was happening, she was giggling like a child in the mad house, standing close to the mirror, reaching for it as it grew swelling and expanding like a rosebud about to bloom.

Raven sang his soul there on the rocky tor that bore his name, and felt the changes unfold, the blocked doors fall away, the locks open that the song had bound upon the golden witch. And when the moment came, he felt more than saw the king nod as a king grants leave to depart. In the midst of the last phrase, he changed first his voice and then his shape, and he leapt into the air, the King's Raven of Faerie with his joyous cry tumbling through the song. The last barrier fell.

But the king of Faerie is of old and subtle mind. The strands of his enchantments are many, the patterns complex. His own voice deep with power took up the song as his image invited the woman into his arms. Revelling, free at last, she threw aside the useless furs and finery and boldly stepped through John Dee's mirror, and into the king of Faerie's mated one.

When the scrying glass saw her there, of course it called her back. Faerie's mirror, jealous of her image, dragged it in again. Howling on the airs between them, she flew from one enchantment to the other, locked in infinite reflection until the forces between them ripped her apart.

Dee's lesser glass succumbed at last to paradox. The greater mirror folded over it, collapsed into itself, closed off her wailing, growing smaller with each change, and was gone.

Deep within his kingdom, Oberon glared at the space and the last thin note left behind. With a breath, he pinched the singularity out of existence.

"Finally," he said.

Raven shouted, "Yes!" and launched himself out over Iveston Vale, turned and powered back like a small black missile. Over the stone circle, he stalled, opened his wings, and dived down under the hill before the gate rumbled closed and the earth was still.

53

In Faerie: Drive the cold winter away

Oberon listened soberly to his gentlemen's report, which left him grieving for the harm his ancient error had led to, for the deaths the witch had caused. On their suggestion, he dispatched a company of hobs to tidy up the British Museum's Enlightenment Room to some plausible degree, and sent the nineteenth century Lord Aubrey's factor to see what could be done with the north face of the Crystal Palace so it would be standing as it should be when the fire came for it in 1865.

For the deaths of honest men, though, he was powerless for their lives. For the families, he nodded. "We'll see."

He thanked them, and asked what boon each of them would claim. Raven only bowed deeply, winked at Ben, and took to the air. Ben Harper looked around at the activity, the music, the wonder at the heart of Faerie, and knew that Mellis wouldn't be home until tomorrow, even assuming the airlines had gotten their act together. He had to pass the time somehow, so he bowed deeply, and said, "I have no plans for Christmas lunch, your grace."

The dancing in the king's banqueting hall was nimble and quick and not a little raucous among the living trees. The musicians, immortal and tireless, had no concept of sets any more than the dancers did, and besides, it was Yule. The world had been saved, sure—again—which would have been reason enough to celebrate, but Christmas is Christmas. Oberon even danced, as he had promised, with his wife.

Having dined on mince and slices of quince, though eschewing the runcible spoon, the King's Raven was ready for lively, uncomplicated music without a hint of spellcraft in it beside the magic all music has to lift the heart and make the world. So he fetched his fiddle and his bow, and sauntered out, loose-jointed and playful, across the flower-dotted meadow toward the stage, already bouncing with every light-hearted step.

The dancers had better look to their slippers, he thought. There would be no stopping as long as he chose to play, which is why he did it so seldom. The mood he was in, he might not stop till Twelfth Night, except by royal decree.

> *"Oh, I am frolicsome, and I am easy,"* he caroled.
> *"Good tempered and free*
> *And I don't give a single pin, me boys*
> *What the world thinks of me!"*

Passing the royal dais, all draped with silks and sables rich and fine, he nodded amiably to other courtiers without much attention. A fae with a mission, not to be diverted, he heard his name and lifted a careless hand and kept walking, gratefully breathing the sweet airs of his home.

"Seriously, I have to ask."

The boy slowed and turned to find Ben Harper seated like an Oriental potentate, and dressed like one, too, turban and all, on a pile of cushions, nursing a drink.

"You want me to peel you a grape?"

"Hmm, maybe later. Could use a fez, though."

"Fez it is." And so it was. Content to be diverted, Raven sat on the next cushion and collected a glass of something cold. "Ask me what?"

Ben put down his drink and leaned forward in that conspiratorial way that usually means a trap is being set. Or sprung. But only in the friendliest possible way, of course.

"Did you really know Marcus Aurelius?" At the raven boy's tolerant grin, he tried again. "Okay, Crystal Palace. You stood there, cold as a stone, and told Perdita you weren't afraid of either of her or the police."

"Yes, I did." Two beats for effect, then the elven grin twitched into delighted laughter. "Are you kidding? Oak and ash, I wasn't afraid of either one, I was bloody terrified of them both! You're the hero, remember? Whilst I, your humble servant, remain the loyal sidekick and trusty native guide."

Ben rolled his eyes, "I should have known."

"You'll learn, human child," Raven said, getting up again. "Now I'm going to make some music. You can sit in or you can dance, as pleases you."

Without waiting for an answer, he trotted down the steps and strolled off, pleased as could be.

The harper had danced quite enough for one day. Content among the soft airs and easy graces of the king's front lawn, he sat back to listen for a change, letting his fingers ripple across an air-harp now and then, and letting his mind go. Eventually, on another level, he could hear his own band down at the Star warming up, wondering where he was. Time to go.

In his own clothes again, he turned back a moment for a last look to the king's Great House, then set his mind on home. Before he had taken more than a few steps, he had company.

"Leaving so soon?" Aubrey said.

"Got a gig, sir," said Ben. "You should come along, if the queen will let you out of her sight. Oh, I talked to Mellis. I'm picking up them up at Gatwick tomorrow afternoon."

At the edge of the Ravenbeck, the creek that marked his property off from Iveston Common and the path to Raven Tor, they thudded across the wooden bridge and jumped the gate into the winter-bound garden at Diamond Cottage, where all the lights blazed gold and white into the frozen night.

"Changed her mind about California, did she? Good to hear."

"She's a Dartmoor girl, sir. She'll never live anywhere else."

"And you?"

"Oh, yeah," Ben said, with feeling. "Me too."

He opened the office door and stopped.

"Daddy!" Sparrow crowed, and cannoned into him with a triumphant giggle. Over the child's head, Mellis, laughing and bright-eyed, flung out her arms.

"Happy Christmas, Ben," said Aubrey, and quietly closed the door.

THE END

For backgrounds, music, and more about the world of Harper Errant, visit www.maggie.secara.com

About the Author

Maggie Secara started out wanting to be an archaeologist. Then a reporter, then an international spy, a poet, an opera singer, a novelist, a historian. She ended up being a bit of each, earning a Masters in English and becoming involved with historical costume and improvisational theatre. When all those passions came together at once, she decided to be a novelist again, and so she did. Her short fiction has appeared in a variety of publications, including New Realm, Unsung Stories, and *Daily Science Fiction.*

Maggie lives in Los Angeles, California, with one adoring husband, two goofy cats, and half a million English words to toy with.

You can find Maggie in all these interesting places:

Facebook facebook.com/groups/maggiesworlds
Twitter   @MaggiRos
Tumblr   maggie-secara.tumblr.com
Pinterest pinterest.com/maggiros
Amazon   Author.to/MaggieSecara

www.ingramcontent.com/pod-product-compliance
Lightning Source LLC
Chambersburg PA
CBHW072112250626
47159CB00007B/2420